# "I don't have time for such nonsense."

Sal rose impatiently.

"Sal," Hana said, "I don't want to consult this powwow doctor, I just want to talk to him—her?"

"Next thing," Sal said, leaning across the table and poking a finger toward Hana, "you'll be telling me it was hex killed those boys. It's not Christian to believe such things, but there are some around here still do."

"Of course it wasn't hex killed the boys but—"

"How long's it been since we had a murder hereabouts because somebody thought they were hexed? Not that many years. Fifteen maybe. Some places the devil dies hard."

"I'm sure this has nothing to do with local superstition," Hana assured her.

"You are, are you? Well, I'm not. Pitchforks are the devil's tools, aren't they? Always on pictures he's got one anyways."

Hana opened her mout

The slam of the door the old house.

Hana sighed. *You'd al*

# PLAIN MURDER

Also by
Roma Greth

. . . *Now You Don't*

Published by
PAGEANT BOOKS

# PLAIN MURDER

## A HANA SHANER MYSTERY

# ROMA GRETH

PAGEANT BOOKS

**PAGEANT BOOKS**
225 Park Avenue South
New York, New York 10003

Copyright © 1989 by Roma Greth

PAGEANT and colophon are trademarks of the publisher

Cover artwork by Robert Crawford

Printed in the U.S.A.

First Pageant Books printing: March, 1989

10 9 8 7 6 5 4 3 2 1

For the Amish people in this book,
I have chosen Germanic family names
not commonly found in Amish Society.

# PLAIN MURDER

# Chapter One

HANA SHANER FOLDED her arms and tried to relax by peering out at the rolling Pennsylvania farmland, now misty and unreal in a drizzle that grayed the pastel tones of early spring. Sal Nunemacher swung the old station wagon onto a dirt road. The car skidded in mud, then straightened to splash through deep puddles.

"How much farther?" Hana asked impatiently.

"We're soon there," Sal said in a monotone.

Really, Hana thought, she had no time for this. She was extraordinarily busy at her plant. The spring had brought an upsurge in carpet sales for Shaner Industries, with orders coming in from all over the country and even Japan, although she wasn't quite sure how that had happened. More time-consuming was the commotion caused by the launch of a line of women's clothing, in Dutch Blue. Then too, Pocky Reilly from the TV station had chosen this time to give her a lot of flak about their next commercial.

No, she certainly didn't need a disruption like this first thing Monday morning. However, if one wanted one's ancestral estate run smoothly, one sometimes had to cater to Sal Nunemacher and Mr. Fred. She did not, could not, think of them as servants. They were more like, as her aunt had said when speaking of the redoubtable Mr. Fred, "thorns in the side."

Sal Nunemacher had arrived at Blue Spring Hill as Hana nibbled her way through Mr. Fred's experimental carrot-raisin omelette. Nervous and excited, Sal had insisted Hana drop everything to come with her. Although happy to drop the carrot-raisin omelette, Hana was not pleased about missing a morning's work. Most irritating of all was Sal's stubborn refusal to go into details. Despite Hana's probing, she would only affirm that things were fine with her own farm and the large family of siblings she and her widowed mother were raising. It was a neighbor who had come to Sal desperate for help.

She had come to Hana.

Hana turned from the haze of landscape to look at Sal's face, pale and strained looking as she stared through the flapping windshield wipers. Whatever had happened must be serious to upset this woman who took even Mr. Fred's absurdities in her stride. Sal wore the small cap and plain dress of the Mennonite sect, a religious group rather more worldly than the orthodox Amish. Hana knew Sal lived her religion, and she respected her for it. As plain as Sal's outfit were her face and the straight brown hair caught in a bun beneath the cap. The face was slightly full as was the figure, which seemed more matronly now that Sal had passed thirty.

The car shuddered into an especially large hole, spewing water, mud, and gravel across the windshield. The seat belt cut into Hana's middle.

"For heaven's sake, slow down!"

As Sal braked, the engine choked and coughed, threatening to abandon them in God's little muddy acre. Sal proceeded more cautiously.

"I don't see how you can call these people neighbors," Hana grumbled, loosening the old-fashioned seat belt. "They're miles from your place."

"That's how it is in the country," Sal muttered. "We're almost there now."

It was a large farm edging a wooded hillside, unusual for the flat, richly cultivated Conover County. The place was so remote it could have been the location for a movie set in the last century. The big limestone house bore a date of 1792. The same stone had been used for the barn. Everything was neat and well kept. An Amish buggy sat in an open shed. No horse was attached. There was no movement anywhere.

Gingerly stepping into wet grass, Hana got out of the car. Her new gray shoes that went so well with the lavender suit and soft gray blouse were designed for meeting important people in industry, not for wading about a muddy farmyard.

"Looks peaceful enough," she observed, clicking open her umbrella.

But it did not look peaceful; it looked deserted. And it felt hostile. She wouldn't give the unresponsive Sal satisfaction by admitting it.

"Come once," Sal said, starting toward the barn.

Hana had expected to go to the house.

Sal's attitude reminded her of another time she had followed this same employee to a body buried

on the Nunemacher farm. God . . . not another
one. Surely not. One set of murders was enough
for a lifetime. After all, she was not a detective, just
a perfectly ordinary woman. Well, not exactly ordinary . . .

Her shoes were a mess by the time they had
crossed to the earthen ramp leading to the second
story of the barn. Wagons full of hay were pulled
up the ramp to dump their contents onto the
threshing floor. Below horses and cows and sometimes chickens were kept.

Sal, ignoring rain, pulled open one of the large
double doors. Hana flipped water from her umbrella, closed it, then followed Sal into the gloom.
Her shoes squished on the dusty floor. She paused,
blinking, suddenly aware of many eyes watching
her.

They stood along the wall. Silent. Unsmiling. The
women and girls all wore the black bonnets,
shawls, black aprons, and plain but bright colored
dresses of their sect. The men and boys wore wide-
brimmed hats and black suits.

Having lived in Conover most of her life, Hana
was accustomed to the Pennsylvania Germans.
They came in many sects, which had been around
since the early 1700s. Her own family was descended from the "fancy" Germans (Deutsch or
Dutch) who followed the ways of the world. Most
publicized were the Amish, who separated themselves from the rest of society. They wore very recognizable outfits, drove buggies, had no electricity
or telephones, and were a tourist attraction in Conover County.

But in all of her encounters with the Amish,
Hana had never seen an assembly like this one,
which had called in an outsider like herself. They

lived at a slower pace, in another time, and dealt with "the English" only when necessary.

Still nothing was said.

Hana turned to Sal and opened her mouth to speak.

Sal shook her head, pointing toward an area of darkness far from the wide-open barn door, a section where mounds of hay were abundantly high even though last autumn's harvest was long past. The stillness was physical, as if even the animals in the stalls below held their breaths, knowing something was wrong.

Something was—terribly wrong.

Hana saw it and let out a long sigh.

Then, feeling all eyes on her, following her, she moved forward, closer to the object sprawled amid the darkly golden hay. She tried to control her suddenly rapid heartbeat. She had found bodies before, in that other case. But she had never wanted to do so again.

Her breath came faster as she stopped at the edge of the pool of blood that had spread through dust and hay and was now congealing to a thick, deep red. She swallowed, trying to force herself to play the role Sal and these people had chosen for her. The impersonal helper called because . . .

She did not know why.

She concentrated on the body.

She did not know the boy. He really was just a child. Maybe fourteen but probably younger, he could even be a large twelve-year-old. His body curved around a pitchfork, which had been thrust into his chest. He was roughly dressed, like most Amish youths who helped work the family farm. Muddy, ankle-high work shoes, rather short trousers as if he were either outgrowing them or they were hand-me-downs from an older brother. Suspenders, a cotton shirt of dark purple. Dark with blood.

She continued to stare, fighting to collect her thoughts, trying to think what to do next. She had been so intent on her own disrupted morning, she had not even asked Sal the name of the family. Ignoring the blood, she knelt beside the boy, feeling for a pulse she knew she would not find. Behind her nobody moved.

How long had these people—obviously his family—kept vigil? That was not an Amish custom. But neither was violent death. Theirs was a peaceful religion, nonviolent, nonaggressive.

It struck her now that something was off center. This boy was dressed for farm chores, but the family wore their best clothes—what they would put on for a trip to market or on Sundays for religious meetings.

Sal had come to the edge of the blood.

"They found him this morning. Came for me because we're the nearest place has a phone. Most Amish families have a phone at the end of the lane they can use for emergencies. But not the Schwambachs. They didn't know what to do. I said I'd bring you . . . that you'd know."

"You should have called the police—"

"They don't want the police. They take care of their own."

Fine. Except there was no way the law would let them take care of this. And there was certainly nothing Hana could do. Sal should have known better. But perhaps they had pressured her. And Sal didn't want to be the one to summon police against their wishes.

Hana rose and turned to look at them. They appeared to be a typical Old Order Amish family. An elderly couple, grandparents undoubtedly. These people took care of their own. Rarely was anybody sent to a nursing home. There was always more than enough work, even for the old. And if they became ill, there were plenty of young people around to provide care. Another couple, who might be in their late thirties but looked older, were surrounded by offspring of various heights and ages, the oldest a sullen-looking boy in his midteens.

Hana edged away from the body to the clear area where in fancy Dutch barns many a square dance had been held.

"What happened?" she asked.

For a moment it seemed no one would reply; then the middle-aged man stepped forward. Looking very neat in his black suit, he wore a shirt in an odd shade of pink that Hana had noticed on Amish men before.

"*Wos—?*" she began in the dialect.

He waved away her attempt with his callused hand and spoke in English with a slow, heavy accent. "Why, now, we always get up early here. Everybody got their chores to do and that's what they done. Like always. The boys milk the cows and feed the livestock while the women get breakfast and rett up the house. We was pretty near finished out here when I come up in the hayloft and found him like so."

"Did you . . . ?" Hana began.

"*Ja.* I felt for his heartbeat. There wasn't none. He was gone."

A farmer who had done butchering would know death and recognize when life had gone from a body.

"What's your name?" she asked.

"Henry Schwambach."

There was just a slight hesitation now, surely

something the circumstances could excuse. Beside her, Sal stirred.

Then he added, "That's my son. Aaron."

"And this is the rest of your family?"

"*Ja.*"

She looked at them, her eyes sliding along the expressionless faces. "Do you all agree with what Mr. Schwambach has said? Did any of you see or hear anything out of the ordinary this morning? Especially here in the barn?"

They watched her with careful eyes. Odd they were all so very neat. Clean dresses. Clean trousers and shirts. They certainly didn't look as if they had been doing chores.

Hana turned to Sal. "Don't they understand me? Maybe you'd better repeat it in the dialect. I speak it but not too well. I want to make sure they understand."

"They understand," Henry Schwambach said. "Like I told you, the women and girls was in the house doing what women do. My father here and the boys was doing what had to be done outside. Nobody come up here but me. Nobody seen nothing. Nobody heard nothing."

Regretting the patriarchal nature of Amish family life, Hana contemplated the head of the family. His skin was darkened, even at this time of year, by sun and weather. A few strands of gray cut through the dark of the full beard he wore as evidence of his manhood. Only when a male married was he allowed to raise a beard, but never a mustache. His eyes were large and brown, defiant and —yes, Hana thought—fearful.

"What was he doing . . . the boy?"

Fear changed to contempt. "What he was supposed to do. Pitching hay down the hole to the horses and cows. I told you the boys was doing chores."

Beyond the body, where she knew it would be because this was her land too and in one sense these were her people, she saw a railing surrounding an open space where the hay was thrown directly to the eager animals below, a rail which was meant to keep errant children from tumbling through to the first floor. If the boy had pitched too enthusiastically it was possible he might have fallen over the rail and landed below on his own pitchfork. But he had not fallen through the hole.

"You didn't carry him up from below?" she asked. "You found him up here?"

He nodded and she suspected the sin of mendacity was tempting him at that moment.

"I'm curious," she continued. "Why are you dressed up if you were just doing your chores? It almost seems as if you dressed for the occasion."

*"Heilich donner wetter nachemal!"* he cried.

A strong curse for an Amishman. For a moment Hana thought he would charge into her, but instead he brushed roughly past her toward his son's body.

Hana grabbed his sleeve. "What're you doing?"

"I'm taking that pitchfork out of the body! I'm going to carry him to the house and the women are going to wash him and—"

Keeping a firm grip on his arm, Hana said, "You're not touching anything! The police will have to be notified."

"It was an accident!"

"I'm sure it was," she said more gently. "But with any violent death there are questions to be answered."

He shook her off. Hana stood between him and

the body. Angrily he turned to Sal. "You said she'd help us!"

Sal looked flustered. "I said she'd know what to do."

Hana moved protectively closer to Sal. "If you talk to me . . . tell me more about this . . . maybe I can help you."

He walked back to stand with his family, their solidarity against the intruder complete.

Hana turned on them the full glare of her recently developed media presence. "I'll help you do what must be done. I'll back you up and assist you in any way I can. But now I want the police brought out here. Sal, you get to the nearest phone and call Sergeant Kochen. I don't know if this is in his jurisdiction but if it's not, he'll know who to contact. The rest of you will please leave the barn but don't go off the farm. And don't touch anything here. There's been too much tramping about already. I'll wait and make sure there's no more of it. Now! Go!"

Sal scurried out as if glad to get away.

Henry Schwambach's defiance faded. Slowly he moved toward the barn door, followed by his obedient family, stirring the dust as they filed out into the mist left by the morning rain. A tentative shaft of sunlight emerged just as a girl of about twelve paused to look back at Hana. The child was silhouetted against the light, her old-fashioned clothing turning the present into the past. Suddenly it seemed so unfair that these people with their strong faith and their placid ways should be forced to endure invasion by a world of which they wanted no part. Hana wished Sal had not come for her.

Alone in the heavy atmosphere of the barn, she turned to look at the body. One fact cried out to her almost as if it had a voice. There was no way that boy could have fallen onto the pitchfork. There was no way this awful thing could have been an accident.

Hana Shaner, who usually did not cry easily, felt tears gathering. Willing them away, she put her hands over her face and breathed deeply.

She had great respect for Sal's intelligence, and knew Sal was loyal to her. Sal must have known. That was why she had not suggested calling the police immediately. She had wanted Hana here when the police came. She had wanted Hana to protect this family, these people who did not know the ways of the world.

Hana felt unequal to the task.

Her hands dropped to her side and she went to pick up her umbrella. Even though the rain had stopped, she was glad she had it. Holding it tightly like a weapon, she moved to the center of the floor and pivoted, looking about carefully and slowly.

But if there was a needle in this haystack, she could not see it. The only things out of place were the boy, the pitchfork, and the blood.

## *Chapter Two*

SERGEANT KOCHEN LOOKED as if the beige turtleneck he wore beneath his brown cord jacket was not enough protection against the breeze that had blown away the clouds and was now troubling early blossoms and sweeping through the barn.

"God, I hate this," he complained to Hana.

Did he imagine anybody liked it?

A photo flash flared from the vicinity of the body. To the Amish photography meant "graven images" and "Thou Shalt Not . . ." Now the violation of the dead boy was complete, she thought bitterly.

Kochen shoved his hands into his pockets. "If the founding families hadn't expected such big things of this city, I wouldn't be here," he said gloomily. "City Line Road is another two miles away and that makes it our murder."

"Maybe it wasn't murder."

He contemplated her with all the superiority of a professor faced with a particularly dense student. "Even you must be able to see the angle of that pitchfork. Someone a lot taller than this kid rammed that thing through him. He sure didn't fall on it at that angle."

Trying not to let this supercilious sergeant see her reluctance, Hana looked again at the body. It wasn't the angle of the pitchfork that bothered her but the fact that he had been a slight child, not the kind one usually thought of as a farm boy. Not that there was a rule which said all Amish children had to be robust and rawboned.

Hana shook her head. "Maybe the boys had been playing . . . you know, fooling around. Amish kids aren't saints although some people pretend they are. Older boys play rough sometimes . . . especially with such a little fellow. Maybe they jumped on him from that pile of hay. Why *couldn't* it be an accident?"

She knew she was groping. Apparently Kochen did too.

"At least it's a possibility," she added sourly because he looked as though he pitied her.

"No way," he replied curtly, then began issuing orders to scene-of-the-crime people. They were looking for fingerprints, which seemed ridiculous to Hana. This—whatever sort of crime it was—required something other than by-the-book thinking.

A draft banged shut the barn door. Somewhere below a cow lowed.

Hana shivered and went on compulsively as soon as Kochen paused. "Unless it was something like that, it makes no sense at all. These people are nonviolent. They're conscientious objectors."

"There are aberrant persons in any society, Ms. Shaner."

Although his words were mild, his tone soft, she was aware of his hostility. It had been present during her brief contact with him when she was searching for her missing friend last fall but today it seemed stronger. He was giving her his full attention now, his eyes sweeping from her short white hair down to the muddy shoes. There were those who found her youthful-looking face an attractive contrast to the white hair, but apparently Kochen wasn't one.

"What are *you* doing here anyway?" he finally asked.

"The Schwambachs are neighbors of my housekeeper—Sal Nunemacher. She thought I might be able to help."

"She thought wrong. There's nothing you can do here except get in the way of professionals who know how to handle a murder case."

Hana let the coldness she felt into her voice. "A murder on an Amish farm just might be beyond your expertise. You don't know these people. As I recall you've only been in the area for about three years."

"This will be handled like any other crime of its kind."

Hana took a deep breath. "That's not the right way to go about it. I have some feelings about this—"

"Feelings!" he exploded. "Deliver me from amateurs who try to solve cases with 'feelings'!"

"Sometimes feelings are all we have to go on."

"Ms. Shaner: leave. And take Sal Nunemacher with you . . . wherever she is. I'll send someone to get your statements later. Meanwhile, I don't want you asking questions around here. I don't want you interfering with police work. I don't want you, period. Do you understand?"

Hana Shaner, at forty the last of a long line of locally prominent Shaners accustomed to giving orders rather than taking them, resisted an urge to threaten to go over his head and have him fired. Instead, she contented herself with throwing out a red herring which, she was sure, would unsettle the unimaginative detective.

She moved a few feet away then turned dramatically, stirring barn dust with her foot to give eerie emphasis to her words, and closing her deep green eyes to slits. "I hope for your sake this doesn't turn out to be a case involving . . . hex."

She took evil satisfaction in how well it worked.

"Hex!" he shouted. "Who said anything about *hex?*"

Everybody stopped what they were doing to stare at him. A uniformed officer on guard at the barn door took a step forward, eyeing Hana suspiciously.

Kochen lowered his voice to a dignified level. "There is no such thing as . . . hex . . . witchcraft."

"There is if you believe in it, Sergeant Kochen. And some of these people still do, you know."

He did not know. She knew he did not, because he had not grown up with the Germanic tales and superstitions that reached beyond the plain sects to include the fancy Dutch. He probably didn't even know what "powwow" meant.

"The very suggestion is irresponsible," he said tightly. "It's a subject which should not even be brought up without damn good cause. And I doubt you have any cause for introducing it. Now you listen to me: if you try to hamper my investigation of this boy's death in any way, I'll see that you're prosecuted to the fullest extent of the law. Understand? Shaners are not above the law, no matter what you think."

He had left himself wide open. She smiled. "Very well. When you need my help, you are going to have to ask for it. I have a *feeling* this is going to be a very difficult case for you, Sergeant."

Still smiling, she left before he could come back with a topper.

She suspected Sal was in the house with the family. The girl of the barn silhouette answered her knock and just stared at her. In the light she was a pretty child, fair and wide-eyed. Her dress and apron looked new. Traces of mud clung around the soles of her shoes. Hana asked for Sal Nunemacher.

Apparently the girl understood English, because she stepped aside for Hana to enter, then carefully closed the door as if shutting out something unpleasant.

Hana followed the child through a hall toward the back of the sprawling house. It was a typical old Amish farmhouse—which meant it was not quite as plain as its occupants. Bright ovals of rags that had been given a glorious rebirth as rugs lay on yellow wood floors. Geraniums and begonias, which the locals called "ice plants," crowded the wide windowsills. Like a green chandelier, one fabulous spider plant hung in a sunny corner of a parlor large enough to accommodate easily the church services that all Old Order Amish took turns hosting. On the walls were bright calendar scenes, some of which had been framed. The furniture was all old but sturdy and well cared for.

In the kitchen Sal and Mrs. Schwambach sat with white coffee mugs in front of them. The child ducked back through the doorway and a moment later Hana heard the clumping of shoes on bare wood stairs.

"Can I get you some coffee?" Mrs. Schwambach asked, slowly dragging out the English words. "There's lots."

"Another time if I may?"

The woman nodded uncertainly. Hana wondered if the rest of the family were upstairs somewhere getting their stories together. Plain People were the souls of honesty but they were also human, and these circumstances might justify a lie, just as sometimes modern transportation was justified in the case of illness or business.

"The police will soon be in to talk to you," Hana told Mrs. Schwambach.

Again she nodded. Sal noisily swallowed the last of her coffee.

Hana hoped Mrs. Schwambach understood English better than she spoke it. She tried to catch the woman's restless eyes and hold them. "Sergeant Kochen and his officers will ask you questions. You'll have to speak to him. Not just your husband. *You* will have to talk to them."

A nervous tongue licked her lips as she nodded once more.

Hana decided to press harder. "Your husband said that all of you women and girls stayed inside the house. I don't believe that's true. I know Amish girls do barn chores too. If questioned by themselves at the police station, I wonder if they'd have something to tell us."

Mrs. Schwambach looked appealingly at Sal.

"There's no need to scare her so," Sal snapped.

"Isn't there? Mr. Schwambach said the boys were feeding the horses and cows. They had to be up there in the haymow to pitch food down to the animals. Don't try to tell me that's not how it's done. And I suspect even Sergeant Kochen will know it. Now if they were up there—any of them—they must have seen something. That's where Aaron was: either with them and alive, or dead before they got there." Hana leaned toward the Amish woman. "You'd better think about it. Maybe you should decide to tell the truth. If somebody was playing too roughly and something happened . . ."

"*Nein! Folsch!*" she cried. "Nobody here done it. None of my kids done it. *Ach, du lieber Gott!*"

The woman put her hands over her face. Sal hesitated, looking as if she wanted to put her arms around her neighbor.

But she didn't.

"Maybe it would be better if she had time to think about it alone," Hana said to Sal. "Kochen will be here any minute, and it might be best if he doesn't find us talking to the family."

Sal nodded, then said a few words in dialect to Mrs. Schwambach. The woman was still sitting with her hands over her face when they left the room.

There was no sign of the rest of the family.

\*   \*   \*

On the return trip to Blue Spring Hill, Hana fast-forwarded her mind to her own business. She could still get everything done if she worked fast and efficiently. She was considering the suggestion of her executive assistant, Cindy Hefflefinger, to do a wedding gown in Dutch Blue, an audacious, daring innovation, and watching a confetti of cherry blossoms blowing across plowed fields when she realized Sal had said nothing since they had left the Schwambach farm.

The set of Sal's jaw and her frown showed that she was concentrating. But certainly not on her driving, for Sal was an instinctively good driver.

"Sal, are you angry?"

"No."

The word was clipped.

Hana sighed. "There was no way we could keep the police out of this. Those people are hiding something. I don't even know them and I'm terribly sorry they have to go through this but I don't . . ."

"I know them."

Sal looked at her for a moment before she returned her attention to the morning traffic. "If I tell you something, will you keep it just between you and me? Nobody else. I don't want to be carrying stories about my neighbors to the police. That's not my way. But I'll tell you if you promise."

The woodland beside the road was turning yellow-green, the gray of limbs blurred by maple blossoms. Hana realized if she made this promise to Sal, it would be sacred. That was the Plain way, and she had to abide by it or lose their respect—maybe even lose Sal. And yet . . . she thought of the sprawled body of the boy. No matter what Kochen wanted or didn't want, she owed something to that dead child.

"I will not give Sergeant Kochen or any other police officer any private information you share with me about the Schwambach family. If I can use it myself to find out who killed the boy, I will. But I won't tell anybody. Unless, Sal, it must come out at a trial. Then you realize I wouldn't lie."

"That's good enough," Sal agreed. "Because maybe it doesn't mean anything. It's just . . . well, now, it bothers me some."

They turned onto the winding driveways of Blue Spring Hill. The famous azaleas were tuning up for spring and their imminent display. Grass, recently and lovingly fertilized by Bottingers' Gardening Service, was actually quivering to grow. For a moment Hana became lost in the love of her ancestral estate and forgot that Sal had something to say.

Sal stopped the car, then suddenly began talking.

"We've been living on the next farm to those Schwambachs for . . . well, ever since my grandfather got our place. We're Mennonite and they're Amish, so we don't go to their meetings and aren't in with them thick, you understand, and they keep to themselves a lot, but still . . . they've been our neighbors. They know our kids. We know theirs. The kids play together once in a while like kids do."

The decision on the Dutch Blue wedding gown was waiting. The TV decisions with Pocky Reilly were waiting. Undoubtedly Jimmy Klopp was waiting at the plant with an emergency that would require her attention.

"Yes, I understand you're neighbors," Hana interrupted. "I understood that when you asked me to go out there with you. But what does that have to do with their son being killed?"

"I never saw that boy before in my life," Sal said without emotion. "I know every one of the Schwambach kids and I never saw him before. As far as I know, they never had a boy named Aaron."

## *Chapter Three*

SAL GOT OUT of the car mumbling something about being behind in her work, leaving Hana to wonder if she had really understood Sal's words.

Two dogs and three cats, lined up as if trained like English servants to greet their mistress upon her arrival, blocked the way to the side door. But no way were these animals trained.

Sal turned to glare at Hana, grunted, then, avoiding the animals, tramped over the grass and into the house.

Dog Ghost, large and shaggy, and Dog Crumb, small and long, looked as if their favorite bones had been taken away from them and they were feeling growly about it. That the three cats stood beside them was unusual. Gray Trouble, Penelope Baskin, a lucky three-colored cat, and Kitty Fisher, a mud-eyed cross between a wayward Siamese and a red alley cat, all stared at her accusingly.

"What's the matter?" Hana asked them with some irritation.

Mr. Fred must have done something; Mr. Fred was always doing something. But what abominations could he possibly commit on a spring morning like this? She looked about apprehensively but all she saw was a strange car in the parking lot. Probably a new day person for cleaning, or somebody servicing something—nothing to concern her. She decided she would avoid Mr. Fred if possible, change her shoes, and get to the office. The animals were perfectly capable of doing battle with him.

Inside, muddy shoes in hand, she was on her way through the front hall to the stairs when she heard voices and the clank of coffee cups from the largest drawing room. My God—was she entertaining today? Had she forgotten something? The *large* drawing room was used only on very special occasions . . .

Gnomelike Mr. Fred, omnipotent and omniscient, appeared at the folding doors, a broad but suspiciously phony smile on his large face.

"Here she is now!" he announced, throwing open both doors.

Her guests, bone white coffee cups from the 1882 service in hands, rose as a unit with smiles as large as Mr. Fred's.

Hana devotedly wished she had that awful carrot-raisin omelette to dump on his big head. He had the biggest head and tallest, thinnest body of anyone she had ever met.

She did not know these people.

Wrong. She did know one of them. A Mr. . . what was it? Something odd even for Conover County, the home of odd names. Pettengill! Yes. Harvey P. Pettengill, head of the local historical society.

And that explained it.

Mr. Fred, who frequently had archaeological students digging up portions of her estate searching for artifacts with which to fill the 1812 Annex of Blue Spring Hill, had obviously struck again.

Damn his soul to writhe forever in a molten mass of eggs, carrots, and raisins.

With dignity she placed her shoes on the stairs and came forward in her stocking feet.

"I have only a few moments," she said, smiling sweetly at Mr. Fred. "I really must get to the office."

There were four of them: Mr. Pettengill, another man, and two women. While Mr. Fred fussed about, making a show of getting coffee for Hana, one of the women rushed up to her.

"I've always wanted to meet you, Ms. Shaner! I can't tell you how exciting all this is."

"It's awfully generous of you," Mr. Pettengill added, beaming through thick lenses.

Inwardly Hana groaned. She really would have to do something about Mr. Fred. Whatever he was planning, he had arranged this meeting for a time when she would ordinarily have been at the office, so his scheme would have been too far along to stop once she heard of it.

"Who are you?" Hana asked the woman. "And just what is it I'm so generously doing?"

"I'm Teddy Jolf."

Coffee was thrust into her hands by the speeding Mr. Fred, who whipped out introductions.

The other two were Josie and Bert Adams, conservative, ordinary-looking folks in their forties.

Hana found Teddy Jolf more interesting. She had inquisitive brown eyes, which matched abundant hair. Hana judged her to be somewhere in her early thirties. There was a competent air about her which the Adamses did not possess, nor did Mr. Pettengill, who reminded her of a benign Mr. Fred.

"I'm new to the Historical Society," Teddy Jolf

said, "but I'm really getting into it. This Open
House is the first project I'm helping with."

"What Open House?" Hana asked Mr. Fred pointedly.

"Ms. Shaner is a busy woman who doesn't like to
be plagued with details," he said glibly, avoiding
her eyes. "I'm sure you can depend upon us to do
all the spadework."

"I'm sure I can," Hana agreed. "Where is this
Open House to be held?"

Mr. Pettengill looked surprised, which meant his
funguslike eyebrows nearly reached his hairline
for a few seconds. "Why . . . here, of course. To
open the museum in the 1812 Annex."

If it hadn't been the 1882 bone china from Great-
Great-Grandmother Clara Elizabeth Fronheiser-
Schoener, Hana would have dropped her coffee
cup.

"And to think you've invited the entire county to
view your beautiful azaleas," Josie Adams chortled, her short sprayed hair bouncing approvingly.
"What a generous gesture."

Mr. Fred looked worried. "We'll have all the
plans drawn up today and you can veto anything
you think inappropriate."

Bert Adams, pleasant looking despite his bland
coloring and features, had apparently been watching her, because he added sensibly, "I can see that
Ms. Shaner is worried about people trampling her
flowers. But we assure you the place will be well
patrolled."

"I had the greatest idea how to do that!" Teddy
announced proudly. "We'll have an absolute army
of Amish kids here to act as guards!"

"We'll bring them in by the busload right from
the farms," Bert Adams agreed.

Although the Amish lived in the midst of Conover County, their ways kept them separate. There were months when they were scarcely mentioned. Odd that on this particular morning . . .

Teddy Jolf went on, "I talked with the oldest Schwambach boy yesterday—what's his name? Jake. He offered to help get them together. We'll pay them, of course."

A coldness seeped through Hana. Just a coincidence. What else could it be? Her mind on the dead boy in the barn, she hardly heard Mr. Fred's carefully worded request for her permission to go ahead. She supposed she must have nodded absently, because he looked relieved.

Hana gently placed her coffee cup on a table.

"There was trouble at the Schwambach farm this morning," she said loudly, her eyes on Teddy Jolf. "One of the boys was killed."

"Farm accidents," Mr. Pettengill said testily. "Shouldn't let kids handle some of that equipment. Asking for trouble."

"The police are sure it wasn't an accident," Hana said. "They think somebody deliberately shoved a pitchfork through his chest."

Josie Adams sat down quickly, looking as if murder had never before come closer to her than a newspaper article, quickly read and discarded.

"Maybe you knew him," Hana said to Teddy Jolf. "The father said his name was Aaron."

She started nervously. "No. No!"

"But apparently you knew his brother. Jake, right?"

"Oh. Well, yes."

"But not the rest of the family?"

"Some of the children," she said cautiously. "But not an Aaron. I don't think so anyway."

Hana waited through the moments of uncomfortable silence. Not even the coffee cups clattered. Then Mr. Fred began talking again about the Open House at Blue Spring Hill.

Later, cleanly shod, Hana drove along the winding lanes of her estate. She had called the office. Appointments had been jostled about and things were reasonably under control, except that Pocky Reilly kept calling, desperately wanting to talk about a new commercial.

Barking distracted her. Across a wide patch of grass between what would soon be massive beds of magenta azaleas, Ghost and Crumb pursued a running figure. They were not watchdogs but companion animals she had adopted from the animal shelter she had founded. However, Ghost and Crumb did not always acknowledge these fine distinctions in dog status and enthusiastically looked for opportunities to defend their property.

Who was it, an Amish boy? Yes . . . the clothing was right. An Amish boy, or young man. Whatever.

She braked, pushed the button to open the window, and called to the dogs. Crumb, always agreeable, came immediately. Ghost, more dedicated to the dog profession, swiped at the lad's trousers as the boy slowed, apparently believing help was at hand. Then he put on a spurt of speed while Ghost triumphantly galloped to the car, a shredded bit of fabric hanging from his mouth.

Hana got out of her car to accept this tribute of the dog's devotion. He'd done it before and he'd probably do it again; after all, why not? He'd never ripped clothing off invited guests. Beyond the azalea bushes, the boy disappeared into the woods. Hana ordered the dogs back to the house. Unnerved and perplexed, she slipped the fabric into the glove compartment.

The dogs were still sitting on the driveway, watching her car as she drove off again. Although she kept watch for the intruder, she saw no one. That this morning's problems involved the Amish disturbed her. She respected and admired these people. They did not trespass. Nor did they steal or molest anyone. They were the best neighbors and the best citizens a country could have. But something strange was happening with the Schwambachs.

As she headed toward the freeway, she wondered if the intruder could possibly have been Jake Schwambach. Had he been coming to her for help? She would have to return to the farm. No matter what the caustic Sergeant Kochen thought of her meddling, she was involved.

She postponed until later thoughts of Mr. Fred's hordes enjoying an Open House among her azalea beds. Come to think of it, had she ever given him permission to open that stupid museum in the 1812 Annex?

"Amish!" Pocky Reilly babbled over the phone as Hana sat at her desk in her plant-filled, window-lined private office. "That's the answer! Your Dutch Blue clothing line needs a real zinger, right? So get this. *A modified Amish dress.* The shops'll go crazy over it. On the ads we'll feature this real-looking Amish girl admiring the outfit. Wow! Is that a natural or is that a natural? Posters! And a commercial to launch it!"

Nancy Reilly, a young woman Hana had brought out of the local community theater to direct her first carpet commercials, was becoming known in her field and, to use a homey phrase, growing too big for her britches. Her most annoying idiosyncrasy was her insistence on the use of her nickname. "Pocky" Reilly she had become when, as a forlorn refugee from a foster home, she had arrived at the Conover Players wearing jeans and a baggy top featuring large square pockets in front. Pocky Reilly she remained because, she said, that name was the first thing anybody had cared enough to give her.

Hana interrupted a flow of descriptions. "No, Pocky! Absolutely not. I've told you how I feel and my decision is final. This would be no different from my friend Bill Longenecker taking tourists on buses to stare at them. We'll launch Dutch Blue without an Amish dress."

"Just hire a designer and look at the idea before you say no—"

"I've already said no!"

Hana hung up on her grumbling.

The remainder of the day she devoted to details of getting Dutch Blue into the marketplace sans an Amish dress. The shade was special; it had made the Shaner fortune in carpets, but to use it in another field was quite a radical decision. So far as Hana knew, no one had ever put out a monochromatic clothing line. She wasn't even sure her staid ancestors would approve of this use of their very special blue.

Cindy Hefflefinger, her executive assistant, certainly did.

"Exciting!" she exclaimed, holding out a design for the controversial wedding gown. "Love it. It's so . . . different."

Hana nodded, feeling tired. The day had begun with murder and was ending with tedious overtime. April, unpredictable as always, had turned to clouds and drizzle again. She realized with surprise that it was already quite dark. Her office staff had gone long ago.

"Why don't you run along?" she told Cindy.

Cindy was willing to stay but Hana insisted. Her assistant, the daughter of one of the janitorial women who worked at Shaner Industries, was at times too ambitious and willing.

After the young woman had reluctantly gone, Hana spent another half hour reading reports from clothing wholesalers.

Hunger. She wondered what Sal had prepared for dinner. The thought of Sal conjured up the events of the morning, but at the moment Hana didn't feel like coping with them. Wearily, she got her coat out of the closet and shrugged into it as she left her private office.

Odd, she thought, how a room that's usually filled with people seems emptier than, say, one's own bedroom, where one is accustomed to being alone. Well, at any rate, *she* was accustomed to being alone in her bedroom. Those romances and flings she had enjoyed had never been brought home to Blue Spring Hill. She sighed and the sound was loud in the silence.

Except that the silence was not complete.

# Chapter Four

HANA PAUSED in the outer office, listening. She heard nothing. Just for a moment, she thought she'd heard someone moving in the hall. Logically it should be a security guard patrolling, except that the sound had been too stealthy. She often worked late and had never been afraid before. Security at Shaner Industries was thorough and good.

Nerves.

Of course. Seeing that poor dead boy this morning had affected her more than she realized. Somehow it was always worse when the young died. The days of spring he would miss, the plowing of his father's and then someday his own fields with a team of mules. Harvest and full barns, as full of pride as of grain. Good times visiting the local farmers' markets when work was forgotten . . .

Damn.

She was well caught up on work now. Maybe she could take off for a few days and see what she could find out.

Hana strode across the glass-walled room. She opened the door. Down the corridor where it turned toward elevators and stairs, she saw—or thought she saw—a movement, a shadow, as though someone had turned the corner.

Hana hesitated.

She remembered the fear she'd felt when she'd been poking around in that other mystery. There'd been an excuse for it then, but why be a hero now for nothing?

Hana closed the door, retreated to her inner office, and called Security. Minutes later, guards and dogs were all over the office and the corridor.

They found nothing.

However, one female German shepherd became excited about something near the double doors that opened onto the parking lot. But once outside she merely circled about with her nose to the ground. Feeling foolish, Hana was escorted to her car by two guards and a phalanx of dogs.

Maggie Nunis, crisp and efficient in her security uniform, watched her sympathetically.

"It's been a long day," she said as she closed Hana's car door.

Hana nodded. Maggie Nunis didn't know how long.

Home to a good meal at the end of day.

Yeah, sure.

Sal, who really ought to have been aware that Mr. Fred had invented an omelette that morning, should not have created broccoli cheese soup and lentil-rice loaf with dill dressing for dinner, Hana thought resentfully. She offered some lentil-rice to the cats, who were sitting watching the progress of her meal with interest.

The dogs were out patrolling, probably looking for another boy to embarrass by the removal of a layer of his posterier clothing. Mr. Fred had eaten long before, apparently an appreciator of broccoli and lentil-rice.

"It's Lent," he said, although she had not mentioned her feelings about the meal.

"I don't observe Lent."

"Sal does," he said.

Trouble tasted the loaf and swallowed it with a thoughtful look on his gray face.

"I can't believe you would actually plan an Open House without consulting me," Hana grumbled. Even if she was tired, the subject had to be dealt with and the sooner the better.

"I intended to consult you," he said stiffly, removing the loaf from the kitchen table and replacing it with a small dish of rice pudding. Hana decided she would have to speak to Sal about her obsession with rice. Of course, Lent would soon be over, for which one had to be grateful.

"When?"

"When we had formulated our plans. After all,

there's no point in discussing things with busy people until one can do so intelligently."

He really was a pompous ass.

"I hate the idea."

"You're tired."

"I'm tired but I also hate it. Tired doesn't stop hate, only makes it more uncomfortable."

He sat in the chair across from her. Behind him a small fire in the open fireplace felt good against the damp spring air. Sometimes Mr. Fred made her feel like a child again, and this was one of those times. To avoid looking at him, she ate her rice pudding.

"The museum is virtually set up. Everything in it represents a part of the history of Blue Spring Hill. Everybody is anxious to see the Revolutionary War remains we dug up last fall. We have display cases filled with bodies and parts of bodies."

Oh, God, when had it all happened?

"Did I ever give you permission to go ahead with this?" she asked curiously.

"Naturally! You can't think that I . . . I . . . who have served the Shaner family on this estate since I was a boy in my teens . . . would involve myself in a project such as this without permission?"

Mouthing rice pudding, she contemplated him. No, of course not. Somewhere, sometime, he had caught her in a weak moment. He knew her vulnerable times as he had known her father's.

Hana swallowed her pudding, knowing objection was useless. Mr. Fred had decided Blue Spring Hill needed a private museum, so a private museum would be there. Death, taxes, and Mr. Fred's museum.

"These artifacts," he said grandly, "belong to the community."

"Then let the community have them. I will gladly donate everything to the Historical Society. More than gladly."

"However," he went on, stroking his thinning hair as if patting himself on the head for a job well done, "they are an integral part of Blue Spring Hill. Your father would have welcomed this display. He'd have been proud to contribute to the enjoyment of historically minded citizens. And every other year during *his* lifetime we had an Open House here. He enjoyed sharing his azaleas. It was only after you took over that the practice was discontinued."

It was more than she could bear. The ghost of her father was irresistible when resurrected by the loyal Mr. Fred.

He had the grace to look worried, as if he had gone too far. He had. She damned his soul to wander forever through the 1812 Annex.

Wow. No, she didn't really mean that.

Leaning forward, he smiled enticingly, like an enormous Disneyesque elf. "If you would just visit the 1812 Annex—"

"Later. Tell me. Where did you meet this woman —Teddy Jolf?"

"She's a member of the Conover Historical Society."

"She gave me the impression that she hasn't been a member long. Did you know her before she joined?"

"Actually just since we've been working on the Open House. It seemed wise to include the society in the planning. And I must say they've come through with fine ideas."

"All right, but how did she get on the committee?"

"I think she volunteered."

"But you don't know for sure?"

"Yes, of course I know. That's how the committee was formed. By people volunteering."

"So an unknown woman from nowhere volunteers for this thing and is invited into my home to view its inner workings, security system, to make notes—any damn thing—without my knowledge and you think nothing of it."

"I will stake my reputation on her good intentions," Mr. Fred sniffed, apparently not realizing how low his reputation had sunk. "Really, Miss Hana. Why on earth would anyone join a historical society for clandestine reasons? Only the most upstanding, culturally minded citizens are interested in historical societies."

While Mr. Fred watched disapprovingly, Hana placed her dish on the floor to let the cats finish off the rice pudding. Kitty Fisher slapped Gray Trouble with a fistful of claws and he backed off while she lapped away. Mr. Fred made small sounds as if he were growling.

That made Hana feel better.

## Chapter Five

GOOD FRIDAY AT the White Unicorn Farmers Market and Auction had become a local tradition. Although a few of the most orthodox Old Order Amish closed their stands and fasted on this holy day, the parking lots surrounding the conglomeration of ramshackle sheds, cinder-block buildings, open stalls, and tables were often gridlocked. Bumper-to-bumper traffic clogged the two-lane country roads and bridges crossing Conover Creek, and the White Unicorn grounds took on the look of a county fair.

The midway displayed everything from produce to clothing and collectibles. A large hay sale occupied one parking lot, and a labyrinthine barn full of animals was the center of interest for children. Tourists came to see Plain People up close, where they could be spoken to for the price of a jar of chow-chow or Pennsylvania Dutch artichoke roots.

It was a day Hana longed to avoid. However, the Fur and Feather Animal Shelter she had founded kept an active interest in certain doings involving live animals. Only constant vigil kept conditions of the animals sold for butchering even tolerable in the barn. Volunteers monitored the agents of laboratories who did illicit trading in the parking lots with farmers careless about spaying their barn cats.

Hana, who seldom pulled rank, took her turn at surveillance along with the other volunteers. That was why Good Friday morning found her in the White Unicorn bar, a sagging one-story frame structure set across the road so that religiously inspired teetotalers would not be antagonized or offended. Opposite her Bill Longenecker sat gulping beer while she drank tepid coffee and contemplated her life which, although it had brought her wealth and success, had also supplied a share of crosses to bear. Or perhaps it was because it was Good Friday that she thought of crosses.

Bill Longenecker.

She had a reason for inviting him along on today's expedition that had nothing to do with the surveillance. Bill operated a travel agency specializing in tours of the Amish areas. She had objected to his turning the Amish into a tourist attraction. He maintained he was respectful of their rights and privacy and only took his buses where members of the sect expressed interest in benefiting from tourism. And certainly some of them did.

Hana knew a number of his contacts had stands here at the market.

The murder of the Amish boy was no closer to solution than the day he died. She and Sal had given their statements to a bored detective who asked few questions. Hana worried that the case would soon be swept away into a file of unsolved crimes and a murderer would quietly go on to kill again. She had decided to try to get inside information by using Bill's contacts.

She sometimes wondered what she had seen in Bill during that summer of their relationship. She wondered again as she watched him swallowing the last of his morning beer. She flicked somebody's potato chip crumbs from the oilcloth covering the small, rickety table and asked, "Started the Amish tours for this season, Bill?"

He bristled, giving her the momentary illusion that his amazingly curly hair rose a little. "First of May."

"But I'm sure you've been talking to people like that woman who sells quilts out of her garage."

"Aha!" he exclaimed triumphantly. "I was wondering what you wanted. It's that Amish boy who was murdered last week. That's it, right? You're trying to do a detective thing again."

There had been the briefest paragraph in the newspaper. No hint of anything except a farm accident. Nothing on the local TV news. Nobody wanted the media intruding in the Amish community.

"I'm here to inspect for animal abuses. You know that."

He grinned slyly. "That's your story. But I know you, Hana. I always look for ulterior motives when you ask me out."

"Then why do you come with me?" she asked curiously.

He hesitated, rubbing his hand where it had stuck to old cola congealed in rings on the table. "Maybe because I'm always interested in what you're going to do next. Maybe because I just like to see you. Even on these terms."

The answer embarrassed her. He was watching her expectantly. She didn't know how to respond.

"How did you know the Amish boy was murdered?" she asked.

"Heard about it from Mr. Fred. He's been calling me every day."

"Mr. Fred calls you?"

"Wants me to promote that Open House at your place. Maybe even include it on one of our tours."

One day, Hana decided, there would be a murder at Blue Spring Hill. And she cast Mr. Fred in the role of victim. Blue Spring Hill on one of Bill Longenecker's tours? Wait until she got ahold of Mr. Fred.

With an effort she pulled her mind back to the market.

"The woman who sells those quilts to tourists has a stand here, hasn't she?"

He shook his head. "Not her. A second cousin or something like that. Sells dried schnitz, chow-chow, that kind of thing. Are you having another drink?"

With disgust, Hana pushed away her cup. "No. Let's go talk to the Dried Schnitz Lady."

Across the road the crowd surged slowly through

the midway. Later that night groups of young Amish and Mennonites, boys and girls, would gather. This was the main recreation of their week, the only place they could go without sin, their only contact with the world beyond their religion and their farms. She noted that girls in their traditional costumes wore pastel sneakers with their cotton stockings. Even here the modern world was intruding.

The Dried Schnitz Woman, whose name was Mrs. Hinklefuss, sold from a small shed sheltered against the weather by plastic stretched over a board framework. Rows of home-jarred goodies rested on sturdy shelves. The dried schnitz (apples) were packaged in plastic bags for sanitary reasons, whereas formerly they had hung in attics as a roost for flies. There were baskets of "old" potatoes, whites and sweets, and in a discreet corner, bags of homegrown cow manure for suburban gardeners who wanted the real thing, fragrance and all.

Bill greeted the woman who, Hana thought, looked annoyed.

He introduced Hana. The woman nodded, then turned away to sell a bottle of sweet homemade catsup to an eager tourist.

"I know you're busy today," Hana said hastily as a noisy crowd pushed into the little shelter, "but I wonder if you could answer just a few questions?"

"What for?" she asked.

"I'd like to help the Schwambach family. Their boy was killed in the barn . . ."

"*Ja*. I know."

"Then you know we should clear up the mystery as soon as possible."

"Ain't no mystery. It was an accident."

Somebody took a flash picture. Mrs. Hinklefuss covered her face with her hands. Without buying anything the group barged out. A man trundled in a wheelbarrow, which he loaded with manure bags.

Bill and Hana retired to a neutral corner while the woman completed the sale.

"You're not going to get much out of her," he murmured. "She's not exactly the talkative type."

He was right. Between customers the farm woman agreed that she knew the family but never noticed kids. The Schwambachs had lots of kids, so she must have seen the boy Aaron but didn't remember particularly. She kept repeating the word *accident*. As they left, she mumbled how city folks were too dumb about farming to know all the "dangerous stuff" that went on.

"She's probably right, you know," Bill said as they turned toward the barn.

Hana didn't want to agree, but unless somebody talked—really talked—it might be the only conclusion they could ever reach.

The cattle sales were over. Many of the animals were still in the largest barn area, lowing mournfully over their fate, which they seemed to understand intuitively.

"This place always gives me the creeps," Bill said as he tramped about after her.

Parents with their children clustered near the front of the barn peering at the livestock. Drovers and auctioneers in overalls were taking a break, sitting about on bales of hay as eager out-of-staters snapped photographs.

Back toward the loading platforms the barn was deserted and quiet. Some animals had already been removed. Hay and straw lay in untidy mounds, and Hana looked carefully at them. Carcasses had occasionally been hidden beneath the straw. If there were dead animals, she wanted to know why.

Bill said, "I didn't think you'd get anything out of Mrs. Hinklefuss. Whole family's like that. Even the kids won't talk to the tourists we bring in. Pop Hinklefuss isn't a talker either, but he likes the money and their farm has a big pulloff so our tour buses can go right up to the little stand he built to display their produce. But now you take that Quilt Woman, she's different. Really chats with the people. And she doesn't mind pictures. Not all of them believe in 'Thou shalt not make any graven images' thing anymore."

"The Quilt Woman is a talker?"

"Oh, sure. She knows that Pennsylvania Dutch is the number one folk culture in this country. Which means she knows which side of the bread has the butter."

Hana ignored the cliché. "When are you going to see her?"

"Could be soon," he said with a grin. "Have to set up our tour schedule. I like to get there in late afternoon. She's usually closing up about then, getting ready to cook their meal. Maybe you and I could have dinner after seeing her?"

Hana nodded, feeling guilty. She really should not be using him this way. Too bad he was so . . . useful.

The barn, like most of the buildings at the White Unicorn, had been hammered together in bits and pieces, expanding as more room was needed. The result was a haphazard cluster of rooms. Hana peered into one. Nothing but hay that she could see. Little light came through the small, high window.

"Hey," Bill said.

"Yes, and I guess that's all. Just hay."

"No, I mean something's over there, in that corner."

Hana squinted toward the mounds of hay that almost hid a dark and huddled form.

"I told them that if I found one more unexplained dead pig, there'd be trouble! People think they can do anything they damn please with butchering animals."

"I don't think it's a pig," Bill whispered.

She looked at him, momentarily surprised. Dusty sunlight turned him into a hovering silhouette. Hana crossed the floor.

Suddenly she knew what she would find. She could see the pitchfork now. She ran, dropped to her knees, and scraped away dirty straw.

Blood had oozed onto the cement. Was still oozing.

The boy was slightly larger than the other one. And, like Aaron, dressed in an Amish outfit—colorful shirt, suspenders, baggy work pants, high rough shoes.

She saw it all at a glance and felt sick.

Then she saw the hand move slightly, the fingers clawing at the ground.

"He's alive," she cried to Bill. "Go get help! Get an ambulance!"

Bill ran.

She brushed curls from the boy's forehead. His flesh felt cold. As she watched, the light in his wide blue eyes went out and he died.

Hana was still kneeling beside him when she saw it—a small homesewn pouch hanging around his neck on thick twine. It seemed as though an eternity had already passed. Another began as she fumbled to insert her fingers into the drawstrings, spreading them. She withdrew a slip of white paper and carefully opened it.

She read:

I.

N. I. R.

I.

SANCTUS     SPIRITUS

I.

N. I. R.

I.

Once, a long time ago, when constant stomach cramps had defied all of Dr. Harold Reifsnyder's remedies, Aunt Sissy had taken her to the cabin of an old woman whose breath smelled of wild chives. It was a cabin in a strange woodland full of oddly shaped hemlock trees with voices of their own. They had gone at night, walking slowly along a path without a flashlight, their only illumination the full moon. Terrified, Hana had clung tightly to Aunt Sissy. She had not understood nor even recalled all that went on in the place, but afterward her stomachaches were gone and she had carried around her neck just such a charm. She could almost hear Aunt Sissy's voice: "It means, 'God bless me here in time, and there eternally.' It's a good hex charm to carry if you've been in any kind of trouble."

Hex.

She had only meant to bait Sergeant Kochen by mentioning the possibility. She hadn't been serious, hadn't for one moment believed any of these people were involved with hexerei. But she'd been wrong. This boy at least had been touched by it before he died.

She put the charm back into the pouch and tucked it gently beneath his shirt.

# Chapter Six

SERGEANT KOCHEN CONTEMPLATED Hana without enthusiasm. They were seated on bales of hay that had been set out for their convenience on the lot at the rear of the barn. Police tapes roped off the entire area. Uniformed police and the official corps of specialists were everywhere, doing preliminary interviewing, taking photographs, searching. Half of detective work was searching, Hana thought.

And rarely finding anything.

Bill Longenecker hovered somewhere behind her.

"Does anybody mind if I get back to my office?" he asked plaintively. "I don't know what else I can tell you anyhow."

"Okay, but don't plan any trips for yourself, Mr. Longenecker," Kochen told him.

"I came with Bill," Hana said. "I'll need a ride home."

"Of course."

"Unless you're willing to let me go now."

"I'm not at all willing to let me go," Kochen snapped.

"Then if it's all right I'll see you later," Bill said and scurried away.

"Don't forget we've got a date," Hana called after him.

"You and Mr. Longenecker are good friends?" Kochen asked.

"I can't imagine what that question has to do with this murder."

He ignored that. "I suppose you think this innocent act has me fooled."

"It is not an act, Sergeant."

He straightened his glasses and leaned forward. "I don't expect cooperation from you—"

"I have always cooperated with the police."

He grunted derisively. "Just tell me his name so we can notify the family. That's only humane. And surely it will not impede your own independent investigations."

Contemplating him for a moment, Hana decided she could understand his point. To him it was perfectly logical that she should know the identity of the boy. Logical that someone had sent her looking for a lost child.

"I honestly have no idea who he is," she said quietly. "I would tell you if I had."

"Is he another of the Schwambach boys?"

Hana considered the suggestion, trying to recall faces from among the knot of kids who had stood silently watching her in the Schwambach barn. She could remember only the older boy and that pigtailed girl.

"I can't be sure. I just met them that one time."

"What the hell were you doing here, woman?"

She looked at him, startled. The man was losing his cool. She told him again about the animals, about the concerns of her animal welfare group for all animals. She certainly had not come to find a dead boy.

It was obvious he considered it a cover story to hide her real motivation. In a sense he was right, she thought, remembering the Dried Schnitz Woman.

"Why don't you send officers around to ask the Amish who have stands here if any of their sons are missing?"

"We're already doing that."

"Nothing so far?"

"Nothing."

"They sometimes hire Amish kids to feed the animals in the barn—"

"Nothing there either. They did hire two boys, but they're at a pizza stand on the midway and have been there for a couple of hours smoking their way through a pack of cigarettes and eating two pizzas each."

"And they heard nothing, saw nothing?"

"Right. Did you?"

Hana tried to visualize the barn as she and Bill had walked through. Piles of straw everywhere. Anyone could have been hiding.

"This place was full of people. Except back where we found him," she told Kochen. "A lot of them were congregated at the entrance, looking at the animals. It's always crowded on Good Friday."

"Thousands of people milling through this area," he said dully. "From every state in the union."

"You could broadcast an appeal for information."

"Don't tell me what I can do, woman!"

"Stop calling me 'woman'! You know my name, Sergeant Kochen." Hana stood up. "And if that's all, I'm leaving now."

He almost smiled. "You have no car, remember?"

"I can hitchhike," she said defiantly, hoping to annoy him.

"Not you. You'd dial a servant," he said, also rising. "But it won't be necessary, Ms. Shaner. I'll drive you home."

"You're finished here?"

"We're past City Line Road this time. Chief Hoffman asked me to come because I'm involved in the other case. He saw a link."

"Apparently you do too."

"Apparently," he said wryly. "We don't get many pitchfork murders."

She wondered if he had been shown the hex amulet. Would he recognize it for what it was? Surely Chief Hoffman would. He had grown up around here.

Kochen escorted her toward the rope that kept the curious in unhappy segregation. Hundreds of people were hanging out in the parking lot, spreading false rumors. A loudspeaker usually reserved for calling errant standholders from the restrooms was announcing that anyone with information about the body in the barn should report to the fish stand.

"Why the fish stand?" she asked as they progressed slowly through clusters of people.

"It's vacant," he said shortly. "The people running it are always closed on Good Friday, Christmas, and Ascension Day. At least, that's what their sign says."

Hana couldn't help smiling at the list, recognizing them as three of Sal's most holy days. She glanced up at Kochen but he was staring solemnly ahead, apparently not amused. It struck her that he was good looking in an idiotic sort of way.

As they got into his old Buick the PA system was announcing, "Will the Sneaker Man please move his wife's Chevy station wagon? It's blocking the Asparagus Woman."

Hana still carried a mental image of a stalky green female as they drove through incredibly peaceful countryside. Hana wondered why he had been so eager to take her home. Surely he had no idea of ingratiating himself, drawing her out with a show of false friendship? He certainly didn't think she actually had anything to do with this awful business.

But in that other case, he had thought just that. More logically, he was probably headed back to

Conover City to fight crime and this was on his way. The silence was almost ticking aloud. He wasn't even talking, let alone questioning her.

"This isn't the way to Blue Spring Hill," she said sharply.

He swung onto a dirt road. "We're taking a detour."

The Schwambach farm. Of course. For some odd reason he had decided to take her with him to the Schwambach farm.

"I don't want to do this," she said.

"Oh? I thought you'd be pleased to be included."

"Suppose it is one of their other sons?"

"I was under the impression that you'd want to be present to protect these people from police brutality. Or coach them perhaps. I'm sure you know more about them than we do. After all, Sal Nunemacher lives on the next farm. You were called in as a friend and consultant. They'll tell you things they would never tell us."

In truth, Hana had been postponing a visit to the farm until the funeral and the Easter holidays were over. But the questions she had couldn't be asked in front of the sergeant unless it could be done so subtly he wouldn't recognize their significance.

Risky.

"That thing around his neck. It has something to do with hex, doesn't it?"

The question was abrupt and harsh.

"It's like a charm," she said. "Nothing bad. Not like a curse or anything. It's there to help."

"Help what?"

"Whatever. If you've been sick or hurt or robbed or threatened—anything. Just a general charm for good luck."

"I didn't know these people were still that super-stitious."

"They take full advantage of modern medicine. At least, most of them do. But there are other things that help too sometimes."

She thought she saw a flicker of shock in his eyes. "You believe in that stuff yourself?"

"Of course not," Hana said, wondering why she felt as if she were lying.

"Strange," he mused. "If you don't believe in it, how did you know hex would be involved here?"

"I didn't know."

"You said so."

"I was just baiting you. I never thought for one minute we'd find anything like that."

"Another unhappy coincidence."

"If you want to call it that."

They were driving over the bumpiest part of the lane. His voice shook. "Ms. Shaner, I don't believe in coincidences."

Nice way to call her a liar.

He went on, "And since we're almost there, you may be interested to know we've found nothing to indicate anybody but the family was in the Schwambach barn that morning. I repeat, noth-ing."

Hana made no response.

The farm had the same deserted feel. Perhaps, despite everything, the family had gone to the White Unicorn. But after Sergeant Kochen's sec-ond authoritative knock the door opened and the same girl, long braids to her waist, stared up at them.

"I'm Sergeant Kochen of the Conover Police De-partment. Are your parents at home?"

Hana willed her to speak but she only backed

away silently, allowing them to enter. Kochen
looked about comfortably.

"Nice place," he commented.

Almost immediately Mrs. Schwambach came
from the direction of the kitchen.

"Mister ain't here," she said as if the English
words were bitter in her mouth.

"Perhaps you can help us," Sergeant Kochen said
politely, moving into the large living room.

Uneasily, the woman followed. Kochen described the boy. Hana could almost see him again
as she listened.

The farm woman shook her head. "Ain't one of
ourn."

Some of the tension left Hana, making her realize how much she wanted this family to be spared
another overwhelming loss. Then she saw a flicker
of emotion in the woman's eyes. It was there for
only a second. Was it possible she had recognized
the description after all?

"You're sure?" Kochen persisted.

The moment had passed. Mrs. Schwambach's
eyes were blank as she looked up again, her arms
folded across her broad body. "I guess I know how
many boys I got. I know where they are too."

"And none of them went over to the White Unicorn today?"

"We don't go over there much. Gives the kids
worldly ideas. And sure not on Good Friday."

While Mrs. Schwambach continued to condemn
the sophisticated activities available to the young
at farmers' markets, Hana wandered about the
room. For whatever reason Kochen had brought
her along, it wasn't working. She supposed he really believed the boy was a Schwambach.

"What a beautiful old German Bible," she exclaimed.

It lay on top of an embroidered cover on a fine oak table.

Mrs. Schwambach turned to her. "It was my *grossmutter's*. It's mine now. Someday it will be hers."

The girl was hovering about her mother.

"May I look at it?" Hana asked.

The woman nodded. Hana was aware that Kochen was watching her closely. Damn. Feigning casual interest, she opened the large book and inspected a colored picture of a robed man facing a barrage of snarling lions. Slowly she turned pages until she found an Egyptian woman parting reeds along a river to discover a woven basket containing a smiling baby.

She spent a long time locating more pictures and even longer inspecting each one. Kochen was asking Mrs. Schwambach where her boys were that minute. Lapsing into the dialect when English failed her, she accounted for them. He was trying to take notes, finding the dialect unintelligible, and no longer seemed aware of what Hana was doing. She flipped quickly through the rest of the Old Testament to pages provided for family histories. Most of the older Bibles included them and this was no exception.

It was all recorded in neat Germanic script, which Hana deciphered with some difficulty. The Schoener family had always kept German as a second language, and now Hana was glad she had followed the tradition. She skipped the generations that had gone before. The years were written plainly enough. *Kinder* of Henry Schwambach and Fannie Dreibelbis Schwambach. Jacob, the oldest. Aaron, the second son.

So Sal Nunemacher had been mistaken. He was here in the Bible, as he had been dead in the barn.

Sal just hadn't noticed him. Hana noted the date of death had not yet been filled in.

She glanced up to find the girl watching her with an odd expression in her eyes.

That other boy . . . Could he possibly be here too? Hana quickly ran down the list of children's names.

No boy of the right age. The next was a girl—Catharine.

"Kate?" she asked the child.

The girl lowered her eyes.

Hana heard Kochen say the word "Hex."

"We don't bother none with that stuff," Mrs. Schwambach told him coldly in very clear English.

Hana closed the Bible.

Kochen seemed anxious to leave. This time he headed directly for Blue Spring Hill.

"Well?" he asked as they sped around a still-dormant apple orchard. "Did you find what you were looking for?"

"What do you mean?"

"In the old Bible—did you find it?"

"I found many pretty pictures."

"And the family records."

"Yes," she admitted. "And the family records."

"Did you find our boy in there?"

"Our boy? No, but I found Aaron."

He slowed down. "Was there any reason you hadn't expected to?"

For a moment, she considered telling him what Sal had said.

He noted her hesitation. "You mean there's a possibility neither boy is a Schwambach?"

"I didn't say that."

He smiled meanly. "Didn't you?"

# Chapter Seven

A FUNEREAL ATMOSPHERE permeated Blue Spring
Hill. Hana paused just inside the door that led to
her parking lot and listened. Usually there was
sound: One of the day-women running a sweeper
somewhere. Or Ghost's and Crumb's toenails tap-
ping against the wooden flooring. Cats racing
around. To say nothing of the omnipresent Mr.
Fred bellowing orders.

The draperies had either been drawn or only
partially opened to the bright day. For the Amish
boy? Had Sal known him better than she acknowledged? Puzzled, Hana walked back along the hall
and down the two stone steps to the kitchen. It was
empty except for Ghost and Crumb, who were sitting near the back door drooping as if they had
been chastened.

"What's the matter with you two?"

She received languid tail-wags in reply. Crumb
gave a short, inquiring bark and looked at the
door.

"I don't see why not," Hana said as she opened it
for them. They bounded out, as though escaping
from a house of grief, nearly colliding with Penelope Baskin, who hissed at them before she continued her regal way inside.

Hana prowled about the downstairs with the cat
padding after her. As she was opening a drape in
the long dining room, Hana suddenly realized she
went through this every Good Friday and it always
caught her unaware. Of course. To Sal's Mennonite
sensibilities, this was a day of mourning for ancient crimes.

Hana closed the drapes again.

So that explained part of the deathly stillness; Sal would be attending services with her family. But Mr. Fred had no such fine religious feelings.

Penelope Baskin, sitting expectantly at the hallway leading to the 1812 Annex, gave a low rumble like a purr crossed with annoyance. Who said cats aren't smart?

Hana went into the Annex, wondering what perverse architectural whim had stirred within her ancestor when he created this limestone protuberance at the side of the otherwise light and airy Colonial mansion. Fortunately this Annex and the Victorian conservatory were tactfully screened from the outside world by forests of shrubbery, mostly rhododendron.

A breath of musty air greeted her as she pulled open a heavy mahogany door and entered a long room, the original purpose of which had been lost. Her father had often speculated on it, as had Aunt Sissy. Their ideas ranged from dance hall (too gloomy) through office (too dark) to chapel (unlikely for business-minded, worldly Schoeners) to a place for unmentionable practices (also unlikely because of a conservative and definitely nonsexual bent in the family). Hana dreaded the day this question would occur to Mr. Fred and he would want to dig up the floor beneath the Annex. She had to grudgingly admit that the room, while unfit for anything else, was perfect for a museum.

Hana squinted in the dim light coming from small gothic windows near the vaulted ceiling.

Gray Trouble and Kitty Fisher, with feline patience, were watching Mr. Fred, who was so involved with his task he hadn't even noticed Hana's entrance. The room was now lined with display cases. Antique by the look of them, therefore hard to find. She'd have to go over the household bills

very carefully; he must have slipped them in somewhere. Shards of Colonial pottery, a moldy jar of
antique pickles, and long-broken kitchenware lay
on shelves above the cases, each carefully labeled.
Most appalling of all, to Hana's mind, were the artifacts dug up from the Revolutionary War graveyard that had recently been excavated on her front
lawn.

"My God," Hana said involuntarily.

Like a misshapen Dr. Frankenstein, Mr. Fred
was bending over a table on which was spread
what appeared to be a body. He was dressing the
thing in a partially decayed and completely moldy
uniform. It was like one of Aunt Sissy's Germanic
tales come to life.

He looked up and smiled lovingly—not at Hana,
fortunately, but at the object before him. Kitty
Fisher commented in Meowese that it was all most
interesting. Hana's eyes, becoming accustomed to
the gloom, saw it was a male mannequin he was
stuffing into the old uniform.

He stepped back to view his work, which was
obviously meant to be laid out in a nearby wooden
box that was as decayed as the garment the figure
was half-wearing.

An amateur artist had painted over the originally
open eyes of the dummy to create the closed eyes
of death. Hana moaned.

"We'll have lights up there at the end of the room.
Green, I think. *This* will be the focal point of the
entire exhibit," he pronounced.

Hana supposed she should be thankful that the
skeletons and portions of skeletons were not the
focal point. At least Mr. Fred had some tact and
taste. Some. A little. Not much.

"And I have another surprise!" he cried joyfully,
bouncing to seize a large black urn from a pedes-

tal, which looked suspiciously like a valuable antique that had graced the Lafayette Room.

He thrust the urn under her rose. A musty-earthy odor rose from its interior.

"What is it?" she asked, backing away involuntarily.

He followed, tilting the urn hopefully toward the light from the windows. "Deathdust."

*"Deathdust . . . ?"*

"We are sure it's remains," he confided. "But it was damp in that particular area—underground spring, you know—and so it was not preserved like the others."

He replaced the urn on its pedestal and beckoned her toward troughs containing the "others" in bony glory.

Hana stood her ground. "Mr. Fred, I was told you asked Bill Longenecker to put Blue Spring Hill on one of his tours."

He paused, then turned with a lofty wave of his hand as if it were of no importance. "Only for the Open House, of course."

"I will not have tour buses at Blue Spring Hill no matter what the occasion!"

"But—"

"And that is final."

"That parking lot is quite large enough—"

"No! I have enough money to keep this house a private home, and private it will stay as long as I'm alive."

"Very well," he said smoothly, "perhaps you are right. Tour buses lack dignity. And, I assure you, everything at the Open House will be done with dignity. Amish youth to keep order. Only booths with Colonial foodstuffs and souvenirs in keeping with the occasion. Crafts perhaps. Authentic ox rides. No tawdry amusements. I agree with you that it must be kept dignified."

He was smiling. She was sure he was smiling.

Of course he was smiling. He'd just gotten everything he wanted. He'd never intended to let tour buses in. What an idiot she was.

He ought to be fired. Now. While she could concentrate on his transgressions and not on his long service at Blue Spring Hill.

"By the way," he said quickly, "I took care of that problem with the roof on the East Wing. I had to stand over the roofers every minute but they did a thorough job and there won't be any more leaks, I assure you. You don't have to worry anymore about that."

Hana sighed.

A finger joint from a skeleton draped over the edge of a trough dropped to the floor. Penelope Baskin leaped to grab the prize. Mr. Fred leaped to retrieve it. Penelope Baskin gave it a whack that sent the bone spinning beneath a case displaying the inelegant remains of somebody's 1779 lunch. Mr. Fred rapped his head sharply on the leg of the display case but grabbed the bone as three cats converged on it.

Hana dropped morosely into a folding chair to wait until Mr. Fred had brushed himself off and the cats had stopped complaining about their lost toy.

Then she said, "There's been another murder."

He frowned disapprovingly as he **began** rewiring the finger onto the skeletal hand. "I wish you wouldn't do that. I hate to think what your father would have to say about this."

"Do what? I certainly didn't kill these boys."

"Therefore, it is no concern of yours." He paused. "Another boy?"

Hana nodded wearily. It was really easier to make carpets and bring out new lines of clothing than to go around discovering bodies.

"Amish?"

"Apparently."

"Odd."

"Sal at services?"

"It's Good Friday."

"I noticed."

"There are a variety of salads and cold dishes in the refrigerator," he said, eyeing his pseudocorpse as if he might be called upon to leave it.

"I'll help myself," Hana assured him hastily. There was something to be said for eating alone. One did not have to hear about open houses and eighteenth-century graveyards.

The finger bone fell again. This time Gray Trouble dived after it. And Mr. Fred hit his head again. An instant replay. Hana rose.

With his darkly dyed hair disheveled, Mr. Fred held the bone aloft like a candle and fretted, "I wish Teddy Jolf were here. She's so good at finger bones."

Not really caring, Hana felt obliged to ask, "Where is she?"

"You didn't see her? She's got the biggest bookstand at the White Unicorn and, after all, this is one of the busiest days of the year over there. I thought you might stop around and say hello."

"A little thing like another murdered child got in the way of my social calls," Hana said as she headed for the door.

She loved to have the last word on Mr. Fred. It made up for some of the other inconveniences. She and the cats retired to the kitchen. She opened cans for them and the dogs, who came scratching at the door, able to hear the electric opener from any part of the estate.

While she was eating bits of Sal's creative salads, Hana thought about Teddy Jolf. That young woman had some connection with the Schwambachs, and obviously her book business placed her near the scene of today's crime. Farfetched and nebulous, Hana thought. Much more important was identifying the boy who had been killed today. And trying to find a link between him and the Schwambach family, if one existed.

Hana decided that if she were Sergeant Kochen or Chief Hoffman, she would set up a farm-to-farm check to locate the boy's family, starting, of course, with the area immediately surrounding the market-auction.

She popped an olive into her mouth. Suddenly she wanted to be moving, wanted to search out those farms for herself. Talk to the people. Find out where that poor boy belonged.

But Shaner Industries had not been built on impatience. It had been built on solid business procedures and delegating responsibility. The police certainly had the most efficient means of conducting such a search.

Maybe, Hana considered as she chewed, if she was nice to the good sergeant, he would share the results of the canvass with her. Of course he would, even if she was not nice, because there would be no point in keeping the lad's identity a secret. No need to go out of her way to charm that obnoxious, suspicious man. She could read about it in the paper.

So what could she do that Sergeant Kochen and Chief Hoffman couldn't accomplish more effectively? Well, she could talk to Mrs. Schwambach again, by herself this time, and try to decide if the woman really knew who the boy might be. The thought of intruding on the grieving mother again, especially on this holy day, repulsed Hana. But Teddy Jolf merited no such consideration. She was probably a solid citizen who had hundreds of witnesses to testify that she had been selling books and had not been near the White Unicorn barn all day. On the other hand, there was always room for one or two more books in Hana's library.

Unfortunately, it was very late before she got to Teddy Jolf's stand at the White Unicorn.


# *Chapter Eight*


IN THE DARK HOURS, the atmosphere of the White Unicorn was far different from the tourist- and family-oriented action of the day. There were many young people about, both Plain and fancy, and even some bikers in search of excitement. Floodlights created shadows and light pools. Some standholders had already gone home and at these vacant stalls the youths clustered loudly. The murder was still talked about but the emphasis was on experiencing life and love, not death.

Sergeant Kochen too had returned to the scene of the crime.

Hana hadn't really expected to see him. He should, she decided, be out working the countryside with Chief Hoffman's forces.

His appearance of aimless wandering about the barn area annoyed her immediately. It could only be forgiven if the boy's identity had been established. It must be. Surely no police officer would appear so casual otherwise.

Hana hurried forward.

A uniformed police officer stopped her at the roped-off area.

"I am Hana Shaner," she said before she realized she had adopted the lofty tone Mr. Fred often used. "I want to see Sergeant Kochen," she added more humbly.

For a moment he looked doubtful, making Hana wonder if new generations were arising to whom the name Shaner meant little or nothing. Then he gave a brief salute and unhooked the tape to allow her to pass.

"Thank you." She smiled.

Kochen's expression, when he saw her coming, was odd. She couldn't place the sentiment on his face but she suspected it was not connected with cordiality. Of course, it could be connected with whatever he was cleaning off his shoes with rumpled tissues.

She decided on polite formality.

"Good evening, Sergeant."

"Well, Ms. Shaner. What are you doing here?"

"I came to find out the boy's name."

"How?"

"By asking you," she murmured, keeping her voice conversationally kind.

"Why me?"

Hana raised one eyebrow and merely stared into his face. This always worked with Penelope Baskin.

It worked with Sergeant Kochen too. He dropped the tissues into a large barrel.

"I don't know any more than you do."

Hana stopped herself from accusing him of being a liar. One of Sal's favorite sayings was, "Honey attracts more flies than vinegar."

"You mean officially?" she inquired.

"No. I mean, I have no idea who he is."

"I thought you'd have everybody available out asking at the farmhouses. That certainly doesn't seem like too difficult a task."

He looked dignified now, the way a real sergeant should. For a change, even his glasses remained pertly in place. "Chief Hoffman has had every person he could spare doing just that, Ms. Shaner. In the past three hours every farm in the immediate area has been checked—Amish and non-Amish. Nobody has any idea who this boy is."

"Well, it's a holiday," Hana said. "Perhaps some of the people are away from home. Maybe they're even here at the market. Maybe they're standholders. Did you broadcast his description over the PA system?"

He looked at her as if she too were clinging to his shoes. "Do you honestly imagine we haven't thought of all this?"

"Oh, have you? It's a relief to know our tax dollars are paying for efficiency and service."

"If you'll excuse me, there are some of us who must work for a living," he said, then turned and strode into the barn, stepping once again into another flat, dark blob. He chose to ignore this one.

It was his attitude which was so annoying, she decided as she made her way into the long, one-story cinder block building that housed Teddy's Used Book Corner. He seemed so inefficient, as if he needed prodding to do his job. She wondered if his lieutenant found him irritating.

Teddy's was a large stand complete with a lighted showcase displaying valuable collectors' items. Narrow aisles between the high shelves would be a challenge to stout book lovers, Hana suspected. At a rough estimate, she guessed the stand displayed about twelve thousand books.

Teddy Jolf, looking tired, was filling a bin with paperback mysteries. There were few regular customers about. At an adjacent automotive stall, groups of teeners were congregating.

Hana accepted the invitation on a sign urging her to browse. She was already at the biography section when Teddy returned to her cash drawer and looked down the aisle.

"Ms. Shaner . . . ?"

Hana replaced a book on Queen Victoria's daughters.

"Must have been a busy day for you," she commented, noting bare places on the shelves.

"It was." Teddy glanced toward the gathering youths. "I usually close about this time."

Hana nodded understandingly. "Do they give you trouble?"

"Oh, once in a while they'll say something. You know how kids that age are. But the security's pretty good here."

"I suppose you know another boy was killed," Hana said casually, watching her face.

Tired turned into exhaustion. "That's all people have been talking about today."

"Any idea who he is?"

She looked surprised. "Me? No, I didn't even see him."

"But somebody coming by the stand may have said something—"

"Not that I heard. You understand, this was a six-hundred-dollar day and, believe me, that's a lot of books going out."

"You mentioned when I met you at my home that you knew the Schwambach family."

"I wouldn't say I exactly *know* them."

"Anything you could tell me might be helpful. Anything at all."

A late but eager tourist bought a twenty-five-dollar book about birds. Apparently both he and Teddy thought they had gotten a good deal.

"I didn't mean to give you the wrong impression," Teddy finally said as she stuffed money into a pocket of her jeans. "I only know the Schwambachs in the most casual way, as customers. They keep to themselves. Not the average Amish family. You know most Plain People love to visit relatives and attend meetings . . ."

"Surely they attend religious services?"

"I suppose they do that, and take their turn to hold them when it comes around, but not much else. At least that's what I've heard. The father's very strict. It's a miracle the kids manage to get here to the White Unicorn. The oldest boy, Jake, brings the young ones once in a while."

"Could the boy Aaron ever have been with those younger ones?"

"Well, sure, he could have. It's just that I don't remember. I get awfully busy sometimes. And who notices all these kids?"

"What do they come for?"

Teddy grinned. "Books, what else? It's the one thing they're allowed to do—read. No TV, tapes, radio . . . nothing."

"Where do they get the money to buy books?"

"Who knows?"

"Their father?"

Teddy contemplated the question as she straightened a row of occult books with enticingly mysterious titles. "My guess would be the mother. Somebody's sure encouraging them to read. As long as they're 'decent' books, of course. Nancy Drew,

Hardy Boys, very old novels from the early 1900s before publishers discovered sex. That kind of thing."

It seemed so meaningless, unimportant.

Teddy Jolf took a broom from beneath her counter and began to sweep the aisles inside her area. As Hana inhaled a sudden dust storm, she decided it was time to leave. The back door of the building opened right onto the lot where she had left her car. The gang of youths was still loitering near the automotive stand.

Hana sneezed good-bye to Teddy then headed for the exit. As she passed, one of the boys giggled. Another said, "Hey, Momma!" A loud question followed her: "Say, Henry, you ever done it with somebody over thirty?"

Hana ignored them. As she stepped out into the cold, windswept night, she considered that she might as well have stayed home. She still had no idea of the identity of the new boy, and what difference did it make that the younger Schwambachs read Nancy Drew? Certainly there hadn't been a duel to the death with pitchforks over the ownership of a Nancy Drew book.

Of course it was possible. Barely.

The White Unicorn Market was surrounded by parking lots on three sides, and this particular one stretched far out toward plowed fields, unseen but smelling of fresh, pungent earth. Most of the holiday celebrants had already gone home. A few floodlights on the rear of the buildings sent weird shadows across the lot but failed in their basic task of illumination. Hana stumbled on the uneven cinders and gravel where rainwater had carved miniature canyons.

The boys had followed her onto the parking lot. No, Hana corrected herself, not followed. They were merely going in the same direction, probably down to the shed that sheltered Amish horses and buggies, although a number of the group had not appeared to be Amish. She would have felt more reassured if they were.

She walked purposefully toward her car.

They moved faster.

Hana turned her head slightly, trying to see them. Six teenage boys. A couple of them pretty big guys.

It was at that point Hana realized she was lost. In her haste she had not taken her bearings. She'd been parked beside trucks but the trucks were long gone. She didn't see her car anywhere.

And she was walking purposefully toward those large, deserted fields.

Hana Shaner refused to let a few kids intimidate her. She slowed, waiting for them to close in. Then she whirled to face them.

"What do you want?" she demanded.

They scattered among the remaining automobiles on the lot, but continued hooting and brazenly mocking her. She hesitated, looking back toward the lighted rear door of the market building. An elderly man and woman carrying bags of produce were approaching an ancient Ford nearby.

She hurried to them.

"Excuse me. This parking lot is awfully dark. Would you walk me to my car?"

"Where is it?" the man asked, shifting his bag.

"Come on, Sam, let's go," the woman urged. "It's late."

When Hana admitted she didn't know the exact location of her own automobile, they scurried the rest of the way to the Ford, flung in the bags, then scrambled inside after them, slamming and locking the doors. Ignoble as it was, Hana realized the best thing she could do was return to the building, perhaps to find Sergeant Kochen or ask Teddy Jolf to drive her around the lot until she located the Chrysler.

She had only retreated a few steps when a stone struck her arm.

It was a smallish stone, hardly leaving a mark, except one of fear. Hana ran. Two boys jumped from behind a farm truck. Others appeared out of the darkness. Like a pack of savage dogs they surrounded her, moving stealthily, menacingly. During her last encounter with crime Hana had bought a .22, and the shock of wounding someone remained. She had been reluctant to carry a gun again.

She had no weapon, not even a stick. A sudden nightmare exploded inside her—a woman's fear. My God, was she going to be gang-raped here on this stupid parking lot?

Hana screamed.

It was a bellow, powered by all the diaphragm action acquired long ago in teenage acting lessons. It stopped only when one large boy slugged her. *Slug-slugged* . . . the words blurred through her mind when she saw his fist coming. She turned instinctively, the blow glancing off her jaw, the bony feel of his knuckles bruising her as she fell to the gravel surface of the lot.

A boy's voice whined, "Come on, Johnny, let's get out of here!"

She heard their shoes crunching cinders. She was breathing again, deeply, screaming as she scrambled to her feet and stumbled toward the lighted building.

She almost fell, then found a VW to which she clung, gasping. From the direction of the barn came the sound of police whistles. People were coming out of the building. Two police were spotlighted by a floodlight mounted near the water tower. Their flashlights found her.

So did Teddy Jolf, wide-eyed, white-faced.

Hana touched her own face. Wow. That was going to be sore. What if she hadn't turned?

A uniformed policewoman asked, "What happened?"

Hana waved toward the dark. "Boys. Six . . . maybe more . . . attacked me."

Teddy had an arm around her. "You must sit down."

Other police followed the first into the depths of the parking lot jungle. Hana meekly went with Teddy and was gently placed in a chair behind the counter of the bookstand. She closed her eyes against the harsh, fluorescent lights. The Asparagus Woman tapped her gently and held out a paper cup full of ice and cold liquid.

Cola. The panacea of America. Whatever had happened to plain water?

But she sipped it, both hands grasping the cup because it was something to cling to in a crisis. As she began to feel better, she held the cup away to inspect it suspiciously. Maybe this really was the elixir of the gods. Maybe it was just what the doctor ordered when one was slugged on the jaw. Maybe it was the caffeine. Maybe the blow had made her a little punchy.

"Go on," the medically minded Asparagus Woman, who wasn't green, urged. "It'll make you feel lots better."

"Oh, this is terrible," Teddy moaned.

"No, it's really quite good," Hana muttered, obediently taking more gulps.

Over the rim of the cup she saw Teddy looking at her strangely.

Then Sergeant Kochen and Murray Schmidt, the owner of the market complex, crowded into her line of vision.

"Somebody call a doctor," Kochen ordered.

Hana gathered her cola-restored wits. "No. I'm all right. Really. I'll check in with my own doctor tomorrow."

"You look like hell," Kochen said dispassionately.

Hana bridled. "It was only one little sock on the jaw. I can take it."

"Well, I can't," Schmidt wailed. "A murder and now a woman's attacked in the parking lot! I'll have to hire more security. It's going to ruin me." He stared as if seeing her for the first time. "Hana Shaner? *Hana Shaner!* Thousands of people use that parking lot and when some goons want to attack somebody they pick on Hana Shaner!"

"You should be glad," Kochen said, his eyes amused. "She doesn't need the money so maybe she won't sue."

Schmidt turned white and began swallowing rapidly.

Kochen helped Hana to her feet. "I'll take you home. You can tell me what happened on the way."

Struggling against his arm, Hana turned to Teddy Jolf. "Those boys . . . you must have seen them hanging around here before tonight. One they called Johnny. Who are they?"

"I don't know," Teddy insisted. "Just kids. There are a thousand Dutch kids named Johnny."

"Were any of the Schwambach boys here tonight?"

Teddy shook her head. But she wasn't looking at Hana.

Kochen held Hana more securely. "We'll talk about this tomorrow. Ms. Jolf, the officers will get your address and phone number. Be available in the morning."

"I want an answer to my question," Hana babbled.

"Later," Kochen said soothingly.

"What can I do to help?" Schmidt worried, getting in their way as they moved into the aisle.

"We'll interview you in the morning too," Kochen told him. "Now let me get this woman to my car."

It was waiting beside the rear door.

"But my own car—?"

"They'll bring it to Blue Spring Hill. You're not driving tonight. Give me your keys."

"I'm fine," Hana grumbled as he helped her into the front seat.

"The keys."

Annoyed, Hana fumbled them out of her bag and slapped them into Kochen's hand. At least the little devils hadn't grabbed her purse. Obviously they hadn't wanted money.

Had it really been attempted rape?

Kochen spent a few minutes talking to other officers. She leaned back, feeling spent. She hoped her jaw wouldn't swell. She also hoped nobody, especially the newspapers, would make too much over this. Maybe it could even be kept away from the media.

She mentioned it to Kochen as he got into the car.

"Don't try to talk. Just relax."

"Damn it, I don't want to relax! I want to find out who those kids were and if they had anything to do with the murder of the boys."

"You think they might have?"

"You're the police. You tell me."

He drove slowly over the gullies of the parking

lot. "That would make it a gang killing, wouldn't it?
I don't buy that. Not in Conover County. Big cities,
sure, but we don't have that kind of thing around
here."

"There's always a first time."

He shook his head. "I don't think so."

"Why not?"

"Doesn't fit. Do you really think it does?" He
didn't wait for a reply. "You've been thinking of
rape, haven't you?"

"What woman doesn't?"

"Tell me exactly what happened."

She did with as much detail as possible.

Would she recognize the boys? Hana hesitated. It
had been dark. Everything had moved so fast. Already it seemed like a blur. If a row of kids was in
front of her, could she pick out even the two oldest,
tallest ones? She wasn't sure.

"Never mind," Kochen said. "Think about it
later."


At Blue Spring Hill, the animals greeted her with
concern. Kitty Fisher was the first to comment on
the scrapes and bruises. Mr. Fred's attitude, however, after being assured that she was basically all
right, became one of censure, as if she had once
again darkened the name of Shaner.

Even worse, Sergeant Kochen refused to leave
until a doctor had been called.

In a mean mood, Hana phoned Dr. Harold Reifsnyder, an old friend of her father's, who hated to
be called at home, hated to make house visits, and
most of all hated to be reminded of all he owed
Hana's father, who had long ago paid for his medical education.

A large, prosperous man, he arrived in a state of
pique and annoyance to wrathfully prescribe an

ice pack—which Mr. Fred had already supplied—
and some nonaspirin painkillers.

Through all of this, Hana had remained in one of
the formal sitting rooms. She would have been
more comfortable in her bedroom or the snuggery,
her informal area for watching TV from soft sofas
and clusters of chairs. But these visitors were not
ones she wanted to see with her guard down.

"Do you know," Reifsnyder asked darkly, "how
many truly ill people have been deprived of my
services this evening?"

Since his practice consisted mainly of assisting
the wealthy to overcome bad dietary habits, Hana
doubted if any truly ill people were hovering by
their phones waiting for his call.

Ghost sat on her feet to make sure she knew of
his sympathy. Crumb lay in the middle of the floor,
rolling his eyes from her to Dr. Reifsnyder. Hana
wondered if he contemplated an attack. The cats
had disappeared, obviously not anxious to be
mixed up with police.

"The best advice I can give," the doctor continued with dignity, "is to get plenty of rest. And to
put these filthy animals outside the house."

Ghost and Crumb growled in unison. Crumb's lip
curled as if the attack were imminent.

"He didn't mean it," Hana cooed at them. "Would
you like a sherry, Uncle Harold?"

Ignoring her, he backed away from the dogs to
turn his glare on Kochen with an intensity usually
reserved for patients who had committed the sin of
banana splits. "This man is from the police?" he
asked.

Kochen admitted to this deficiency in his person-
ality.

"Once was bad enough," the Good Doctor declared, returning the evil eye to Hana, "but twice is

unforgivable. Whatever are you thinking of, Hannah Elizabeth Clara, to mix with police business? It is unbecoming in a Shaner. Your father would be shocked." He plopped his heavy frame into a delicate Queen Anne chair. Mr. Fred winced. "I'll have that sherry now," he said as if conferring a favor.

Mr. Fred served. Kochen also accepted a glass. Hana sighed. She knew Harold Reifsnyder's curiosity, now only thinly disguised in his greedy little eyes. And the only way to get rid of him was to satisfy it.

Without preliminaries, Hana told him of the two dead youths while Kochen and Mr. Fred listened soberly. When she had finished, Reifsnyder was silent for a moment, staring into his glass as if it contained foreign objects.

"Odd," he said.

She hoped he didn't mean the sherry. He didn't.

"Odd that the family didn't hear him scream. And that nobody in the White Unicorn barn heard the other boy scream."

"The pitchfork pierced the heart," Kochen told him. "At least in the first case. We don't have the PM report on the second boy as yet."

"Even so," Reifsnyder objected pompously, "death is seldom instantaneous. It can happen, of course. But to have both boys die silently? I find that hard to accept. The family must have heard something. Victims can scream bloody murder."

He had the grace to look embarrassed by his choice of words.

"Even if they knew where to strike . . . I mean, which part of the chest?" Hana asked.

"They're farmers," he said testily. "How could they know?"

"Farmers are often butchers," Kochen suggested.

"Well, it's your problem."

The doctor shrugged, swallowed the last of his sherry, and rose.

"Thanks for your expert opinion," Hana said dryly. "I'm sure you've had a lot of experience with pitchfork killings."

"I've had a great deal of experience in medical matters," he said stiffly, looking resentfully at Crumb, who was sniffing his trouser leg.

Hana smiled fondly at the dog. "He bites. But only people who don't like dogs."

The doctor, shrugging into his coat, stepped quickly away from Crumb. "My office will send you the bill," he said icily.

"An overcharge as usual?" Hana asked just as icily.

"If you don't want to pay for proper medical attention, I suggest you try a powwow doctor next time."

Jamming his hat on his mottled gray hair, the doctor marched from the room. Dourly Mr. Fred went after him. Hana leaned back and closed her eyes, hoping Kochen would take the hint. There was silence broken only when they heard tires ripping gravel from the parking lot.

"Charming fellow," Kochen said with a grin. "Strange man for a family doctor."

Hana opened her eyes a slit. "A family . . . friend, I guess you might say. I usually go to another doctor, but that one never makes house calls."

She wondered why the man was still hanging around, why he was staring at her.

"What do you want?" she demanded. "Do you think I know more than I've told you about what happened this evening?"

He hesitated, then took off his glasses and

dropped them into his coat pocket. She decided he looked better with them on.

"I was concerned about your welfare," he said formally.

The man was human after all.

Hana assured him she was in good hands, and when Mr. Fred returned, Kochen finally left.

Later, alone in her room, where the cats had been waiting for her, Hana lay in the soft glow of her bedlamp, thinking. Outside the wind roared, reminding her of winter rather than spring. Kitty Fisher flung herself against Hana's side and lay there in an ecstasy of friendship. Cats purring made a night less dark.

Dr. Reifsnyder had sneered when he mentioned powwowing. She wondered if Aunt Sissy had ever spoken to him about it. She frowned, trying to recall the word her aunt had used . . . *braucherei* . . . Yes, that was it. White witchcraft. She hoped that's where the boy's charm had come from. But whether it was good or evil, the person who gave it to him would know his name.

# *Chapter Nine*

GRAY TROUBLE LAPPED at the milk in Hana's cereal bowl. But then, Hana had never really liked mushy cooked cereal, even though it was Sal's answer to morning vigor and had been dutifully fed to every Nunemacher under fifteen—at which age most of them rebelled. Sal ignored rebellion only in her employer.

Mr. Fred averted his eyes and protected his own cereal bowl by pulling it close to his chest and lowering his head over it, while he slurped from a large spoon.

Sal had eaten her own nutritious goop at home. It was understood by all that she had come in for only a couple of hours to make sure Blue Spring Hill and its occupants were able to survive the holidays without her.

Penelope Baskin landed on the table beside Gray Trouble.

Sal promptly scooped her up and deposited her on the floor, to the accompaniment of angry cries.

"Maybe one. Never two," she said, hesitated a moment, added, "Better not even one," and grabbed the gray cat to drop him on the floor.

She picked up the cereal bowl. "Guess you're not so hungry this morning."

"Just toast," Hana said, pulling the coffee cup toward her. Her jaw hurt enough to make eating a chore.

"Toast isn't a real breakfast," Sal sniffed. "Sure you don't want to come out to the farm for dinner tomorrow? We're making a big ham. Plenty to go around."

Mr. Fred looked interested but Hana shook her head. "You just enjoy your holiday."

When Sal placed the plate of toast in front of her, Hana asked casually, "Sal, were any of the Schwambachs sickly?"

"We all got troubles sometimes."

"When they had trouble, did they consult a doctor the way most Plain People do?"

"Why, sure . . ."

"They never powwowed?"

Sal looked uncomfortable. "What gave you that idea?"

"They seem like unusual people, and sometimes unusual people do unusual things." Sal put the cover on the toaster. Hana grew impatient. "I told you another boy was killed and we don't even know who he is. Maybe I'm grasping at straws but there's nothing else to grasp. Anything you can tell me about the Schwambachs may help us find out about this other boy. Think of his parents, Sal."

"Well, there were stories . . ."

Sal sat at the table. Hana knew she was worried because she automatically reached down to pet Gray Trouble, who arched his back in surprised gratitude.

"Yes?" Hana prompted.

"The old woman . . ."

"The grandmother?"

"*Ja.* She's Mister's mother, you know, and if you ask me all Schwambachs got an odd streak in them. Last winter she had arthritis so bad she could hardly get around. I saw her one day at market and I says, 'Sadie Schwambach, you'd best see a doctor right away or you'll be laid up right.' Didn't even answer me. Not so much as a nod. I went over next day with willow tea. Figured if she wouldn't do something sensible at least she could do *something.* But she wasn't there. I got it out of that girl Katie that she'd got her son to take her to a pow-wow doctor."

"Where?"

Sal rose impatiently, pushing Gray Trouble aside with her foot. He hissed with betrayal.

"I work here. I work at home. I got a big family to help Mom raise. I don't have time for nonsense."

"Sal, I don't want to consult this powwow doctor, I just want to talk to him . . . her?"

"Next thing," Sal said, leaning across the table and poking a finger toward Hana, "you'll be telling me it was hex killed those boys. It's not Christian to believe such things but there are some around here still do."

"Of course it wasn't hex killed the boys but . . ."

"How long's it been since we had a murder hereabouts because somebody thought they were hexed? Not that many years. Fifteen maybe. Some places the devil dies hard."

"I'm sure this has nothing to do with local superstition."

"You are, are you? Well, I'm not. Pitchforks are the devil's tools, aren't they? Always on pictures he's got one anyways."

Hana opened her mouth in astonishment.

Sal was already heading for the door. "You want to know about anything else, you'll have to ask the Schwambachs. I'll see you Easter Monday, Miss Hana. Mr. Fred, dinner's at noon sharp Sunday if you'd like to come."

The slam of the door echoed after her through the old house.

"You'd almost think she was afraid," Hana said.

Mr. Fred began collecting breakfast dishes and taking them to the sink. "She is."

"Of what?"

"Maybe her neighbors."

It was then Hana decided to return to the Schwambach farm that morning.

# Chapter Ten

IT WAS ONE of those perfect days when early warmth spreads across the land. If she had been on any other errand, Hana would have enjoyed her drive through a countryside already showing promise of the plenty which the Plain and fancy farmers would pull from the rich soil. Rain enough. Sun enough. Hana breathed deeply of the air. That this land should have a darker side seemed unbelievable on such a day.

This time the Schwambach farm was not deserted. Despite the impending holiday, two teams of mules were harrowing a far-off field. It was too distant to tell for sure but the straw-hatted figure on the harrow looked like Mr. Schwambach. The other team would be driven either by the grandfather or one of the older boys. She wasn't sure whether or not they had spotted her.

Not that it made any difference.

She hoped.

She pulled up to the farmhouse. Tulips she had not noticed before had opened in the yard. A boardwalk led to an outhouse and continued on to a kitchen garden.

Three figures were working there. The girl Katie, apparently self-appointed or parent-appointed as her mother's companion, was concentrating on dragging a three-cornered hoe through recently turned earth. The grandmother came behind her, carefully dropping kernels into the furrow. A little apart, Mrs. Schwambach herself was raking fertilizer into another patch of ground. In Conover County the odors of blossoms were often overwhelmed by the fragrance of horse and cow manure.

Taking a deep breath, which would have to last for a while, Hana headed toward the garden. They glanced up. The fact that they were aware of her didn't interfere with the rhythm of their labor. Hana paused at the edge of the overturned soil.

"Hello," she called. "Remember me? Hana Shaner."

They looked at her. They went on with their chores.

"I'd like to talk to you."

Katie glanced at her elders, apparently decided she was chosen spokesperson, and said, "We got work to do."

"This won't take long."

The old woman straightened quickly, if somewhat stiffly. Powwowing had obviously been effective.

She said something in the dialect. Hana translated enough to understand that she was planting early peas and early peas had to get into the ground early.

Hana took from her bag the swatch of fabric Ghost had removed from her intruder's britches and held it toward the younger Mrs. Schwambach.

"I think this belongs to you. My dog ripped it off the pants of a trespasser who looked very much like your son."

That got action. Mrs. Schwambach dropped her manure and came forward, to Hana's horror wiping her hands on her apron. Nothing was said until she stood right before Hana, who still held out the fabric. Slowly the woman took it, then awkwardly stuffed it into the large pocket of the apron.

"I have a few questions," Hana said stubbornly.

"I want to ask the older Mrs. Schwambach about her visits to a powwow doctor."

*"Koom,"* the woman said.

It appeared Hana was not to be allowed to talk to the grandmother. Reluctantly she followed the younger Missus to a back porch shaded by a pear tree whose buds seemed to grow as one looked at them. With a loud sigh, Mrs. Schwambach dropped into one of many wooden porch chairs.

"I'd like to talk to your mother-in-law."

She shook her head. "She don't talk English so good. In her time it wasn't so important to talk to the English."

Hana sat opposite her. "I understand the dialect."

Mrs. Schwambach looked surprised. She surveyed Hana's beige pantsuit and brown turtleneck, then averted her eyes.

"It's best I talk to you," she said.

"All right. Why was your son at Blue Spring Hill?"

"I don't know."

"I'd like to ask him."

"He ain't here. He's working out in one of the fields. He didn't take nothing, did he?"

"He trespassed."

The eyes came back to rest on a sterling pendant and chain around Hana's neck. "You wasn't exactly invited here yourself."

Hana couldn't help smiling. "Do you have any idea why he would come to my place?"

"Maybe to ask *you* some questions?"

"Like what?"

The woman shrugged.

Hana waited, then finally said, "We'll let that go for now. I understand your children buy books at the White Unicorn."

"You got something against kids reading?"

Hana decided she was not having the best of this interview. "Of course not. I'm always glad when young people read. Aren't you?"

Mrs. Schwambach hesitated, then nodded.

"I suppose both you and your husband encourage them to read?" Hana asked pointedly.

She nodded again, her eyes more wary.

"Are you the one gives your children money for books?"

"Sometimes."

"Yesterday?"

"No, not yesterday! Yesterday was Good Friday. Nobody went over there yesterday. I said so before and it's so."

Her eyes defied Hana to prove otherwise. Her workworn hands picked at her apron as if she were sewing it.

Hana said reluctantly, "The day your son was killed . . ."

*"Ja,"* she breathed. "That day . . ."

"Did you hear anything? I mean, a cry? A . . . well, sounds?"

"No."

"I was talking to a doctor. He said the boy would probably have screamed. He told me that in this kind of death, there is often a scream."

"There was no scream! Nobody heard nothing. We'd of said."

With finality the hands smoothed the apron across her lap. "Now I got to get back to work. Don't have time to set around yammering like city folks."

Hana realized the interview had gone completely out of her control. And she hadn't found out what she most wanted to know.

"Please, Mrs. Schwambach! I need the name of

the powwow doctor who treated your mother-in-law."

Again surprise flickered across the woman's face. "Why?"

"I might want to consult a powwow person sometime," Hana said lamely.

This time there was a very long silence.

Hana gave in. "You win. The reason I want the name is because we still don't know the identity of the boy who was killed in the White Unicorn barn. The one Sergeant Kochen asked you about."

"So what's the powwow doctor got to do with that?"

"Probably nothing," Hana admitted. "But I saw an amulet on the body. Something such as a powwow doctor might give."

"Ach, Gott . . ."

Hana tensed. "Do you know who he is?"

"I told you I didn't."

"As I recall what you told us was that wasn't one of yours. There's a difference."

Mrs. Schwambach was watching the kitchen garden, where Katie and her grandmother had finished one row of peas and were beginning another. Once more she smoothed nervously over her apron.

"If I tell you the name of the powwow doctor," she said slowly, "will you promise to go away and let us alone?"

"I'll go away for now. But I can't promise I won't be back. I think you know I can't."

The Amish woman considered this thoughtfully for a few moments and apparently decided these were the best terms she could get.

"Ach well," she murmured. "Her name's Betty Schlicher. She ain't Plain. We don't have Plain People doing that, you know. She lives in Bruchberg."

"Where in Bruchberg?"

"Just ask around. Everybody knows her."

With that she abruptly rose, left the porch, and strode purposefully toward the kitchen garden without looking back. Hana had no choice but to return to her car.

She was off the Schwambach property, traveling along a two-lane road winding through acres of winter wheat, when she sensed it.

Someone was hiding in the backseat of her Chrysler.

# *Chapter Eleven*

PERHAPS WHOEVER WAS hiding behind Hana had stirred slightly in his cramped position. Perhaps it was only the sense of another being close at hand. She, who never got into her car in the CarPark in town or the lot at Shaner Industries without carefully checking to make sure no one lurked inside, had this time hopped into her unlocked vehicle without a thought. After all, it had been parked in farm country. If one couldn't trust these peaceful people, who could one trust?

But murder had been committed there. How could she have been so careless?

The gun. She had resolved to start carrying it but had been reluctant to act on that resolution. If she got out of this, no more Ms. Nice Guy, she thought bitterly.

Ahead was a pulloff used by the slow-moving

farm machinery that sometimes clogged this road. Abruptly she jammed her foot on the gas pedal. The car zoomed forward. She swung onto the gravel of the pulloff, slammed on the brakes. The Chrysler skidded, a front wheel spinning into a ditch. Hana turned off the motor, opening the door at the same time, then stumbled into the ditch. Damn—mud and water to her ankles. She squished to the road again, quickly looking about. No farm buildings were in sight, but across one field was a patch of woodland that probably marked a rocky outcropping of limestone, making it unfit for plowing.

Back into the ditch and across to the other side, feet sliding around inside her mud-filled shoes. Behind her as she ran she heard the car door slam.

"Hey," he shouted.

Youthful voice. Dutch accent. One of those kids from the parking lot? She ran faster.

"I ain't going to hurt you! I wouldn't do nothing like that!"

His voice sounded farther away, so he wasn't running after her. Hana chanced a glance over her shoulder. He stood beside her car, on the other side of the muddy ditch—which was smart—his hands still cupped about his mouth. She slowed, then stopped and turned to look at him. At this distance, she couldn't be sure but it looked like the oldest Schwambach boy. That made sense because whoever he was, he had concealed himself in her car while she was interviewing Mrs. Schwambach—if one could call that unsatisfactory conversation an interview.

Still she hesitated. Not that dashing into a patch of forest was exactly Lesson Number One in how to save oneself when pursued by a teenage assailant. Again she scanned the landscape. Off in the distance she did see a farmstead amidst a haze of blossoms. But it was much too far away.

"I'm Jake Schwambach," he shouted. "I just want to talk some to you!"

"Then why didn't you talk instead of hiding in my car?" she screamed back.

"Because I ain't supposed to, that's why! Pop . . . he don't want none of us saying nothing to you. Can I come over there?"

Hana suddenly felt ridiculous shouting across a field of winter wheat.

"I'll come to you," she shrieked, then, with as much dignity as possible, she strode back the way she had come.

At the ditch she hesitated.

"Can I help?" he asked.

She pictured this rough-hewn country boy putting his purple shirt across the mud for her to step on.

Disregarding him, she scrambled into the ditch and up the other side.

"I guess your car's stuck," he said unhelpfully.

"Talk," Hana said, panting a little.

He looked at the ground with embarrassment as he drew a line in the gravel with the toe of his work shoe.

Hana was no longer afraid.

"Get in the car," she said more kindly. "If we can ram out of that ditch, you can talk to me while we drive."

He looked uncertainly at the Chrysler.

"In the front seat this time," she suggested. "Not on the floor in the back."

He had the grace to grin. "I'm sorry. I guess I just didn't think."

It took Hana five minutes of slamming in and out of reverse to get on solid ground. Her feet were very uncomfortable now. She whirled the wheel and headed for home.

"I'm going to Blue Spring Hill," she said. "I assume you've been there before."

*"Ja,"* he admitted sadly.

"When my dog tore your pants?"

*"Ja."*

"I think your conduct has been ill-advised and you can be glad nothing worse happened. You could have lost more than a pair of pants."

*"Ja."*

Hana glanced at him. His large hands hung between his legs. Already callused from work, they were the kind of hands she suspected were seldom still.

"You have something to tell me about your brother's murder," she prompted. "Is that why you came to Blue Spring Hill?"

He looked as if he might be sorry he had persisted. *"Ja."*

"Say something besides *'ja,'* Jake."

He spoke in the dialect, caught himself, and switched to English. "Sal Nunemacher says you can help us. That's why she got you to come. She says you know the police and that you helped before when some lady got herself killed or something. But Pop don't think so. He says it will all be okay if we just keep still and don't say nothing to nobody. But I'm scared. I'm a man and I know I ain't supposed to be scared but I am. Because it happened at the farm. And it seems like that policeman thinks one of us done it. Maybe that's what you think too."

"People are bound to suspect the family. Because you're lying."

"That's what I told my pop. Only he don't listen to me."

"What happened that morning?"

He swallowed loudly. "I don't know what happened."

"Jake . . ."

"I don't! I just know it wasn't none of us done nothing to Aaron. We was out at five-thirty. Soon as it got light. Like Pop said. Except for Aaron . . . he wasn't supposed to be up there in the haymow. That was my chore. Throwing down the hay. I'm strong and I'm fast. Pop says I can do it twice as fast as any of the other kids."

"But for some reason he beat you to it and was pitching down the feed—?"

"No. He didn't pitch nothing. He didn't."

"So tell me, Jake. Don't make me drag it out of you."

"Well, we was coming out through the yard. Except for Aaron. He wasn't with us. But we come out together like always. Then we usually split up at the barn and go do different chores. That's how Pop likes it. So's he knows where everybody is and that nobody's staying back and not getting stuff done. So we was all together, see, when we heard him scream."

"You *heard* him . . . ?"

"Screamed like a stuck pig at butchering time. Didn't know what it was at first. None of us. We just stopped and looked at each other. I thought maybe somebody'd got in and was doing something to one of the animals. That's what I thought."

"But you were all together when you heard this?"

"Pop too. So's it couldn't have been none of us."

"At least not one of the boys."

He looked shocked. "A girl wouldn't do nothing like that."

"Don't the girls help with butchering?"

"*Ja.* Sometimes."

"Then why couldn't it have been a girl or a woman?"

"Because they wouldn't, that's why," he said stubbornly. "And because they didn't. That's another why. And I can prove it."

"You can?"

"*Ja*, sure. Because he was killed with a four-pronged pitchfork!"

Hana looked at him blankly. "So?"

He was triumphant. "Why, hardly nobody in the county uses a four-pronged pitchfork. It's hard to even find them if you wanted to use one. All ourn are three-pronged. So it wasn't one of us done it. No, sir. Couldn't have been. Ain't even our pitchfork."

He beamed at her as if he had delivered a speech to the jury exonerating the entire family. Hana hadn't the heart to tell him the evidence of the pitchfork would mean little to any jury. The evidence of hearing the scream was better. *If* he was telling the truth and *if* they all stuck to the same story. The idea that he could be lying grew in Hana as he answered the rest of her questions. He told of finding the body. He didn't touch anything. He hardly looked. He hardly seemed to feel grief. No, they had seen nobody—heard nobody. No strangers had been about.

Apparently Mr. Schwambach, instead of sending for help, had ordered everyone into the house. First they prayed. Then, while the women prepared breakfast, the males returned to the barn to tend the livestock, even going into the haymow to throw down feed. It seemed incredible to Hana how their regular routine had been so little disturbed by Aaron's body lying there with a four-pronged pitchfork through his chest. They had returned to the house and eaten a big breakfast. After this

Mr. Schwambach had ordered them to wash up and dress in their best. Even then they had not raised the alarm directly but had gone to Sal Nunemacher and discussed matters with her and her mother.

Hana noted that Jake was becoming increasingly nervous as if he now realized their actions did not sound convincingly innocent. Yes, this could be what country people who kept rigidly to their own might do, but Hana thought they could equally well be the actions of people who had something to hide.

Jake denied being anywhere near the White Unicorn at any time on Good Friday, then refused to answer any more questions. He seemed afraid—perhaps of his father—and declared he had to get home. It was with difficulty Hana prevented him from getting out of the car at a stop sign. Only by persuading him that he'd get there faster if she drove him could she keep him in his seat. Trying to ignore the mud caking her ankles, she spun the car in a circle and headed back to the Schwambachs'.

He insisted she drop him at the top of their long lane and not even pull into it to turn around.

Hana and her muddy feet exceeded the speed limit on the return trip to Blue Spring Hill.

Later, with her feet comfortable in fuzzy slippers, Hana leaned back on her bed pillows. She smiled at the animals surrounding her as she dialed Sergeant Kochen.

This was just too good an opportunity to pass up. He was always acting so superior about his official capacity. The cats and Crumb all purred their approval. Hana suspected it was Kitty Fisher who had taught Crumb to purr. Nice sound, if a bit on the doggy side. Only Ghost seemed skeptical.

"I just thought you might want to know that four-pronged pitchforks are never used by the Schwambach family," she told him after she had established her identity.

"How do you know?"

"I never divulge my sources," she replied smugly.

He threatened her so violently, Hana considered she might have cause to sue for damages. If only she had turned on her recorder. She was finally forced to resort to lying, telling him it was a rumor Sal Nunemacher had picked up around the neighborhood.

"It certainly is a point in their favor," she said in her most soothing voice.

He sounded dangerous. "I'm not so sure of that. The boy at the White Unicorn was killed with an ordinary three-prong job."

Hana sighed and hung up. After a moment she gently pushed aside the animals and got out of bed. She padded across the room to her small wall safe, neatly hidden by a large framed photograph of Shaner Industries in winter when one could see the buildings through the parklike surroundings. Inside the safe was her .22. Whatever happened next, Hana intended to be prepared.

# Chapter Twelve

THEY STOOD ON a corner of what was obviously the main street of Bruchberg.

Bill Longenecker asked, "Now what?"

To say that the town was small was to exaggerate. It was hardly a town at all, rather a row of unbelievably neat single houses at a crossroads, one branch of which went on to the White Unicorn while the other served those people anxious to lose themselves meandering through farmland on unmarked byways. The only building of any size was an old stagecoach inn, which had anchored the crossroads for generations. In the yards of the houses daffodils, stirred by the arrival of warm days, swayed rhythmically. The brook, which had given the town its Germanic name, cut through green watercress, which pulsed in full running water. These were the only movements.

"I wonder where everybody is," Hana said.

"Watching TV."

"It's Saturday evening . . ."

"What else is there to do in a town like this?"

"I guess we're going to have to ask somebody where to find this woman."

"Who is there to ask?"

Her eyes fixed on the inn.

Bill moved his brows rapidly up and down. "I thought wc were going to have dinner. I never heard of the Bruchberg Inn being noted for its cuisine. Actually, I never heard of the Bruchberg Inn."

Hana winced at the Groucho Marx imitation. "We can have cocktails here, then go back to the highway to find someplace to eat."

90

"Cocktails? You've got to be kidding. A beer is more like it."

"You like beer."

"I was hoping for something special this evening."

"Bill, where's your sense of adventure?"

Unhappily he followed her inside.

It was a typical country bar. Whatever remained of the original interior had been covered by plastic paneling. Only the wide windowsills, crowded with cardboard beer advertisements, hinted at what real restoration might achieve. A row of booths, worn where weighty customers had devoted their time to contemplation of the large TV high in one corner, stood empty and waiting. A few rough-clad males sitting at the bar with ritual glasses of foam before them looked curiously at Bill and Hana, then returned to meditate on an early ball game, which had blossomed like the daffodils. A long modern bar, hopelessly out of touch with its environment, supported scummy jars of red beet eggs, pickles, and sausages.

"Better not order anything fancy," Bill advised as they slid into a booth.

A grinning fellow who looked to be about forty and had one tooth missing on the right front asked, "What'll it be, folks?"

"Rum and Coke," Hana ordered confidently.

"Sure thing."

"With lime."

"Lime?" he repeated slowly, frowning.

"If you don't have it, just the rum and Coke will be fine."

"Beer for me," Bill added. "Whatever's on tap."

While their host assembled the order on a tin tray whose chipped paint betrayed its age, Hana said in a low voice, "I'm going to ask him where to find Betty Schlicher."

Bill groaned.

"That's good," Hana approved. "You've got to convince her you're ill."

"Why don't you consult her yourself?" he demanded. "Women's troubles. I understand powwow doctors are big on that."

"You know something about them?"

He became instantly cautious. "Well, working with these people as I do, you hear talk, sure."

"Ever hear of the one I'm looking for?"

He shook his head. "I never paid too much attention because these hex types just aren't cooperative. Refuse to see tourists."

Her opinion of powwow doctors rose considerably. Still . . .

"They make me nervous," she admitted. "It's the thought of going down some weedy path to a shack in the woods and having some ancient woman mixing magic potions out of God-knows-what."

"Yeah, well, don't think I'm going to drink any God-knows-what."

"Just pay for it and take it home."

"And flush it down the toilet."

"What about our sewage system?" she inquired whimsically. "You want to ruin it?"

Apparently this was no time for whimsy.

"You think this is a joke," he snapped, "but it's not. I don't like it at all, Hana. I don't like lying to one of these hex people. They are odd, believe me."

"Bill, do you think they have real power?"

"I didn't say that. I just said they're odd. Maybe," he added darkly, "we won't be able to find her. Then we can go visit the Quilt Woman. I thought that's where we were going today. I thought you wanted to talk to her."

"I did . . . do. But this is more important."

"Not to me," he pouted.

The barman brought their drinks. Bill put five dollars on the table.

"I'm looking for a woman who lives around Bruchberg somewhere," Hana told the man.

He blinked, his mind apparently occupied with counting out change.

She patted his hand. "Just keep it."

"All of it?"

"Sure."

Bill grumpily watched a big fist scooping money into a pocket.

"Who're you looking for? I guess I know everybody in town."

"Her name is Betty Schlicher."

"I don't feel so good," Bill said, his eyes still on the man's pocket.

The bartender grinned broadly. "You want Betty Schlicher?"

"Yes, if you can give us directions. Maybe even some kind of map if it's hard to find."

Little things certainly give some people great pleasure, Hana thought, because he seemed to be enjoying this very much. The dear soul probably loved being helpful.

"I guess maybe you can find it without a map," he chortled. "Go up these stairs back here, then down the hall. Last door on the right."

The picture of the weed-choked path abruptly faded.

"This Betty Schlicher . . . she is a powwow practitioner, isn't she?" Hana asked.

"Oh, yeah. Ask anybody. She's good."

The assembly at the bar turned as if ready to give choral testimony.

"That won't be necessary," Hana said quickly.

He leaned closer. "She charges pretty good though," he whispered, eyeing the finely knit green suit Hana was wearing. Her only ornament was a simple silver pin, which he noted too.

"We'll manage," she said with what she hoped was finality.

Bill groaned again, quite authentically.

There was a call for more beer. The barman winked then returned to his tap.

"You're going to pay a lot for nothing," Bill said, wiping foam from his lips. "I'm glad it's your party."

Hana took a swallow of her drink and gasped: three-quarters cheap rum, one part cola.

Bill grinned wickedly. "I saw him pour it."

The man was a sadist.

She pushed away the drink. "Let's go."

But he insisted upon finishing his beer. Bill had been a poor boy and in some ways had never gotten over it.

It was fifteen minutes before they started up the brown-painted, creaky stairs. The hall was not as wide as she had expected and Hana guessed the age of the building as mid-1800s. It was certainly no Blue Spring Hill. Nor was it anywhere near the moonlit shack she recalled from her childhood.

Nor was the woman who opened the door her concept of a hex.

She appeared to be about thirty-five. Her eye makeup and lipstick were skillfully applied; her jeans were tight; her T-shirt advertised a good brand of cat food. Her hair was short, windblown. Attractive in an offbeat way with strangely pale eyes, unfortunately she too had a missing tooth. And in the same location as that of the bartender downstairs. Hana hoped it wasn't a sign of some secret hex society.

"Betty Schlicher?"

She nodded. Bill groaned. Both women eyed him with disfavor for a moment before Betty invited them inside.

"Inside" turned out to be an apartment as paneled and modern as the bar below but done with more restraint. The furniture was of excellent quality. Business must be good.

"The man at the bar told us you're a powwow practitioner," Hana began tentatively.

"Only as an avocation." Betty Schlicher glanced at her watch. "Other times I tend bar. And Barry's due to go off in ten minutes."

Hana noted signs of double occupancy of the apartment.

"Barry's your husband?"

"Quaint of you to ask. This is our place. Nice, huh?"

"Oh, indeed," Hana agreed awkwardly. "I'm Hana Shaner. This is my friend, Bill Longenecker. He's having stomach problems. Someone told us you could help."

"Who? Who told you?"

"A Mrs. Schwambach."

"Really?" Suddenly Betty was no longer in a hurry to take up her stint behind the bar. "Would you like a drink?"

"Yes," Bill said, apparently relieved. "Beer. Plain beer."

The woman looked at Hana with those well made up but peculiar eyes. Hana agreed to accept a rum and Coke. There was even lime this time and the proportions were reasonable. The doctor herself drank a bubbling pink concoction that Hana eyed suspiciously.

"Wine cooler," Betty said, taking a long sip. "Now then." She spent some moments palely sur-

veying Bill, who moved uneasily. "My advice is to
take two antacid tablets you can buy anywhere
without a prescription and call me in the morning." More wine cooler. "Little joke there."

"I don't understand," Hana said. "Can't you do
anything for him?"

"No."

"Why not?"

"Because he's not sick."

Hana said, "Maybe you're not what they say you
are. I don't see anything in this apartment that
proves you're a powwow. And I've been to one."

She didn't add how long ago.

"You want cauldrons? Bats? Cobwebs? That shit
went out years ago."

"I'm sorry. I guess things have changed."

"In some ways." The woman smiled lopsidedly
as if trying to hide the vacant spot among her teeth.
"So. Mrs. Schwambach—whose son has recently
died—sent you to me. Interesting."

The pupils of her eyes were dilated. Hana wondered if the hex doctor was on drugs.

"I told you it wouldn't work," Bill said cheerfully
as he settled back with his beer. "I knew she'd figure it out. You can't fool them."

Honesty was the only policy now available.
Hana put on her best smiling face and sales per-
sona as she went into an explanation of the second
murder and how, sadly, they were having no luck
identifying the victim. How his family must be in a
torment of anxiety. She described him in detail,
not forgetting the charm she had found around his
neck.

"Have you recently treated a boy like that?"

Betty Schlicher said cautiously, "I may have.
There's a family named Longsdorf over around the
Scotch Mountains. Last farm off Rain Road. They

have a son named Matthew who answers that description."

"What was wrong with him?"

Apparently powwowing was thirsty work, because she took a long drink of wine cooler without answering.

Bill said, "Maybe she figures it's none of our business."

"It is our business," Hana insisted. "If not ours, then the business of the police. There have been two murders. You could be in trouble, Ms. Schlicher."

It was as if a veil dropped across the eyes and they became darker. "He was disturbed in his spirit. I gave him a charm like the one you described. Sometimes, if you believe, they help."

"Disturbed? How disturbed?"

"Disturbed."

"Afraid of something? Someone? Violent himself?"

"I only noted the disturbance. I did not address the cause."

Hana felt sure the woman was lying. Impatiently she asked, "Did your charm help?"

"I wouldn't know. I never saw him again."

"Was the Schwambach boy also disturbed in his spirit?"

Betty Schlicher's voice was soft. " 'True happiness and perfect rest cannot be found on earth . . .' "

Hana wondered if the quotation might be from the Sixth and Seventh Books of Moses, hex volumes that even Aunt Sissy had been superstitious enough not to permit on the bookshelves at Blue Spring Hill.

"But you did treat Aaron Schwambach, didn't you?" Hana persisted.

"Ask the Schwambachs," Betty Schlicher said.

"I'm not sure they'll tell me."

Her only answer was a cold smile.

Bill finished his beer and rose. "Come on, Hana. We've got a dinner date."

He was right. There was nothing more to be gained here. At least not now. As they headed for the door, Betty said, "That'll be forty dollars, please."

Hana's mouth dropped open. "For what?"

"My time."

"I don't suppose you take credit cards?"

A lazy smile answered her. "A check will do fine."

As she scribbled in her checkbook, Hana said, "I'd like to see you work sometime. I mean, really work."

"Would you?" The woman traced a circle in the moisture gathering on her glass. "Maybe you will. Yes. I think you will."

A black cat padded softly out of the bedroom and paused to stare at Hana. Its pale eyes matched those of Betty Schlicher.

# Chapter Thirteen

HANA WAS ON the road early, although she knew the narrow, winding backways of Conover County would be filled with buggies and cars—church Amish going to their meetinghouses, house Amish heading for whichever farm was hosting the ser-

vices that week, and an assortment of other Plain
and fancy Dutch going to Mennonite, Lutheran,
Episcopal, and Unitarian Universalist churches.

It was about twenty-five miles to the pockets of
Amish over by the Scotch Mountains, not far on
the highway to Philadelphia, but slow driving
when behind a buggy. Crawling along in low gear,
Hana had time to observe the dazzling springtime
in the countryside and the holiday happiness of the
people. On a farmhouse porch she saw quaintly
dressed Amish children cracking open colored
Easter eggs.

She had decided to come alone. This could, after
all, be a red herring. For reasons of her own, the
hex woman might be lying. It was quite a journey
in a horse and buggy. How would the boy have
found his way from the Scotch Mountains to the
White Unicorn?

An unexpected and uncommonly straight stretch
of road gave Hana an opportunity to pass the latest
buggy in her way. She always proceeded slowly,
cautious about pulling back into her lane. Horses
can be skittish. Nobody needed another tragedy.

Even when she finally reached the area, the farm
was difficult to locate. Many crossroads had no
signs. By the time Hana pulled up at yet another
unmarked crossroad, the buggies and cars were
gone and the road had degenerated into a narrow
strip of macadam filled with potholes. Wondering
if she had made the wrong turn miles before, Hana
decided to keep going in the direction of the low-
slung mountains in front of her. Betty Schlicher
had described it as the last farm on Rain Road,
which could be the road she was on but then again
. . . Just when she had decided to give up and
backtrack, she came over a small rise and in front

of her was a farmhouse before which a neat mailbox bore the name "Longsdorf."

"I won!" Hana cried.

But what had she won? The place had the deserted feel of the Schwambach farm. Outwardly, like all Amish farms, it was neat and well kept. The buildings were neither as old nor as solid as on the Schwambach property. Both house and barn were constructed of wood. As different as they were, something gave both farms an atmosphere of tragedy and isolation.

Hana parked on a grassy area reserved for mail delivery and got out of the car. She had hoped, with her early start, to arrive before the family left for their church service. If she had missed them, it would be a long wait, because religion for the Amish included eating and visiting until milking time in late afternoon.

As she clicked through the front gate and walked past flower beds struggling upward from winter, she could see a buggy near the barn. Hana went up to the front door and knocked. The door was opened by a teenage Amish girl of the type artists and tourists adore. Her fair hair curled upward beneath her cap. Summer farm work had not yet darkened her skin, which retained the pale rosy shades peculiar to her ancestors of the European river valleys.

"Is this the Longsdorf farm?" Hana asked.

Warily the young woman nodded.

"May I see your parents?"

A teenage boy came around the side of the house and paused when he saw Hana. For a moment Hana thought it was Jake Schwambach. That was why it had been hard to identify the boys on the parking lot that night: the similarity of ages, identical haircuts, their clothing (which was almost a uniform) made them hard to tell apart. Hana couldn't see an Amish boy now without feeling again the fear of Good Friday.

"I'm Mary Longsdorf," the girl said. "That's my brother Johnny. Come once."

Hana followed her inside. The boy came after them. They paraded through austere rooms, unbrightened by calendar pictures or plants. In the kitchen a woman was gathering the remains of a large breakfast from a table covered with a checkered plastic cloth. When she saw Hana she dropped a cup, which smashed on the floor. She continued to stare as if she hadn't even noticed the accident.

She was not an old woman, but she gave the impression of age. Her shoulders were already stooped, puffiness beneath her eyes seemed to indicate . . . what? Sleepless nights? Worry? Illness? Tears? The eyes themselves held an expression of apprehension.

"Mom, this here lady wants to talk to you and Pop," Mary stated flatly.

Johnny said, "Pop's out by the barn. Shall I get him in?"

The woman nodded. The boy banged through the back door. Somewhere in the house a younger child cried out.

"He'll be in right off," the woman said and quickly left the room.

"Wait," Hana began.

Mary moved forward as if to intercept Hana if she had any plans to follow the older woman.

"Mom's not much for strangers," she said.

A clock on the wall ticked loudly. Hana looked at the girl, who turned away and stooped to pick up bits of broken cup. Finally, uninvited, Hana sat in a chair at the table. The hex woman was right. This had to be the home of the murdered boy. They were all nervous, uptight—as if waiting for the other shoe to drop.

It was fifteen minutes before Pop Longsdorf and the boy Johnny came into the kitchen. Mr. Longsdorf was a fierce-looking man with frown lines etched deeply between his eyes and flecks of gray in both beard and hair. Lines running from his nose to his mouth gave him a dour, somber expression.

"What'd you want?" he asked bluntly.

Hana rose, facing him squarely. "Have you a son named Matthew?"

"*Ja.*"

"Is he at home?"

Despite the lack of hospitality, Hana had no intention of giving these people a jolt if none was necessary. There were hundreds of Marys, Johnnys, and Matthews in Amish families. Repetition of names was a trademark of the sect.

There was more silence. Nobody moved. Hana stared into the eyes of the patriarch. If it takes all day, she thought, I'll stare him down. It didn't take all day, but it must have taken all of five minutes. Mary started to speak.

Longsdorf's voice rose above hers. "No, he ain't home. What for do you want to know?"

"Do you know where he is?" Hana asked patiently. "When did he leave?"

A muscle twitched in his cheek and, despite herself, Hana felt sorry for him. They were proud people, which made this hard for them to bear.

"Why don't we sit down?" she asked. "Wouldn't it be easier?"

"I'm sorry," he said, rubbing his forehead with a roughened hand. "*Ja.* Please. Sit. Mary, coffee."

He dropped heavily into a chair across the table

from her. Hana waited. The coffee was apparently still hot from breakfast. Clean white mugs were placed in front of them and filled to the brim.

Gratefully Hana took a swallow before she asked, "Can you tell me when you last saw Matthew?"

"Thursday night," Johnny blurted out.

*"Gott verdumbsei nochamal!"* his father cursed. Johnny backed away.

The man stared angrily at his son for a long moment before he turned back to Hana. "Tell me why you want to know about Matthew."

Keeping her voice even, Hana said, "A boy was killed in the livestock barn at the White Unicorn Market on Good Friday. He hasn't been identified but I have reason to believe he may be your son."

She looked from one to the other. They were all staring at her now. She had the impression they were not surprised, that she had only confirmed something they already knew. It was a weird feeling. She began to describe the boy.

The father rose. "It could be Matthew. *Ja.* Maybe. *Danke.* You go on now."

"It isn't that simple, Mr. Longsdorf. I'll have to notify the police. They'll want to ask questions—"

"You go on and do what you got to do, woman. And we'll do what we got to do and that's an end to it."

"You'll have to go to the morgue to identify the body—"

He smote the table with his fist, endangering a cup that was close to the edge. "Why are you going on about it still? The law is the law and we obey the law. Everybody knows that about our people. Let the police come and we'll do what they say. Not what you say."

Hana glanced at Mary. She was looking at her

father benignly without the fear her brother showed. Maybe Pop Longsdorf was easier on his girls than on his boys.

Hana took another swallow of the good coffee, then regretfully rose.

"I'll see you later," she said crisply.

They did not look as if the thought gave them any pleasure. Mary trotted after her to the front of the house. The girl even politely opened the door.

Hana paused. "Aren't you going to services this morning?"

Mary shook her head.

"Don't you attend services?" Hana persisted.

"Why, sure now! But if you're sick or got troubles you don't have to go."

"Is someone here ill? Or is it because you people knew Matthew was dead?"

Mary moved closer, effectively edging her out of the house.

"My little sister's sick," the girl said stoically.

Hana, now standing on the porch, studied her.

"Will you at least tell me why your brother left home on Thursday evening? Where was he going?"

"I don't know. Maybe he went because he was one who didn't feel Amish inside," Mary said softly. "Some don't, you know. Especially some kids don't."

The girl firmly closed the door, leaving Hana alone and unwelcome outside. Frustrated, she returned to her car.

Of course, she would have to notify the police and report everything. But how do you talk about hex over a telephone? Hana wondered what the police would make of Betty Schlicher.

She considered the problem as she meandered along unmarked roads. Twice she took the wrong turn. Although the buggies were off the road now,

it took her nearly as long to get back to Conover
City as it had to find the Longsdorf farm. By the
time she reached the suburbs people were coming
out of churches—women in flowered hats, men
and children in spring colors—reminding her
again that it was Easter Sunday. Holiday spirits
were in the air.

Hana discovered they penetrated even to the police when she finally made up her mind and dialed
Chief Hoffman on her car phone. After all, he was
a native of Conover County, so he should understand the hex angle. But Hoffman was also a family man. His calls were being taken by Lieutenant
Singh.

Hana hung up and dialed the Conover police station. Sergeant Kochen was not on duty either but
had left his home number in case somebody required his personal attention. It was really a pleasure to dial the number. She hoped he was having
a wonderful holiday and she was interrupting his
entertainment. It might make up in part for their
last phone conversation.

He answered with a businesslike "Kochen."

"Shaner," Hana monotoned. "Are you busy?"

"Shaner? Oh. Yes." He sounded surprised. "Not
really busy."

"I'd like to see you for a few minutes. It's a little
hard to explain over the phone."

There was a moment of silence before he gave
her his address. At least this time he wasn't shouting at her. Maybe that would come later.

Annoyingly he lived in the part of town through
which she had just come. She swung the car in an
illegal U-turn and drove rapidly to one of the many
suburban apartment complexes in the area. Most
of them were rumored to have been constructed to
last for thirty years and, although this one looked

all right from the road, up close it appeared to be nearing the end of its twenty-ninth year. She parked over a puddle of somebody's transmission fluid. Kochen was waiting for her before a mock Colonial doorway.

For a moment Hana hardly recognized him. Instead of the usual turtleneck, he wore a brown T-shirt decorated with a white beer logo, jeans, and a disreputable pair of loafers without socks. The outfit gave him an attractive boyish air.

Feeling uncomfortable, she said politely, "I'm sorry to intrude on your holiday . . ."

He shrugged. "Come on up."

She followed him into the building to carpeted stairs. Cheap, she noted, worn areas repaired with wide bands of brown tape. Accustomed to Shaner quality, she could hardly bring herself to walk on it.

He had a corner apartment on the second floor. She wasn't fond of modern apartments, but this one gave an impression of space and light. Windows met at the corner of the living room with nice effect. The carpeting here looked new, but what Shaner Green Glory would do for this room! Furnishings, although spare, had been chosen with care—a decor which might be called Sturdy Modern. At his invitation, Hana sat in a surprisingly comfortable easy chair with broad wooden arms. A large-screen TV was reporting news. He switched it off.

"Just checking on what they had to say about our second murder," he told her. "We've been downplaying it as a possible accident. They haven't picked up on anything yet."

"Surely they soon will."

"At least it buys us time. Nobody here is anxious to make a circus out of this."

"No inquest?"

"Not now anyway. Thank God Pennsylvania still has the old coroner system and the coroner feels the way we do. May I get you something? Beer? Coffee? Mineral water?"

Recalling her unfinished cup at the Longsdorfs', Hana agreed to black coffee. He shuffled into a small area behind a counter. As he heated water and rattled an assortment of cups, Hana began to feel foolish. All that would really have been required was to supply him with the dead boy's name. Why was it so important to her that the police know about the hex angle? And to imagine that she could talk to this man about it was totally unrealistic.

He brought two cups of coffee, which he placed on a dust-free, ornament-free, wooden coffee table. Hana took a sip. Awful. How could anybody create instant coffee that seemed . . . gritty?

"Look," he said abruptly, "I want to apologize for the way I blew up at you over the phone. It was uncalled for. It happened because I'm really uptight about these two dead kids. That kind of thing —killing, injuring children—always gets me worked up. I'm glad you told me about the four-pronged pitchfork. It was something we didn't know, and God knows we need all the information we can get."

She hadn't expected an apology. He seemed different on his home territory, more relaxed.

"Apology accepted," she told him lightly.

He took a swallow of his own coffee, looked thoughtfully at the cup, then replaced it on the table. "Now then, what've you got this time?"

"I want to talk to you about hex," she said. He looked startled, so she repeated distinctly, "Hex. Witchcraft."

"Oh."

"It's part of the folklore of this area," she explained. "Brought with our people from the old country. These traditions can be traced right back to medieval Germany. There are local cases where a person was murdered because someone believed the individual was a witch who had put a spell on them. Barns have small windows high up to let the witches out, and don't ever let anybody tell you that hex signs on the fancy Dutch barns aren't there to ward off evil."

"Why are you telling me all this?" he inquired mildly. "Not that it isn't an interesting way to pass an Easter Sunday afternoon."

"It's something you ought to know. Especially since you're an outsider." She hesitated. "Where did you come from, Sergeant Kochen?"

"Call me Will."

"Will?"

"Short for Wilford. I'm that rare breed—a native New Yorker. So I can believe almost anything. When you work in a Manhattan precinct for ten years, you get all kinds."

Ten years? Interesting. He couldn't be as young as he looked.

"You told me," he continued, inspecting her over his glasses, "that you didn't believe in this sort of thing yourself. Are you now telling me that you do?"

She tried to sound dignified. "It's hard to describe how I feel. You don't need to believe in incantations to feel there are forces we don't understand. I believe people can be helped if they have faith in a talisman of some sort. I also believe people can be hurt if other people concentrate on evil."

He pushed his glasses into place. "But you didn't

come here to discuss the philosophy of superstition. Did you?"

He sounded brusque, the way he did on the job.

Hana felt a sense of triumph as she let him have it. "I came because I've found out who the second boy is and I felt I had to discuss with you how I got the information."

He sat up straight, suddenly tense. She took another sip of the instant-awful, making him wait.

"Who is he?" he asked.

"I have to tell this in my own way."

"Damn!"

"Or I can wait and tell Chief Hoffman when he's finished playing Easter Bunny for his kids."

There were sparks in the air between them. For the first time Hana was acutely aware that his eyes were a smoky gray. Unexpectedly, he laughed. "I've got to hand it to you, Hana," he said, using her given name for the first time. "You do things in the damnedest way. But it seems to work. What the hell, I'm not even on duty, so do it your way. But first let's get rid of this lousy coffee. I've got a bottle of pretty fair German wine back here."

"Fine."

"After all," he said dryly, "it goes with the territory."

She waited until he was reseated and they had wineglasses in front of them before she told him about Betty Schlicher. She had his full attention. He seemed unhurried and was even amused by the part about the missing teeth. But when she told him about the Longsdorfs, he stopped being amused.

"I've got to call Lieutenant Singh—he's taking over for Hoffman today—"

"I know."

He paused. "You know everything, don't you?"

She shook her head. He went into what was obviously the bedroom, closing the door behind him. Hana rose and wandered to the window. Two small girls in fancy pastel dresses were searching beneath bushes on the grounds. Each had a basket filled with lavender Easter grass. While Hana watched one found a foil-covered candy rabbit. Aunt Sissy had always made much over holidays when Hana was little. On Easter the conservatory had been filled with hyacinths and all sorts of toys and goodies had been hidden there. Holidays were for children. Perhaps, after all, she should have gone out to Sal's farm. She could have brought extra sweets for the children. Unattached people like herself just wandered through days like these, apart from the celebrants and always a little lonely underneath. She thought about Kochen. Maybe he was glad she had come.

Hana returned to her wine. The deaths of these Amish boys had gotten to her. She was becoming maudlin.

When Kochen came back, he looked unaccustomedly happy.

"Singh and another man are going out there right away. Sorry—habit. The other man is a woman. They thought it would be good to have one along."

"I hope Singh doesn't get lost."

Kochen picked up his glass. "Unlike me, he's a native."

"I didn't know. His name sounds Indian."

"It is. His parents emigrated here from Madras. And I'm glad you didn't know. That means there might be a few things I can teach you."

Hana decided not to ask what those things might be. "Are you going with them?"

"I wasn't invited. By the way, I told him you

were the one who got the information. So they may want to talk to you."

"Anytime." She drank the rest of her wine. "Guess I'd better get back home."

"You have family coming for Easter dinner?"

"No."

"Want to stay and dye Easter eggs?"

She looked at him uncertainly, not sure he was serious.

He was. "There's a family here in the complex that's having a pretty hard time of it. Parents both out of work, so I do things for the kids when I can. I bought candy and I was going to dye eggs and make up baskets. But with these murders . . . I just didn't get around to it."

Hana laughed. "Oh, my God—"

"Will you?"

The wine was quite good. The apartment pleasant. And, after all, maybe she could pick his brain and learn more about police procedures.

"I used to love to dye Easter eggs," she mused. "I was very clever at painting faces on them."

He grinned. "So was I."

It wasn't until she was back in Blue Spring Hill that evening that Hana remembered she had forgotten to talk to Kochen about police procedures or the case. Instead they talked about the Easters of their childhoods. She had helped him create beautiful baskets decorated with bunches of fresh violets they had found growing in the grass behind the complex. She had gone with him to deliver the goodies and had found loving people who, despite their troubled times, were hospitable and friendly. Kochen had brought along wine and they had hard-boiled egg sandwiches for their supper with the family. Hana couldn't remember when she'd had a better time.

# Chapter Fourteen

HANA FLICKED THE switch on her intercom and said to Mary Hafer, the receptionist, "Get me my private eye."

Things were very calm around the plant and office for a Monday morning. Even Jimmy Klopp, her plant manager, had lapsed into an unusual placidity. Maybe their three-day spring holiday was just what everybody had needed. The first thing Hana had done that morning was contact Personnel to give them the names of Kochen's unemployed neighbors. Shaner Industries could always use good people.

Ralph Sensenig must have been having an uncommonly crime-free morning, because Mary had him on the line almost immediately.

"How was your holiday?" he inquired in the same tone in which he had often led suspects into dangerous admissions of guilt.

But Hana refused to allow herself to be trapped into an admission that she had spent her Easter dyeing eggs with a sergeant of police.

"I have a sensitive job for you," she told him in her all-business tone.

He made comforting, inviting noises low in his throat.

Accepting these sounds as an answer, she continued, "I want you to shadow two teenage Amish boys."

There was silence at the other end of the line, then he repeated, "Amish?"

"Old Order Amish. Plain People. The ones you see driving buggies about the countryside—"

"I know who the Amish are, for heaven's sake.

But I don't ever recall being asked to . . ." He paused, clearing his throat. "However, with our latest surveillance techniques, we can arrange anything. For example, we could give the horse a listening device in its food. If it was for a short-term job only, of course, because naturally the device would . . ."

Hana resisted a strong temptation to hang up. "I don't want you getting after their horses. I don't want you using all those electronic gadgets you're so fond of."

He sounded shocked. "But surely you realize sophisticated electronic devices are the only effective means of surveillance. Following people in cars or on foot—spying—all that's TV fantasy in our technological age."

A picture of mules plowing, of kerosene lamps in windows of farmhouses in April dusks, came to Hana. "Regardless, I want a flesh-and-blood human being for a change. How about that young man who worked on Nunemachers' farm as a bodyguard last fall? He was a real farmer. He'd fit in."

"Unavailable. His grandfather died and willed him a large farm in Nebraska."

"Well, surely you have someone else like him."

He sounded grieved. "That kind is so rare. But we have any number of electronic geniuses. We'll bug their buggies! Our latest sounding devices are so sensitive we'll be able to tell you everything that's done or said in the house or barn and—"

"I'll let you know," Hana said and hung up.

She sat glaring at the phone. She wanted the killer found but not to invade the privacy of these families, these people who didn't even permit electric lights because electric lines would connect them directly with nonbelievers. These peaceful people, whose very religion was tied with the seasonal flow of the living things of the earth. The thought of ordering such an invasion repelled Hana.

But that did not change the fact that she suspected Jake Schwambach and Johnny Longsdorf knew something about the killings and felt equally sure that the police were doing nothing about that angle. However, whatever she did had to be aimed at the boys themselves without violating the privacy of their families.

Restlessly Hana rose and moved to a window. Outside, what farmers called a "land rain" was falling. This was a gentle rain, which soaked into the ground rather than running off, eroding precious topsoil. Grass and new leaves on trees were vibrantly green in the glistening wet. In the parking lot, beneath a sheltering roof, was a row of bicycles some of the more athletically inclined employees rode to work.

They gave Hana an idea.

She spent the morning focusing on details of marketing Dutch Blue wearing apparel. She tried to call Pocky Reilly without success. Either Pocky was still angry over Hana's rejection of her idea for a pseudo-Amish dress or she was adding an extra day to the Easter weekend, which seemed more likely.

At lunchtime Hana returned to Blue Spring Hill.

Rain still fell, which didn't suit her purpose. New leaves were popping all over the place. The woods would be full of fragile white flowers of bloodroot, and the umbrellas of mayapples would soon carpet wet areas. She'd have to take time to walk her trails one day soon.

Trotting along the edge of the woods were Ghost and Crumb, looking wet but happy. Padding after them was Kitty Fisher, her reddish fur dark and damp. More and more, since Gray Trouble had moved into the house, Kitty Fisher allied herself with the dogs.

Shaking her head over the idiosyncrasies of living creatures, Hana drove to the house. She dashed through the rain to the side door and hurried inside, hoping Mr. Fred and Sal would cooperate with her plans.

They were in the kitchen having lunch.

"Hi!" she greeted them in her most friendly manner.

They became immediately wary.

Five minutes later they were both angry.

Hana considered her plan to be the best under the given circumstances. It also had the benefit of simplicity and the involvement of few people. Mr. Fred would go about the countryside pretending to be a salesman, perhaps of surplus groceries at inexpensive prices. Hana suggested damaged cans and past-date crackers. His territory would be the neighborhood around the Schwambach farm. His main purpose was to keep an eye on Jake Schwambach and follow him if he went anywhere.

Hana herself would dress in one of Sal's Mennonite outfits and ride around the Longsdorf area on the old bicycle Mr. Fred sometimes used when patrolling the estate.

"You are not Plain!" Sal cried. "And I am not giving you my clothes so you can go around spying on folks and giving Plain People a bad name!"

Mr. Fred was more calm but equally negative. "I have served the Shaner family in many capacities, but I have never been asked to assume a role of detective, which is certainly better left to professionals. Nor have I been asked to jeopardize the

health of entire families by selling them damaged
cans that may contain tainted food."

Hana considered herself a master at handling
mutiny in the ranks.

"I thought you would want to help me," she said
sadly. "There's no one else I can turn to. It means
so much to me to find out who killed these boys.
After all, they were hardly more than children. I
thought it might mean something to you too. You,
Sal, you're the one who involved me in this in the
first place."

The plea, though well acted, did not work. Hana
had to go as far as insisting she would obtain an
actual Amish costume from a theatrical shop for
her charade and to muse about hiring one of Pocky
Reilly's actors to play the part of the salesman.
There was also mention of subsidizing a hired
hand during spring planting at the Nunemacher
farm, and carte blanche for Mr. Fred in setting up
the museum in the 1812 Annex, before they gave
in. Even then, it was with bad grace. Mr. Fred fretted that he had a million details to attend to for the
Open House. However, he could spare perhaps a
day and a half for this ridiculous enterprise. After
all, he didn't wish to be thought uncooperative in
the light of such tragedy. He insisted that the groceries he would sell be first class all the way. Hana
agreed.

Sal grudgingly admitted that she kept extra outfits at Blue Spring Hill in case, as she said, "one got
dirty." If there was anything Sal Nunemacher
could never be accused of, it was being dirty. She
had her own room in the mansion, set aside for the
rare occasions she stayed overnight or in case she
wanted to take a nap, also a rare occurrence.

Later, in this room, Hana stared at her own image in the full-length mirror on the closet door.

Mennonite outfits were less severe than Amish dress. Sal declared that no conservative Mennonite would have such short hair, but most of it was hidden by the small white cap. Hana's face was rather round, her cheeks full. With the white cap on her white hair, her green eyes were startlingly prominent. The "wash dress" and white apron gave her an earthy look she had never thought possible. Clothes do indeed make the woman. In oxfords and tights, her legs looked thicker.

If Bill Longenecker or Sergeant Wilford Kochen could see her now . . .

Sal pinned a small ball of pale gray yarn at the back of her head, beneath the cap, to suggest a knot of hair.

She eyed Hana critically, as did Penelope Baskin, who had come to see what all the fuss was about. "That's as good as it's going to get."

"Will I pass?"

"If nobody looks too close," Sal said with a grunt. "It's not your style."

Hana wondered just what Sal considered her style but decided it wasn't the right time to ask.

Mr. Fred was more difficult. He would have to rent a van and fill it with the suggested groceries. He insisted on a written note that he was acting on the orders of Hana Shaner, just in case he was picked up by the police for peddling without a license. He was certain it would take all afternoon just to get ready for the job. And since he had only promised a day and a half . . .

Hana left before she lost her temper. He was conferring with Sal about what a well-dressed peddler might wear as she slammed through the side door. With some difficulty she loaded the bicycle into the trunk of her car and set off for the Scotch Mountains.

# Chapter Fifteen

DURING A LONG afternoon Hana cycled along country roads. Rain had settled into a dull drizzle. She wore a raincoat with a hood that also belonged to Sal, but she soon felt damp and chilled. As often as she dared, she passed the Longsdorf farm. She had spotted both Johnny Longsdorf and his sister Mary. The boy was apparently repairing something in the barn. Once she saw him carrying wood and twice she heard hammering. On a third pass, Mary, shawl over her head, was crossing from house to barn with coffee—two steaming cups—so Mr. Longsdorf was probably also working inside.

A few buggies went by in the fast lane. Their occupants, comfortably dry behind plastic like windshields, stared at this crazy woman peddling through the rain. Hana found herself thinking constantly of the coffee at the Longsdorfs'. She even considered knocking on their door and asking for a cup. When she began to think kindly of Ralph Sensenig and his electronic gadgets, she decided it was time to go home. The light was fading fast. Hana checked the Longsdorfs one more time. A kerosene lamp glowed yellow in the kitchen, giving the place a warm, lived-in appearance. Intermittent hammering still came from the barn. The horses were in their dry stalls. The buggy was in the shed. Nobody was going anywhere.

Wearily Hana peddled on to her car, which she had parked in a lane that cut through a peach orchard. It was harder than before to shove her bike into the trunk. She suspected that by morning she'd be stiff. Once more she thought of Ralph Sensenig. Once more she rejected his all-consuming, intrusive surveillance, although this time with less vigor.

Warm air flowed about her from the heater as she drove home. She dialed her office on the car phone, found things moving well, sneezed as she hung up, and wondered why she was doing this.

She hoped fervently the sun would shine the next day.

Mr. Fred was right, she sadly admitted to herself. If these boys didn't move in the next two days, something else would have to be done. The Longsdorfs were bound to notice a woman, Mennonite or not, cycling past their home much too frequently. And how long could Mr. Fred's van dally near the Schwambachs? Mr. Fred, tall yet gnomelike, with his large head and slicked-back dyed hair, was very noticeable.

Gratefully Hana turned into her own driveway. A good hot shower. A meal on a tray in the snuggery in front of the TV. Happy thoughts. She glanced at her watch. Sal had already gone home. God knows where Mr. Fred was.

Hana pulled into her parking space. No animals were about, which was a good sign that they, unlike herself, were warm and dry inside the house. She crawled out of the car rather stiffly and shook herself to limber up as she went to the side door. Maybe this was good for her. She really should exercise more often.

She fitted her key into the lock and went inside. The hall light had not been turned on. She closed the door and looked toward the kitchen. There was a faint odor of cooking in the air but no light and nothing stirring back there.

Two small furry figures streaked by without stopping to say hello and blended into the darkness of the kitchen—Gray Trouble and Penelope Baskin.

She wondered what had frightened them.

Moving forward, she switched on a light. Everything looked normal. She went into the large front hall. Near the main stairs her welcoming committee waited—Ghost, Crumb, and Kitty Fisher. They came snuffling and wagging. Kitty Fisher rubbed against Hana's legs.

Upstairs Hana's bath and warm robe waited for her. But she hesitated. She trusted the instincts of her animals. Why had the two cats run to hide? Yet, if a stranger was inside the house, surely the dogs would be barking. Instead they were acting as unalarmed as Kitty Fisher, who was obviously playing dog today. What this meant to Hana was that if somebody was actually inside the house, it had to be somebody known to Ghost and Crumb. Somebody like Mr. Fred, except it couldn't be Mr. Fred because he never forgot to turn on the lights.

With cold fingers Hana took her .22 pistol out of the pocket of Sal's apron.

## *Chapter Sixteen*

HANA STOOD VERY still, listening. But she heard nothing except the silence of a very large, very old house. She stooped beside Crumb and rubbed his head and ears with one hand, her .22 ready in the other.

Keeping her voice very low, she said, "Crummy-

boy, go. Who's here? Show me who's here, boy.
Go."

The dog hesitated, looking at her with fond, in-
telligent eyes.

Hana put more urgency into her voice and repeated her order.

Crumb shook himself, circled a few times, then
trotted off toward the 1812 Annex. Hana followed,
turning on lights as she went. Ghost and Kitty
Fisher joined them.

If Mr. Fred was working in the museum on his
damned bones . . .

But before they reached the Annex, Crumb
stopped in front of the conservatory door and
whined. Hana glanced at Ghost. He too was looking at the door but, like a fool, wagging his tail.

Hana switched on the lights of the conservatory
and opened the door quickly. Kitty Fisher streaked
past into the warmth of the sweet tropical air.
Hana stepped inside, .22 ready. The dogs followed
more slowly, confused about the human signals
they were getting. Crumb whined low in his throat,
as if afraid he had, after all, been remiss in some
duty.

Hana skirted a large fern, grown almost to tree
size, and looked down the walkway.

In front of her, Kitty Fisher was rubbing about
the legs of Teddy Jolf.

"Hey," Teddy said. "Hey, Sal . . . don't shoot!
It's me—Teddy Jolf. You know . . . the person
helping Mr. Fred." She paused suddenly. "*Hana?*
Hana Shaner? Is that you? Why are you dressed
like Sal?"

Hana stood still, her .22 pointed. "What the hell
are you doing in here?"

Teddy Jolf licked her lips and ran a hand
through her somewhat wild curls as though to

comb them. "Easy answer. Mr. Fred . . . he called
. . . asked if I'd come over. He was going to be
busy doing something else. I'm great on fingers,
you know. Bones? Wiring up the fingers of the Revolutionary War skeletons. Maybe he told you. I
mean, it's not long until Open House, is it? He
didn't want to lose today. So I said okay because
I'm pretty well caught up on book sales at the moment. He let me in and I've been working in the
1812 Annex all afternoon. Hey, I was not crazy
about doing it either. This is one weird old place
when you're alone. I was never alone here before.
How do you stand it? Wow, if I lived here I'd have a
gun too."

Hana waited calmly until the woman had
stopped talking, then asked, "But what are you doing in the conservatory?"

"Nothing! Well . . . I mean, what I'm doing is
just looking around. I love places like this. Green-
houses all full of exotic plants. I'd stopped working, you see. How many bones can you do in one
day before you start getting crazy? Look, you can
search me if you want."

It made sense. Or would have if the lights had
been on and Teddy had been casual about it. Hana
put her hand into her pocket and moved forward.
Crumb, confused, went up to Teddy Jolf and lay
down whining. Teddy reached down to pet him.

"The dogs like you," Hana said dryly.

Kitty Fisher was sharpening her claws on a banana tree, right next to the secret panel that Hana
had used as a child to get in and out of the house
unobserved. Hana hissed at the cat and Kitty
Fisher ran.

Around the base of the banana tree were footprints of a human as well as a cat in the soft loam.

It appeared somebody had stood there searching for something.

"I daresay Mr. Fred has told you a lot about the house," Hana suggested.

"Yeah. He really loves this old place."

"Did he tell you about an adventure we had where we were forced to use the secret entrance in this conservatory?"

Teddy looked uncomfortable, then nodded.

"Is that what you were looking for?"

"Okay, okay! But just out of curiosity! I have no designs on you or your house or anything in it. This place is so much like a museum, one forgets . . ."

"Apparently you also forgot to turn on the lights. Did you hear me come in? Heard the car perhaps, or saw car lights through the rhododendrons? You thought you'd wait quietly and maybe I'd go right upstairs?"

"No—"

"Then why didn't you turn on the lights?"

Ghost looked at Hana then importantly went up to Teddy Jolf, sniffed her pant legs, and growled.

Teddy said nervously, "It wasn't all that dark in here. It's just twilight and I was working in the museum and it's always dark there so I really didn't notice."

Hana took the .22 from her pocket again and motioned Teddy toward the conservatory door. "I want you to leave this house and I don't want you to come back."

"But I've been working so hard on the Open House and the museum—"

"Get out. Now. Or I'm calling the police."

Her eyes on the weapon, Teddy gave Hana a wide berth, stepping into the moist earth around a bird-of-paradise, then scurrying to the door. Hana and the two dogs escorted Teddy into the hall. Kitty Fisher, apparently tired of playing dog, had climbed the banana tree.

"Where's your car?" Hana asked. "I didn't see it in the parking lot."

"Mr. Fred picked me up in some kind of van."

*Oh, God*, Hana thought.

Teddy went on, "I was supposed to stay here until he came back. I thought sure he'd show up by this time."

"So how did you expect to get home, since he hasn't?"

"I thought I'd call a cab."

Hana felt a surge of weary exasperation—toward Teddy Jolf in particular, Mr. Fred and the entire world in general. She could shove this young woman out the door, in which case she was free to roam the grounds for reasons of her own. Or Hana could drive her home. Galling thought.

She was saved from the dilemma by the timely arrival of Mr. Fred, like a skinny superman in jeans, plaid shirt, and masculine apron so large it nearly reached his ankles.

"What in heaven's name are you wearing?" Hana demanded as she slipped the safety on her pistol and dropped it into her apron pocket.

"I'd like to know what you're both wearing and why," Teddy said cheerfully, quickly returning to normal.

"Wait until you see the van," he told them proudly. "I had the most marvelous idea—"

"Tell me later," Hana snapped. "Right now I want you to take Ms. Jolf home. And I don't want you to talk to her about what we're doing. Is that clear?"

Mr. Fred blinked and fussed with his apron. "But—"

"Neither do I want her inside this house again."

"Now just a minute," he said assertively. "She's indispensable to the fingers of my skeletons. Nobody can do fingers and toes like Ms. Jolf."

"I did something dumb," Teddy said hastily. "I just wanted to see the conservatory. Then I was going to hunt a phone and call a cab, that's all. Hana thinks I was snooping, but I wasn't. Really."

"Of course you weren't." He fixed a malevolent eye on Hana. "We of the Historical Society hold this young woman in the highest regard. She is one of the joys of our committee—creative, innovative, talented—"

Before he declared her to be Saint Teddy of Conover, Hana waved a dismissal.

"Just get her out of here. We'll talk about it later."

Offended and indignant, Mr. Fred, at his fussiest best, ushered Teddy Jolf to the side door. From the conservatory came an indignant wail. Hana let Kitty Fisher out, then went uptairs.

By the time Mr. Fred returned, she had showered and was wrapped in her quilted robe, with fuzzy slippers on her feet. She was in the kitchen chewing dandelion greens with bovine determination when he came in. It was a dish that Sal served with almost religious fervor each spring.

"Thins the blood," she always said. "It's as good as any tonic."

No matter that it tended to be tough and stringy, it had to be endured on at least three occasions to keep Sal contented with their diet. Hana had been rather nonplussed to find it waiting on the stove for her. But, after all, she did enjoy the sweet and sour dressing that covered the greens, and there were always the baked potatoes and hard-boiled eggs as a garnish.

"This unusual interest in crime has ruined your

faith in the goodness of human nature," Mr. Fred charged stuffily. "When you were a child—except for a certain lack of intellect, which you fortunately overcame during your college years—you were known by everybody for your kindness. To use a weapon to threaten a person admiring the conservatory—"

"She was admiring it without lights."

"She didn't know where to turn them on."

"That's not the story she gave me. Mr. Fred, do you realize you know nothing whatever about this person?"

"I know all I need to. I suggest that if you have real suspicions, you get your firm of private investigators to scrutinize her background with their computers. That should ease your mind and not rob us of a valuable volunteer."

"Don't think I won't do just that."

"Good." Mr. Fred helped himself liberally to the strands of slippery dandelion from the pan on the stove as Hana watched, fascinated. "Then we can settle this once and for all. You've been unfair to her right from the beginning and I can't think why."

"She was at the scene of the crime for the second murder."

"I believe the same thing might be said for several thousand other people."

Hana might have continued the conversation if she had not at that moment choked on a dandelion leaf that she tried to swallow whole because it was impossible to chew. She grabbed her water glass. The rest of the meal they ate in silence, broken only by the sound of masticating. Mr. Fred was right, however, Hana decided, munching along as she thought of Ralph Sensenig and the electronic heart of his organization. Even though they could not deal with the simple world of the horse-and-buggy Amish, they could track the history of thoroughly modern Teddy Jolf. Hana would have to see about it.

Mr. Fred, having accomplished the feat of eating everything on his plate, asked, "Aren't you curious about what I've done for my charade? You were so anxious to send me on this mission I would think you'd have some interest in ascertaining how I'm going about it."

"Forgive me. It's been a long day," Hana sighed. "How *are* you doing?"

"I am a baker."

"What?"

"I even had a sign painted that I have attached to the side of my van. I just happened to pass one of those little shops specializing in Italian and French pastry. I bought out their entire stock then and there, and they will furnish me with more in the morning, even though it means overtime for them. I felt sure that since we've gone this far, a little additional expense would be acceptable. My cover story is that my wife bakes these culinary delights and she and I are cooperating on this new venture."

"You're going to sell Italian and French pastries to the Amish?" Hana asked faintly.

"Isn't it a wonderful idea?"

Viciously Hana tried to thrust her fork through some dandelion, which immediately slithered off her plate. "No, it isn't. The Amish will never buy such things. They're meat and potato and raisin pie people."

Stubbornly he shook his head. "I intend to open their world a bit. At least I can do that, even if I can't do anything constructive toward solving this crime."

"I'm sending you out there to shadow Jake Schwambach! Not to sell cannolis."

"Did you," he asked pointedly, "find out anything useful about the other boy?"

Hana refused to answer as she ate the last bit of hard-boiled egg, then rose with her plate. She'd shove the rest into the garbage disposal and Sal would never know. Even Mr. Fred wasn't foolhardy enough to tell.

# *Chapter Seventeen*

THE NEXT DAY was a preview of summer. Dandelions thrust open yellow eyes all over the county except on the pampered, spongy lawns of Blue Spring Hill. They were a happy sight to Hana, who rejoiced in their flowering. It meant no more meals such as she had enjoyed the evening before. A good Pennsylvania Dutch cook like Sal Nunemacher would never use dandelion greens once they were in bloom. They were too tough by then, according to tradition, although Hana wondered if this was possible.

Mr. Fred in his van and Hana in her car set off for their adventures while Sal and the animals watched from the side door without a great deal of enthusiasm.

Feeling hopeful, Hana once more drove the narrow roads of Conover County toward the Scotch Mountains. On a day like this, the natives were restless. It was a promise of all the good things of summer. Surely if a boy was going to do anything, go anywhere, it would be on such a day.

The whole countryside was alive with activity. Farmers busily planted. Cows moved through sweet pastures. Farm women had opened windows and doors. Drying wash and airing bedclothes stirred in a gentle breeze.

As Hana parked in the same lane she had used the day before, she realized she was not as stiff as she had expected and was actually looking forward to cycling.

On her first pass by the Longsdorf farm she nearly fell off the bicycle. The barn door was held open by Mary. Through it came Johnny and his father bearing a plain wooden casket.

Horrified, Hana realized what had been going on in the barn the day before. They had been making the coffin in which Matthew would be buried. Apparently they did not notice her, so intent were they on their burden. Hana pedaled faster, the day no longer so beautiful. Down the road, beneath a tree, she stopped.

She knew that years ago the Amish had always constructed their own caskets. Now almost every funeral director in the county stocked these unvarnished wooden coffins suitable for Plain use. But obviously the Longsdorfs and, Hana suspected, the Schwambachs continued to do things in the old way. She felt sure the body had not been in the coffin. They couldn't go so far as to bury it without embalming. Ever obedient citizens, the Amish allowed their dead to be preserved, even though they considered it a contradiction to their Lord's command: "Dust thou art and unto dust shalt thou return."

Hana mounted her bicycle and thoughtfully continued along the road. . . . The funeral would be this morning. Amish funerals were always in the morning. Johnny Longsdorf would certainly be too busy to go anywhere today. Or would he? Under the cover of funeral activity, a lot of things might happen. She decided to continue her surveillance. She wasn't sure whether the activity would make her task harder or easier.

On her next pass by, carriages had already begun to arrive. If it was anything like other Amish funerals Hana had known, soon the barnyard would be full of them. These early arrivals carried casseroles, pies, and other foodstuffs into the house.

The sun was higher now, and the uncommon warmth of the day made Sal's midcalf skirt feel cumbersome. Buggies and a few cars were now clogging the road. Even if a family was unpopular —and Hana was not reassured about the Longsdorfs' popularity—their church of perhaps thirty families would attend services.

Hana wished she had rented an Amish costume. If only she'd known! This Mennonite dress would stand out in an Amish crowd, and the last thing Hana wanted was to be noticed. She parked her bike beside her car, waited for half an hour in the shade of orchard trees, then walked slowly down the road. By the time she reached the farm, people had congregated inside. Through windows open to the warm air, she heard the words of a hymn being read in High German. There was no music of any kind at Amish funerals.

Hana hesitated, looking up and down the road. It was deserted, except for the steam rising as the hot sun vaporized puddles from yesterday's rain. Horses, unhitched from a collection of buggies, were visiting their fellows in the barnyard and making soft horsey sounds to each other.

But the horses were not what tempted Hana to

open the neat picket gate and go into the yard. Two
modern automobiles were parked anachronisti-
cally beside the waiting buggies, which meant, of
course, that non-Amish people were attending the
funeral. Hana wanted to know who they were. She
felt it might be important. Very important. Surely
just a quick look through one of those open windows would go unnoticed.

She glanced guiltily over her shoulder. But nobody was around to observe such an indiscretion.
Unfortunately, however, the wooden part of the
farmhouse was constructed on top of a sturdy
stone base, where generously wide cellar windows
must have been a comfort to people without electricity. It meant, however, the first-floor windows
were too high for Hana to see through without
standing on something. The yard held nothing but
stepping-stones, grass, and beds of pansies, basket-
of-gold, and fading tulips.

Hana wondered if Mrs. Longsdorf or the youthful Mary had planted the flowers. Grateful that
Amish funerals were drawn-out affairs, Hana crept
to another gate, which opened into the barnyard.
Free-running, healthy chickens scurried away
from her, objecting loudly to the invasion. Horses
moved restlessly and one whinnied.

"Shh!" Hana said, glancing back toward the windows of the house. "Friends, okay? Hey, I like
horses."

No faces appeared at the windows. Hana moved
slowly, speaking softly to the creatures, and it took
her some little time to locate a small wooden crate
beside a chicken house. Carrying the crate, she
found herself walking on tiptoe across grass that
couldn't possibly echo sound. Carefully she placed
the crate beside a rosebush full of shiny new
leaves, looked about again, then stepped onto the

crate in a crouching position. The thought of Kochen and what he would say about this crossed her
mind as she straightened slowly until she could
peer into the room.

It was a sight Hana would not soon forget.
Benches facing away from her and toward the
wooden coffin were filled with motionless figures,
all in black, still as death or those who waited for a
Day of Judgment. There were no flowers, nothing
to relieve the somber scene. The casket was built
with the lid in two pieces, the hinged upper half
open for viewing the body. Hana stared at it, for a
moment forgetting her situation and remembering
only the instant of Matthew's death. He was
dressed all in white, white shirt, white vest, and
surely white trousers below. A man as stern and
bearded as Michelangelo's patriarchal god was
speaking High German, which Hana understood
better than the dialect.

It was mesmerizing but finally Hana focused on
the rest of the room. Chairs, marginally more comfortable than the benches, were at one side. On
them sat four members of the Conover Historical
Society—Teddy Jolf, the two Adamses, and Mr. Pettengill.

As Hana stared in surprise, Josie Adams turned
her head and looked directly at her. Josie gave an
involuntary cry and pointed.

Hana didn't wait to see how many people would
pull themselves out of their grief to turn around.
She jumped off her crate, ran to the gate, fumbled
with the catch for a moment, then dashed through
and down the road.

Nobody chased her. Nobody left the house of
sorrow. After chancing a few backward glances,
Hana slowed to a trot and finally a fast walk. When
she reached her car, she threw the bicycle into the

trunk, leaped into the driver's seat, and got out of there. She could only hope Josie Adams hadn't recognized her.

To intrude on a funeral, to spy on people attending a funeral . . . God, what was she coming to? To get her mind off her iniquities, Hana turned on her radio, which immediately and ecstatically informed her tomorrow would be another day as beautiful as this.

Tomorrow.

If she could do something—anything—to solve these awful killings it would be a beautiful day. But something sensible, not like the undignified position she had put herself into today.

What had she not done that she had planned to do?

The Quilt Woman. She had never talked to the Quilt Woman. Interviewing Betty Schlicher had distracted her, and she had never gotten around to it. She'd remedy that now. As soon as she reached home she'd call Bill Longenecker and ask him to take her to the Quilt Woman tomorrow afternoon.

Bill would be so pleased.

## *Chapter Eighteen*

HANA, SATISFIED THAT the next day was planned, and worried about Kitty Fisher's recent identity crisis, played cat games with a catnip mouse tied to the end of a string. When Gray Trouble and Penelope Baskin came to share the fun, Kitty Fisher disdainfully rejected their company and joined the dogs for a stroll around the grounds.

Hana wondered if she could find an animal psychologist in the county.

While twirling the mouse high above the cats she thought about the quartet at the funeral. Teddy Jolf seemed to be popping up all over the place. Of course, there was no reason she and other representatives of the Historical Society shouldn't attend the funeral. On the other hand, why should they?

Gray Trouble leaped magnificently into the air and seized the toy.

Hana applauded. "Lions: 1. Christians: 0!"

Penelope Baskin wrathfully grabbed the mouse and ran into the hall. Howling over the loss of his prize, the gray cat followed.

Hana settled back on the snuggery sofa and pulled the phone toward her. First she checked in at the office. According to Mary Hafer, Pocky Reilly had finally called and had sounded quite excited. Hana tried Pocky's home and office numbers without success. Then she got in touch with her private detectives and ordered a background check on Teddy Jolf. Wondering how people functioned before the days of the telephone, she next dialed Bill Longenecker at the travel agency.

As usual his secretary connected her immediately.

"Hi, Bill," she said cheerfully. "How about dinner tonight?"

"Sorry. I'm busy."

It was rather a shock.

"Oh," she said awkwardly. "Well, how about tomorrow night?"

"Just what is it you want, Hana?"

He sounded so cool and un-Bill-like.

"I haven't seen much of you since our last murder," she told him.

"Right. But what is it you want?"

"I need to talk to the Quilt Woman."

"I thought it was something like that."

"And it would be really nice if we'd go together," she added quickly. "After all, you know her and I don't. We could make a social evening out of it. Have dinner and—"

"All right. I'll try to get around to it one of these days."

Hana wondered if it was really Bill she was talking to.

"When?"

"I'm not sure. I'll call you."

Through the window she saw Mr. Fred's bakery van pulling into the parking lot, but she was hardly aware of it. Bill Longenecker was too busy to go out with her?

He continued smugly, "You see, I've had quite a few dates with Pocky Reilly. I'm seeing her again tonight. And tomorrow. A remarkably talented young woman, Hana. You don't really appreciate her many talents."

Chuckling, he hung up gently without even saying good-bye.

Slowly Hana replaced her receiver. *Bill (as in Good Old Bill Longenecker) and Pocky Reilly?* What an unlikely duo. She'd always thought of Pocky as wild and unorthodox. What on earth did she see in Bill?

The next instant she felt ashamed and guilty. After all, what had she herself seen in him? His good qualities, of course, were many. Bill did not exist for her convenience. And despite his weird curls, he was a reasonably attractive man.

Mr. Fred appeared at the door of the snuggery.

Hana was accustomed to seeing him in his neat black suit. She couldn't get used to this ridiculous outfit.

"Please take off that apron."

Grinning, he complied, neatly folding it.

"I've had a very successful day," he announced, digging into pockets and producing wads of folded bills. "And you thought the Plain People wouldn't go for French and Italian pastries! These women are into baking, but this was a new world to them, one they found fascinating. I was sold out by one o'clock. I've made four hundred dollars' profit!"

Hana stared at the money cascading onto her coffee table.

"What about the Schwambachs?" she asked.

"Schwambachs? Oh. Nothing. I didn't even see them. Somebody said they were attending a funeral somewhere. They must have left at dawn." He began to arrange the bills into piles. "I've decided I should devote a few more days to this project. It's a pleasure to be helpful."

Hana gritted her teeth, rose, and went upstairs, leaving the snuggery to Mr. Fred and his money.

The next morning Mr. Fred was happily off to spread his canolli gospel among the Plain People, whose taste in pastry was proving to be not plain at all. Hana, no longer wearing Sal's clothing, was less happily off to her peach orchard. She would have preferred not to go near the place but decided she had to devote one more morning to sitting and waiting. Yesterday had hardly been a typical day for Johnny Longsdorf. Nor had the one before, when he'd been in the barn hammering on his brother's coffin. Maybe he was ready to break out now.

Considering the Peeping Tom episode, Hana decided it would be prudent to sit in the car. From the orchard she could view the road that passed in front of the Longsdorf farm. Of course she couldn't actually see the house over the rise, but neither could they see her. And she assumed that if Johnny went anywhere it would be in the direction of town.

It was.

She had been there only for about an hour and was half-dozing in pleasant sunshine.

She had also assumed he would be driving a buggy. Instead, he came striding briskly along, hands in pockets, whistling a tune she could not identify. She sank down, hoping he had not spotted her. When she finally poked up her head, he had passed, the whistling continuing without pause.

Now what? Ralph Sensenig had been all too right. How could she possibly follow a boy strolling along a little-traveled country road? Impatiently she drummed her fingers on the steering wheel. There had to be a way. Maybe she could wait until he had walked a good distance, then drive to the next turn in the road and keep him in sight until the road curved again, drive there and so on. It would be a long leapfrog into town, but she could think of nothing else.

She knew there was a relatively straight stretch of road beyond the next curve. Since he had been walking fast, she waited another five minutes, then started the car and headed after him.

When she rounded the curve, the road lay straight between two plowed fields for about four city blocks. But Johnny Longsdorf was nowhere to be seen. Hana braked and looked around. At the roadside, still damp from recent rain, were fresh tire tracks. A car had been waiting, probably with motor running, for a prearranged pickup.

Hana put on speed.

They'd been driving fast, too fast for this narrow road. She didn't catch up with them for nearly ten miles. Then she could only assume the old Ford pickup rattling along at a truly amazing speed was the one she wanted. She didn't dare approach too close but thought she saw three boys inside.

Hanging back, Hana barely kept them in sight. She wished she had one of the detective agency's bugs on that car so she could follow in peaceful security.

One of Aunt Sissy's homilies came to mind. "If wishes were horses, beggars would ride . . ."

As they neared familiar territory she took a few chances. In one small village she turned off and drove along a parallel street, returning to the through-road at the edge of town. At another place where she knew of an unpaved lane, she left the road again for a few miles. This time she had trouble locating her Ford. The road was less winding and they were picking up speed. Traffic was also increasing.

Hana's luck held and she spotted them just as they turned onto a larger, more heavily traveled highway. She had been sure they were heading for Conover, but this turn took them in the opposite direction. Hana swung after them. A truck inserted itself between her Chrysler and the boys. She watched sharply at each intersecting road but didn't see the Ford turning off.

They were approaching different country now, leaving the flat farmland of Conover County and crossing into the more hilly areas of Grover County. The truck slowed at an incline and Hana pulled around it. With just a few cars between them, Hana followed the pickup a few more miles to a crossroad where a sign proclaimed that Mount Grunwald was five miles away.

Hana was familiar with Mount Grunwald. While Conover was Colonial, Mount Grunwald was entirely Victorian. It had been established by a railroad company, which had been determined to lure summer people to a woodland and small lake that it owned but had found to be of no financial benefit. By judicious cutting, a gingerbread town had been built, every house surrounded by trees and laurel bushes. Once there had been an amusement park; now only a theater remained in that area. Art festivals held every July still attracted crowds. The gingerbread houses themselves had become highly prized residences.

A tall fence guarded a swimming beach where beneath ancient oaks mossy picnic tables proved that the Victorians built for the ages. On summer days people still swam there, changing in the wooden bathhouse (circa 1890) and putting their clothing in wire baskets in use since 1920. Boardwalks ran along the front of this bathhouse and Southern-style pillars held up the porch roof. These same boardwalks ran right out over the waters of the lake where swings, platforms, and diving boards, all of white-painted wood, demonstrated that what had been enjoyed in the nineteenth century could still be enjoyed in the twentieth.

Ever since she had been a child, Hana had been coming to Mount Grunwald. She had often met Amish people here, the youngsters in conservative bathing suits, older folks placidly enjoying the novelty of sitting and not working. It was attractive to them, she supposed, because it retained the placid pace of an older day. Nor was any sin to be seen. There were bars and other entertainments, but they were situated on the other side of the hill in a newer part of town.

A town, however unusual in character, has traffic on a perfect spring day. Hana, feeling successful, confidently followed at a distance, allowing other cars to pull in and out. She dropped even farther behind when they turned right at the general store, passed along a wooded area, then swung off on a lane that led to the swimming beach.

She pulled over beside a large memorial boulder in a broad meadow. On the boulder was a plaque which she read while she waited. It proudly announced that at the turn of the century this field had been used as a parade ground for National Guard encampments. She passed ten minutes thinking of the lively boys who had paraded here behind their drums, then gone on to die at the Marne River or some other World War I battleground.

Then, feeling depressed, she drove to the section of the field devoted to a parking lot for the swimming area. A rather surprising number of cars were there, considering that the beach would not open until Memorial Day. Included among them was Mr. Fred's new bakery van. Puzzled, Hana parked in the shade of an edging of trees. Why the van? Why, in fact, any of these cars?

The wire gate in the fence was propped open. Nobody presided at the ticket window. Hana walked along, keeping a row of budding spyria bushes between herself and the picnic grounds. When she reached the stairs that led down to the lawn, she peeped around snowlike blossoms.

"Oh, my God," she exclaimed involuntarily.

# Chapter Nineteen

IT WAS NOT the gathering of brightly shirted Amish youth she could see beside the lake at the farther edge of the grove that dismayed Hana. It was the group occupying two long tables near the closed concession stand. These tables were covered with plastic cloths and topped with overflowing baskets of picnic food. On the benches sat an assortment of people. Mr. Fred was offering around a large plate of elaborate pastries. Mr. Pettengill blinked with anticipation as he accepted a mound of confection that must have contained at least ten thousand calories. Teddy Jolf was there, as were Josie and Bert Adams, along with a scholarly assortment Hana could only guess were additional enthusiasts from the Conover Historical Society.

These people were haunting her like a recurring nightmare.

Before Hana could retreat, Mr. Fred caught sight of her and waved, then loudly called her name. Everybody at the table turned to stare.

Damn his hide.

Even some of the kids at the other side of the grove were looking at her now.

So much for anonymity.

Stretching her mouth into a smile, Hana strolled down the steps and joined the group. Mr. Bigmouth Fred proceeded to introduce her to the people she didn't know. Smiling tentatively, Josie Adams handed her a plate. Bert Adams moved to make room beside himself. Hana sat down. A cup of real lemonade, as proved by the fact that seeds were floating about in it, was thrust into her hand.

"What's a picnic without lemonade?" Josie chirped.

Hana looked into the woman's eyes then at Bert's benign face. There was no hint in either that they knew about her Peeping Tom act at the funeral. After all, Josie'd had only a glimpse of this supposed Mennonite woman at the window. It was possible—just possible—they hadn't recognized her. Feeling more confident, she turned her attention to Teddy Jolf, the Ever-Present.

Teddy avoided her eyes.

"It's rather early for a picnic, isn't it?" Hana asked. "In fact, two picnics. Those kids by the lake seem to be having one too."

Bert looked puzzled. "Well, of course."

Mr. Pettengill beamed over his whipped cream mustache. "We're certainly glad you could join us."

"So am I," Hana said. Then she decided to chance a bluff. "I have, you know, always supported the Historical Society even though I haven't been really active. But when I heard about this meeting . . ."

Thank God for Josie Adams. She took the bait with a smile. "Yes, everybody's happy that we have our spring picnic here at Mount Grunwald. This place is a rare historical treasure."

"A bit Victorian for some tastes," Mr. Pettengill said petulantly. "Especially when you consider all the Colonial buildings remaining in the area. Some people feel we should concentrate our conservation efforts on those."

"Victorian is coming into its own," Bert and Josie said in chorus as if it was an argument they had rehearsed many times.

Dishes of potato salad, chow-chow, and red beet eggs flowed by Hana, making her realize she was hungry. So, she thought as she helped herself, the

Historical Society had decided to hold what was apparently an annual event. To have this much food, it must have been planned for some time. Mr. Fred should have told her. Unless, of course, he hadn't meant to attend this delightful social function and was only present because he had followed the Schwambach boy here.

She looked toward the other group but found it impossible to pick out Jake Schwambach or Johnny Longsdorf. She thought of the boys who had attacked her in the parking lot. She had supposed most of them were Amish by their clothing. Yet Hannah herself had been dressed as a Mennonite for two days, so what did the clothing actually prove?

"What are the kids doing here?" Hana asked Mr. Pettengill, who was delicately licking his fingers.

Since Pettengill was busy, it was Bert Adams who explained. These were the young people recruited for the Open House. They were mostly Amish and Mennonite but also included fancy Dutch. There were not as many girls, since Plain girls were encouraged to confine themselves to traditional women's activities. Youths participating had been invited that day for a training session. The Plain People liked their young to learn the value of earning money, so there had been no trouble getting them excused from farm chores. Lunch was being provided, after which Bert would give a lecture on what misdemeanors they were to watch for at the Open House and how they were to conduct themselves in the event such occurred.

"But why a training session now?" Hana asked. "This thing isn't for a couple of weeks."

"We didn't feel one training session was enough," Josie said.

"Right," Bert added self-righteously. "We want to make sure your property is protected."

There was a sudden blare of rock music from the young folks' tables.

"Who supplied the tapes?" Hana inquired. "The Historical Society?"

Mr. Pettengill, his fingers as clean as Penelope Baskin's paws after a bath, bristled. "Certainly not! I for one think we should put a stop to it."

Josie said defiantly, "Let them have a little bit of freedom. Most of those kids work hard on their farms and if they want to act like other kids for one afternoon, what's the harm?"

Pettengill pursed his lips. "It's shocking. That tape recorder belongs to one of them. Big enough to be a Wurlitzer. I daresay he's got it hidden at a non-Amish friend's house."

Bert said mildly, "If their parents look the other way, I think we should too."

Teddy Jolf joined the conversation. "The Amish are afraid if they come down too hard on the teenagers, they'll drive them right out of the church. And I think they're right. Most of them settle down when they get older."

Hana ate her lunch listening to the talk bouncing about her to the accompaniment of quite fierce rock. Teddy Jolf began discussing techniques of wiring finger and toe bones together with a woman who looked a little green and stopped munching on a cold chicken leg. Hana gathered from what Mr. Pettengill said that there was to be a business meeting after lunch.

She excused herself and went around the table to where Mr. Fred was plotting a publicity campaign with a young woman who seemed more interested in her wedge of rum cake.

"May I speak to you for a few moments?" she asked with a very friendly smile. "Privately."

He accepted the summons with rather poor grace but followed docilely enough as she led the way up the worn wooden stairs to the old bathing house. There were no doors because there was nothing to steal unless one wanted a collection of wire baskets.

She moved along the counter toward the wide dressing room beyond. The interior was dim, the only light coming from louvers below the roof. Long benches had been arranged near large mirrors whose silver was cracking from their backs. Down the middle and along the sides were private changing booths with plastic curtains that celebrated the Bicentennial of the Constitution in red, white, and blue, the only "modern" touch in the place. The rest of it, including the plumbing in the toilets and showers, had been in place for decades.

Hana sat on one of the long wooden benches. Mr. Fred hovered a short distance away.

"What's going on, Mr. Fred?" she asked conversationally.

"It's the annual spring picnic of the Historical Society. Certain members are most interested in Mount Grunwald—"

"The Adamses."

"And others. Victorian is coming into its own."

"I heard. How did you get here? You didn't follow the Schwambach family to the funeral yesterday and now it seems you're not working on it today either."

He looked offended. "You told me to stay near the boy. Therefore, I arranged to have him included in this. After all, I've got my responsibilities to Blue Spring Hill and its Open House to consider.

This way I can attend the meeting and keep up with that young man at the same time."

"But why didn't you tell me? I followed the Longsdorf kid all over two counties to get here!"

"I didn't know he was on the list too. A number of people worked on the project. I can't do everything."

"Didn't Jake Schwambach think it odd that the baker should invite him here?"

"But I didn't," Mr. Fred said loftily. "Certainly not. It would—shall we say?—blow my cover. I had Teddy Jolf go around to the farm and do it. The family knows her."

"I'm sure your cover's blown anyway since he's seen you here."

"The youths have been told *I* am catering this event."

Mr. Fred blinked triumphantly at her. He should be running Shaner Industries. He should be running the entire world. Hana turned from the dizzying thought of Mr. Fred actually running the governments of Earth.

"Now, if you will excuse me," he announced, "I must get back to my meeting. I am permitting Mr. Adams to show our youth corps a map of the grounds I have made up."

Hana let him go, then stretched, noticing that her legs felt stiff from all the bicycling she'd been doing recently. She looked around. It had been years since she'd been inside the old bathhouse. She felt strange sitting in this building, which had seen so many generations of girls primping before the old mirrors. It was almost as though an aura from earlier summers had remained, worn as smooth as the boards of the floor through the cracks of which, as in all good old summer buildings, one could see the dirt a few feet below. She had a feeling . . .

Hana's skin prickled. A feeling. Yes, such as she'd had when she worked on that other case. She thought of Betty Schlicher. Was Hana herself part hex woman? If she concentrated on that part of herself, as she had concentrated for years on her business acumen, what might she find?

The feeling was strong now and she let it come through. This wasn't "woman's intuition," which was, after all, just a stupid catch phrase. This was something far older, far more dangerous.

Not all of those kids had come here to be lectured about the Open House. Not all had come to listen to forbidden rock music. This was not just a delightful spring picnic beneath budding trees.

Hana knew all these things as surely as she now heard a movement in the dim recesses of the rows of curtained booths. The room stretched before her toward the lavatory and showers at the rear. Dark. Like an underexposed photograph.

Hana had only a short distance to the front entrance and escape. But she didn't go that way. She took the .22 out of her bag and carefully got to her feet.

Ears straining and eyes wide open, she walked down the center aisle between the curtained booths.

There was movement in the aisle on the other side of the row of booths. Footsteps retreating. She recalled a rear entrance into the lavatories near the showers. Hana ran in that direction. The footfalls were running too, like ghost feet, unseen. She opened her mouth, breathing silently. She was perceiving everything in slow motion. It was an odd sensation, as if she had run into a film and this was only a shadow of herself, automatic poised, safety off, striving to reach the end of this row before the other runner. An Amish boy. Had to be. With a pitchfork perhaps . . . and she would shoot him. Shoot the boy who ran through the bathhouse.

Hana stopped, grabbing hold of a stall curtain. The large room snapped back into normal motion. The footsteps ran on through the lavatory. A wooden door squeaked and banged. Hana ran again, through the lavatory, and jerked open the protesting door. The wide veranda, made of the same smooth boards as the floor of the bathhouse, stretched before her. Empty.

Bushes grew thick beyond the railing. In front were evergreens, full even at this time of the year. A leap over the railing and he would be hidden.

Hana stepped back inside. The building was quiet. She stared down the shadowy aisle through which the boy must have come. At the other end of it was the daylight of the entrance. So he must have been here. He certainly hadn't entered through the noisy lavatory door while they were sitting talking. He'd been here already.

Doing what?

Hana walked along the aisle, lifting the plastic curtains and looking into each booth. She estimated there must be room for hundreds of changers. At one time probably hundreds of people had come here on excursion trains.

She was halfway to the entrance when she found it.

In one booth, neatly hanging on ornate metal pegs, were the trousers, shirt, suspenders, and hat of a teenage Amish boy.

Hana lifted them carefully. The trouser pockets were empty. There was no identification at all. But then, she had expected none.

One thing was sure. Either not every boy who

looked Amish really was, or a real Amish lad was walking around naked. Or it could be that this old bathhouse was a place where many an Amish kid changed his Plain clothes for a secular outfit when he was headed for a day on the town.

# Chapter Twenty

THE BOYS WERE perched on top of unused picnic tables staring at Bert Adams, who was solemnly addressing them. Looking self-conscious, a number of girls clustered together on benches. Mary Longsdorf was not among them, which did not surprise Hana since Johnny had left home alone. Bert Adams pointed importantly to an enormous chart of the grounds of Blue Spring Hill. Hana groaned inwardly. If anybody wanted to infiltrate, here was the blueprint. She tried glaring at Mr. Fred, who was pointedly ignoring her. The Conover Historical Society had split into groups, with stacks of papers and clipboards spread over tables as they planned God-knows-what to be done at her estate.

Hana, lurking between the groups, turned her attention to the youth. Since they were being paid for this preliminary day, they were obviously attempting to be interested in Bert's monologue. Jake Schwambach's mouth hung slightly open as if he were having a hard time comprehending all of the instructions.

Hana didn't blame him. She could detect Mr. Fred's pompous manner in all this.

". . . in this area is a rare white azalea with pale pink stripes. It is designated by the striped lines on the map. Under no circumstances is anyone to go into this area. It will be roped off as designated by this line of orange on the chart. Now the green and purple darts denote where the portapots will be located. Green for men, purple for . . ."

Hana drew a shuddering breath, then tried to get her mind off portapots by concentrating on Johnny Longsdorf. Legs stretched out before him, feet bare, he was listening with a sardonic, cynical look on his face.

There were a number of fancy Dutch kids, but she could think of no subtle way to find out if they might be Amish in disguise. She glanced toward the bathhouse. Nobody but herself showed the slightest interest in it. It stood there year-round, unlocked, an open invitation for use. True, there was the high chain link fence around the entire area, but when did something like that ever keep out enterprising kids? Especially if they had an urgent need for a private place.

Hana decided there was nothing further she could do about Johnny Longsdorf that day and as unobtrusively as possible slipped out of the grounds and went to her car.

She was in her library at home when the call came. She had gone to the office for a few hours before returning to Blue Spring Hill. It was the thought of the omnipresent Teddy Jolf prowling through the house that had driven her to the library.

Hana's grandmother had collected many of the volumes, and Hana's father had continued her interest. Hana herself was proud of the mint condition collectibles, especially the large section of books that were printed and/or written locally. Nothing of enormous value, she reminded herself, like a first folio of Shakespeare or that little paperback of Edgar Allan Poe's, but respectable. Very respectable. Maybe the fact that Teddy Jolf was a used and rare book dealer had nothing whatever to do with her interest in Blue Spring Hill, but then again . . .

Hana had taken down a rare hymnal printed in the early 1700s by a cloistered Conover religious sect when the phone rang. Gently she replaced the book on the shelf before she picked up the extension.

"Hana . . . ?"

Bill Longenecker.

"Hi," she said lightly, determined to be cheerful despite the fact that he had not dropped everything to take her to the Quilt Woman. "Did your date stand you up tonight?"

He sounded shaky, which was unusual for Bill. Anybody who could juggle tour groups as he did had a deep well of inner calm.

Except when it came to finding dead bodies.

"Hana, I need you."

It was almost funny. Turnabout. How often had she called him when she needed something? So, all right. She owed him.

"Okay, Bill. Anybody you want buried, I'm your woman."

"This isn't funny," he squeaked. "Can you come right away?"

"Where are you?"

"The Crescent. 124."

"That's Pocky's address—"

"Please hurry!"

"Bill, what's happened—?"

But he had already hung up.

It just wasn't like Bill, she repeated to herself as she went to the kitchen. The odors there were delicious. Sal was peeping into the oven. Kitty Fisher sat with the dogs watching Sal expectantly. Gray Trouble sat on the table, also watching Sal. Penelope Baskin was stuffing herself at a bowl of dry cat food. Penelope B. was working on a case of "fat fur," as Aunt Sissy used to call overweight in cats.

"I'm going out and may not be home in time for dinner," Hana announced. "What're you making? Smells good."

"Corn pie."

"Corn pie," Hana repeated unhappily.

"Last of the season," Sal said, ignoring the tone. "I thought it was cold enough still."

"Too many calories. I was hoping the one in March was the last. Mr. Fred home yet?"

Sal sniffed. "I haven't seen him. *He* loves my corn pies."

"He's thin."

"And you're not, I suppose?" Sal demanded, eyeing Hana's size-twelve beige dress with its high 1890s collar.

"Difference is I have to work at it."

Hana left the disgruntled Sal shooing Gray Trouble off the table.

Hana knew she wasn't being asked to Pocky Reilly's place in order to join Pocky and Bill on a dinner date. As she drove she kept telling herself they must have discovered something. About the murder, of course. Maybe Bill had talked to the Quilt Woman by himself. She'd have to give him a piece of her mind about worrying her this way.

After all, it was ridiculous to suppose that anything had happened to Pocky Reilly. She wasn't involved with the Schwambachs, the Longsdorfs,

Teddy Jolf, or even the Historical Society. She was only involved with community theater and her budding TV career.

The Crescent was a curving cobblestone street that had once been a country lane before the city of Conover had stretched itself beyond the square mile that had comprised the original city settlement. The small bricked houses had been meticulously restored. Barrels beside front stoops had already been planted with the seedlings that would be bouquets of color by summer.

Pocky's house was at the very end of the row. A high board fence in an odd shade of wood green surrounded the back garden. She had purchased the house only six months before, and Hana knew she was worried about the large mortgage. She needed her TV work to continue to live in her new luxury.

Hana used the discreet wrought iron knocker on the door.

Bill Longenecker opened the door immediately. Without a word, he quickly looked up and down the street, then pulled her unceremoniously into the house.

"Bill . . . what on earth . . . ?"

"Oh, God," he said. "Why did I ever become involved with you?"

"It's Pocky Reilly you were going out with tonight," Hana reminded him coldly. "What does that have to do with me?"

"It's got everything to do with you! What else could it have to do with? Since you began this crime business, nobody's safe!"

Hana turned from him and entered the small living room, which opened off the even smaller foyer. Pocky Reilly lay stretched out on a sofa.

Pocky . . . ? Dead . . . ?

The woman raised a hand to her head and groaned.

Only then did Hana realize the tension she had been under. Her knees felt weak, and for a moment she thought she was going to topple right on top of Pocky. Bill was correct in a sense. Since she'd begun to dabble in crime, people around her were dropping like flies.

Pocky was holding a damp cloth over her forehead and eyes. Hana knelt beside her because it was easier than standing up. Bill cracked his knuckles.

Gently Hana drew away the cloth. Pocky had two black eyes. There was a laceration on her cheek and a swollen red bruise on her arm.

"Who did this?" Hana asked.

"I don't know," Pocky sobbed. "Oh, Hana, they got it! They took it away with them!"

"Took what?"

"My design!"

Hana looked at Bill. "Is she hysterical? Did you call a doctor?"

"I couldn't get my doctor to come to the house," he said miserably, popping his index finger. "Or hers. And she won't go to the hospital."

"Stop cracking your knuckles," Hana said, lowering her voice to a threatening level.

Bill put his hands behind his back. Hana thought of Dr. Reifsnyder, then rejected the idea in favor of a saner approach.

"I really think you should go to the emergency room," she told Pocky. "They won't keep you unless you're badly hurt, you know."

Pocky struggled to a sitting position. "I'm not hurt! I'm mad! And I'm not going to any hospital. I *hate* hospitals."

Hana hated to call Harold Reifsnyder more than Pocky Reilly could ever hate hospitals. However, there seemed to be no other alternative. Sadly she picked up the phone on the table beside the sofa. It was Aunt Ethel who finally cautiously lifted the receiver after about twenty rings. They were going out, but if necessary Uncle Harold would speak to Hana.

What Uncle Harold did when he got to the phone was shout at Hana. Even the old arguments of duty to the Shaner family sounded thin to her ears, so Hana resorted to an appeal to his curiosity. Ponderously he agreed to stop around on his way to the dinner of the Pioneers of the Spirit of Conover.

All through the phone call, Pocky continued to sniffle.

Hana hung up. "Now tell me what happened."

Pocky wailed. And Hana had always thought of her as so cool.

Bill said nervously, "When I got here the front door was open. I called. Pocky didn't answer so I came on in. Real slow. I thought of calling the cops but . . . Well, I was afraid to wait for them. I thought there might be . . . uh . . ."

"He thought I might be dead!" Pocky cried. "And I might have been!"

"I found her here on the floor," Bill continued. "It didn't seem like she was hurt too bad but she sure was scared."

"Mad!" she howled. "I'm mad!"

"Okay, okay," he agreed. "Mad. She was mad. I got her up on the sofa, then went back and locked the front door and called you. I thought that was better than calling the cops. I tried to help her . . . got water and a cloth for her face."

Hana asked Bill to find ice cubes and a towel. As

he obediently scurried away, she turned to Pocky.
"Why are you so angry?"

"My design was stolen."

"What design?"

"The Pennsylvania Dutch dress for your Dutch
Blue collection!"

Hana, unaccustomed to having subordinates fla-
grantly disobey orders, stared at her. "But I told
you I didn't want to include it."

"Yeah, I know," Pocky said, pushing back strands
of hair that were falling over her face. "But it was
such a great idea. I thought if you could just see
what could be done with it, you'd change your
mind. So I played around with material and my
scissors. I haven't been a member of the Conover
Community Players since I was fourteen for nothing, you know. You wouldn't believe how many
shows I've costumed. And, what I mean, I came up
with something really good this time."

"And that's what they took?" Hana asked incred-
ulously.

"The mannequin and everything."

Hana glanced about the room. Pocky enthusiastically embraced everything in which she was interested and it showed in the decor. Here were no
Colonial furnishings, either original or repros.
There were a couple of director's chairs and the
sofa, which Hana suspected opened into a bed. The
brick walls were covered with theater posters and
photos. A long table in front of the windows was
littered with scraps of material, drawings, old play
scripts, and incredible piles of notebooks and papers. Most arresting, however, were the manne-
quins, which Pocky purchased at flea markets and
which made moving about the space dangerous
and difficult. One was a dressmaker's dummy with

no head, one was scaled down to three-fourths human size, but three others were life-size and wearing what were probably costumes designed by the incomparable Pocky. Beside a stocky male figure in a doctor's suit from last year's local rendering of *The Heiress* was an empty space outlined in dust.

Hana privately wondered if the culprits hadn't done her a favor by absconding with Pocky's latest creation. If only they had come at night and not resorted to physical violence, she might have sent them a thank-you note.

"And you have no idea who did it?" she asked.

Pocky shook her head. "No."

"But it's daylight. You must have seen them."

"Sure I saw them. Kids."

"Amish?"

"Who knows? They were kind of in their teens, I think. Guys. Dark pants. A little baggy, so maybe they were Plain or just farmers. But their tops were dark too. Maybe turtlenecks, I'm not sure. I got excited. Okay, so I was scared too."

"Any possibility you'd recognized them if you saw them again?"

"None at all. Ski masks."

Hana took a second to consider how convenient the sport of skiing had become to the amateur miscreant.

"Any idea how they got in here?" she asked.

"Sure. The door chimes rang. I thought it was Bill coming early. When I opened the door these kids crowded right in. Almost knocked me over. Later on, they *did* knock me over."

"Blunt instrument?"

"Fist."

"How many were there?"

"Four. I think. But who was counting?"

"This is a city street—"

"Yeah, I know. And in Conover, the Safety Zone of the East. Oh, Hana, people don't notice what's going on at the neighbors'."

"And you really believe that's what they came for? The dress?"

"I'm sure of it." She pointed to the dust-free spot. "It was right there. And they went right for it. I shouldn't have gotten in the way but it was a little hard not to. It was pretty crowded in here."

"How many people were aware you were doing this ridiculous design?"

"It wasn't a ridiculous design! It was good!" Pocky rubbed her sore arm. "Oh, I don't know. I was pleased with myself. I guess I told a lot of people."

Bill returned bearing an ice pack.

They fussed with Pocky until she lay down again and put the ice pack over her eyes.

"Maybe," she mumbled, "I could do it again. I've still got the sketches."

"Rest," Hana ordered. "We can talk about it later."

Pocky lowered her ice pack and peered above it. "You mean you'll really talk about it? You might consider my Amish dress?"

"I just said that to keep you quiet until the doctor gets here."

"Hana's really pigheaded when it comes to the Amish," Bill grumbled to Pocky. "You'll find out."

"I found out already," Pocky said.

"We'll have to report this to the police," Hana reminded them. "It's an assault and a theft. Bill, you should have done that right away."

"I was more concerned with Pocky," he said.

Ignoring that, Hana said, "I'll call them now."

She had thought Pocky might protest, but instead the young woman seemed relieved to think of the police becoming involved. Before Hana had finished her call Dr. Reifsnyder had arrived. Bill let him in and hovered diffidently behind his presence.

Harold Reifsnyder leveled a baleful gaze on Hana. "I understand Jack The Ripper was from a very good family too."

"We'll leave you with your patient, Uncle Harold," Hana said brightly and pulled Bill with her into the kitchen, where they found Puff, Pocky's white Persian cat, crouching nervously beneath a small table. Hana stooped to pet her. "Poor baby. Don't be scared. Pocky will be all right."

"Shall I make coffee?" Bill asked.

"Great idea."

She and the cat watched him puttering about. He really was a good soul.

"When can we see the Quilt Woman?" she asked kindly.

"I'm awfully busy right now," he muttered as he added water to the kettle.

Of course, even good souls have mean streaks.

"I could go see her by myself," she told him, rising as Puff decided she was in no mood for friendly overtures and ducked into a conveniently open cupboard.

"No way! I don't want you messing around my Amish contacts. I don't want you giving them ideas that I'm exploiting them or something like that."

"They might want a bigger cut?"

"They sell their stuff. That's enough for them."

They argued about it until Dr. Reifsnyder opened the door and glared at them.

"I am ready to leave. As usual, I will send you the bill."

"Won't you stay for coffee, Uncle Harold?" Hana asked suavely.

"Ethel is waiting in the car. We're late now."

"How's Pocky?" Bill worried.

"Miss Nancy Reilly will be sore for a few days and certainly her face will be discolored," he reported stiffly. "As is usual with victims Hana encounters. I'll want her to rest tonight. Quite a charming young woman. Most cooperative and pleasant."

He glanced at Hana significantly.

She suspected Pocky had filled him in on what had happened, probably adding imaginatively lurid details. Since he was such a convenience, Hana followed him out to the car to say a word to Aunt Ethel. That worthy woman, large and solidly girdled, looked more like Uncle Harold's sister than his wife. They had soured on life together—or at least on the kind of life Hana Shaner represented.

After a quick attempt at pleasantries, Hana waved them off.

Inside, Bill was serving coffee and telling Pocky he was going to scramble eggs for a light meal. She was beaming at him out of her puffy face. Hana felt left out, especially since Bill had brought only two mugs into the living room, and she had to go to the kitchen for her own cup. Hana considered whether or not she should wait for Kochen or his alternate to show up. She could add nothing to Pocky's story, and she wasn't ready to report the Amish suit in the bathhouse at Mount Grunwald. Kochen probably wouldn't even consider it relevant.

Everything considered, it seemed like a good time to leave. She'd tackle Bill about the Quilt Woman another time.

"Lock your doors, kid," she advised as she put down her cup and picked up her bag.

Pocky gulped. "I don't think I want to be alone tonight."

Hana left before she heard Bill's answer to that one.

# Chapter Twenty-one

AT FOUR O'CLOCK the next afternoon Hana assembled the cats in the snuggery. She had bought an especially good brand of catnip in an effort to convince Kitty Fisher that she was a cat, always would be a cat, and her recent endeavors to emulate the dogs were not only beneath her dignity, they were futile. Gray Trouble swatted at Kitty Fisher. Penelope Baskin twitched her tail impatiently, eyes on the catnip.

Hana scattered it lavishly. All three were rolling drunkenly when there was a discreet rap on the door.

"Yes?" she called.

She had wanted to talk to Mr. Fred about the boys at Mount Grunwald, but he had eluded her the evening before, obviously making a night of it with the swinging Conover Historical Society. This morning he and the bakery van had set off early. She had given up the idea of shadowing Johnny Longsdorf. Yet the uncomfortable question remained: if she had followed him from Mount

Grunwald, could the attack on Pocky have been prevented?

But what in the world did Johnny Longsdorf or any other boy want with a mannequin dressed in a pseudo-Amish outfit?

Mr. Fred opened the door of the snuggery.

"May we come in?"

"We" turned out to be Mr. Fred and Sergeant Kochen.

A more-than-odd couple.

She assumed Mr. Fred had come home earlier and had let in the sergeant. She assumed wrong.

"There's been a bit of trouble," Mr. Fred began.

Hana tensed.

Kochen smiled. "Let me. I have apprehended this man peddling without a license."

Hana noted that Mr. Fred looked ruffled and unlike himself.

"Since when does a sergeant assigned to violent crimes go about harassing people for minor infringements?" she inquired.

"A criminal act is never minor," he said, comfortably seating himself in an easy chair.

"I tried to explain," Mr. Fred said tartly.

"Oh, yes," Kochen agreed. "Let's see—you're helping the police investigate the deaths of two kids. You're assuming you're in a position to know more than those who are trained to conduct investigations."

Hana liked him better with an Easter egg in his hand.

"He was introducing these people to French and Italian pastries. That's no crime."

"Selling without a license is a crime."

"Hardly a *crime*, Sergeant."

He looked unfriendly. "There's also a report from Chief Hoffman concerning complaints about a woman who was acting suspiciously down around the Scotch Mountains. We understand she was lurking about in a car. An observant Amishman who owns a peach orchard in the neighborhood took the license number. Guess whose car."

God.

"I took my bicycle out into the country to get some exercise," Hana stated with dignity. "Once one hits . . . Well, thirty-five . . . one needs to do things like that."

"In a Mennonite outfit?" he inquired.

"I didn't want to be recognized."

"No doubt, since you were sneaking around the Longsdorf farm while they were conducting a funeral service for their murdered son. You created a disturbance by dragging about a crate upon which you stood while playing Peeping Tom."

Mr. Fred looked shocked. Hana avoided his eyes.

"I'm sorry," she said. "But I didn't create a disturbance. I was simply trying to—"

"I know what you were trying to do," he said, rising angrily. "And I know what Mr. Fred here was trying to do. And I want it stopped! If it isn't, we will prosecute. I'll concede you haven't committed any major crimes, but we can occupy your time with so much red tape you won't be able to harass these good people."

"Have you considered not all of them may be good people?"

"That isn't the point! I want this business stopped. Now. Either that or I'll make you wish you had!"

Hana stared at him. He was vehement far in excess of the misdemeanors involved. Mr. Fred looked extremely uncomfortable. Obviously Ko-

chen had been giving him a hard time even before
they reached Blue Spring Hill.

Kitty Fisher opened her mouth as if she might be
about to bark. Gray Trouble went to the door and
cried.

"Mr. Fred, why don't you take the cats outside?"
Hana suggested. "I'm sure Sergeant Kochen and I
can settle this."

Mr. Fred looked relieved. So did the cats. The
four of them left together, Mr. Fred firmly closing
the door behind them. Hana turned her attention
to Kochen. His face was flushed, his eyes dark and
moody.

"Why," Hana asked calmly, "are you making so
much over this? When we talked on Easter Sunday,
I was under the impression you welcomed my
help."

"On Easter Sunday you hadn't started this harassment."

"We were not harassing anyone."

"The hell you weren't! These people have a right
to their lives, dammit!"

Kochen strode to the window to stare out. Not
quite sure how to respond, Hana waited. Finally he
turned to her again.

"I'm sorry, Hana. I realize you didn't mean to do
it."

*"But what did we do that was so terrible?"*

His glasses were slipping again. He pushed them
up but the gesture lacked humor now. It was, in
fact, rather pathetic. His eyes were pathetic too.

"What did we do?" she asked again.

"Do you know why I moved here from New York
City?"

The switch in topics surprised her. "No, of
course not. We've only really talked one time, on
Easter. And you never mentioned it."

"I came out to the Pennsylvania Dutch Days they hold every autumn in Kleinfelterstown. A lot of New Yorkers do. Bus service right there from midtown, you know."

She nodded.

"I really got into it," he went on, dropping into the chair again. "Hired a car, drove around the countryside. I felt like I'd come home. The older women in those bonnets and long dresses reminded me of my grandmother. She raised me, you know. Okay, so she was Polish and these people are of German descent. But she was . . . real. Just like they are. Close to a rhythm of life most of us have forgotten." His voice tensed. "She was killed. Mugged. Died of it. That's what got me into police work. Seeing this place made me realize how fed up I was with the city and all the shit. So I relocated. Conover was glad to get me. I had a very good record over there. What I'm trying to tell you," he added tightly, "is that I respect and revere the Plain People."

Hana stared at him helplessly. "Well, so do I. I've fought that highway they wanted to put through their farmland and—"

"You frightened them! You and Mr. Fred frightened them. The people who own that orchard, they were uptight or they wouldn't have watched you and then gone to the police."

"But they had no need to be frightened."

"Didn't they, Hana? Don't they?" He was leaning forward now. "In the past year, Amish horses have been stolen, tortured, and slaughtered. Buggies have been smashed. This is not an organized thing against the Plain People. I know that. It's just another sign of our civilization coming apart at the seams. It's what happened to my grandmother. It's kids who are desensitized. Who don't know the difference between TV blood and real blood. Who can get out into the country in cars and on motorcycles and torment people who look different. Anybody who's different can be a target. These days the Amish are wary and they're afraid and they have every reason to be. When strangers show up in the neighborhood and are obviously spying on them, they react. Now I'm reacting to their call for help. I don't want these people bothered anymore. Is that clear enough for you?"

"Mr. Fred and I will stop shadowing the boys," Hana promised. "That is what we were trying to do."

"Yes, I realize that."

"I'll admit it didn't work too well. It's awfully hard to tail an Amish kid. I'm really sorry if we bothered anybody. I guess I just didn't realize the extent of these problems."

"It's been in the papers."

"I know," she sighed. "But even when I see an article like that, I tend to think of it as an isolated case."

He didn't seem to be listening. "I want to protect them. I don't want to lose them. We'll all be poorer if we lose them."

Hana cleared her throat. "Would you like coffee? Or a drink?"

He shook his head and got to his feet. "I must get back."

"Still working?"

"Sure."

"You put in long hours."

"There's a lot to do."

She rose. "How's it coming? The investigation of the boys' deaths? Is there anything you can tell me I don't know about?"

"It would probably be the other way around," he said morosely.

"Hey, you're the one who's got all the official information." She followed him toward the door. "For instance, what about the autopsies?"

"What about them? You know what killed those kids as well as we do."

"But all kinds of odd things can show up in autopsies."

He paused. "Okay. Odd thing number one: both kids ate candy before they died."

"Candy?"

"Nice big chocolate bars. With almonds."

Hana frowned. "That sounds like it might have been one of those unsavory people who lure kids with treats."

"Sexual pervert? You're right except the boys were not molested. Want odd thing number two?"

"Sure."

"They didn't seem like Amish kids."

"What do you mean?"

"Well, the Amish kids I know work on the farm. I don't mean they're abused, but that's the family business and they learn it early."

"So what are you saying?"

He leaned against the door frame as if boneweary. "These boys had no calluses. They just didn't have the bodies of farm kids."

"I noticed that, but we know they were."

"Do we?"

"Of course," she said impatiently. "And even if Matthew Longsdorf's body wasn't found at home, we know where he came from."

"We know where everybody says he came from."

She stared at him. "They had the funeral at the farm. They built a casket for him with their own hands."

"Yeah, I know. But something's wrong." He closed his eyes for a moment. "I wish these people would talk to me. But they won't. Not even the kids. I never saw such a closemouthed bunch in my life."

"You were just explaining to me some reasons why they're so clannish."

"But *I'm* the police!"

She smiled.

"Oh, shit," he said. "During your snooping around, did you get a look at the Longsdorf family Bible?"

"No."

"Too bad."

"Are you asking me to go out there again and see if I can—?"

"No! Dammit, no!"

"A visit is a bit different from riding around on a bicycle giving everybody the impression that I'm a weird woman up to no good."

"You *are* a weird woman up to no good," he said as he opened the door. "And never mind about that Bible. Forget I mentioned it."

# Chapter Twenty-two

AFTER KOCHEN HAD GONE, Hana went in search of Mr. Fred. Not surprisingly, she found him in the 1812 Annex. What was surprising, however, was the fact that he was puttering about a sophisticated lighting panel she had never seen before. Most of the cases and shelves were now orderly. The mannequin in the moldy uniform lay at peace in its place of honor. Skeletons and parts of skeletons had been reconstructed and hung reverently. Their finger and toe bones were a marvel. Hana wondered if Teddy Jolf was also good at beading necklaces.

A truly incredible display, on which Hana quickly turned her back, was an assembly of amputated body parts. It was accompanied by a collection of medical instruments of the time which, according to a neatly printed sign, was on loan from the Conover Historical Society. The room really did look like a museum. Unusual. Macabre. But, still, a museum.

"Wait'll you see this!" Mr. Fred cried joyously as he flipped a switch.

Instantly the room was in total darkness.

Hana cried in exasperation, "Are you crazy?"

Mr. Fred cackled as if auditioning for Halloween. She stood still, afraid a step in any direction would bring her in contact with some historical horror. She became aware of a mauve light that began as a small gleam on the mannequin's chest then increased in intensity until the entire figure in its coffin was visible. The light quivered slightly, giving the illusion that the figure was moving. Even though she knew it was a mannequin and that Mr. Fred, outlined in blue, was manipulating his controls with obvious glee, the effect was eerie and startling. Music began on a minor key, softly throbbing through the room. Around the walls, blue lights slid into brilliance, illuminating skeletons that grinned as if awakening from a long sleep.

Hana opened her mouth to howl a protest when the mannequin in the moldy uniform began to move. As she watched, her mouth still open, it slowly rose to a sitting position.

It was ghastly.

"Stop it!" Hana screamed at Mr. Fred. "Stop it this minute!"

She fumbled toward a light switch on the wall. As she turned it on, bright overhead bulbs overwhelmed Mr. Fred's display. The mannequin fell back with a plop.

"Why did you do that?" he asked plaintively.

"You're demented!" Hana cried. "Alzheimer's. That's what it is. You've been becoming more aberrant every year. But this is just too much! The only thing I want less than a museum is . . . is . . . this. Whatever it is! Turn it off. Take it out."

Deliberately he clicked switches on his panel then rose, remaining on the platform where the obscenity was installed. The added height contributed to an illusion that he himself was part of the display, a giant in black, dark eyes sparking wrathfully.

Hana stood her ground.

"May I remind you," he said haughtily, "that you gave your permission to create this unique display."

"I did no such thing!"

"When you approached me about assuming the role of detective, you guaranteed that no questions would be asked in setting up this museum. You gave me your word."

He said it heavily, threateningly, and in another moment he would be bringing up the ghost of her father to vengefully condemn any Shaner who would break such a tradition of fidelity. The trouble was, he was right. But she had never expected . . . this. She was never prepared for the length to which his criminal mentality would go.

"Where did all this equipment come from?" she asked weakly.

"The fund."

"What fund?"

"My discretionary fund for the upkeep of the estate. For repairs and other minor matters so that I don't always have to keep bothering you."

"You call this upkeep?" she asked, overwhelmed by his audacity. "You have a sick mind, Mr. Fred. Only you could come up with something like that thing sitting up in the coffin."

"I only wish I had."

"You didn't design that?"

He looked as if he were admitting to a great flaw in his character. "Unfortunately, I'm not gifted in that direction. Pocky Reilly did it for me."

"Pocky Reilly!"

*Et tu Brute.*

"Well, I knew we didn't want to spend a fortune," he said, nodding as if agreeing with himself. "So I asked her if the lighting people at the community theater could come up with something. And they did. For very little money, I might add. But it must be seen to be appreciated. If you'd just watch the entire performance—"

"I don't want to watch any of it!"

He stepped down from the platform. Maybe it was the lights, because he did not diminish in size.

"Everybody else loves it," he announced.

"Like what everybodies?"

"Well . . . the entire Historical Society."

"You've been in here giving light shows to the entire Historical Society?"

"It's going to be the main attraction of the Open House." He went on quickly, "Did I mention that I discovered something rather important and possibly quite relevant to your investigation? But then, perhaps all you're interested in is belittling my efforts to create a modern historical display here at Blue Spring Hill."

With dignity, he moved down the room toward the door. Hana was forced to follow if she wanted to hear his news. Mr. Fred was good at putting people at psychological disadvantage. As a child, when discovered in a misdemeanor, she recalled how he had walked away and she had been forced to follow, head down, eyes on the ground.

She tried to recover her authority by demanding, "What did you discover?"

He marched on and out of the museum without replying. Hana hurried after him into the hall. He paused to close the door of the Annex and turn off all lights.

"Unfortunately," he said, "the discovery was marred by the matter of the indignity of being picked up by the police in connection with this matter."

"That was just a ruse on Kochen's part. He wouldn't dream of prosecuting."

"Nevertheless, I was subjected to personal degradation while attempting to cooperate with your rather incomprehensible orders and instructions. I was asked to take part in a possibly dangerous mission—"

"Oh, for heaven's sake, selling pastries to Amish women is not dangerous."

"Excuse me."

He left her standing there and walked rapidly down the hall. Hana took several angry breaths to control herself. She even counted to fifty before she followed him. Seldom in her life had she bested Mr. Fred. As a child, she had learned to work around Mr. Fred, elude Mr. Fred, but if faced straight on, he always won.

He was already making coffee when she reached the kitchen.

Coffee and humble pie. Good combination.

"If the Historical Society has already approved the light display in the museum, I suppose it's too late to change anything," she said, hoping she had kept her sense of bitter defeat out of her voice. "And it certainly is . . . unusual."

He nodded graciously. Hana sat at the table. Someday he would have to go. She'd fire him and get somebody sane, sensible, and subservient to run the estate. It was definitely on the agenda. She was really going to do it.

But not before Open House. That would be a disaster.

He said almost kindly, "Perhaps you'd like to know what I learned during my career as a pastry salesperson."

"Oh, indeed," she murmured. "I was hoping you'd get around to mentioning it."

He gestured impressively with a jar of coffee beans which he was holding. "I have learned that Johnny Longsdorf and the Schwambach boy— Jake, I believe—are very, very close friends despite the fact that they live rather far apart."

Hana stared at him. "That's it?"

He was annoyed. "That's a great deal. Don't you understand? They spend a lot of their spare time together. There's a strong connection here, and both their brothers were killed with pitchforks."

He was right. It was important. Even more important, perhaps, was the fact that nothing had been said by anybody about their friendship.

"I am glad to know that," she said. "Did you tell Sergeant Kochen?"

He looked offended. "He was much too busy

fussing about my activities to encourage any exchange of ideas."

She spoke louder, over the whir of the coffee grinder. "Do you recall what time the boys left Mount Grunwald yesterday?"

"About three o'clock in the afternoon, I should judge. Some of them had to be home in time to milk the cows, I understand, so we didn't keep them long."

Three o'clock. Plenty of time for any one of them to get into town to assault Pocky Reilly. Not in a horse and buggy, but Amish kids had access to cars.

Mr. Fred seemed to have recovered his good humor and, as the coffee perked, brought out exotic samples of pastry.

Almond flavored.

Wasn't there a poison that tasted like almonds? Arsenic . . . ? Hana looked at Mr. Fred. No. If murder ever happened here, he was certainly the victim. She wouldn't have it any other way.

Hana took a bite of her almond-flavored pastry. Tasty. Then she told him what had happened to Pocky Reilly.

# Chapter Twenty-three

IT WAS MIDAFTERNOON of the following day before Hana was free to drive over to the Longsdorf farm to attempt an assault on the family Bible. Even though Kochen had denied it, she was sure he'd be glad after the fact.

It had been an interesting day at the office, highlighted by a report from the computers at the detective agency. Teddy Jolf, despite her presence at embarrassing times and places, was everything she claimed to be. She had been a school nurse for some six years before she quit to establish her own rare and used book business. It was a respectable enterprise with a decent profit from collectibles she sold by mail and a lesser amount from her stand at the White Unicorn. She had never defrauded or cheated anyone. Her record as a school nurse was excellent, and the county indicated it would take her back any time. Before she had been caught prowling the rooms at Blue Spring Hill, her life had been an open book. Hana read the report twice, then had Cindy Hefflefinger, her executive assistant, read it to make sure she had not missed a subtle criminal activity. She hadn't.

By the time she was finished Pocky Reilly had arrived, bruised and swollen but determined to recreate her Amish outfit. Even though Hana had not changed her mind about using the dress, she decided to allow Pocky the therapy of working on it. She supposed the least she could do was look at it since Pocky had become so obsessive. Maybe it would even help solve the mystery of the murders, although Hana couldn't imagine how.

Pocky was ecstatic over the care Bill Longenecker had given her, an enthusiasm Hana found quite annoying.

On the drive to the Scotch Mountains, she pondered the problem of maneuvering herself into a position of browsing through the Longsdorfs' family Bible. She could think of nothing but playing it by ear. She felt positive and optimistic. For one thing, it was a relief to be herself, able to drive right up to the door instead of lurking in somebody's peach orchard.

She had dressed for the visit. Not only would she feel more confident if she knew she looked well, but Hana had the theory that Plain women surreptitiously enjoyed seeing other women's clothes. Since it was a warm spring, Hana and Sal had rummaged about and dug out some of last summer's outfits. This cool, clean navy pantsuit had been one of Hana's favorites last year. The jacket was belted in back, a style she always favored. On her white turtleneck she pinned two tiny dark blue enamel hearts. Her shoulder bag and shoes matched the suit.

At the Longsdorfs' she parked beside the road. In contrast to the day of the funeral, the place seemed deserted. She got out of the car and paused for a moment, looking around. She hoped no nosy neighbor was spying, ready to notify the police that she was here again.

She wanted to walk around to the back of the house but Kochen's warning sent her to the front door. The good sergeant probably had eyes in the back of his head, as in the old saying Aunt Sissy used a lot in reference to Mr. Fred. For one fanciful moment Hana thought of getting close enough to stroke the back of Kochen's head to find out. Annoyed with herself, she knocked loudly on the door. Her annoyance spread to the Longsdorfs, and the inconvenience of not being able to call them on the phone.

The door was opened by Mrs. Longsdorf, who had a welcoming smile on her defeated features. The smile drooped immediately, along with the corners of her mouth. Obviously she had been expecting somebody but it wasn't Hana.

"Remember me?" Hana asked brightly. "I was here a few days ago about your son Matthew."

The woman said nothing, her eyes focused somewhere beyond Hana. Hana turned but saw nobody.

"May I come in?" she asked, turning back again. "I'd really like to talk to you."

This time there was no mistaking the quick, frantic glances down the road.

"It won't take long," Hana added helpfully.

The tired eyes looked relieved at the thought. "What do you want to talk about now? Matt's dead. I can't say no more about him."

"I'd like to talk about your other son. Johnny."

She looked alarmed. *"Er iss net in druvv'l?"*

"I'm not sure whether or not he's in trouble," Hana admitted.

"Well . . . come once in."

As Hana entered, the woman looked down the road again before she closed the door. Hana was led quickly back to the kitchen where she had been before. She didn't see the Bible anywhere as they dashed through the rooms. She wondered what would happen if she simply and honestly asked to see it.

"Want coffee?" Mrs. Longsdorf asked grudgingly. "It's still pretty good. I made myself a pot this after."

Hana accepted the offer of the afternoon's brew, then asked, "Is Mr. Longsdorf around? I didn't see him in the fields."

Mrs. Longsdorf had already grabbed a cup and was quickly filling it, spilling a little, which sizzled on the hot coal stove. "Why, him and Mary went off to town. Now what's this about my Johnny?"

"You know he's a very good friend of Jake Schwambach's?"

"*Ach, ja,* and why shouldn't he be?" she asked defiantly, placing a mug on the table before Hana.

This time the coffee was so black and heavy it hardly needed the sides of the mug to lean against. She took a sip, coughed, and squeaked, "Do you know both of them have a job patrolling my estate when we hold our Open House?"

Mrs. Longsdorf poured herself a cup of her lethal liquid. "This'll put hair on your chest. And wake you up, if that's what you need."

"Perhaps I could have a little milk?"

"Milk I had in this morning soured. There's some in the springhouse but . . ."

She sat wearily at the table.

"Please don't bother," Hana said after a moment.

The woman glanced nervously toward the front of the house and stirred in her chair. She picked up her cup, then set it down again without drinking. Hana didn't blame her.

"You do know your son has a job at my Open House?"

This time the woman nodded. "It's good for kids to do stuff like that. Money ain't so easy to come by and they best learn that young."

"We had a picnic for these young people at Mount Grunwald," Hana said glibly as if it had been her own idea. "To show them a map of the estate and tell them what's expected. It's important for them to do a good job because, after all, it is a private home."

"Wouldn't want nothing like that here," Mrs. Longsdorf said distastefully.

The fire in the old iron cooking range made the room unnaturally warm. The coffee was very hot. Hana found herself sweating. So was her hostess, she noted.

"At this picnic," Hana said, "the young people were playing rock music on an expensive tape recorder. I wasn't aware the Amish were allowed to do that."

"You think we ain't got trouble with our kids like everybody else?" Mrs. Longsdorf demanded with sudden bitterness. "It ain't easy for the young ones to follow our ways. They don't live inside the barn and never get to see what other folks got, you know. *Ja*, they listen to such dumb music sometimes and they drink beer too. But that don't make them bad kids. So if you got no more to say to me about Johnny, I'm busy today."

Hana hesitated, wondering if she should make excuses to linger and meet whatever mysterious visitor the woman was expecting. But Mrs. Longsdorf had already risen and had taken away Hana's cup, which was something of a relief.

"Just how much would you tolerate?" Hana asked.

"Why, what'd you mean?"

"Suppose your son was involved in an attack that was made on me on the White Unicorn parking lot? How would you feel about that?"

Mrs. Longsdorf dumped Hana's coffee into a sink, sending some of it splashing over her apron. "You know for sure he done something like that?"

"A boy named Johnny was there."

"I could name you twenty Johnnys right around here. Amish, Mennonite, and English," she said with more spirit than Hana thought she was capable of.

Hana rose, forcing a friendly smile. "You're right, of course. I just wanted to talk to you and try to get your feelings about your son. Apparently you feel that underneath he's a good boy, and I'm sure that's something a mother knows by instinct."

Without looking at Hana, Mrs. Longsdorf took a swallow of her own coffee. She grimaced, but whether because of the coffee or the thought of her son Hana couldn't tell.

"Oh, one other thing," Hana said, moving toward the doorway to placate her unwilling hostess. "I'm very interested in old German Bibles. I have a collection of my own, and I try to see other people's Bibles whenever I get the chance. Do you think I could see yours? It would only take a couple of minutes and then I'll be on my way."

"We ain't got one."

"But every Amish family has a Bible."

"Not the big ones you're talking about." She moved forward, effectively forcing Hana into another room. "We had once but I used to let the kids look at the pictures by themselves when they was little and it got all torn up."

Shocked, because she knew what old German Bibles were worth, Hana asked, "Didn't you have other books for the children?"

"The Bible's the best book there is. It's good for kids to look at such pictures. Then they grow up good and don't give their parents no trouble."

Hana was slowly but persistently being pressed toward the front door. Giving up, she moved voluntarily in that direction.

"Thank you for your time, Mrs. Longsdorf."

In two more seconds she was on the porch with the door closed behind her. As Hana returned to her car, there was still no sign of the expected guest. She drove away slowly, heading down the winding Rain Road, away from the Longsdorfs'. She had a vague plan of driving for a while, then turning and passing the house once more. Surely that wouldn't be considered harassment.

When she came to a patch of woodland beside a stream, a different idea came to her. Here one of Conover County's famous wooden covered bridges crossed the picturesque, meandering creek. And right beside it was a grassy turnoff, patronized by fishermen and used by Hana herself as a resting place on her recent bicycle expeditions. She pulled in, maneuvered herself behind a sumac thicket, and shut off the motor. The afternoon was quiet and sleepy. A few early flies buzzed about. A mayfly born in April fluttered toward a meadow where small yellow buttercups promised drops of honey.

Hana got out of the Chrysler and crossed to the meadow. She knew she was taking a chance but, after all, what could Kochen or Chief Hoffman do to her? Her lawyers were more than a match for either of them. She felt confident Mrs. Longsdorf would be busy looking for her visitor and in any case would not expect Hana to circle back, especially on foot. Hana assumed that the land on this side of the road was Longsdorf property. If she was right, even Mr. Peach Orchard wouldn't see her.

A few cows glanced at her curiously. The mayfly had found sweet flowers. Hana herself found mud between the clumps of meadowgrass. She slogged along but got into a worse mess in a freshly plowed field beyond the meadow. She crossed to a hedge-row where brambles and small trees separated neighboring fields. From here she could see the house. She could also see lilacs. Apparently some-

body—Hana wondered if it could possibly be the
taciturn Mrs. Longsdorf—loved lilacs, because a
miniature forest of them grew behind a spring
house where water flowed coolly between stone
walls. It was, Hana thought, the prettiest spot on
the farm. Keeping low, she scurried along a hedge-
row. When she got close she saw that the lilacs
were old, with thick gnarled trunks. No, she decided, it hadn't been Mrs. Longsdorf who had encouraged these, but some woman probably long
buried in a simple Amish grave.

Hana crept behind the lilacs and lowered herself
to the ground. It was relatively dry here with a
sweet grassy odor. She wriggled for a short way
into the thicket until she could see the front of the
house.

A small modern imported car, classy and well
cared for, was parked where her Chrysler had
been. She did not recognize the car and nobody
was in sight. If only she had been able to delay a
few more minutes . . .

Sitting on the ground, lilac branches poking her
at odd places, Hana hoped that whatever conference was taking place at the Longsdorfs' would not
be a long one. Perhaps Sergeant—Will—Kochen
had bought a new car. Heaven knows, he needed
one. She could picture him coming out of the
house with a cringing Mrs. Longsdorf, who would
point directly at Hana. Kochen would furiously
drag her out of the lilacs to lecture her about
crimes against the Plain People.

For a while Hana passed time, between glances
at her watch, considering how she could find out
whether or not Mrs. Longsdorf's Bible story was
true. Since Jake and Johnny knew each other, it
followed that the parents too were acquainted.
That was no surprise, because everybody within

the Amish community seemed to be acquainted. Also, everybody knew where everybody else lived, so they might know who had an old Bible and who did not. It could be that it didn't matter a hoot, because Matthew's name would be recorded with those of the other children. Still, it wouldn't hurt to talk to the Schwambach women and ask. She wondered if she could possibly get a word with the old grandmother.

Hana had glanced at her watch every five minutes for forty-five minutes when the door opened and Mrs. Longsdorf and her guest came onto the porch. Even at three hundred yards, Hana recognized Betty Schlicher, the hex woman.

So. Like old Mrs. Schwambach, Mrs. Longsdorf consulted a powwow.

Hana couldn't hear what they were saying. Mrs. Longsdorf's apron was thrown up over her arms, country-style, as if she were cold. Betty looked slick and modern beside her, somewhat like a mannequin in a shopping mall. She wore a longish brown skirt and brown turtleneck with a white linen overblouse. A silver belt dangled low on her waist. Silver bracelets flashed in the sun when she moved her arms.

Hana wished they'd raise their voices. They didn't.

Very slowly, Hana moved her cramped legs and slithered out of the lilac clump. She tore her jacket and scraped her arm but kept going. When she reached the grass she crawled on her hands and knees until she was out of their line of vision. Only when the outbuildings were between her and the women on the porch did she thankfully get to her feet.

Stumbling a little, Hana ran.

It wasn't easy after crouching for nearly an hour.

Neither was it easy to slide over muddy, plowed earth. She slowed to catch her breath but, even then, kept moving. She was making pretty good time when she reached the meadow. A group of robins congregated there, chirping about possible nesting sites. Hana wished them well.

She crossed the clumps of grass with a philosophic consideration of costly shoe replacement in a detective's life. How did the pros cope? Private eyes, the ones she hired at any rate, obviously did it by rarely leaving their computers to march through the mud. Someday she'd have to discuss it with Kochen.

She reached her car, short of breath but triumphant. Mrs. Longsdorf's conversation with Betty Schlicher had seemed intense, and Hana could only hope they were still at it. She got in her car, sent mud and grass flying as she backed out of the parking place, then spun in a quick turn and headed back the way she had come.

As she slowed, nearing the edge of the woodland, Betty Schlicher's sporty car came toward her. She clearly saw the hex woman's face as she flashed by. Hana waited until the other car was out of sight, then backed up swiftly, swung into the turnoff beside the covered bridge, and once more dug up grass as she turned and took off after Betty.

Hana reflected contentedly that Kochen had no such tender feelings toward hex doctors as he did toward Plain People. She rumbled through the wooden bridge, then drove fast until she spotted Betty's car. Being red, it was easy to keep in view.

And if she lost it, it probably didn't even matter.

Except that perhaps Betty was going on a mission for Mrs. Longsdorf. Someplace where the Longsdorf family with their religious sensitivities could not go. Hana liked the thought. She liked it so much, she considered setting her private detectives on Betty. Might be interesting to find out what the woman was up to and even more interesting to test electronic bugs and PI devices against Betty's occult powers.

Hana grinned as she rounded a curve to see a long straight stretch of road but no red car.

She slowed, looking about.

This was a different part of the county. Maybe they had even crossed the county line. Tidy farms had been replaced by small houses and mobile homes. Hana passed a garage and a small settlement around a bar that boasted country music every Friday and Saturday night. She stepped on the gas.

Could the spirits have warned Betty that she was being followed? Or had the woman merely spotted an inept amateur? Strange, abandoned warehouses now dominated the landscape. Beyond them, a rusted, dilapidated, and very high wire fence did what it could to keep a littered woodland protected from trespassers. Signs on the fence warned of prosecution.

As Hana swept by, her peripheral vision caught something red among the light green of the springtime woods. If it had been later in the year with more leaves on the trees, she never would have spotted it. She slowed, looking for a place to turn. She found it farther along, where the fence gave way to what had been swinging gates into this place, whatever it was. The gates were secured by a series of rusted padlocks but there was plenty of decaying macadam for a turn.

Hana again headed back the way she had come.

From the road it certainly looked like Betty's car. Behind her an impatient VW sounded an angry horn then whipped around. Hana flicked on her signal and turned onto a cindered one-lane road, rutted and little used. At one time the road had been guarded by a smaller gate but it had been broken and hung useless in the weeds around the fence.

Bouncing along, Hana looked sharply about. On both sides of the road was an unkempt grass verge. Litter was everywhere, most of it fast food containers and empty beer cans. Betty had parked amid the debris on what appeared to be reasonably solid ground. Hana pulled in right behind her. Attempting to hide her car would be useless.

She put down the window and listened. People. Laughter. But it seemed to be at some distance. She closed the window again, got her gun out of her bag, and slipped it into her jacket pocket. She crammed her shoulder bag beneath the seat, then got out of the car and closed the door as quietly as possible. Now she noticed paths—just ordinary dirt paths, only moderately overgrown—leading off into the woods. One seemed wider, more traveled than the others.

Another, edged with the shiny leaves of new poison ivy, seemed much less used but appeared to lead in the same general direction. Hana chose this path, quietly padding along in her muddy shoes and avoiding the poison as much as possible.

She was slowly getting closer to the sounds. Whatever it was, it was still some distance from the road. She was puzzled. The voices sounded happy. The playful shouts reminded her of an amusement park she had visited as a child. A sudden blast of sound sent her hand flying to her gun.

Then she realized what it was.

Rock music.

Somewhere ahead, somebody had suddenly turned on a tape.

She was glad she had taken the lesser trail. It would even be worth the itch of poison, although she was not particularly susceptible to it. She paused but it was useless to try to hear if anybody prowled this woodland with her. Ahead, the path sloped upward. Cautiously she moved forward. The music was unbearably loud now. She was almost there. Only a patch of thick brush separated her from the human and inhuman sounds.

Hana crouched low, carefully parted the curtain of bushes, and looked through.

Looming in front of her, obliterating everything else, was the totally nude behind of a young male. It was definitely a male, she noted when he bent over and disappeared from her view. In another second she heard a distant splash.

# Chapter Twenty-four

DAZED, HANA BLINKED. Before her was an embankment of rocks, gravel, and cinders. Across a void lay more of the same. A caldera. No, a quarry! Suddenly she knew where she was; the old Baggenstose Quarry. It had been abandoned during the Great Depression of the 1930s and never reopened. Hana was at a high point on the lip of the quarry, which was very deep and filled with water. The raucous music came from a radio hanging on a branch of a scarred tree. To Hana's left appeared more young males, all stark naked. In this group were Johnny Longsdorf and Jake Schwambach.

Oh, God. This was worse than being a Peeping Tom at a funeral. Much worse.

They were laughing, horsing around. Kids who had found a private place for an illegal dip on a warm spring day. But why select such a dangerous place when Conover County was full of streams? As soon as the question occurred to her, Hana thought she knew the answer. Most streams that flowed through the county's meadows and fields were muddy from soil erosion and, especially in spring, ripe with fertilizers that had washed in with the rains. In the quarry the water was cold and pure from the seepage of deep underground springs.

But where was Betty Schlicher? And why had she come here? God forbid that she was skinny-dipping with these boys.

A worse suspicion occurred to Hana. Had Betty known Hana was following and deliberately led her here? Suddenly Hana felt very vulnerable. Suppose Betty was even now taking pictures with a telephoto lens? Blackmail. Or at the very least, adverse publicity.

She was about to retreat when more boys began to leap over the edge of the quarry into water at least thirty feet below. Then, suddenly, to Hana's horror, she had a glimpse of a short, heavyset child among the older youths.

Instead of retreating, Hana scrambled forward, shouting, to the edge of the quarry. But she was too late. The small boy was arching through the air, then he splashed into the water below and disappeared. Boys still on the bank scattered with cries, but she was hardly aware of them as she stared downward, willing the small lad to surface.

It happened so quickly there was no time for thought or defense. One moment she was standing staring into water far below, and the next there was a sharp blow below her shoulder blades. Then she was falling sickeningly through the air, hurtling toward the dark water. She was aware of air rushing into her open mouth, of panic, of flailing her arms and finding nothing to grab. Then the all-consuming sight of water. It seemed to rise up to her, striking her. She hit with a force harder than the blow to her back. She struggled to close her mouth and hold her breath. She seemed to be traveling even faster now, through frigid water toward some bottom perhaps a hundred feet below. Water forced itself into her mouth and nostrils. Her clothing felt like dead weights. She began struggling with her arms and kicking.

It seemed an eternity before her direction was reversed and she was moving upward. She saw lighter water above. Her lungs were shuddering, as if forcing her to open her mouth and take in gulps of something, even water.

Nothing mattered except survival. All her energy was focused on reaching that light. She hated her shoes with primeval loathing and kicked viciously to rid herself of them.

Hana was a strong swimmer. Although an anachronism such as a swimming pool had never been allowed to violate the historical purity of the grounds at Blue Spring Hill, Aunt Sissy had, every summer, taken her to the YWCA for lessons three times a week. That was, Aunt Sissy said, what the YWCA was for and, despite the lack of a pool, no Shaner had ever died by drowning.

*No Shaner had ever died by drowning.*

It was as if Hana heard Aunt Sissy's voice inside her own ringing ears. She felt exhausted, her legs unable to push against the heavy weight of her shoes.

Hana struggled again. In another moment she burst above the surface of the water and opened her mouth to gulp air. She sputtered, coughing, spitting, hardly able to keep her head above the water.

She tried to cry for help. Everything looked fuzzy. Blinking water from her eyes, she looked for the boys.

She saw no one as she sank below the surface again. She reached down, digging into the flesh of her heels, forcing the leaden, slimy shoe off her foot.

One free.

She surfaced, breathed again, ripping at her jacket and tearing it off. It was easier now. She managed the other shoe, then began to tread water as she looked about.

The rocky sides of the quarry rose around her, steep and sharp to the water's edge. She scanned the lip above but saw no one. Nor did she hear the music. Everybody had gone. Run away.

She experienced overwhelming panic before her mind began functioning. The boys. They didn't dive into this quarry if there was no way to climb back up. Some of them had been in the water when she fell. There must be a way out. Pivoting slowly, she inspected the sides near the water level. About fifty yards away was an area of clay and dirt. It was small for a beach but at least she could get out of the water.

She was shivering. Probably turning blue. Those kids were crazy to swim here this early in the season. Crazy to swim here at all. Then she remembered the small boy. Had he gone through this? Had he been able to struggle upward toward the light?

She tried to concentrate on the beach. It seemed

far away. She felt as if she must be standing still.
But as she swam the water seemed less cold. Even
friendly. Luring her. She was tired . . . It would
be so easy to slide downward and rest. Let all the
murders of the world go. Let Shaner Carpets be
swallowed up in some giant corporation. Let the
secret of Dutch Blue coloring slide into this water
and be lost forever. Such an incredible shade of
blue . . . more brilliant than the sky . . .

Hana's hands clawed at dirt and clay. The ledge
was solid but sloping. Slippery. She groped toward
a protruding boulder, grabbed it, and held on. Now
that she had something solid to cling to, the water
seemed less threatening. Looking down she saw
another ledge about ten feet below her in the water.

And something or somebody was down there.

Oh, God, if only she wasn't so cold. If only she
could see.

Clinging to her rock, Hana squinted into the water. An arm. A face. Eyes staring at her through
water forever in motion.

If she'd had the breath she would have screamed.
Frantically she looked around again. Nothing. No
one.

She couldn't stay in this water much longer. No
way. And yet, if that child was down there . . .
and if she was in time . . .

Hana turned off her mind. If she thought about
it, she knew she couldn't do it. Put yourself on automatic. The only way. Hana-the-robot. She took a
gulp of air, released her hold on the rock, and sub-
merged, forcing herself downward toward wide-
open eyes staring up at her.

Her hands slid along the wall of rock. She had
only to sink a few feet to get a better view. A dress

waved slowly in the water. Hair billowed. An arm lay severed. Eyes still stared out of a broken head.

Hana shot upward, grabbed the rock, and pulled herself out of the water to fall onto the clay, gasping and shuddering. What she had seen had registered in her brain but would have to be assimilated when she was warm again. And safe.

The fact that Pocky Reilly's mannequin, still wearing its pseudo-Amish dress, was lying on that ledge in pieces like something sacrificed to an ancient water spirit seemed almost unimportant. Ghastly but unimportant. What was important was the fact that she had never been so cold in her life. Every muscle and nerve was twitching with cold. Couldn't stay here. Had to get to the top of the quarry. Somehow had to get to her car. Turn on the heater.

Hana realized she was crying at the thought of her car heater. She sat up shakily, breathing deeply. After a moment, she felt a little more in control and looked at the rocks around her. She couldn't get back into that water again.

But there was a path. In her desperation she had overlooked it at first, but now it was clear. Between the rocks a trail led upward, marked by generations of youths who had clambered up this cliff to take their lives in their hands with another dive.

Weakly Hana got to her feet, surprising herself by her ability to stand. Slowly she began the climb. There were plenty of rocks to hang on to, but the trail was narrow and difficult in places. As she rose higher she felt giddy and sat down to rest.

She began shivering almost immediately and forced herself to go on. Her stocking feet hurt from stones. She stubbed her toe. She no longer dared to look downward but kept her eyes on the lip of the quarry, which was coming within reach although maddeningly slowly. Near the top she slipped and slid downward for about ten feet before she managed to stop herself by grabbing a boulder.

She crawled up again and hoisted herself over the lip.

She dug her fingers into an area of soil and clay and lay there, exhausted and shivering, eyes closed.

She heard footsteps.

In her condition she knew anybody could just roll her over the edge. Should have staggered into the woods. Should get up now and do it. Hide.

She opened her eyes and lifted her head. A figure loomed above, shutting off the warming sun. A figure with a big cape.

No. Not a cape.

Her eyes focused on the face. The mouth. The smile. Smile? Yes. Big smile. Missing tooth. Hana heard herself croaking something but it didn't sound like English. My God, she was babbling in the Pennsylvania German dialect, the original tongue of her people.

Unglued. She was unglued.

And Betty Schlicher was answering in the dialect. And she wasn't wearing a cape. It was a blanket. A car blanket by the look of it, which she was wrapping around Hana.

It felt rough and warm. Hana hugged it to herself.

The woman was still smiling. Why didn't she have that damn tooth replaced? Or keep her damn mouth shut?

"Why didn't you help me?" Hana rasped, in English, her throat feeling sore and unnatural. "I thought I was going to drown. I didn't know the way up."

"Oh, I knew you'd get out," Betty said cheerfully. "Although I did think you'd use the stairs. This is the old path. Too difficult. The boys carved steps in the clay on the other side of that nice outcropping of rock. Now open your mouth."

"I don't want to open my mouth!"

"Do it anyway. I want to look at your throat and listen to your chest."

Hana wanted Uncle Harold. Uncle Harold was always around when nasty things happened. Instead she had this hex person prowling over her body, thumping her, peering down her throat, placing an experienced ear next to her heart.

Finally Betty said, "You'll live."

"No thanks to you."

"I went to my car for a blanket, didn't I?" She helped Hana to her feet. "Let's go. Lean on me if you want."

Galling as it was, Hana found she did want to do just that. No, not *want*. Need. Big difference. She let Betty guide her along the well-used path through the woods. There were small stones and twigs on the way. Hana no longer hated shoes. Even slippers would be a treat.

"When did you go for the car blanket?" she panted.

"When you went in."

"Somebody pushed me."

"Oh? I thought you slipped."

Hana looked at her. "I didn't slip. I was shoved. By the limb of a tree. Dead limb maybe. Anyway, something. It was a hard blow. If you saw me go in you must have seen who pushed me."

"I was watching the boys. And then I saw movement. Saw you going over the edge."

Well, maybe. And then also maybe it was Betty

herself who had been behind Hana in the woods. But at the moment it didn't seem prudent to pursue that interesting possibility. She felt unequal to doing battle with a hex woman.

"There was a young boy," Hana said. "A boy much smaller than the others. And he jumped in with them. Where are those kids?"

"Halfway home by this time. One of them has an old truck they all use. They scattered fast when you went in. Don't want their folks to find out they come here."

"The parents don't know?"

"Oh, they know all right. But they ignore it. It's a policy of theirs to ignore a lot of things the kids do. However, if somebody like you got hurt when the kids are here, maybe it couldn't be ignored anymore."

They had reached the lane. Betty guided Hana to the red car and opened the door.

"Get in."

"But my car—"

"Get in."

Too exhausted to resist, Hana flopped into the front seat. Betty closed the door, walked around to the other side, got in, and turned on the motor and the heater. From a basket on the backseat she got out a thermos. A strange sweet odor filled the car as she poured fragrant tea into a plastic cup. Her bracelets jangled when she offered the cup to Hana.

"What's that?" Hana asked suspiciously.

"Hot herbal tea. It'll make you feel better."

She forced the cup into Hana's hands. Hana sniffed it. Through steam she saw Betty grinning crookedly at her.

"It's not poison," the hex woman said softly.

"Well, how come you have a thermos of hot herbal tea all ready? Were you expecting somebody to go into that water today?"

"I always carry a thermos of medicinal tea in my line of work," Betty said. "That'll be three dollars, please."

"Three dollars?"

"For the tea."

"Three dollars for one cup of lousy tea?"

"It isn't lousy." Betty jangled her bracelets in irritation. "It's very good for you and very special." She took the cup from Hana, drank a swallow, then handed it back. "Now drink."

The cup felt warm in her hands. The rising steam seemed to be making her throat and head feel better. "I can't pay you. My bag's in my car. I hope my bag's still in my car."

"I'll trust you," Betty assured her. "I'm sure you're good for three dollars."

"Why did you come here?" Hana asked.

"Why did you?" Betty countered.

"I followed you from the Longsdorf farm."

"You shouldn't have done that. It was wrong."

"And I deserve to be punished?"

Betty shook her head. "The spirits provide their own punishments. It's not up to me."

On impulse, perhaps because it smelled so good, Hana took a sip of the tea. It slid softly down her throat and she could feel it melt into her stomach, easing a nausea she'd had ever since getting out of the water. She took a bigger swallow.

Watching her, Betty smiled. It wasn't possible . . . No, people didn't sit smiling while one drank poison. Even so, Hana decided she'd take no more of the stuff.

"You haven't answered my question," she said,

glad her voice now sounded quite normal. "About what you're doing here. Unless it's because you enjoy watching naked boys."

"I do," Betty admitted and her smile widened so that Hana could again see the space among her teeth. "Some of those kids . . . they sure are developed for their age."

Since Hana could think of no reply to that, she drank more tea.

Betty laughed aloud before she went on. "But that's not why I came. Mrs. Longsdorf is real worried about her Johnny. Thinks he might be getting himself in some kind of trouble. I think you gave her that idea. After our session, she asked me to look into it. She told me where he was."

"Session?"

"Uh-huh."

"What kind of session?"

"A doctor never reveals confidential information."

"You're not a doctor."

"Oh, but I am. As far as these people are concerned, I am."

"And how much do you charge for quarry calls, Doc?" Hana asked flippantly.

"Plenty. They can afford it. The Amish are good farmers and they're very thrifty."

Hana realized she had drunk even more of the tea. The woman was hypnotic. Maybe it was that smile. Or the way the sun gleamed on the silver bracelets that moved as she moved her arms . . .

Hana recalled she had asked about the smaller boy she had glimpsed so briefly. After all, he was much more important than the mannequin. Because she was already dead in the water. No, that wasn't quite right. You cannot kill a mannequin. Or maybe you can. She thought of consulting the hex doctor about it, but Betty hadn't even answered the question about the boy and that came first. Hana took another drink of tea and asked again.

Betty's pale eyes were slitted as she looked at Hana. "I didn't see a little kid. Only big boys."

"He wasn't exactly little. Just younger than the others."

"Maybe I was too busy watching ass."

Hana felt offended. That was no way for a good, authentic hex doctor to talk. Aunt Sissy would have been horrified. Hana drained her cup.

"I wouldn't mind having more of that stuff."

"Sorry, no."

"Think I can't afford your prices?"

"You've had enough."

"Enough for what?"

"To make you feel better. To counteract the effects of the cold and the water."

"Twice as much ought to do twice as much good."

"Twice as much might send you sailing away on that blanket."

"What is that stuff?"

"My secret formula."

Sadly Hana set her cup on the dashboard. "Do you have a lot of secrets?"

That damn smile again. And the jangle-jangle.

"I hear a lot of secrets from the people I work with. But I'm not telling."

"Not ever?" Hana asked softly. "Not even if it includes murder?"

"Not even then."

Hana's mind was racing. If she could go on thinking with so much clarity, she could solve this case in minutes. Yes, there was something odd . . .

something she should have noticed before. She'd have it in a second. If only she had another cup of tea, it would be right there. Maybe inside the cup.

Watching her, Betty smiled. Hana smiled back.

"How are you feeling?" the woman asked. "Are you able to drive?"

"Indianapolis. I could drive at Indianapolis. In the whatchamacallit."

"I want you to promise me you'll drive carefully. No speeding."

Funny this woman should mention speeding.

"Certainly not," Hana replied soberly.

She opened the door and floated out of the car. She was surprised to find Betty out of the car too.

Hana's gun had gone to the bottom of the quarry but her car keys were in the pocket of the navy slacks. She whipped them out and Betty opened the door for her. Trailing her blanket, Hana regally took her seat behind the wheel.

"Sure you feel all right?" Betty asked.

"I shall be fine. Your blanket—"

"Bring it to the bar next time you're in Bruchberg. Unless you want to pay for it along with the cup of tea."

Hana dug her bag from beneath the seat. "I'll have it laundered and returned to you."

She'd send Mr. Fred. It would serve him right.

She carefully counted out three dollars and handed them to Betty. "I'd like a receipt."

"Be careful or I might put a curse on you," Betty said, hissing a little through the empty space.

Then the Guardian Angel of Quarry Swimmers and Tea Drinkers returned to her own car.

Hana started the motor, backed around deftly, and headed for the main road. As she drove through the opening in the fence Betty was right behind her. The red import stayed behind her until

they were clear of most of the traffic and Hana was
nearly home.

Hana was whistling. She felt wonderful. Obviously a swim in your local quarry had great restor-
ative powers.


# *Chapter Twenty-five*


HANA DID NOT return to earth until long after dinner. The cats, meanwhile, had been avoiding her
and the dogs asked to be let out of the house. Sal
obviously thought she had been drinking. Mr. Fred
tactfully found things to do in the 1812 Annex.

Hana was alone in the snuggery when she realized she had been staring at the TV screen for half
an hour and the set wasn't even turned on.

What in heaven's name was Betty Schlicher dispensing in her tea?

She had to admit, however, that she felt fine.
Even the place where she'd been struck on the back
wasn't really sore. But while she'd been floating
through the evening in a daze, nothing had been
done about the boy in the quarry.

Probably he was a younger brother who always
tagged along with the older kids and could swim
like a fish. Probably he had run away with the others and was safe at home this very minute, chores
done and attending to his homework. But then
again, maybe there was a young body floating near
the plastic hair of Pocky's mannequin.

It was dark now. Hana had no intention of

spooking around an abandoned quarry at night. Nor did she feel justified in calling Sergeant Kochen. Perhaps she should report the location of the stolen mannequin, but it seemed so trivial compared to the safety of a child. Staring at her TV screen, she saw there the scene in which she first noticed the boy heading for the edge of the quarry. It had been only a glimpse because of the naked crowd about him. Jake Schwambach. Jake had been right beside the boy. He would know. Even at the risk of making trouble for Jake and further upsetting the Schwambach family, she had to talk to him. He could tell her if the child was safe at home.

It would also be a good opportunity to ask about the Longsdorf Bible, and maybe a few other things.

With the fickleness of springtime, the night had turned cold. Clouds trailed across the moon, hinting that showers might be on the menu for tomorrow. A wind had risen, moving new leaves in patterns of sound.

Before Hana left, she called Ghost and Crumb and insisted they go inside. They eyed her suspiciously as they obeyed. Kitty Fisher was greeting them joyously as Hana closed the door.

Although she felt more normal, she was still experiencing a strange afterglow. She tended carefully to her driving but noted that it did not seem to be affected.

Spring rains had not improved conditions in the Schwambachs' lane. It was considerably more rutted than the day Sal Nunemacher had driven her down this road to find the first dead boy. His face returned to Hana, haunting the dark. Other memories trickled through as if blown among the leaves of night. Her father's fight for the right of the Plain People to handle the schooling of their own young.

He had hired good lawyers to argue the elimination of the rules that applied to the other school-children in the community.

But the Schwambachs and the Longsdorfs were not typical of the Amish families she had known before. As she approached the old farmhouse at the end of the lane, she remembered how she had felt when she had first seen it: a sense that the place was deserted. Why should she have that feeling when such a large family lived here?

She parked on the same grass verge and sat for a few moments contemplating the house. Even though some windows were lit with coal oil lamps, the place still had a forlorn air. Was it possible for an entire family to lose its soul? Hana caught herself up short. She couldn't imagine why such a thing had come into her mind, unless she was still under the influence of the afternoon's narcotic tea. That was hex talk.

She wished she had listened more carefully to the stories Aunt Sissy used to tell about bad witches, the hexerei who did not lay on healing hands but who cast evil spells.

Hana stepped out of her car into shafts of moonlight shining like spotlights through the gathering clouds.

Best to keep her mind on realities like the teen-age boys in the parking lot. Like the naked child leaping into the quarry. Like the broken mannequin thrown into the water. These things even Will Kochen would understand.

Standing in the shadow of the house, she knocked on the door. She found herself afraid to look back into the light of the half-hidden moon shining whitely on the shaggy lawn.

And she hated herself for the fear.

Old Mrs. Schwambach opened the door, squinting at her through modern plastic-framed bifocals. The odor of the kerosene lamps intruded on the night air. A yellow cat sneaked out of the house and frisked off into the shadows.

Hana addressed the old woman in the dialect. She reminded her who she was and asked to see Jake. The woman had a soft, oddly youthful voice. Also speaking in the dialect, she invited Hana into the house.

Some of the fresh air moved inside with Hana, diluting the acrid smell of the lamps. She was ushered into the parlor, where she found herself an intrusive presence in a picturesque family group. For a moment they sat motionless before her, the yellowish light giving an impression of a faded photograph, frozen in a different time, a century past. The father was seated at a round table reading his Bible. The younger Mrs. Schwambach placidly knitted. The grandfather was dozing in a comfortable chair. Young people were scattered artistically about the room, reading and sewing. One boy was whittling. Katie was flat on her stomach doing homework. The cat should have stayed, Hana thought. It was needed on that oval rag rug to complete the picture.

The tableau moved as Mr. Schwambach rose, after deliberately closing his Bible.

Hana introduced herself again.

He frowned. *"Ja.* We know who you are."

"May I please speak to Jake?" she asked humbly. These Plain patriarchs were overpowering.

"Why for? What's he done?"

"Nothing," Hana assured him, hoping she spoke the truth. "I need information about somebody."

"Somebody Plain?"

"I'm not sure. If I could just talk to him in private . . . ?"

Jake Schwambach looked scared as his father turned toward him.

"Come once, Jake," he ordered. *"M'r gaina im kich."*

Hana smiled at the room in general, then singled out the younger Mrs. Schwambach in particular. "I'm very sorry to disturb you this way. It's just a simple matter. Nothing to worry about."

The woman did not look reassured. Jake shuffled to his feet and meekly followed his father toward the kitchen. The old woman still stood near Hana and looked as if she might be tempted to join them.

In the dialect, Mr. Schwambach suggested she return to the parlor. Actually, it was more than a suggestion but not quite an order. As Hana followed toward the rear of the house, she wished she hadn't come. Even if Mr. Schwambach already knew that the boys swam in the old quarry, his pride would force him to finally do something about it when she brought it up. And it could very well be for nothing.

He rasped a large match into flame and lit another lamp. Jake stood, his large hands hanging limply by his side.

*"Setz dich*, Jake," the man ordered.

Hana tried again. "I'd like to speak to the boy alone."

Frowning, Schwambach shook his head. Jake sat. So did Hana. She turned to the boy, shutting out the father as much as possible.

"Jake, this afternoon you were with a group of boys taking an early swim at the old Baggenstose Quarry," she said with assurance, hoping he wouldn't deny the whole episode.

He glanced at his father, then shifted his eyes back to Hana. *"Ja.* We go there sometimes. Not much. Just sometimes."

Mr. Schwambach said nothing.

"I saw a younger boy there. It was just a brief glimpse before you jumped into the water."

"What was you doing up there?" Mr. Schwambach demanded. "The boys go there alone and swim naked."

Oh, wow, Hana thought. Aloud she said, "I found that out. I hadn't known."

"Well, what did you want up there anyhow?" he insisted.

The old woman came into the room.

There was a sharp exchange between her and her son. They spoke too fast for Hana to get all of it, but she gathered the old woman declared she had to go through to the outhouse. She seemed to be a feisty old soul and closed the back door behind her with annoyed emphasis.

"I'm trying to find out who killed your son and the Longsdorf boy," Hana said, taking advantage of the silence that followed Mrs. Schwambach's departure. She suspected the old woman might be listening at the door. "The investigation takes me to strange places." She turned again to Jake. "Do you know which boy I mean? He was much shorter than the others. I'm really concerned about whether or not he got out of the water all right. That's a dangerous place to swim."

"I don't know nobody like that," Jake said as he stared at the flame in the lamp.

"You must know him. You were right there beside him. You were swimming with him."

"I don't know everybody." His eyes slid to his father. "I got to work most of the time. I don't go running with the other kids much."

She tried to will him to look at her. "Somebody nearly killed me up there today. I was pushed over the edge into that water."

"Maybe they didn't like you looking at naked boys from the bushes," Mr. Schwambach said.

"How did you know I was in the bushes?"

"Why, where else would you be now? These boys wouldn't stand around without their pants on if they knew some English woman was hiding there, watching them," he said triumphantly, something in his eyes daring her to disprove his statement.

"Did you see me?" Hana asked Jake.

He still didn't look up. "No. Didn't see you. Didn't see that kid you're talking about."

"You must have seen something. All you boys disappeared fast enough when I was pushed into the water. Didn't you realize you should have helped me? Didn't you know I might have drowned?"

He licked his lips. "We . . . heard some splashing. Didn't know what it was or anything. Thought maybe somebody come to chase us away. We got out of there real fast."

"You didn't even try to see who had fallen in?"

"I had to go. It's too far to walk back here so I had to go with the guy who had the truck. We all got out of the water and up the steps as fast as we could. We got steps in that clay now so we can go up real fast."

"I didn't see a truck."

"We hide it. There's a shed on one side of that road near the quarry."

"Did you see Betty Schlicher?"

"Who's that?"

Hana repeated the name.

He shook his head. "I tell you I didn't see nobody except kids. I don't know who that is."

"Of course you know who she is," Hana snapped. "She powwowed for your grandmother and I bet she has powwowed for you."

Darting another glance at his father, Jake shook his head.

The back door opened noisily and Mrs. Schwambach reentered.

"That was a short trip," Hana said agreeably to her.

She grunted, then continued on her way.

Mr. Schwambach rose. "If that's all you want, I guess we're finished now."

"He hasn't answered my questions."

"If Jake says he don't know, he don't know," the man said. "And maybe you'd best stay away and not go spying on naked kids."

Ignoring him, Hana asked the boy, "Did you see a broken mannequin in the water? It was on a ledge about ten feet down."

He looked relieved. "*Ach, ja.* That dumb thing. I guess somebody threw it away. People are always throwing junk in the quarry."

It was a good reply. Hana decided to try one more appeal.

"Jake, I'm sure you know the name of that child who was with you. Won't you please tell me so I can check with his people? I'm not trying to make trouble for anybody. I just want to know if he's all right. Did you see him get out of the water as you ran away?"

Jake clenched his big fists. Behind Hana, his father stirred.

"There was no young kid with us!" the boy cried. "I don't know nobody like that!"

Mr. Schwambach let out his breath with slow relief. Hana rose and turned to him, in time to see a flicker of triumph in his eyes.

"I'll ask your mother to let me out," she said and quickly left the kitchen.

The old woman still hovered in the hallway.

Again Hana spoke in the dialect. Mrs. Schwambach seemed almost enthusiastic about showing
her to the door. On the way, Hana paused at the
parlor. They were still there in their places. She
stared straight at the younger Mrs. Schwambach.

"I understand you attended the funeral of Matthew Longsdorf. We could have identified him
much sooner if you'd told me who he was when I
first described him to you."

"I didn't know—"

"Didn't you really?"

"Well, I wasn't sure," she said with spirit. "And I
wasn't going to make trouble for nobody unless I
was sure. It ain't always so easy for us to get in
touch with people."

"Maybe you should get a public phone at the end
of the lane like most Amish people have."

"There still wouldn't have been one over on Rain
Road," she muttered.

In the kitchen Hana could hear the rumble of
Mr. Schwambach's voice. The grandmother put a
hand on her arm.

*"Koom,"* she said.

Hana yielded to the pressure, but once outside,
she paused. She did an "Oh, by the way" in German
and asked the old woman if the Longsdorf family
had a beautiful Bible such as she had seen in this
house.

Mrs. Schwambach looked surprised at the question but nodded. *"Sie hen en shainie Bev'l. Besser
don unsara. Mai bilder."*

Hana smiled, thanked her, and ran through a
light pattering of rain to her car.

# Chapter Twenty-six

LATER THAT NIGHT, Hana lay in bed staring into the dark. Every time she closed her eyes, she felt as if she was underwater. Finally she forced herself to imagine wide blue skies and tufts of clouds. This helped and she managed to drift into a restless sleep.

But worry nagged at her and she slept fitfully, finally jarred awake by a nightmare about water covering her as she was pulled downward by a one-armed mannequin come alive like an evil puppet. She sat up in bed, gasping for breath, remembering the final vision—the body of a short, rather stout boy, whose dead eyes stared at her through watery light as she sank.

Hana grabbed her robe from a chair. A cup of tea. Yes, that's what she needed. Maybe it would calm her, get her mind on something else so she could go back to sleep. She put on the robe and went into the hall. Dim lights in the sconces created shadows everywhere. Hana paused, realizing she had no weapon. Her gun lay at the bottom of the quarry along with her jacket. But this was Blue Spring Hill, her home. Surely she didn't need one.

Penelope Baskin and Gray Trouble, who had been sleeping in her room, padded after her. Downstairs, where a priceless antique Persian carpet covered a portion of the wide entrance hall, Kitty Fisher lay curled up with the dogs, who wagged tails in acknowledgment of friends and went right back to sleep. Penelope Baskin and Gray Trouble flicked their own disdainful tails at the trio.

While Hana's tea brewed, the gray cat batted a

stalk of herbs Sal had hung near the large fireplace to dry. Penelope Baskin sat on a chair at the table, alertly watching Hana as if inviting confidences.

"You understand all about being up at night, don't you?" Hana asked her. "What am I going to do? I can't even prove there was such a boy. And even if there was, I don't know that anything happened to him. How can I persuade the police to drag that quarry just because I think I glimpsed a kid who may have drowned?"

Penelope Baskin wisely said nothing.

Hana patted her calico head. "The only one who might be willing to listen is Will Kochen and I'm not even sure about him."

Anyway, nothing could be done for the boy. It was much too late for that. His terror would be over. Yet something within her wanted him found. It was even more important than the fact that someone had tried to kill her—or frighten her, perhaps, not caring if she lived or died in that water.

Could there be something in the quarry which somebody wanted? When she began to conjure up mental images of buried treasure or even a Loch Conover monster, Hana knew she'd better get back to bed.

Her pondering out loud had put Penelope Baskin to sleep. Gray Trouble had managed to pull down Sal's herbs and was rolling in them. The odor of crushed herbs brought Betty The Hex to mind. The woman probably had some absolutely marvelous stuff to use in place of sleeping pills . . .

"No!" she cried. "Not that!"

Penelope Baskin opened one eye. Gray Trouble looked at Hana and hiccuped. By that time Ghost, Crumb, and Kitty Fisher had arrived to see if anybody was eating.

Hana gave the animals a snack from their treat boxes, then forced herself upstairs.

This couldn't go on. In the morning she would go into the city and talk it over with Sergeant Kochen. Since Easter Sunday she had considered him—almost—a friend. Once you have dyed Easter eggs with a person, a certain relationship is established. She would report the location of the stolen mannequin. It would be a good opener.

Having made up her mind about that, Hana tried to think of something pleasant: her beautiful azaleas ripening into their blossom time. But that reminded her of the fast-approaching Open House. She groaned. Despite everything, she finally fell asleep.

Perhaps, Hana thought as she drove through a fine rain the next morning, she was obsessed with the young fellow at the quarry because of the deaths of the other boys.

But morning, even a morning like this, made things seem brighter. Considering what she had been through, she felt reasonably alert and healthy. She decided that if Kochen assured her, with his friendly smile, that she was inventing doom where none existed, she would accept his decision.

She was passing a disgusting plethora of fast food chains and convenience stores when she noticed the red car following her at a discreet distance. She had noted it absently before but had been too deep in her own concerns to register the fact. Just to make sure, she dodged around a few blocks of small, neat homes. The red car dodged with her.

Annoyed, Hana returned to Fast Food Avenue.

She could understand why Betty Schlicher had followed her the day before. But why was Betty on her tail again this morning? What did the woman want? For an anxious moment, Hana considered the possibility that Betty had administered a slow-acting poison along with her merry tea and was waiting to witness the results.

Making no further effort to shake the red car, Hana drove to the police station. She had the good fortune to find nearby street parking. Betty had apparently forgotten to order the spirit forces to reserve one for herself, and Hana had the satisfaction of seeing her frustrated expression as she drove by. As Hana pumped money into the smiling face of a meter, she saw Betty parking at a fireplug.

Hana wondered if she had enough pull here to see that Betty got a ticket immediately.

Kochen was in, going over papers on his desk, behind his private partition with its covering of carpeting. He looked glad to see her.

She sat in the plastic molded chair which, despite appearances, was vaguely comfortable.

"I'm glad you're here," he said. "You're a hard person to get ahold of."

"I've been busy."

"I understand. You have a very time-consuming hobby, after all."

She looked at him sharply but he was smiling. "You can always leave a message at the office."

" 'The cops called you again, Ms. Shaner.' No thanks."

"How about 'Tell her Will called'?" she murmured.

His glasses slipped as he wrinkled his forehead. She noticed he was wearing a blue turtleneck. It reminded her of her own Dutch Blue clothing line.

Maybe someday they could branch out into men's items.

"Did you ever consider contacts?" she inquired curiously.

"I hate the idea of poking myself in the eye every morning. What did you want to see me about? Speaking as a police officer now, of course."

Hana decided to be brief and businesslike. After all, it's what she did best. She began a clear, concise recitation of the events of the day before, keeping unimportant details out of the narrative. She had reached the edge of the quarry when Kochen's assistant, Officer Alcorn, appeared at the opening in the partition.

"Excuse me, Sergeant, but there's this woman—"

Betty Schlicher whipped around him and strode to the desk with her hand extended. Automatically Kochen took the hand. Pressing it against her bosom, Betty leaned forward to stare into his eyes. His glasses oozed downward.

"I'm the hex woman," Betty said with warm passion.

And she looked it. In dismay Hana stared at her. Today Betty wasn't at all like the with-it woman who tended bar. She had on a flowered wrap-around skirt that nearly reached her rope sandals. She wore an earth-colored blouse ornamented with layers of necklaces from which dangled odd charms. Large looped earrings and her jangling bracelets completed the picture.

"She's been following me," Hana said loudly to break any spell Kochen might be under. "And I demand to know why!"

Betty straightened, still holding on to the sergeant's hand, bringing him with it across the desk. She ignored Hana. "Ms. Shaner and I were at the Baggenstose Quarry together yesterday. She nearly drowned. A woman of her age swimming in such a place! Unwise. If it hadn't been for me—"

"You didn't do anything!" Hana cried, rising, colliding with Officer Alcorn.

"Sergeant," he babbled, "do you want me to do . . . anything?"

Kochen extracted his hand with difficulty and fell back into his chair. Betty leaped around the desk to lean close to him.

"She wants you to dredge the quarry to look for the body of some lad she fancies she saw. *I* did not see him myself nor do I know of such a boy. But I am here to offer my considerable services if you do wish to go ahead and search. Perhaps we should, even at the risk of making fools of ourselves. Perhaps she is right. I will sit on the edge of the quarry and meditate on possible locations of the body. I can use the publicity. After all, the hex business just isn't what it used to be."

Hana shoved Alcorn out of the way and moved in to drag Betty from Kochen. "You crazy woman . . . why are you doing this?"

"Will you two—?" Kochen began in a strangled voice.

Hana had Betty's arm. Alcorn fumbled after her.

"Shall I arrest them?" he asked feebly.

"Get out of here!" Kochen roared. "I'll handle this."

Alcorn retreated as far as the doorway. Betty's arm slipped out of Hana's grasp as if it was greased. She slithered to the other side of the desk. Hana moved to follow but Kochen rose between them.

"Is that true?" he demanded. "Hana, did you come to ask me to drag that quarry for the body of a boy?"

"Not exactly—"

"Have you sufficient reason to believe a boy was drowned out there?"

"Well . . . I have this feeling . . ."

He growled. Betty's hands were on him, moving like snakes, pulling him around to her, pressing her against him. "She's so much like me, Sergeant. She has these feelings too. Sensations of impending doom. She could be a hex woman, you know. Hana Shaner has the gift! If there's a body in that deep, dark water, we will find it. I will ask her to work with me. I will gladly share the spotlight with her. All publicity. I will accept her as my sister and indoctrinate her into the mystic workings of magic—"

Hana stared at her in horror.

"Shut up!" Kochen said angrily, trying to elude her without success. "I want both of you out of this office! I'm going up to the Baggenstose Quarry with a couple of police officers and nobody else. Is that clear? If kids have been using the place, we'll secure it. If either of you shows up during this operation, you will be arrested for trespassing. And if I hear any more crap about hex, I'll see that you're charged with practicing medicine without a license. And that goes for you too," he snapped at Hana. "Now get out!"

Officer Alcorn stepped forward, apparently trying to achieve a look of authority but succeeding only in looking silly. He also looked as if he might be afraid to put his hands on Betty.

"You're so closed-minded," she sighed, releasing Kochen. " 'There are more things in heaven and earth . . .' "

Hana rushed from the office. People in other cubicles were peering out, obviously having heard enough of the scene to whet their curiosity. Head held high, eyes straight ahead, she left the building. She snapped open her sedate black umbrella, glad it hid her face. There was a ticket on her car. The meter had malfunctioned, accepting her money but not registering. Maybe it was hexed. Hana refused to acknowledge that the thought had even crossed her mind.

While she was still rummaging in her bag for her keys, Betty sauntered up to her. She carried a green umbrella edged with small tassels. It cast an interesting color over her face. The pale eyes, looking now like green glass, were mocking.

Hana located her keys and unlocked her car. "Do you want to tell me why you gave that remarkable performance in there?"

"Doing my civic duty. Saving taxpayers' money. Take my word for it: there's no dead boy in that quarry."

"I wouldn't take your word for anything!"

Betty smiled, displaying the empty space in her mouth. The woman was crazy. And now, Hana thought ruefully, Sergeant Kochen was probably putting her in the same category.

"Who is he?" Hana asked. "That boy?"

"There is no dead boy in that quarry."

"But there are going to be plenty of angry boys when the police close that hole in the fence," Hana said.

"Whose fault is that?"

Hana studied her. "You put on this scene because somebody doesn't want that quarry dragged. I'll bet he is in there."

"Think what you like. But I doubt you'll get much police cooperation now."

"Somebody paid you to do this. To keep them from really looking for that child."

"Prove it," Betty said, turning away.

Hana watched her walk up the street. Everybody who passed watched her too but she seemed unaware. Later when Hana drove by, Betty was just getting into her car. There was no ticket on the windshield.

# Chapter Twenty-seven

POCKY REILLY POKED her head around the door of Hana's private office with a grin that transformed her plain face.

"Are you ready?" she asked.

Hana loathed guessing games during office hours. "For what?"

"My Amish design! I did it again!"

"All right," Hana said with dismay. "Let's see it."

The door banged open. Pocky disappeared for a moment then reappeared with Cindy Hefflefinger, a member of Hana's office family. Together they wheeled a mannequin into the office. She had been mounted on a platform to which had been attached what appeared to be old roller skates. She was life-size, whole, and wearing a modified Amish outfit.

"Isn't this wonderful?" Cindy cried. "I just love the dress. I'd buy one myself. Hey, we could all wear them here in the office!"

"That will do," Hana told her.

Cindy winked at Pocky and left the office.

Pocky said proudly, "I draped the material around, cut it, and used some pins and Velcro. I mean, it's not really finished but it gives you the idea."

Hana faced the new mannequin. It was clever, she had to admit. Pocky had taken all the elements of a traditional Amish dress, then modernized them for style and comfort. In vivid Dutch Blue trimmed with black the effect was stunning. Pocky saw approval in Hana's eyes and pressed her advantage. Slowly turning the mannequin on its roller skates she began outlining the TV commercial. Hana had to be the one wearing the dress. In a country setting. All sorts of big-city types would be in the commercial, all suddenly transformed in their Dutch Blue dresses. A literal blue-out of the TV screen. Saturation blue. Blue sky, blue flowers. A little blue gate.

"My God," Hana said. "The Amish don't paint their gates blue to show there's a marriage-age daughter in the house."

"You know that. I know that. But it's such a romantic tradition the tourists think it's true. So why not take advantage of it? We've always used fantasy. TV commercials are pure fantasy. Why are you saying this is one fantasy we can't use?"

Why indeed?

"It's a good idea," Pocky continued stubbornly. "And I'm not going to let those freaks who broke into my house scare me out of it."

"Pocky," Hana said, "I found the other mannequin—the one they took."

"Oh, wow! Where?"

"In the old Baggenstose Quarry under ten feet of water. Whoever did it just threw it away."

"Vandals!" Pocky howled. "Destroyers!"

"Well, you've got another one now," Hana said comfortingly.

"Do I ever! And this time I took pictures of it and

put them in my safe deposit box. What d'you think, Hana?"

Talented, creative Pocky Reilly who, when Hana had found her, had been doing community theater at night and working at a cash register in a local outlet store by day. She'd had no education beyond high school and had grown up unhappily with a foster family. Hana thought of the broken, soggy mannequin in the quarry. Pocky didn't deserve that.

Pocky apparently took Hana's silence for disapproval. "Hey, I know how you feel about the Amish and, believe me, I respect that you don't want to exploit them. So I'll understand if you won't go along with it. Really I will. I was carried away before but maybe that beating I took knocked some sense into me."

Hana's phone rang. She picked it up, her eyes still on the mannequin. Mary Hafer's voice said, "The cops are here, Hana."

"Cops?"

"A Sergeant Kochen. Says his name's Will."

Hana's dark eyebrows shot up almost to her white hairline. "Tell him to make himself comfortable, Mary. I'll see him soon."

Mary Hafer chuckled.

Hana hung up and turned to Pocky. "We'll do it."

Pocky gave a triumphant hoot.

"But I won't wear the dress myself," Hana said. "Doesn't go with green eyes."

"Wear blue contacts."

"Get a younger woman. I'll lead the big-city types and be transformed by a Dutch Blue pantsuit."

Impulsively Pocky dashed around the desk and hugged her. "I don't even care that they wrecked my first one! This is much better."

Hana laughed at her enthusiasm. "We'll talk

about money and other nasty details later. On your way out, tell Cindy Hefflefinger to get started. Right now I've got business with the law."

"May I tell everybody?"

Hana nodded, her eyes on an asparagus fern nearly popping out of its pot because of Cindy's new Ferngro. "Don't dash off. You owe me one. Maybe you owe me more than one. I need a favor."

"Well, sure. Anything."

"I'm having trouble connecting with Bill Longenecker these days. He never returns my calls, so will you please tell him that I want to see the Quilt Woman. He'll know who I mean. I want to see her now. Or even yesterday." Hana shifted her eyes from the plant to Pocky's startled face. "You may come along if you wish."

"Hey, I don't know if I can get him to drop everything and—"

"Oh, I'm sure you can, Nancy. Do try."

Pocky winced at the use of her given name. "I guess I can handle it."

"Good. I'll be expecting Bill's call." Hana waited until Pocky rattled away with her mannequin, then picked up the phone again. "Send the cops in, Mary."

"One cop coming up," Mary drawled.

While she waited, Hana wondered if, instead of pressuring Pocky, she should have gone to the tourist office to lie in wait for Bill. Demanding favors from subordinates was something Hana hated to do. But she had no time to lurk around Bill's haunts and, after all, he had promised. There had to be something somebody could tell them. If the Quilt Woman was a gossip . . .

Kochen, looking more relaxed and Easter-Sunday-like than he had earlier, entered. He held a corduroy cap which, combined with the inevitable turtleneck, gave him the appearance of someone she had dated briefly in Paris one summer.

"Here I stand, hat in hand," he announced.

"Want to sit down? You may still hold the hat."

He came forward to drop into the comfortable upholstered chair at the side of her desk. "Nice office."

"So's yours."

He laughed. "Now you're pulling my leg."

"You've come equipped with all sorts of clichés today, Sergeant. Have a case that's getting to you?"

"You know it," he sighed. "I mean, seriously, you do know it. But that was no excuse for me to lose my temper this morning. I'm sorry."

"You really were way out of line," Hana said, not wanting to make this too easy for him.

"On the other hand, you shouldn't have dragged that crackpot woman down to my office."

"I didn't drag her. She followed me. Besides, I'm not at all sure she's a crackpot," Hana said stiffly. "That's what she wanted you to think and it appears she was successful."

He raised his hands expansively. "You're right. I'm a narrow-minded slob. I need some education in these delicate matters. I'm ripe for conversion. How about working on it tonight over dinner?"

A parody ran through Hana's mind. "When in spring a young cop's fancy lightly turns to . . ."

"Well, I have to eat somewhere, so why not?"

"What a gracious acceptance."

"Isn't it what you expected?"

He smiled. "Just about. I'll pick you up at eight." He rose leisurely. "By the way, we checked out the quarry."

"With scuba divers?"

"We had no reason to go that far. No report of missing kids. Everything was calm and peaceful and normal out there, except for a mannequin we found in the water. Dressed kind of strange."

Hana nodded. "I saw it. I'm sure it's the one that was taken when Pocky was attacked."

"Why didn't you tell me about it this morning?"

"I intended to. But I was asked to leave before I had the chance." Smugly she opened a desk drawer and took out a neat report, which she handed to him. "So I had my assistant type out my statement."

He took it humbly. "Thank you. You'll be glad to know we repaired the old gate where the boys go through."

"Wonderful."

"Not everybody thinks so. According to the kids who use that place, you were seeing things. And they're angry that you've spoiled their fun. You might want to be a little careful and look over your shoulder a lot."

Annoyed, Hana rose. "Why did you tell them I was involved?"

"They knew already. It impressed those boys when you popped out of the bushes while they were standing around stark naked." He grinned. "We talked to Jake Schwambach, who told us about your visit to the family and your assertion that you were pushed into the water. So we asked around about that. Nobody noticed who shoved you. They were all too busy running for their clothes."

He was still smiling. The man had the damnedest sense of humor. Hana glared at him.

"I'm glad you're such a good swimmer," he said. "See you at eight."

# Chapter Twenty-eight

BILL LONGENECKER WAS driving, his crazy curls ruffled by the breeze that came through the car window. Sunlight slanted across farmlands, turning new leaves to a golden chartreuse. A team of four mules in a field cast a long shadow. An Amish girl with muscular arms was driving them. Barefoot in the plowed earth, her skirts and apron blowing in the breeze, she looked like a daughter of Demeter. Hana turned to watch her. She had let Bill drive so that she could relax. He hadn't called until Shaner Industries was shutting down for the day, and she felt weary. Jimmy Klopp had pulled one of his famous tantrums that afternoon. His assistant of fifteen years had retired and he didn't like the woman Hana had promoted to the position. For some reason, Jimmy had wanted an outsider brought in.

Demeter's Daughter passed from view and Bill broke the sulky silence he'd maintained since he had picked her up at the office.

"I don't want you to think you can just whistle and I'll come running any old time. Those days are over."

"You did promise to take me to the Quilt Woman," Hana said soothingly.

"And you put me off."

"And now I'm putting you on."

"You're always putting me on, Hana. I shouldn't have tolerated the situation as long as I did."

Secretly Hana agreed with him, but this was hardly the time to say so. As she watched with fascination, he ran a hand through his hair, which bounced up again like coiled wires.

"How much farther?" she asked. "I must be home by eight."

"Almost there."

It was on a relatively well traveled road. Hana had been expecting another Amish farmhouse, but this was a neat brick bungalow of the sturdy 1950s kind with no more than a large kitchen garden behind it, a portion of which had been taken over by a brick garage. Annuals had already been planted in broad flower beds bordering the house. The Plain love of flowers reminded Hana of the gardens of old Germany. A neat wooden sign, handsomely carved, announced that handcrafted buggies could be ordered here. Below it another sign, this one painted white, stated that quilts were for sale. Between lawn and flower beds was an enormous, well-paved driveway and parking lot.

"We can accommodate two tour buses here now," Bill said with satisfaction. "Before they put in the new drive we used to have to park on the road."

He pulled to the rear of the lot near the garage. A sign above a white door invited them to "Enter Here."

"She's expecting us," Bill assured Hana.

He led the way. Remembering Demeter's Daughter, Hana experienced a jolt of culture shock. Inside, bright neon lights were reflected in a modern cash register. One section of the building displayed magnificent quilts that featured classical patterns in use for generations, all handmade by Amish and Mennonite women. Another section catered to those tourists not affluent enough to invest in those works of art. There were postcards, coloring books, faceless Amish dolls, scarves, and embarrassing T-shirts that made double entendres out of the name of the small town of Intercourse.

The woman who greeted Bill familiarly was dressed traditionally but Hana sensed a kindred soul. The heart of a businesswoman beat beneath the neat pins that fastened her apron to her dress. She had a pleasant face featuring sharp but genial eyes. Hana guessed her age somewhere in the fifties. While Bill and the Quilt Woman discussed the coming tourist season and details about percentages, Hana looked around the shop.

She found a quilt that was truly arresting. She loved brown tones, and this was full of them—a brown and rust sunburst against ivory, with the neatest stitching she had ever seen. She pulled it out of its plastic bag to inspect it more closely.

The next instant the Quilt Woman was behind her.

"It's a nice one, ain't so?" Her accent was broad—intensified, Hana suspected, for the wonder of innocent tourists. "That one's seven hundred dollars. It's special."

Bill belatedly introduced them. The woman's name was Lizzie Brubaker. Hana bought the quilt, suffering further culture shock when the woman accepted a credit card in payment. Bill seemed amused at Hana's reaction.

"Did Bill tell you I wanted to ask you some questions?" Hana inquired, glaring at the offending tour director.

Briskly attending to the business of the purchase, the Quilt Woman nodded. Hana hoped the sale would lubricate her cooperation. While the woman was wrapping the quilt with professional precision, Hana asked, "Do you know the Schwambach family?"

The Quilt Woman paused to look at her in surprise. "Why, sure now."

"How about the Longsdorfs?"

Lizzie Brubaker laughed as if Hana was telling jokes. She said, "Why, sure now" again, finished the quilt, and dropped the package on the counter beside the cash register.

"Have you visited the Longsdorf home?"

"*Ja*. Lots."

"Have you seen their Bible?"

The Quilt Woman looked as if she thought Hana was slightly demented.

"*Ja*."

"Do they have the family statistics, births and deaths, recorded in the Bible?"

Hana wondered if the strange surroundings were fueling her imagination or if Lizzie really looked suddenly wary.

"Why wouldn't they?" she asked.

"Have you seen it? Is the boy Matthew listed there?"

"That's a pretty dumb question. He was one of their kids, wasn't he?"

"Was he?"

"Why, sure now."

"Are you positive?"

The Quilt Woman glanced at Bill as if to ask where he had found this one. He shrugged, disassociating himself from Hana.

"Well, I guess I am," she said. "I put it in the book myself."

"You were there when he was born?"

"We always go. Fannie and me. No matter what chores we got at home. And they come to me, too. We was always together when little ones come."

"Then you're a very close friend of both Mrs. Schwambach and Mrs. Longsdorf?" Hana asked.

"Why—we're sisters. Didn't you know that?" She laughed, a jolly robust sound Hana could never imagine hearing from Mrs. Longsdorf. "But how

could you now? You're English and it's so that
Plain folks keep to ourselves."

Hana was staring at her in amazement. Sisters.
These three women were sisters and nobody had
mentioned it.

"Why didn't somebody tell me?" she demanded.
"Bill, did you know?"

He shook his head. "We talk business."

"That's mostly what we talk with the English,"
Lizzie Brubaker agreed comfortably.

"You don't seem like sisters—" Hana began.

"Sisters under the skin," she said crisply.
"Scratch us once and you'd see. Just married different is all. Now, Elam and me—we got our business
and no farm. But that don't change how we feel
about other stuff."

Lizzie's fingers were absently caressing her new
cash register. Hana asked more questions but the
answers took her around in a circle. The boys were
just ordinary boys. Nobody knew anything. Nobody saw anything. Hana realized she was dealing
with a keen mind.

As they returned to Bill's car, Hana grumbled, "I
thought you told me she was a talker."

He sounded puzzled. "Well, she is. To the tourists
anyway. And I guess I never listened to what she
was talking about before. Market gossip, crops,
and tourists. The weather sometimes. Now that I
think about it, she never did say much about the
family."

"It seems to me you should have known they
were related."

"Hey, don't put it on me, Hana. I never even met
those Longsdorfs. How about Sal Nunemacher?
Even she didn't know they were sisters, now, did
she?"

"Apparently not."

"Because she's not Amish. You ought to know these Amish people keep to their own. They wouldn't survive if they didn't. I do business with them but I'm not one of them. Now, is that all? I've got a date tonight."

"So do I," Hana snapped. "Take me back to my car."

As Bill swung in a wide circle on the tour-bus-sized parking lot, Hana glanced back toward the entrance to the shop. Lizzie Brubaker had come to the door to watch them leave. Although she had said little, she was standing there holding her hands over her mouth in an instinctive gesture of dismay at having talked too much.

"The weird sisters," Hana said.

"Huh?"

She shook her head. "Nothing. These Brubakers don't seem very orthodox. They've even got electric lights."

"A few of them do."

"Her sisters don't."

He looked unhappy, as if some of his own world was coming apart. "I heard talk over at the White Unicorn that Lizzie and Elam Brubaker are joining a Mennonite church. Less rigid, you know."

# *Chapter Twenty-nine*

WILL KOCHEN HAD made reservations at a good restaurant in downtown Conover. The restored area had a number of nice places, but this one was different in its decor, which was distinctly Victorian. The fact that it fit in with its Colonial neighbors always amazed Hana.

They sat in front of an enormous gilt-framed mirror that hung on a brick wall and was surrounded by a jungle of hanging plants. In the mirror Hana could see the reflection of an orange-and-yellow Tiffany lamp, which gave her white hair a golden glow. Recalling Kochen's turtlenecks Hana had dressed casually in dark green slacks with a black "sweatshirt" in soft material. It had a scalloped neckline and had been handpainted with imaginative green foliage around the scallops and across the chest. With this she wore two emerald rings—a tiny one on the little finger of her right hand and a much larger one on the middle finger of her left. Kochen wore a dark turtleneck and a light suit. She thought she had noted some admiration in his eyes but as he sat looking at her quizzically, she wondered if she had imagined it.

They were drinking what was called a Renaissance wine from a local vineyard. A ricky-tick piano played somewhere in another room.

"I," Kochen announced, "do not know what to do."

A surprising admission from a detective.

"We've found out a great deal," she objected. "After all, we know now that Mrs. Longsdorf lied about her Bible."

She noted in the mirror that the back of his head

looked vulnerable. She had noticed that about
strong men. They looked so vulnerable from the
rear.

"Sure," he agreed dismally. "Wait'll I take that to
the lieutenant. 'This woman, sir, has lied to the police about her family Bible.' I'll get a promotion for
that one."

"You asked me to find out," she reminded him.

He was on a roll. "A search warrant to locate all
Bibles in Conover County! Maybe we can stake out
church meetings too. Find out what's going on in
those places. And let's close all the swimming holes
we can find. Get those kids back on the streets
where they belong!"

"You're getting carried away," she said coldly.

"When I said I didn't know what to do, I wasn't
talking about the case."

Hana had seen that look in men's eyes before,
although it was seldom accompanied by the reflection of a Tiffany lamp. It was always interesting to
see which Courtin' Cliché (Aunt Sissy's term)
would follow.

His was: "I was talking about you."

Except that he should have added: *and me.*

She took a sip of wine. "You could arrest me for
interfering with a police investigation."

He nodded solemnly. "You are interfering. Apparently you have a thing for it. But I don't want to
arrest you. Believe me, I don't."

The next line was, "What would you like to do
with me?" but Hana had no intention of giving that
one. At least, not yet.

"You're feeling frustrated about the case, aren't
you?" she asked.

"I'm feeling frustrated all right."

She went on quickly, "It is a very unusual case.

Not many children are murdered that way. And certainly not many Amish. And then there's the hex angle."

His eyes glinted behind his glasses. She knew she had lured him away from personal matters.

Not quite.

"Oh, yes. Hex," he said distastefully, then took a large swallow of wine as if to wash it away. He set down his glass and moved uncomfortably in his plush chair before he went on. "You know, Hana Shaner, you're an amazing woman. You're by far the most successful businesswoman in the county, maybe the state. Your company is booming with American products when foreign imports are everywhere. You're modern. Sophisticated. And yet I have the ungodly feeling you actually believe in this witchcraft every bit as much as these farm women."

"And the farm men," she added.

"Okay, okay. Let's not get into that."

"Why not? How many policewomen and women detectives are there on the Conover force?"

"Quite a few. Don't change the subject. I would really, seriously, like to hear how you feel about . . . hex." He seemed to have trouble with the word. "I would like to understand why you feel the way you do. At least, I'd like to try to understand."

When a question was asked seriously Hana always believed in replying in kind. But this one wasn't going to be easy.

"Maybe you can never really understand if you're not from around here. It's in our blood, I think. We carry the past around with us more than other people. The Amish certainly do, but it goes for the rest of us too in lesser degrees. These beliefs go back to Celtic Europe. The Germanic people were more isolated than the coastal dwellers, less influenced by the outside culture of Rome, for example. They kept to their old ways on isolated farms and vineyards in the river valleys. Then later they just transplanted everything over here. They still hold local Oktoberfests that are actually harvest festivals predating Christianity. They brought their language along, of course. Our dialect is what was spoken in the lower Rhine valley two hundred years ago. Really archaic. Funny. There it changed. Here it didn't, except for adding some English words."

"A lot of what you're saying could also be said of the Polish people. We've kept the old festivals, dances, folk traditions. But it's the witchcraft that goes with yours that blows me away. You not only brought the language, you brought the hex tradition. Why have you people continued to believe in it today?"

"And tomorrow," she smiled. "Don't forget tomorrow."

"You're teaching the young people?"

Hana thought about it. Teaching the young . . . Were they? Was somebody? Could it be a motive for these killings? Was it possible in this modern, strident society that young people would take a giant step from incantations to murder?

"I don't know," she admitted. "Anyway, I would hope they'd be taught the benign white witchcraft."

"You believe dabbling with the occult can be benign?"

"It's all a matter of intent. My Aunt Sissy did some of it. So did your grandmother, I daresay."

"Never!"

"No? When you were hurt as a child, didn't she ever 'kiss it to make it better'?"

"That's not the same thing—"

"It *is* the same thing. I've seen bleeding stopped. When I was about twelve Mr. Fred was hurt by a power mower and Aunt Sissy stopped the bleeding with a Bible verse."

She told him about her childhood visit to the hex doctor. He listened. They had more wine.

"This Aunt Sissy of yours," he said, "sounds like a very interesting person."

"She was. She raised me after my mother ran off. With another man, I think. Aunt Sissy was tall and thin. She dressed in black, good black. Silk, high-neck blouses and fine jewelry. If she'd been English one would have called her Edwardian."

"Sounds like a witch herself."

Hana laughed. "Oh, she was much too dignified for that. But she believed her world wasn't bounded by telephones and typewriters, just as I believe our world isn't held inside computers and television sets. I believe those ancient people who sat around and contemplated the stars gained knowledge we're too busy to listen for today. Just because we've closed our minds to a certain kind of learning doesn't mean it's not real. Maybe people like the Amish who live closer to the rhythms of the land and the seasons and don't have so many modern distractions have a wisdom we aren't even capable of understanding."

He looked impressed. They both had more wine. Hana was about to rise to further heights of philosophy when their meal came. She was almost sorry, even though the restaurant was noted for its sea-food broiled in the best Conover County butter and served with a large dish of lemon slices. After all, how often did one get to preach about one's favorite subject (after carpets, of course) to such an interested and interesting young man?

*  *  *

They returned to Blue Spring Hill relatively
early. He pulled up beside her Chrysler and turned
off the motor, which did really require an invitation to come in for another cup of coffee. After the
euphoria of discussion and wine had worn off,
Hana felt uneasy. She prided herself on being able
to handle men in both her business and personal
life. After all, one didn't reach forty with stars in
one's eyes. But there was something about this
man she found disturbing. If she didn't keep herself in tight control she could like him very, very
much despite his obvious flaws, among which were
lack of variety in dress, lingering obstinacy toward
being assisted in investigation, and lack of well-
fitting eyeglasses. Even if Hana had been promis-
cuously inclined she felt the time for such freedom
was long past and actually foolhardy in today's
world. Which meant a real relationship. And even
if he was willing . . .

He seemed so young. What was she thinking of?
A gigolo relationship perhaps? Aunt Sissy had once
tartly called it that when, during Hana's college
days, she had dated a construction worker to
whom she had lent a sum of money to buy his own
welding machine.

The house was quiet. And again, darker than
usual. Annoying, but Hana had matters like Will
Kochen on her mind and gave only a quick thought
to Mr. Fred's lapses. In the kitchen they found the
hearth still glowing. Mr. Fred had obviously rewarded himself with a fire that evening. If he had
gone to Bruchberg to return the hex blanket as she
had directed, he had returned early.

Two dogs and three cats followed them into the
kitchen. The dogs, wagging languid tails, looked as
if they had just awakened. But the cats were inter-

ested in Kochen. Although they had shown little preference for police officers in the past, they seemed to sense that he was not here in an official capacity and needed to be inspected on another level.

Hana invited Kochen to a seat, then put on water for instant coffee. She was unprejudiced in coffee matters. Anything from specially ground beans to instant was all right with her, just as long as it was coffee.

Kochen stepped cautiously over Kitty Fisher, who was sniffing his trouser leg, and sat at the table. Gray Trouble immediately leaped onto it and stared into his face.

"I hope you like animals," Hana said cheerfully.

"Well . . ."

"They know when a person doesn't like them."

"Oh, I like them well enough," he said quickly.

"But you don't have a companion animal."

"It's my hours. Long and erratic." Gray Trouble stared hard into his eyes. "It wouldn't be fair to the animal," Kochen finished lamely, speaking directly to the gray cat.

Penelope Baskin jumped onto his lap. She stood there for a few seconds to gauge his reaction, then wound her calico body into a ball and lay down.

"She can lie like that for hours," Hana told him.

"Oh. Really?"

The dogs asked to be let out. Mr. Fred had obviously retired, even though he customarily stayed up until about one o'clock. Sometimes Mr. Fred could actually be thoughtful.

"It's just us and the cats," Hana said as she poured water into dark crystals. Then she wished she hadn't said that. Somehow it sounded like an invitation.

"I guess one does get used to having them around," Kochen remarked uncertainly.

Gray Trouble yawned in his face.

"If he bothers you, just move him. Sal's forever putting him on the floor but we just can't seem to break him of getting on this table," Hana said indulgently as she placed Kochen's cup in front of him, beside the cat.

Gray Trouble sniffed at it. Kochen reached toward the cat. Gray Trouble hissed. Kochen withdrew his hand. Penelope Baskin looked from one to the other, then she too hissed and leaped off Kochen's lap.

He drank his coffee quickly. Conversation dragged.

"Would you like another cup?"

"No, thanks. It's getting late and I must be at work early." He rose and stepped away from the cats. "Will you walk me to the door?"

Hana grinned. "For protection from my beasts?"

The dogs asked to be let in by dramatically throwing themselves at the door. When Hana opened it they came rushing inside, smelling faintly of fertilizer.

Hana, Kochen, and the animals went into the hall. He turned abruptly, very close to her. He took her hands and leaned toward her face.

Before he succeeded in kissing her, Hana asked, "Will, how old are you?"

He paused but did not withdraw. "Thirty-six. Why? How old are you?"

His eyes were very close now, gentle. "Really?" she murmured. "Thirty-six?"

"How old did you think I was?"

"You seem very youthful. You look very young."

"So do you."

He kissed her quietly. For seconds they stood,

looking at each other before he said, "There's no hurry, Hana."

There was charm in the moment because she knew what he meant.

That charm was shattered the next instant when he turned toward the door and stepped on Kitty Fisher's tail. Both Kitty F. and Kochen were quite startled. The hollering touched off a chorus of barking, and cries from the other cats.

Kochen left quickly. Hana picked up Kitty Fisher to soothe her injured feelings. The tail was not damaged.

"I told you not to sneak around under people's feet," Hana chided. "You see what happens when you don't listen?"

Ordinarily Kitty Fisher was quite vocal in her reaction to any sort of scolding. Now she just quietly nuzzled Hana, putting her head under Hana's chin and hiding her face.

"What's wrong?" Hana asked. "Are you really hurt?"

The calico cat, still clinging to Hana, turned her head to look down the hall toward the front of the house. Hana heard Kochen's car pulling away.

Hana knew her cats. They communicated with her in body language and sometimes even verbally. Kitty Fisher was telling her that something was wrong. Had Mr. Fred tactfully retired upstairs because she had brought home a date? Or wasn't he in the house? Was she alone with the animals?

"Ghost. Crumb," she said in a low voice.

They came to her side, Ghost's toenails clicking on the wooden floor. Hana put down Kitty Fisher, who immediately scurried back toward the kitchen and the laundry room. Hana shooed the other two cats after her and closed the kitchen door to keep them safely out of the way.

Followed by the dogs, she went softly along to
the wide hall and foyer at the front of the house.
Two standing lamps usually turned on here were
dark. Only the small sconces on the wall were lit.
Quickly Hana ran upstairs and through another
hall to Mr. Fred's door. She tapped, then opened it.
No Mr. Fred.

She stood still, listening. Silence. The dogs did
nothing to support her uneasy feeling. But then,
they had ideas of their own about who was acceptable and who wasn't. Surely whoever was here had
heard Kochen and her come in. Why hadn't they
left? Were they waiting for her to go to bed? Or just
waiting for her?

Ghost and Crumb, brave watchdogs, meandered
into the unfamiliar territory of Mr. Fred's room,
where they were not allowed, jumped on his bed,
and lay down together.

Across Hana's mind suddenly flickered a memory of icy water, of her struggles to get out of her
jacket. Of the jacket sinking into darkness below
her, taking her pistol along with it.

Oh, God. She should have arranged to get another .22 immediately.

Then she remembered Mr. Fred's gun. She felt
almost like a child as she slipped into his room to
the old oak bureau. As a child she had often rummaged among his things, pleasantly startled by
some of his odd treasures, some of which she suspected now had been put there for her dismay.
She'd been a horribly inquisitive kid and wasn't
proud of it. She sometimes wondered why Aunt
Sissy had permitted such conduct.

Although Mr. Fred was self-righteously fond of
declaring that he kept his gun under lock and key,
the drawer where he hid it beneath old receipts,
travel folders, antique postcards, and a college cat-

alog from 1940 was not locked. She groped through the ephemera for a few panicky moments before she found it. Wow. It felt as heavy as a small cannon. It was nothing like her dainty, almost pretty weapon, but Mr. Fred had given her shooting lessons with this monstrosity. She checked and was surprised to find it loaded. Did Mr. Fred have fears that his display of moldy bones might be ripped off?

On the bed, Ghost rolled onto his back and sighed happily. Crumb washed a dainty paw and closed his eyes.

"Crumb," Hana said.

He opened one eye.

"Come," she ordered.

For a moment she thought he wasn't going to obey then he rose, stretched, and jumped to the floor.

Feeling somewhat more protected, Hana went into the hall with Crumb dutifully following her.

## *Chapter Thirty*

AT THE BOTTOM of the stairs, Hana hesitated. Crumb stopped, wagging his tail.

"Sic 'em," Hana whispered.

The dog perked up his ears, then sat on his haunches.

Hana appealed to his watchdog instincts, to any hint of bloodhound in his veins, and to the concept of protecting one's own turf. When that didn't

work, she reminded him of the BEWARE OF DOGS
sign on the front gate of Blue Spring Hill. Crumb
yawned and glanced regretfully up the stairs in the
direction of Mr. Fred's bed.

"Heel," Hana snarled.

Since she had nothing else to go on, she let her
instincts guide her in the direction of the 1812 Annex. At the entrance to the conservatory, she hesitated. This was where she had found Teddy Jolf
lurking. And she would have taken a bet now that
it was Ms. Teddy Jolf, the used book dealer, who
was again in the house. It would explain the indif-
ference of the dogs, who liked Teddy, and would
also explain Mr. Fred's absence. Apparently Teddy
could talk him into anything, even deserting the
premises at night.

Hana looked down the hallway toward the Annex with its bones, relics, and new light show. She
didn't want to go in there. There was something
very weird about the place now that Mr. Fred had
turned it into an above-ground graveyard. She
turned toward the nearby library door. She had
asked herself before why Teddy Jolf had gone to
the conservatory rather than the library. Perhaps
this time . . .

Cautiously Hana tiptoed to the door, took a deep
breath, then flung it open and leaped into the
room. With her left hand she reached for the light
switch. In her right she held Mr. Fred's .45 as
steady as possible.

The huge, comfortable room was illuminated
with wall brackets and glowing lamps. Trying to
keep her back to the shelves of books lining the
wall so that nobody could creep up behind her,
Hana moved forward, looking everywhere—before, behind, around chairs and sofas.

Agreeably, Crumb followed for a little way then

jogged on ahead. At a neat brown sofa he paused, wagged his tail, and gave a friendly bark.

Both hands now holding the increasingly heavy gun, Hana said, "I know you're there, Teddy Jolf. So just get up slowly and save both of us a lot of trouble. Because I'll shoot. Maybe not to kill but I'll shoot."

Teddy peeped above the back of the sofa.

"Okay, okay," she said.

Hana felt ridiculous but hoped Teddy wouldn't realize it. Her arms were quivering from the weight of Mr. Fred's miniature cannon.

"Come out," she ordered gruffly.

Hands raised, Teddy came from behind the sofa. Crumb greeted her affectionately.

"Sit," Hana ordered, edging toward a telephone on an end table.

Looking surprised, Crumb sat on the floor. Teddy dropped onto the sofa.

"Can we talk?" she asked.

"No."

Hana awkwardly shifted the gun to one hand as she picked up the phone.

"But you don't even know why I'm here," Teddy said desperately.

"You're a used book dealer. You're skulking around my library at night. I'd say it's pretty obvious why you're here."

"I'm not stealing your books! I've never stolen a book in my life." Teddy seemed to take heart from the fact that the .45 was no longer pointed directly at her. "I know how this must look, but you see Mr. Fred had this appointment to interview a young man. This guy's discovered some very interesting old maps of Indian burial grounds. It seems there was one in the area of your biggest spring."

Hana stared at her, aghast. Not more digs. Steal the whole library but not more digs.

Teddy Jolf pressed her advantage. "I was busy in the Annex and the Open House is almost here, after all. It seemed dumb for me not to finish what I was doing, so I persuaded Mr. Fred to let me stay, okay?"

"No way is it okay. But I'll talk to Mr. Fred later. Right now I'm talking to the police."

Teddy spread her hands in a gesture of defeat. "I'll confess! Only please don't call the cops."

Hana replaced the receiver and gratefully clasped the gun in two hands again. "Very well. Confess."

"I'm not trying to steal anything. I swear. But it's true I did arrange this interview to get Mr. Fred out of here. You stopped me before, when I was looking for that entrance to the conservatory from outside. If I'd found that I could have come anytime, but this way all I could do was play games with Mr. Fred so I could hunt."

"Hunt what?"

"Your Aunt Sissy's notebook."

Hana nearly dropped Mr. Fred's .45. Aunt Sissy, dead for a decade, was part of the past as surely as the bones in the 1812 Annex.

"Did you know my Aunt Sissy?"

"Well, actually, no. Since we're being honest. But I've heard so much about her, I kind of feel like I do."

"From Mr. Fred?" Hana demanded.

"And from my grandmother," Teddy said with dignity. "She respected your aunt very much."

Hana was almost afraid to ask. "Who is your grandmother?"

Teddy smiled. To Hana it seemed like a wicked,

eerie smile more befitting the 1812 Annex than the warm library.

"You met her," Teddy said in a low voice. "She was the old hex woman your aunt took you to when you were a child."

Hana sat in a chair facing Teddy Jolf and rested the gun in her lap as all sorts of unpleasant sensations rippled through her. That Teddy had something to do with the dead boys she had no doubt. More awful was the feeling that somehow her own dear, long deceased aunt was involved with these recent murders. The analogy of tossing a pebble into water, she thought bitterly, was appropriate here, and the ripples were reaching into her own past.

"Be careful what you say about Aunt Sissy," she said unsteadily. "She was like a mother to me. I know she took me to a hex woman one time but—"

"More than once."

"No. I'd remember."

Teddy shook her head. "You were very young when she started taking you along. They were great friends, your aunt and my grandmother. They visited a lot. She told me."

"You're lying!"

Teddy looked puzzled. "Why are you getting so upset? I'm not saying anything against your aunt. According to my grandmother, your aunt was a wonderful person. So they were friends. What's so terrible?"

Hana rose. "I don't know. Let's go to the kitchen and get coffee. I don't feel well all of a sudden. I was out this evening drinking wine. Maybe a little more than I should have."

"Please. Can't I stay here? You see, I haven't found it. Honestly, I wasn't going to take it out of here, just look at it and copy parts. If there was a

lot of material and I thought I had to Xerox it, I
intended to ask your permission. Really I did."

"I don't even know what you're talking about!"

"The notebook. Your Aunt Sissy's notebook!"

"I don't know anything about a notebook. I never
even knew she kept a notebook."

"Maybe your father didn't approve. Maybe she
thought she couldn't show it to you."

Hana was staring down at her. "Why not? What
was in this alleged notebook?"

But she knew. As Teddy Jolf spoke, the words
sounded familiar. Had Hana seen the notebook? As
a child, had she been aware of what Aunt Sissy was
doing? Was it all there beneath layers of memory?

Teddy said, "You know your Aunt Sissy didn't
spend all her time being hostess here and raising
you. I mean, everybody's got a life of their own and
other interests besides the house and the kid. So
her interest was powwow, hex, that kind of thing.
That's how she met my grandmother. Your aunt
was even thinking of writing a book about it. She'd
get my grandmother to talk to her by the hour and
she'd take notes. That much I know for a fact. She
kept a very detailed record of the conversations."
Teddy's eyes wandered restlessly to the shelves
with their rows of books. "It must be here somewhere. Maybe in the back or in some stack—that
notebook's got to be here."

"Let's go to the kitchen," Hana said firmly.

Teddy looked at her searchingly for a moment,
then reluctantly got to her feet. Crumb, apparently
deciding his duties were no longer required, left
the room ahead of them. Dragging the gun, Hana
followed Teddy. It was a shock to find herself again
thinking of Aunt Sissy as alive and involved in
today's problems. The pebble in the pond. Aunt Sissy's notebook. She felt grief all over again for Aunt

Sissy, who had not lived to write her book. Had she ever intended to write it? Or had she wanted the information for other reasons?

Hana turned off the lights and closed the library door. Teddy started to say something but Hana silenced her. In the kitchen she put wood and paper in the still glowing fireplace, then filled the kettle with water for coffee. Silently Teddy watched her. Crumb had disappeared, probably already lying in the unaccustomed luxury of Mr. Fred's bed. The cats were apparently nesting in the laundry room.

Hana left the kitchen door open because she wanted to see Mr. Fred when he came sneaking in. She placed his gun inside a kitchen drawer devoted to tea towels decorated with cats and dogs. She didn't fear Teddy Jolf. Not physically anyhow. As she got out cups, the memory of Aunt Sissy was so strong with her that she almost added one for her.

"I know that my aunt was acquainted with a hex woman and I believe your story that she was your grandmother. Also, I do recall Aunt Sissy writing a lot. She did keep notebooks—lots of housekeeping records and that sort of thing. So maybe she kept the one you're talking about. But, believe me, if it exists it's not in the library. I spent a fortune a couple of years ago having that entire collection cleaned and catalogued. If there had been such a notebook it would have shown up in my inventory. So you see, all your sneaking around and machinations for getting Mr. Fred out of the house were useless."

Teddy looked into her eyes. "It was rotten of me. I'm really sorry."

"It's why you joined the Historical Society and tried to get next to Mr. Fred, isn't it?"

"Not entirely. I love history. It's my subject. But some of that was there of course. I know now I should have come straight to you and asked. But, you're pretty unapproachable."

Hana was startled. She had never thought of herself that way.

Teddy explained, "I mean, from my point of view. Hey, you are one rich, successful woman. And here I am, just me and my little book business. I really hated to lay all this on you. I didn't know what you'd think."

"I still don't know what to think," Hana admitted. "You tell me my aunt kept a notebook that apparently contained a lot of occult information she got from your grandmother. She must have done some of those interviews nearly forty years ago. Why are you after it now?"

"This is the part I didn't think you'd swallow," Teddy said with embarrassment.

"It's the part I'm anxious to hear. And it had better be good, because I can still call the police and charge you with trespassing. This is my home and I didn't invite you here. In fact, I specifically ordered you to stay away."

Teddy sighed. The clock ticked. Hana grew impatient but kept her peace. She wondered if Teddy was killing time, waiting for Mr. Fred.

Finally the bookdealer said, "You're really not going to believe this."

"For God's sake," Hana said irritably, "get on with it."

"Yeah. See, I was as close to my grandmother as you were to your Aunt Sissy. I learned as much as I could from her but she just wouldn't teach me to powwow. My parents . . . I think they were ashamed of her. Real middle-class. Conservative. Finally they even forbade me to go visit her. I had to sneak off. I was just a kid and it was really hard to spend the time with her that I needed. Don't you see?" she cried with sudden passion. "Your Aunt Sissy's notebook is the only way I can get to be a hex woman."

Hana sucked in a breath. "You want to be . . . ?"

"Right."

"That's ridiculous," Hana said, glad to hear herself sounding sensible. "It's something out of the last century. Nobody does that anymore."

"Betty Schlicher does."

Yes, Hana knew well enough that Betty Schlicher did. So did others. But one never asked how they did it. Or where they learned. Only vague mentions of knowledge handed down through generations. PhDH. Doctor of Hexerei. Hana drank her coffee.

Teddy leaned across the table. "Don't you know that I was aware of the chance I was taking by prowling around this place? Do you think I wanted to end up in jail or in the hospital because somebody mistook me for a thief? I unstrung a whole arm of Mr. Fred's favorite skeleton so I could stay here and rethread it. I didn't want to do that. I don't want to beg, but *please* help me find that notebook. *Please* let me read it."

Hana leaned back to escape Teddy's intensity. "My God, my aunt's been dead for years. The chances of finding her notebook are pretty slim, wouldn't you say?"

"But there is a chance. Isn't there a chance? Isn't there someplace we can look?"

"Why is it so important to you?"

Teddy's fist smashed against the table, rattling the cup. "Because Betty Schlicher is evil! And she's doing harm to people. See, they think she's a white witch, but she isn't. Believe me, she isn't. My grandmother worked with these people her whole life and she cared and I care. I want to help them like she did. I'm a nurse, Hana. I can combine the knowledge. I can really help."

Firelight flickered across Teddy Jolf's face. Midnight madness, Hana thought. Teddy looked mad and *was* mad, so obsessed with becoming a hex that she broke into Hana's home to search for a nonexistent notebook. Hana was mad for listening to her. And yet, truthfully, there was something about Betty Schlicher that was a turnoff. It was possible that she was evil.

And then Hana recalled something she rarely thought about.

In one sense Aunt Sissy had never died. Aunt Sissy was still here at Blue Spring Hill.

## *Chapter Thirty-one*

MR. FRED WAS obviously tired. He had to be, because he accepted without comment the sight of Teddy Jolf and Hana sitting together at the kitchen table. He even accepted a cup of coffee. He was also angry. He declared that Teddy had sent him on a fool's errand. The young man he had gone to interview had no real evidence that there was an Indian burial ground anywhere around the Blue Spring. He had old maps all right, but they were obviously not of this area.

Hana allowed herself a few moments of relief before she said coldly, "It was just an excuse to get you out of the house. You walked out on your responsibility to Blue Spring Hill. You should be more careful in the future."

His sputtering was another indication of his fatigue. Mr. Fred never sputtered. He always had his dignity to fall back upon. Hana took pity on him and explained briefly about Teddy's quest, leaving out the bookdealer's passion and her career hopes for the position of Number One Local Hex.

When he realized the direction the conversation was heading, Mr. Fred became more wary, withdrawing his scrawny neck into the collar of his coat so that his big head appeared to be sitting directly on his shoulders.

What Hana had recalled were the special bedrooms, known in the family as the "Dead Rooms." Besides the servants' quarters, Blue Spring Hill contained numerous spacious bedrooms. Some were kept up as guest rooms. Hana had her own rooms, of course. Mr. Fred, because of his years of service and the fact that Hana's father had wanted him close by during the last years of his life, had long ago graduated from the servants' area to his present comfortable accommodations. At the other end of the hall, existing in an eternal twilight of closed shutters, was the Grandmother's Room. Really a great-great-grandmother, she had died a generation or more before Hana was born, and no one remembered just why her room had been left intact as if waiting for her to return.

Perhaps the grief of her passing had been particularly intense, or perhaps everybody had been preoccupied with their own affairs and it had been permanently neglected. Whatever the reason, it had established a tradition at Blue Spring Hill. Since the rooms were not needed they remained the property of the dead. There was also the Grandfather's Room. And a room called simply

"Dorothy's room," although even Hana's father could not recall a relative of that name. There were other rooms too, including Hana's own father's, which was just as it had been the morning he suffered his fatal heart attack. She knew that Mr. Fred attended to that room, airing it at times, cleaning it. Mr. Fred had charge of all the Dead Rooms.

Including Aunt Sissy's.

"Her room is still here?" Teddy asked in disbelief after she had heard Hana's explanation. "Her things are still there?"

"No one but family has ever gone into those rooms," Mr. Fred said, obviously including himself in that select company.

As a child, Hana had been taken into the various Dead Rooms by the necrologically inclined Aunt Sissy. She recalled being confused as to whether or not these people had really gone. She avoided the excursions whenever possible.

"Please!" Teddy appealed to Mr. Fred. "Please, let's look. It's so important."

Mr. Fred, who apparently had a soft spot in his heart as well as his head in matters concerning Teddy Jolf, looked inquiringly at Hana.

"Why not?" she asked. "What harm could it do?"

But she felt nervous. She made sure that the doors of the house were locked and the alarm system turned on. As to the question of what harm it could do, she fancied a battle between Good Witch Teddy and Bad Witch Betty might have an unsettling influence on Conover County.

Hana had not been in Aunt Sissy's room for years. But it was the place to which she had run for comfort and companionship during her growing up. It remained in every detail the way she remembered it. The pictures on the bureau—Hana with wavy blond hair, grave green eyes staring into the camera. And Aunt Sissy as a young woman in an old-fashioned dress waving to her across the years.

Hana wondered if she should do this. Especially tonight. Another time perhaps. In daylight with the shutters opened. But Teddy Jolf and Mr. Fred were already at the old rolltop desk. It had been Aunt Sissy's pride, and it still stood where light from a window that was now shuttered had once found it every day. Hana remembered the golden oak gleaming in morning sunlight. She sat on the bed, recalling how often she had crawled into it, welcomed into the safe circle of Aunt Sissy's arms.

She hoped she wouldn't embarrass herself by bawling out loud.

Dimly she heard Mr. Fred's voice saying ". . . be very careful. I want everything replaced exactly as we found it. This is a shrine, you know."

Hana let the memories come as her eyes traveled slowly about the room.

Mr. Fred's instructive voice faded as another came through to Hana, very loud and clear. "No, Hanny, there are things in here that little girls wouldn't understand. Let's get out the old bead box instead. We'll make a pretty necklace to show your daddy when he comes home."

There was a small, very ancient chest, decorated in the old style with wallpaper, on the bottom of a bookshelf. Hana had, after Aunt Sissy's death, opened the box and taken a quick look inside. The will had been on top and underneath there had been notebooks, among other personal things. At the time she'd had no heart to investigate them and, unless Mr. Fred had looked through them . . .

Feeling strangely numb, she slipped off the bed and went to the small drawer in the bureau. The key was still there, beneath fragile lace handkerchiefs an unlucky Shaner cousin who had died in Belleau Woods had sent to Blue Spring Hill during World War I. Slowly she took out the key and carried it to the old chest. Gently she lifted the chest from its shelf and placed it on the floor. Hana pushed the key into the stiff lock. Teddy Jolf and Mr. Fred were mumbling over things they were finding in the desk. It took Hana some minutes to work the lock.

Even without touching the notebooks, she knew she had found what they were looking for. She sat with her own thoughts, staring into the chest. Aunt Sissy, despite her love of black clothing, cemetery picnics, and excursions into the past of Blue Spring Hill—she would have loved Mr. Fred's museum— had been very modern in her own way. She always had her hair done at a beauty salon, always drove a new car . . .

Hana lifted out the notebooks. Beneath them were the very old, very valuable but well-used volumes of the Sixth and Seventh Books of Moses, occult writings Aunt Sissy had publicly vowed would never be part of their library. Hana was tempted to lock up the chest, declaring it off limits. She might have done it, except for the knowledge that in one of these notebooks were words which had come down to them from Teddy Jolf's grandmother. Fairness dictated that the grandchild be allowed access to them.

Hana lay the notebooks tenderly back inside the chest and said, "I've found it."

Mr. Fred and Teddy were beside her immediately. Mr. Fred turned on another lamp. Hana sat back, letting them into Aunt Sissy's secret life, watching as Teddy lifted a notebook and reverently paged through it.

"Wow," she said.

Yes. Wow.

Hana got up and moved toward the door. She needed sleep. Even more, she needed to get out of that room. She paused.

"Mr. Fred, take that chest down to the library. Keep it locked in one of the cabinets except when Teddy wants to come to read the notebooks. I don't want these things ever to leave this house nor to be copied. Is that clear?"

Teddy looked bewildered. "But how am I going to . . . ?"

"Memorize them," Hana said. "I'm sure that's what your grandmother did. What any good witch would do. Mr. Fred, I'm holding you personally responsible for this material. And watch her. She's a tricky one."

"No," Teddy vowed. "I promise . . ."

Hana left the room, closing the door on Teddy's declarations of virtue and honesty. She was glad her own room was so close. She felt exhausted.


# Chapter Thirty-two


THE APPARITION OF Mr. Fred in his dressing gown tearing into the kitchen caused Hana to spill her coffee and Sal Nunemacher to give a startled cry.

"Where's Old Ugly?" he cried.

"Look in the mirror," Hana snapped as she grabbed her napkin and dabbed at the coffee spreading across the polished boards of the kitchen table.

He sputtered, clutching at his yellow-and-green plaid robe, which was threatening to reveal more of Mr. Fred than either Hana or Sal cared to see. His bare spindly legs suggested that there was little beneath the robe except Mr. Fred himself.

"Why, you should be ashamed!" Sal exclaimed. "Coming down here in front of ladies like that."

He placed his big bony hands at strategic places on the robe but held his ground as he demanded, "Who took Old Ugly?"

Hana paused in her mopping operations. "Is that what you call your gun?"

"It's what everybody calls those guns," he informed her. "Even in World War II. And before that. It's an affectionate term for a reliable weapon and mine is missing."

"It's in the kitchen drawer under the tea towels," Hana said, helping herself to more coffee.

"*Ach!*" Sal exclaimed in dismay. "What's a thing like that doing in my towels?"

Mr. Fred rushed to the drawer, opened it, and rummaged until he found the .45.

"Don't ever take Old Ugly again," he said.

"Then don't make it necessary by permitting somebody like Teddy Jolf to be alone in this house."

"Well, you best keep that ugly thing out of my drawers," Sal told both of them as she furiously straightened towels, whipping out those that had touched the gun for a purification rite in the automatic washer.

Ignoring her, Mr. Fred marched toward the hall in his yellow terrycloth slippers, fringed and tied with bows, which had been a homemade gift from Sal the preceding Christmas. He paused at the doorway and turned to glare at Hana.

"Furthermore, there is dog hair on *my* bed," he announced before he made a dramatic exit.

Hana snickered and looked at Sal. In another moment they were laughing together. Sal finally wiped her eyes on her apron and headed for the laundry room. Hana finished her breakfast in good humor, then checked with her office by phone. She had decided to spend the morning with Mr. Fred, a not entirely delightful prospect however necessary.

He took much longer than usual to get downstairs in full black-suit uniform. Hana suspected he had been dawdling, hoping to avoid her after his appearance in dishabille. She was in her at-home office with the door open as he passed. She let him go and waited a decent interval before following him to the kitchen. She even permitted herself to think kindly of the poor soul, who very obviously was working unusually hard on the Open House. At any other time he was the first to be up in the morning and always properly attired. She was filing his performance this morning in mental notes to be used as blackmail if he began another archaeological dig on her property.

He looked at her unhappily over his bowl of yogurt, wheat germ, and apple sauce.

She grinned.

He looked down again.

"I need your help," she told him.

"I'm busy," he said curtly. "The Open House is almost upon us."

"Too bad," she sighed. "I guess that means I'll have to use—what did you call it?—'Old Ugly' again when I need a weapon."

He paused with a large spoonful near his mouth. "What do you mean?"

She leaned across the table. "I've lost my .22. Irretrievably. And I need a weapon. I want you to help me get one. This morning."

He resumed eating. "I don't know why you're in such a hurry. You never had a real weapon. That was a toy. The minimum that's needed for impact is a .38."

She smiled. "Anything you say. As long as it's this morning."

"Impossible. I've got to be at the Historical Society at ten o'clock," he objected. "There's an important meeting."

"Who's paying your salary?" she inquired pleasantly. "Me or the Historical Society?"

"The meeting is to finalize plans for the Open House."

"With all the work you've done surely that won't take long," she said pointedly.

"Actually, I don't think it will be a long meeting."

"Then we'll go together and after your meeting we'll get my gun."

"Pistol."

"Whatever you say, Mr. Fred."


The Conover Historical Society was housed in a twelve-room mansion built around the time of her own 1812 Annex and, in Hana's opinion, just as ugly. A basic square box, not bad in itself, but where those people had found dark green stones for building blocks she couldn't imagine. It wasn't mossy green, which would have been attractive, but a dark, somber color. Nobody had ever seen fit to change the trim from its original dungeon brown but had faithfully, through the years, repainted in the same color. A heavy black wrought iron fence surrounded the property where ancient oaks towering above the house had long since

killed off any enterprising grass that had attempted
to grow.

If there was a local chapter of Druids, this was
surely where it would meet. Hana decided Mr.
Fred looked right at home here. So indeed did Mr.
Pettengill, who emerged from a dark corner of the
foyer to stare at her through his thick glasses.

Although new lights and wiring had been installed, the interior always seemed dark.

The committee was gathered in a schoolroom-
like conference area, which was decorated with
photographs of former presidents of the society
staring from their frames with malevolent hauteur.
Teddy Jolf, looking prim and bookish in a navy
suit and white blouse with a Peter Pan collar,
greeted Hana as if they shared guilty knowledge.
Bert and Josie Adams arrived late and breathless,
full of enthusiasm for the booth they would be op-
erating.

Hana sat through twenty boring minutes, then
left when they began wrangling about numbers of
trash receptacles needed. Despite her reservations
about the building itself, Hana had a high opinion
of the exhibits. Her particular favorite was a large
diorama depicting the center square of Conover in
the days when open market stalls attracted people
from the surrounding countryside to the excitement of market day in the town. A retired school-
teacher had researched and labored for ten years
to complete the project.

Since the building was only open afternoons, except on Saturday, Hana had the entire place to herself. First she checked the conference room again,
to find the committee had moved from the subject
of trash to the matter of first aid facilities. Then she
tiptoed past and began to prowl.

In a closet storage area she found boxes of bot-

tles from the old Conover Brewery, which had
never reopened after Prohibition. This prompted
her to open more doors. She found a janitor's
closet and the basement door. Steps led into the
darkness below. She recalled hearing that treasures not considered important enough for perma-
nent display were stored down there.

Hana turned on the light switch just inside the
door. The stairs felt solid. Down below she could
see boxes and what appeared to be a broken cigar
store Indian.

Hana went down.

It was so much less formal than the glassed display cases upstairs. Here she could touch things,
open old ledgers, hold cut glass up to the light. She
was having a marvelous time. When she glanced at
her watch she realized forty-five minutes had
passed.

The basement had been partitioned off into
rooms, and before her was an odd little door with
an enameled handle. It was too tempting to resist.
Gently Hana turned the old handle and pushed
open the door. The room was dark, but enough
light came from the main part of the basement for
her to see the contents: farm implements. Antique
by the look of them, and some with soil still clinging to them. She was about to close the door when
Jake Schwambach's triumphant voice came to her
again. ". . . ain't our pitchfork . . . couldn't even
buy a four-pronged one if we wanted . . ."

Hana stepped into the room. She could find no
light switch. Squinting, she saw that dirt covered
the floor. Her footprints showed clearly. Apparently the Mr. Pettengills who ran this place
through the years thought little of gifts of antique
farm implements. Propped against an old egg
sorter of the kind still used by most Amish families

stood a four-pronged pitchfork. In the dust on the floor were four small marks where another had rested. And behind that, another. Hana stood still, looking about. Since her own footprints showed clearly, if somebody had actually come in here looking for a murder weapon, their prints should be here too. But they were not.

Then she realized why.

A trail led to the pitchforks. Somebody had brushed away whatever prints there might have been. Hana backed out of the room and closed the door, trying not to touch the handle any more than she had already.

It had been a farm tool, and the killing had been done on a farm. Nobody had thought of the Historical Society. But somebody here at the Historical Society had been thinking of murder.

# Chapter Thirty-three

HANA PLACED THE Beretta 9mm automatic pistol on Kochen's desk and said, "I want a proper permit for this thing."

He stared at it and said, "That's not my department."

"I didn't think it was. But I thought you could facilitate things for me."

It was not, she realized, really tactful to remind him that with her connections she could go over his head and get just about anything in this town. But she had wanted to see him, and this had

seemed an effective way of saving time by doing
two things at once. The Beretta had Mr. Fred's
blessing. He had declared it to be almost a .38. She
had settled on it quickly because she had hated the
gun store. The Beretta was expensive, reliable, and
about five inches long, which meant it would fit
into her bag. Mr. Fred seemed to think it would
stop most assailants. "It will be a shock, like a
punch," he had said.

She wondered why Kochen appeared to be so
put off by it.

"Mr. Fred said it was a good weapon for me," she
told him somewhat defensively.

"I hate to have civilians carrying these things,"
he grumbled. "I suppose you think you need protection."

"I do need protection. Anybody who lives in a
museum needs protection."

He grunted derisively but dispatched Officer Alcorn for the proper papers.

"Then you'll take care of it for me?" Hana asked.

Kochen looked at her bleakly. "You're asking for
a special favor."

"As a friend," she assured him. It seemed like a
good time to change the subject. "There's another
matter. About that four-pronged pitchfork which
killed the Schwambach boy . . ."

After he heard her story, Kochen and Officer Alcorn took off for the Conover Historical Society so
fast, Hana was, after all, left to deal with her gun
permit by herself. She felt abandoned and furious
as she stood in line before a desk, then filled out a
form under the bored eyes of a policewoman who
obviously loathed paperwork.

Hannah Elizabeth Clara Shaner had never been
expected to deal with the trivia of life. Even after

the permit was in her possession and she was back at the office, she continued to think wrathful thoughts about Will Kochen. Adding to her discontent were some initial reactions to the Dutch Blue line of women's apparel. Two well-known stores, one in New York City and one in Dallas, refused to consider handling monochromatic clothing. Also, a leading fashion writer in LA poked fun at the idea in a syndicated news story.

Hana arrived home angry and upset to find her lawn bustling with activity. For a moment she froze, fearing that Mr. Fred had organized another dig for archaeological students. But these people were not digging. They were building funny little structures and running electrical lines and . . .

The damned Open House.

Her mind had been full of other things. Yes. The Open House was tomorrow. Mr. Fred and the Historical Society members, all wearing bright orange vests for identification, directed the activity. Four large and beautiful oxen, of a rich red color, were nibbling contentedly at an ornately trimmed hedge. Hana immediately transferred her wrath from Sergeant Kochen to Mr. Fred.

Her lot was so full, Hana was forced to park on the grass. Relative calm prevailed inside the house, except that Sal was still there directing a corps of daily workers in their duties, some of which apparently included preparing a meal for the Historical Society and filling with gas hundreds of white balloons, each stamped with a picture of pink azaleas.

Balloons filled the front hall. The door to her snuggery was barricaded by stacks of boxes containing Lord-knew-what. Teddy Jolf drifted past from the direction of the kitchen. Her eyes were glazed; clutched to her bosom was Aunt Sissy's notebook and in her hand a cup of tea. She wafted down the hall toward the library.

Hana, trailed by two nervous cats, escaped to her room. She called downstairs, finally got an answer from Sal, and ordered a supper tray be sent up. She wanted no more contact with humans. She fed Penelope Baskin and Gray Trouble treats from the drawer in her bedstand.

After she had showered and put on her red flannel nightie and matching robe, she felt better. She could not shut out the sound of hammering, but she could pull her drapes so she wouldn't see the abominations being committed. A smiling daily woman named Maude arrived with a tray done with Sal's usual talent. She had even included cat dishes.

At seven-thirty Mr. Fred discreetly knocked on her door. The sounds, even the scurrying house noises, had stopped. She felt sure, however, that her dining room would be full of the Historical Society chomping away. Hana did not answer until he coughed a few times then called through the door.

"Sergeant Kochen is on the phone."

"I told Sal I didn't want to be disturbed."

Mr. Fred coughed again. It was a habit he had picked up from watching British butlers on PBS television series. "He's quite insistent."

"Oh, all right."

Kochen partially redeemed himself and a portion of humanity by immediately thanking her for her discovery at the Historical Society.

"And," he chuckled, "I understand you got your gun permit without any difficulty."

"Of course," she said loftily. "Such small details can usually be handled best by oneself. Was there anything else?"

"You might want to know there were no finger-prints. Except a few of yours on that crazy door handle. And we found your footprints. I guess you realize whoever took those pitchforks brushed around that confounded dirt on the floor so that his were erased. *But* he stepped around the side of that other thing—"

"The egg separator."

"Yeah. That. And of course it was dark in there— the old room doesn't have a light—and he left a couple of prints back there. Rough shoes. Like work shoes."

"But how did he get in?" Hana asked, thinking of Jake Schwambach in the back of her car and feel-ing a little cold.

"It doesn't look as if he broke in. We checked everything."

"Somebody let him in."

"An inside job at the Historical Society?" he asked dryly.

"It could be. Don't you wonder what happened to the other pitchfork?"

"Uh-huh," he admitted.

"Do you think we'll ever find out?"

"There's a definite possibility."

"Oh, God," she said.

"Don't jump to conclusions," he advised. "I'll see you tomorrow."

"Tomorrow?"

"The public is invited to the Open House and I'm part of the public."

She could picture him grinning and perhaps pushing his glasses into place. Before she said goodbye she suggested he be sure to take an ox ride.

Hana put her tray outside her door. Since the

house was now quiet Gray Trouble and Penelope Baskin went into the hall with it.

Hana stretched out on her bed with an English mystery.

She awoke with a start, and the notion that she'd been asleep for hours. Her lamp was still lit. The book lay on the bed beside her. Groggily she groped for her clock, picked it up, and peered at it.

Two A.M.

Fumbling, she replaced the clock and sat up.

Something had awakened her. Dimly she remembered that a noise had intruded itself into a dream. An outdoor sound . . . Surely they weren't still building those cursed booths at this time of night.

Hana went to a window and opened a shutter.

The white spring moon was so brilliant she could see the colors of the azaleas ringing the lawn and, out beyond the conservatory, beds of lavender displays looking almost blue in this light. Wooden skeletons of booths for the Open House were everywhere. But, as far as she could see, nothing moved among them.

Hana raised the old window as quietly as possible and stood listening, while her eyes searched for anything out of place. She was about to give up when she saw it. It was so subtle, she wasn't even sure, but off beyond one section of woods there was the dimmest kind of glow. Slightly yellowish, an artificial intrusion into the moonlight. Just a reflection, perhaps, or even her imagination, lingering from a dream. She knew that woods. A path led to a clearing.

Hana hesitated. Mr. Fred, she suspected, was exhausted. And, anyway, this was probably nothing at all. She wouldn't bother him. She had four-legged friends she would call upon.

Hana put on stockings and shoes, and her jacket. Although she'd had no time to practice with the new gun, she loaded it and slipped it into her pocket. She found the flashlight she kept in the drawer of her bedstand and left the room.

# Chapter Thirty-four

GHOST AND CRUMB were agreeably surprised at Hana's suggestion of a nighttime prowl. Kitty Fisher slipped out with them when Hana opened the door. Hana always had feelings of uneasiness when she turned off the alarm system at night. She supposed that someday when she did it, legions of bad guys would leap from the woods and sack Blue Spring Hill.

But this time at least, nothing of an extraordinary nature happened. The four of them crossed the parking lot. Hana walked in the shadows of the azaleas when they reached the lawn and took a roundabout path to the woods.

An Anglophile her grandfather had known—a beautiful woman who might have been Hana's grandmother if she had not spent so much time in England only to return after many years to make trouble in Grandfather's marriage to a local suffragist—had loved the work of Capability Brown, who had transformed so many English Stately Homes, and the woman's hand was all over the landscaping at Blue Spring Hill. It accounted for much of the arrangement of meadows, mounds, woods, and ponds. It also accounted for the miles of pathways.

The woodland was still spare with spring, but overhanging trees gave the path through it a cavernous, foreboding appearance. Hana did not want to advertise her presence with her flashlight. Crumb, who took his dog business seriously, was at her side, warily looking about. Ghost ran in happy circles, celebrating this adventure. Hana hissed at him. He came reluctantly. She grabbed his collar, shook it a little, and whispered orders. Perhaps the unusual nature of the expedition impressed him, because he fell into step with them as they moved into the woods.

Hana went forward cautiously. At first she heard the furtive scurrying of night creatures, but even this sound ceased as they went deeper into the trees. Hana had almost forgotten Kitty Fisher until she checked the path behind and saw the cat padding after them.

They passed an area where small springs gurgled. Lush with cresses, the springs watered patches of Indian moccasins and spring beauties. Maybe tomorrow, if she could get away from all the splendid festivities Mr. Fred had planned, she could see this place in daylight. Another sound was beginning to intrude into the bubbling of the springs. Hana paused. Obediently the dogs stopped with her. It was what had awakened her. It had to be hammering. The path curved gracefully, which was fine for strolling but prevented a view ahead. Hana stumbled over a rock that had somehow intruded on the walkway and swore under her breath. Ghost sniffed at the offending rock, then wagged his tail.

Hana continued with greater caution. The hammering sound grew louder. She estimated they had come about three city blocks. Around another bend in the trail, she could see the clearing ahead. And she had been right. There was definitely some sort of artificial light in the meadow.

The dogs were now alert. Ghost's hair was standing up and he issued a growl low in his throat.

"Shh," Hana whispered.

Her own hair felt as if it were rising a little too because she knew what she would find at the clearing in the woods.

The dogs stayed very close to her. When she was several yards from where the trail entered the meadow, Hana left the path to creep among the trees. Although dry leaves from last year rustled, she hoped that the sound of the hammering would cover her movement. A protecting hedge of wild, thorny raspberry bushes edged the woods at this point. Standing in shadows, Hana could see over the raspberries into the meadow.

Even though she had been expecting something like this, the effect was uncanny. In the open, where the woods curved around to provide a private place unseen from any driveway, a cabin had been built. Two people were still working on finishing it in the yellow light of a kerosene lamp. The building was so like Hana's childhood memory of the hex woman's shack to which Aunt Sissy had taken her, that she felt sick. Wooden shingles. A porch. Everything. It couldn't have been constructed in just one night. They must have worked on it for days, their activity covered by the commotion of preparing for the Open House.

They. Even in the dim light, Hana recognized them: Betty Schlicher and her barman, Barry Moyer. He was hammering the last board of the steps to the porch into place. Betty, in a long, tattered-looking gray skirt, was hanging bundles of dried herbs about the porch.

Something moved in the meadow. Hana had assumed that Kitty Fisher, who knew more about the grounds of the estate than Hana, had gone about her own business. After all, cats were not dogs and could not be expected to involve themselves as thoroughly in human affairs. But there was Kitty Fisher walking sedately toward the cabin. A few feet from the steps she stopped and sat down. From within the dimly lit interior of the new cabin, a figure slipped out to sit on the edge of the porch and stare at Kitty Fisher. It was the pale-eyed cat Hana had seen at Betty's apartment.

The barman stopped working and looked at the cats. Betty too paused to watch Kitty Fisher. Hana held her breath. Hair bristling, the two dogs stared through the raspberry thicket. For moments nobody moved. Then the cat on the porch challenged Kitty Fisher in a low, almost human, voice. Kitty F. yowled back.

Still nobody moved. Hana could see her own cat's tail expanding. Betty Schlicher came slowly off the porch and down the steps. She stared at Kitty Fisher then raised her eyes to the woods. Hana would have sworn she could not be seen and yet the woman appeared to be looking directly at her. Hana's hand slipped into her pocket to touch the Beretta.

Betty's cat followed her mistress off the porch, moving stiff-legged, right toward Kitty Fisher. Both animals howled in condemnation. Ghost growled. Hana put a hand around his muzzle. Betty was smiling toward the woods.

Then an unusual thing happened. Kitty F., who had the fighting instincts and the voice of her Siamese parent, turned and dashed back into the shelter of the trees. The hex woman's cat did not follow but stood at attention, staring after her opponent. Barry, the barman, started to say something. Betty gestured him to silence and the three of them went into their cabin.

Hana continued to hide, sure they were watching. She wondered if Mr. Fred had given them permission to build this shack for the Open House. But why was it so far from the others, and why hadn't she been told? Or had this been Betty's own idea?

Crumb fidgeted and finally lifted his leg at a nearby tree. Hana waited for another fifteen minutes. The light still shone from the shack but she saw no movement. Taking a chance, she crept back the way she had come with the dogs ambling after her.

When she reached the path she walked faster, pausing every few feet to look behind. She saw nothing and heard nothing, although every shadow and sound startled her. It took a long time to reach the house. Kitty Fisher was waiting at the side door, anxious to get inside.

It was only after Hana was inside and had turned on the alarm system with shaking hands that she realized how unnerved she had been. She wanted to waken Mr. Fred. Call Kochen and get him out of bed. Get everybody out here—police, her private detectives and their computers, bodyguards. She decided to have a drink instead. She went to a sitting room and helped herself to brandy. But her ancestors' eyes in the portraits on the wall seemed alive tonight.

Damn Betty and Teddy Jolf and all of them!

Quickly she carried her glass to her room and locked herself in, along with Ghost, Crumb, and

Kitty Fisher. She swallowed her brandy neat and felt a little better.

Slowly she took off her stockings, shoes, and jacket. She put the new gun beneath her pillow.

She sat on her bed. She knew she needed sleep. Tomorrow was going to be a big day.

# Chapter Thirty-five

IT WAS THE commotion outside that broke through a pleasant dream of carpeting an indoor athletic field with Spider Brown. Hana peeped above the covers to find sunlight beating against the closed shutters of her bedroom windows.

Yeech. Sunshine.

Her reaction shocked her further awake. Why was she having such an averse emotion to a beautiful day? Then she remembered the Open House.

Ghost, Crumb, and Kitty Fisher, clustered at the door, set up a simultaneous yelping. Hana squinted at her clock, then squinted again. It was the obscene hour of six o'clock on a sacred Saturday morning. The sun was just up.

She closed her eyes again. Maybe she could hide in her room and when she got up tomorrow it would all be gone.

The animal chorus began again. Hana scrambled out of bed and staggered over to open the door. After they had dashed into the hall, she slammed the door behind them. Her inclination was to drop back into bed, but curiosity drew her to the window. Cautiously she lowered the louvers of her shutters so that she could see out but the invaders could not see her.

Last-minute details were being hammered and stapled onto the booths. An incredible assortment of people were trundling things into these booths via shopping carts, hand trucks, dollies, and even small automobiles, which were parked on the sacred lawns of Blue Spring Hill near the even more sacred azaleas.

In the midst of this gaggle of questionable guests, Mr. Fred floated about, looking like an emissary from Middle Earth in a flowing gray cape that he apparently hoped would make him recognizable as The Director. Not that Mr. Fred wasn't easily recognizable in any outfit. Scurrying to do his bidding was the promised "army" of Plain and fancy youths. Members of the Historical Society strutted among them with large round ID tags.

Beyond this earthly tempest bloomed a heavenly sight. It was an arch of azaleas, lovingly encouraged through the years by a succession of geniuses from Bottingers' Lawn and Garden Service and which had, overnight, fully opened into a pink blaze, cascading over its trellis, which was more than fifteen feet high. Outside the Deep South nothing like it was to be seen.

In the first rays of the sun, it was breathtaking. Fanning out from this central display azaleas clustered colorfully everywhere, in every shade from lavender through the purples and oranges to white and pale pinks. Apparently Mother Nature smiled upon Mr. Fred, because these temperamental, evanescent blooms were cooperating magnificently with his Open House.

Suddenly Hana felt better.

Perhaps it was fatigue and interrupted sleep, but

she even experienced a positive love toward the
motley crew below. They were right and she was
wrong; bad-tempered too. It was proper to share
this beauty, to allow the people of her hometown
to enjoy the unique display.

She would cooperate and be the sparkling hostess they expected on this perfect day.

Hana lingered long over her clothing, trying to
decide which outfit best suited her role as Lady of
the Manor. Automatically pantsuits were discarded
in honor of the occasion. Influenced by visions of
English garden parties, she selected a flowing,
flowery, pastel skirt to midcalf bought in some
mood of whimsy best forgotten. It had been hanging forlornly near the rear of her walk-in closet
close to some retired army jackets from college
days.

After finally enlisting the aid of the overbur-
dened Sal, who had a phenomenal memory for
Hana's fringe wardrobe, they located an off-white
overblouse that could be belted and draped nicely
over her hips. The neck was high but a border of
eyelet kept it from being austere. A cameo long ago
rescued from a Dead Room gave it an old-fash-
ioned/new-fashioned look. She wore off-white
stockings and matching shoes with two-inch heels
wide enough for comfortable turf walking.

Surveying herself in the mirror she said dream-
ily, "I ought to have a wide-brimmed picture hat."

"What you ought to have," Sal said briskly, "is a
sweater. It's nice out, but it's early still."

Hana graciously acknowledged the suggestion
by selecting a knit stole in a rainbow of colors,
some of which matched the shades of the pale flowers in the skirt.

As she was ready to go into the hall, Sal asked,
"Got your gun?"

Hana blinked. "Really, Sal. This is our Open House. It's a celebration. A springtime festival."

Sal grunted. "You got an awful lot of teenage kids out there running around loose."

"They are here to keep the peace."

"*Ja?* Now it just could be some of them are here because they're mad at you for closing up their swimming hole. Mr. Fred had me serving them coffee and doughnuts this morning—I got up at four o'clock to get here before sunup, I want you to know—and from what I heard maybe you ought to be wearing camouflage dungarees instead of that fancy getup you got on."

"But there's safety in numbers, Sal. Surely nobody would do anything on a day like this."

"A word to the wise . . ." Sal murmured as she left the room.

Of course Sal was right about the Beretta. Not just because of possibly wild teeners but also because of that presence in the clearing beyond the woods. Her excursion there during the night seemed like a dream in this dazzling day. In Aunt Sissy's tales such things disappeared with the coming of the dawn. Fairy-tale days must have been convenient when one only had to guard against evil things at night.

Hana exchanged the dainty drawstring bag she had intended to carry for a purse large enough to accommodate her new weapon. She was now anxious to join the activity. She could not really believe anybody would violate her hospitality. Surely the Open House would go off as a memorable day in the history of Conover County.

Although Sal had disappeared, fresh coffee awaited her in the kitchen. Ghost and Crumb were nowhere to be seen but the cats, even Kitty Fisher, asked to be let into the laundry room, which they considered to be an excellent refuge.

"You're not joining us for Open House?" Hana asked them.

They were not.

Over a breakfast of coffee and toast, Hana decided the first thing she would do was speak to Jake Schwambach. She wanted to know just what the kids were saying, and Jake seemed to be a boy who would talk.

After her quick bite she made a dramatic entrance into the Open House through her front door, then paused on the portico. Nobody applauded. Nobody even noticed. Although people still darted about, the displays seemed complete and ready for the crowds. She was happy to note that the oxen were now nibbling at bales of hay. She had never known they had such large mouths.

Teddy Jolf dashed past. Mr. Pettengill fussed up to Hana, profusely thanking her for the beautiful day as if she alone had control of the weather.

She edged away from Mr. Pettengill and over to a long table where Sal was presiding over more coffee and doughnuts. While sipping another cup of coffee and nibbling at a strawberry-creme pastry, she looked about.

She noted a few fancy kids, but for the most part the young people were anonymous in their Plain clothing. She tried to concentrate on their faces. She thought she saw Johnny Longsdorf and walked toward him, but he disappeared around a stand where Josie and Bert Adams were adding calico Dutch sunbonnets to their display of T-shirts with the Conover Historical Society logo tastefully imprinted on the upper left near the region of the heart.

"Have you seen Jake Schwambach?" Hana asked.

"Who?" Josie blinked as she turned from a peg-board where she had been concentrating on an ar-tistic arrangement of sunbonnets.

"The oldest Schwambach boy?" Bert asked. "He's around somewhere. He was hauling boxes for us."

"Oh, yes," Josie agreed. "He was here."

Beyond a stand featuring West German imports run by the local Deutsch-speaking society which had turned out in dirndls and lederhosen, Hana stopped to stare.

Pocky Reilly and Bill Longenecker had a small booth of their own in which was displayed the mannequin wearing the Dutch Blue Amish dress.

"Surprise!" Pocky cried.

"It certainly is," Hana agreed. "I'm not sure this is wise."

"Why not?" Bill asked belligerently. "It's Pocky's design and this is a very special occasion."

Pocky looked worried. "You said I could tell peo-ple. So I thought, we'll have the TV crews here later when the crowds come. It seemed like a perfect opportunity to share it with the community."

"Suppose somebody steals the idea?"

"Nobody can ever steal Dutch Blue," Pocky de-clared. "And without Dutch Blue it wouldn't be the same."

Hana shook her head at the woman's naiveté but decided against making an issue of it. She'd have a private talk with Pocky about who made such deci-sions, but that could wait for another day. After all, Hana had never been enthusiastic about the de-sign. It was more of a gimmick than anything else. Dutch Blue clothing would rise or fall on other de-signs, not on this special outfit.

Hana left Pocky and Bill holding hands as they

stared enthralled at their mannequin. It was altogether a disgusting display. She decided at that point that the Lady of the Manor had special privileges and located Mr. Fred, who was a lot easier to find than one particular Amish boy amidst the many.

"I want to speak to Jake Schwambach," she informed him.

"I'm much too busy to—"

"I want you to find him for me. I will wait right here."

Mr. Fred surveyed her critically, and apparently she passed his own Lady of the Manor test because, without further argument, he nodded and went in search of Jake. It wasn't until he had gone that Hana realized she was standing with a good view of the portapots that were between the parking lot and a long bed of orange azaleas.

She wondered what the lovely ladies of the PBS English specials did about their portapots. But perhaps the English, being so well bred, did not require facilities at their garden parties.

Jake Schwambach's was not the next familiar face she saw. Will Kochen appeared quite startlingly, popping out of the azalea bed.

"Were you hiding there?" she asked curiously.

He unconsciously pushed at his glasses even though they were neatly in their proper place.

"Just investigating."

"The flower beds?"

"Keeping my ear to the ground."

She groaned. "Well, stay out of my azaleas."

He flecked a blossom from his sleeve. "Nice color."

"Will, am I to gather that you're here in an official capacity?"

"Only partly."

"As in 'half-cop, half-curious'?"

" 'Half-friend' may be putting it more nicely."

She hesitated, wondering if she should tell him about Betty Schlicher's cabin in the clearing. Or maybe he knew. But he was already past her, going in the direction of the portapots. As he opened a creaky plastic door, Hana and her flowered skirt floated away toward the crescent of temporary booths. But the confusion she had noted earlier was nothing compared to what was happening now. People were marching up the drive. Masses of people. She glanced at her watch. It wasn't ten-thirty, the hour the gates were scheduled to open and cars would be allowed in the parking areas of the lower meadows. Something had obviously gone wrong.

At the head of the Plain and fancy brigade, like a maddened general, ran Mr. Fred, his cloak fanning out. He was coming directly toward her. By his side were Ghost and Crumb, jumping and barking. She had the momentary illusion that Mr. Fred and his followers would roll over her and proceed to the mansion, where they would ooze up the walls and over the roof.

Before the waves engulfed her, she grabbed Mr. Fred's arm.

"Where's Jake Schwambach?"

"They opened the gates early," he babbled. "Those kids. One simply cannot talk to young people today!"

"Did you see Jake Schwambach?" she hollered above the barking and the commotion of the crowding celebrants.

"Somebody said he went to that booth down the Lake Path—"

"The witch's cottage? Be quiet, Ghost!"

"Yes, yes. That Betty Whoever. Her place. Selling herbs."

He pulled away, straightened his cape, and moved forward into the mob with all the assurance of an 1812 general, the faithful Crumb like a sergeant at his side. Ghost happily chased his own tail into the crowd. A two-wheeled oxcart rumbled into the area, garlands of cut azaleas around the necks of the huge animals, one of which was reaching around to eat it.

The rarest, newest, brightest ruby . . .

Hana fled toward the woods.

She would fire Mr. Fred! Or hire whoever had charge of those giant beasts to have him trampled to death beneath the feet of an azalea-munching ox.

As she hurried along the path, sounds of the festivities quickly became unreal and far behind her. Or seemed far from these woods. She wondered what devil had prompted Mr. Fred and his Historical Society cohorts to allow Betty Schlicher to set up at such a distance from the rest of the booths.

Betty had probably hexed him.

Hana slowed. She wished she had brought Ghost or Crumb. Or even Kitty Fisher. She had thought she'd feel different now in daylight, but the eeriness of the night still lay on the woodland. In the new green of the trees and bushes, even the air appeared green. The brook among the cresses and rocks was a guttural voice, warning her.

Angry with herself for these fancies, Hana kept to the path and walked into the clearing. The hut had not disappeared at dawn. It was still there, its evil aura hardly diminished by the sun.

Jake Schwambach came out of the cabin and stopped when he saw her.

"Hex!" he shouted. "You took away our swimming hole. But you won't get away with it. They're going to get you!"

Before Hana had recovered from the shock of his words, he cursed her in the dialect, then went crashing into the woods, running fast. Green air closed behind him and he was gone. When Hana turned back to the cabin, Betty Schlicher and the bartender were standing on the porch. Even though she realized they had followed Jake out of the cabin, Hana had the illusion they had materialized out of the air. They stood smiling at her. Fascinated, she stared at their mouths. In the empty spaces that had been there, gold teeth now gleamed. And even at this distance she swore there was some sort of symbol etched into the gold.

Hana cleared her throat. "What are you doing here?"

"We're part of the Open House," Betty said.

"The Open House is up around the lawn and the 1812 Annex, where the main displays of azaleas are."

"We registered with that funny old guy," Barry Moyer said, sounding surprisingly human. "He said it was all right for us to be down here."

"For the atmosphere, you know," Betty agreed. "There are signs."

Hana was momentarily tempted to look up into the sky to see the signs but reason suggested that Betty meant directional signs put up by the Amish youth.

"Won't you come inside?" the hex woman invited throatily.

Hana came forward as far as the steps. From there she could see inside the hut. There were shelves of jars containing odd-looking things. Even though she was outside, Hana could smell a heavy incense. What it must be like inside, she could only guess. She wondered where the cat was.

Betty's eyes glittered with what might have been amusement. Her gold tooth flashed in the sunlight. "Are you afraid?"

Hana shook her head impatiently. "I must get back. It's *my* Open House."

Barry came down the steps. "But we'd like you to see our place."

"What does he do?" Hana snapped. "Sell home brew?"

"He's my assistant," Betty said lazily as if she'd been sniffing her own incense.

Hana stepped backward, away from them. From the path through the woods, Mrs. Schwambach, Mrs. Longsdorf, and the Quilt Woman emerged, pausing to stare at Hana.

Betty was suddenly behind her, hissing in her ear.

*Who comes for my sister, came before,*
*We are three but we should be four!*

The woman was daft. Teddy Jolf had been taking her far too seriously. Nursery rhymes indeed! These people had only the power one permitted them to have.

Hana turned and laughed in Betty Schlicher's face.

The hex woman drew back.

"Have fun," Hana told Betty and Barry. "But keep in mind that you're on my property. I don't want any of my guests frightened. And watch how much of that potent tea you dispense. It's powerful stuff."

"Very powerful," Betty murmured.

The Amish women were coming forward again.

Behind them on the path, Hana thought she glimpsed a short Amish boy.

She hurried to the women. "Are your children with you?"

"*Ja,*" Mrs. Schwambach said. "Up with all the stuff and the nice flowers."

"Not here?"

"They didn't want to come down here," Mrs. Longsdorf said.

"Maybe it's just as well. You're grown women so you should be able to take care of yourselves." Hana glanced back at Betty, who now stood alone before the cabin. "Don't let her scare you."

"Why should she scare us?" Mrs. Schwambach asked. "We've been coming to her for—"

Mrs. Longsdorf poked her sister.

The Quilt Woman smiled brightly. "I've got a booth with lots of real nice quilts—"

"Not today, thanks," Hana said, then excused herself and went into the woods. At the first turn in the path, where she could not be seen from the cabin, she paused to look around for the child.

Why, she wondered, was she so sure the boy she'd glimpsed was the same she had seen at the quarry? Something about his short stoutness. Something in the way he had moved. Not quite . . . what? Hana didn't know.

She walked along the path, searching as she went. She had almost reached the brook and cresses when she caught sight of him again. As before it was only a brief flash. He had left the path and was moving among trees and bushes in the direction of the house. She could hear him or at any rate hear something or someone.

A smaller path veered off sharply toward one of the many springs. Hana was hurrying, stepping lightly in her neat little shoes. She came to the spring, which gurgled out of rocks into unfolding ferns and mosses.

Hana saw the boy clearly for the first time.

He was crouching among the ferns as if they could hide him. For a few seconds he and Hana stared at each other.

He was not a child. He had to be at least Jake Schwambach's age. But he was a dwarf. Broad and short, with a large head. Slowly he got up, one hand against a tree trunk to support himself. Extra fingers on the hand. What was that called?— Polydactyly. His Amish clothing had been sewn to his own proportions. He seemed to belong there in the forest setting, old-fashioned clothing and all, as if he were a character from one of Aunt Sissy's tales come to life.

"Who are you?" Hana asked.

He turned and slipped away into a laurel thicket. Hana hesitated. If he kept going in a straight line he would come out near the red and white azalea display. He must have a family. Somebody had brought him here. She couldn't chase him through the woods, but with luck, she could intercept him when he came out.

But the dwarf had moved too fast for her. When she reached the edge of the woods, she saw him dashing away between two concession stands. Hana followed in time to see him duck into the Historical Society booth.

By this time hundreds of people were milling about. They were taking hundreds of pictures of each other in front of the azaleas. The oxcart went by filled with an uproarious group of children and two dogs who barked a greeting at Hana. Azaleas entwined in their collars, the traitor-dogs seemed to be having a marvelous time. The azalea arbor at the other side of the lawn had attracted a large crowd grouped about what looked like Mr. Fred on a platform, lecturing about something.

Abruptly Sal Nunemacher's grinning face inserted itself between Hana and the horrible scene.

"Look who's here, Miss Hana!"

"Who" turned out to be Mrs. Nunemacher, Sal's mother, and a cluster of Sal's siblings, including a foster daughter, Honey, in whom Hana had taken an interest. Now nine and in Mennonite garb, Honey looked so much like the others, it was hard to realize she was not one of the family by birth. She was chatting excitedly with Annie Nunemacher, who was only slightly older than herself, but when she saw Hana, she paused to smile shyly.

There was no way Hana could avoid a brief visit. Mrs. Nunemacher was effusive about the azaleas.

"Why, now, it must be such a good year for them," she enthused.

"I want the children to have anything they'd like," Hana told her. "Sal, you'll see to it for me."

Hana finally escaped after promising to visit the Nunemacher farm soon, a promise she meant to keep. As she started for the Historical Society booth, she was sure the trail of the dwarf-child must be cold by this time. She narrowly missed being discovered by a group of local politicians but avoided them by sneaking around to the side of the booth and slipping in through the canvas.

Startled, Bert and Josie Adams stared at her. Josie was just bagging a T-shirt she had sold. Bert was beaming in outdated salesman fashion as he distributed colorful flyers printed by the society for this occasion.

They were alone in the booth.

"Where's the dwarf?" Hana asked.

"Dwarf," Josie repeated.

"We don't have anybody helping us," Bert said, managing to sound injured. "We're staffing the booth by ourselves."

"I followed a youth—a dwarf—and saw him duck in here."

"If this is some kind of joke, we're too busy," Bert told her coldly.

Of course it was possible, Hana thought, for a short person to duck in and duck out again without being noticed. Especially if the Adamses were busy, as they obviously were.

Then she saw Josie's eyes.

They were worried eyes as the woman darted a look toward a corner of the canvas side. Hana lifted a flap to look out. She saw nobody she knew except Bill Longenecker, who was a short distance away, at the edge of the crowd, helping a young man adjust a sandwich board that advertised Longenecker's Amish tours.

Angrily Hana dropped the flap. She'd attend to Bill later. Josie Adams had put on one of the sun-bonnets to demonstrate how they looked to a young woman in T-shirt and jeans. They were not Amish bonnets but they framed the face much as the Amish bonnets did and this one was dark blue, nearer the Amish black. Watching Josie, for a moment Hana thought she was looking at Mrs. Schwambach. Betty's hissing voice came back to her: "Who comes for my sister, came before . . . We were three, but we should be four." Many people, for many reasons, left the Amish church. Was Josie one of these?

The Quilt Woman, Mrs. Schwambach, and Mrs. Longsdorf. Could Josie Adams be a fourth sister who had left the faith?

"You're Amish," Hana said. "Or, rather, you were

Amish. Mrs. Longsdorf, Mrs. Schwambach, and Mrs. Brubaker are your sisters, aren't they?"

She was not prepared for Josie's violent reaction. The woman screamed, ripped the bonnet from her head, and threw it at the customer in jeans who, startled, also screamed. Josie grabbed the canvas cover and scrambled out of the booth.

"Now see what you've done!" Bert cried.

He ducked out of the booth, Hana close behind him.

## Chapter Thirty-six

BERT RAN after Josie. Hana ran after him. Bill Longenecker and the man with the sandwich board were directly in their path. Bill leaped agilely out of the way but the sandwich board man was encumbered and slower. Josie ran right into him and both of them went down. Bert Adams fell over them. Hana landed on top of the pile.

Crowds surrounded them. One of the youths assigned to keep order pushed his way through to jerk Hana roughly to her feet then untangle the others. Josie was weeping. Hana, still disheveled, put her arms around her.

"I'll take care of Josie," she said quickly. "Bert, you help straighten out this mess and get somebody over to the booth."

The sandwich board was split and the lad inside bruised and a little dazed. Bill Longenecker was urging people to move on. Bert Adams looked as if he would like to follow them, but Hana maneuvered Josie into the crowd. With her arms tightly about the woman, she led her toward the house. Josie no longer cried but was gulping as if she either could not get air or had been weeping so long she had what Aunt Sissy always called the "dry heaves." She came docilely enough, as dazed as the sandwich board youth.

The house was cool and quiet after the confusion on the lawn. Hana felt relieved, glad the swarms outside could not invade her sanctuary. Gently she guided Josie into the snuggery and lowered her into a comfortable chair.

"Would you like a brandy?" she asked.

Josie looked about as if wondering where she was.

Hana got the brandy and held the snifter to the woman's lips as she would help a sick person. Josie swallowed, coughed, then took the glass herself and downed the rest.

"Maybe you can have more later," Hana said cautiously.

Josie Adams nodded jerkily.

"You're a sister of Mrs. Longsdorf, Mrs. Schwambach, and Mrs. Brubaker, aren't you?" Hana asked.

Another nod.

"Which means you're the aunt of the boys who were killed."

Stricken eyes stared up at her. "Please. May I have another drink? I . . . need . . . it."

Hana poured another brandy and waited while she sipped, slowly this time.

"Perhaps that's why you're so involved with the Historical Society," Hana suggested. "Your heritage is very deep in this community, isn't it?"

Josie cupped her hands around her glass and

lowered her head. "Our family's been here for a hundred and fifty years. Right here. On the land. I love my people."

"But you left the Amish faith."

"Lots do," she mumbled.

"Yes, I know. It's very hard to keep to the old ways in this world. Sometimes even if you love your family very much, you can't stay with them. It's not anyone's fault. I hear that even your sister who sells quilts is leaving."

Hana felt as if she were talking to a child. She wondered if she should call Dr. Reifsnyder to get something to calm Josie down. Perhaps he was on the grounds and she could have him paged . . .

"Outsiders can't understand. Nobody can understand," Josie said.

"I'd like to try."

"I loved the farm. I mean, our farm when I was a little girl. We were way back in the country so far. Out of the way. We didn't get around other people much but that didn't matter. It seemed safe back there. Safe."

Hana slipped into a chair, watching the woman.

"That boy—the dwarf—he's your son, isn't he?"

Josie took a deep breath and suddenly seemed more calm. "Yes. His name's Eli."

Hana said gently, "Any child who isn't perfect is disappointing for the parents. But there are musicians, scientists, artists—many noted people who have been handicapped. I'm sure your son will grow up to do something meaningful with his life."

Josie spoke slowly, sadly. "He won't grow up. Not that way either. He's retarded."

"I'm so sorry . . ."

"Back on the farm . . . we girls . . . there was just one thing an Amish girl could do. And that was get married. Mom said we weren't to marry too young because then you got more babies than you could manage. But even so, there was plenty of pressure by the time you were twenty or so. Seems there were a lot of us girls around that time and not so many fellows. I liked Henry Schwambach but my sister got him. And I thought Moses Longsdorf wasn't too bad but my other sister got him. And Lizzie got the best of all—Elam Brubaker. So there wasn't much left for me except my second cousin Amos Moyer. He seemed funny to me even then but everybody said there wasn't much wrong with him that a good wife wouldn't cure."

"But surely if you felt that way, you could have found someone else?"

"How?" she asked irritably. "You have to marry Amish and how far can you go in a horse and buggy to look for Amish someplace else? You marry one of your own. We all did that. All us girls. And that's where the trouble is. Oh, my God, don't you see?"

Hana nodded. She was beginning to see and wasn't sure she wanted to look.

Josie went on, "After we were married maybe a year I noticed that Amos had some trouble walking sometimes. But still, he could do the farm work all right. It wasn't until a long time later we found out he had Mast Syndrome. You know what that is?"

"It's a genetic disease, isn't it? I read some pamphlets. It's mostly among the Amish people, I remember. Because of inbreeding—marrying second cousins and sometimes even first cousins."

Josie shuddered. "It's a terrible thing. They just get worse and worse. Can't get around, laugh like crazy when there's nothing funny. Can't manage the farm or anything. Finally Amos couldn't do much except feed himself and shave."

"It must have been very hard for you."

"What was hard was the babies." She was staring at Hana now. "I had three. Want to know what one birth certificate said? 'Monstrosity; stillborn, normal delivery.' I saw that baby and I'll never forget it. Then the next one lived two months. It was all messed up inside but at least it looked like a baby. And then I had Eli."

Hana exhaled slowly, a wave of compassion overwhelming her. "I know the Amish don't practice birth control but surely after the first—"

"There was no way. Amos was . . . well, that was one thing he could do and he was a mean man. Moses Longsdorf was no prize but he was a saint alongside of Amos. I stood it as long as I could. Then one day I just up and ran away. Away from my husband. Away from the farm. Away from being Plain. I'd saved my egg money and I took more he'd had around the house to buy a new buggy with. I got a job and went to night school and finally I married Bert."

"Maybe you should have left this part of the country."

"I just couldn't," Josie said sadly. "My sisters were here. And Eli was here with his grandparents. Amos' people. Amos had to go back there because he got so bad. He's dead now. And I felt so sorry. For everything. For everybody. I studied about it. Our recessive genes. We can all trace our families back to a few founders that came to this country. And there's been so much intermarriage. It's cumulative. After you marry second or third cousins often enough, it gets like . . . well, like it was brothers and sisters. And these things happen more often. When a baby like that comes along they say it's God's will. God's will? Seems more like the work of the devil to me."

"Those boys who were killed. Your sisters' boys. Were they ill? There was nothing on the autopsy report that I heard about . . ."

"They were both retarded. Our family seems to have more than its share of trouble. They had to be watched and kept locked up sometimes, Matthew Longsdorf especially. He was often violent."

"There were other Longsdorf children who were affected by some of those dreadful illnesses, weren't there?" Hana asked. "That's why your sister didn't want me to see their family Bible. She didn't want me to know about the dead children. She was afraid I'd realize why the boys had been killed. About the genetic illness because"—Hana stared at Josie—"that's why they *were* killed, isn't it? Because they were such a grief to the family. Matthew hurt your sister, didn't he? A number of times. And she suspected that's why he was murdered."

"What are you saying?" Josie cried.

Hana's mind moved swiftly. Telephone. Police? Sergeant Kochen was here. Maybe somehow she could reach him. Even if the murders had been committed with pitchforks and Josie Adams had no pitchfork with her now, it didn't mean she wouldn't use some other weapon. It did not mean she had not used other methods in the past.

When she had come into the room, Hana had placed her bag on top of the TV. Her gun was in it.

Slowly rising, she said, "They were like mercy killings, weren't they? You thought you were doing right. You were helping your sisters."

She continued to talk soothingly. She was almost within reach of the bag. With a cry, Josie jumped up and shoved Hana. Hana stumbled and hit the

TV. It crashed to the floor. By the time she had recovered her balance, Josie had run out of the room.

Hana scrambled for her bag, grabbed her gun, and ran after Josie.

# Chapter Thirty-seven

IN THE HALL, Hana paused, listening. The beautiful old wooden floors of Blue Spring Hill always echoed footsteps but she heard none now. Then she remembered that Josie had worn walking shoes with rubber soles.

Not even a door slammed. Hana moved warily but as fast as she dared. Because of the crowds expected for the Open House, the mansion was more secure than usual. The library, the conservatory, and even the old schoolroom and nursery above the 1812 Annex had been locked.

Hana wasted precious time searching unlocked rooms before she faced the fact that she would have to get help. She had hoped to find Josie Adams cowering somewhere but it had been a foolish wish. Not only were there hundreds of places to hide inside Blue Spring Hill but there was always the possibility that Josie would get out of the house. A woman who has killed two boys by thrusting pitchforks through their chests is not the kind to cower.

Josie must have a maniacal sense of purpose in life and of the rightness of her cause. Perhaps she had kept her Amish connections secret because they were too painful for her to talk about. Even when she had gone to her nephew's funeral she had taken Historical Society friends along to make it appear that a group had come to offer condolences. She must have been at the quarry that day. Hana wondered if she had come there to kill her own handicapped son and Hana had merely gotten in the way.

Hana shuddered and decided she had better page Will Kochen. She crept into the front hall, took a final look around, then went out through her front door.

The Conover Carnival.

Despite Mr. Fred's vow that everything at the Open House would be in keeping with the spirit of the times in which the estate had been built, and despite the effort of the ox team to operate like historical animals representing their own ancestors who had pulled Conestoga wagons out of the county and toward the western plains, dignity had been swept aside. Hordes of terribly modern-looking people milled about the lawn. A juggler in a medieval jester's outfit was at center stage in front of the delicately blooming arbor. Through the crowd galloped Pocky Reilly's TV crew.

"Here she is!" Pocky shrieked.

Hana turned her back and shoved her gun into her bag as the news team sprang up the steps and a young crewman shoved a microphone into her face.

"Is this a happy day or what, Ms. Shaner?" he bubbled.

Hana turned to him with a big smile. "Sure is! Exciting, too!"

Mr. Fred came pushing through a cluster of people who were maneuvering to be included in the TV picture.

"Where on earth have you been?" he cried. "We're waiting!"

In his excitement he grabbed her arm, pulling her down the steps and along the house toward the exterior door of the 1812 Annex. The TV crew followed enthusiastically.

"What's wrong?" Hana asked in alarm, because only an emergency of a dreadful nature would cause Mr. Fred to lose so much of his cool that he would actually take hold of her. "What's happened?"

"You should have been here," he said as they hurried along.

Hana matched his stride, driven by a horrified vision of Amish youth being slaughtered by a pitchfork-wielding Josie Adams in front of the 1812 Annex. Besides the TV crew, at least two hundred people were hurrying along with them.

The heavy medieval-looking doors of the Annex were unbolted behind a yellow ribbon.

Uncle Harold Reifsnyder, the good doctor, stood beaming beside the ribbon. His hands held the biggest scissors Hana had ever seen. With him were local officials she had avoided earlier, who now looked strained and fretful. Hana had only seconds to recall that Uncle Harold had become politically active because he fancied himself a likely candidate for the office of coroner.

A band began to play a jolly Sousa march. She suspected her arrival had signaled this assault on the senses. Sunlight glinted from their brass instruments. A young percussionist slammed into his drums without regard to beat or the frantic arm movements of a uniformed conductor wearing a high chimney sweep's hat in purple and pink. High school girls in what looked like sequined bathing suits cavorted in front of the politicians.

"Ah, Ms. Shaner," Mayor Gerald Kleinhaus bellowed at her. "They've finally located you."

Beaming, Mr. Fred stepped back. The band played louder. The assembly, hundreds of voices strong, began to sing along with the band even though the number had no words. Conover County had taken John Philip Sousa to its heart since he had brought valuable publicity to the area by dying nearby during one of his tours.

Sergeant Kochen edged through the crowd.

Hana wanted to scream at him above the din, "There's a murderer in my house!"

She tried to get to him through the line of twirling batons. The crown applauded her effort. The mayor rushed after her, but a baton escaped its owner and slammed into his head, knocking him to the ground. The crowd loved it. Hana helped him up and together they retreated to the comparative safety of assembled city council and county commissioners.

As she soothed the ruffled mayor, Hana saw Kochen salute her cheerfully then turn his attention to a group of boys doing a not very competent job of keeping the crowd from barging into the band.

Those stalwart musicians abruptly ran out of Sousa. The mayor, after waiting a moment to make sure the batons stopped with the band, stepped forward to a microphone and began to speak through a cacophony of metallic whistles. Feeling trapped, Hana fidgeted. She wasn't particularly fond of Mayor Kleinhaus. He had gotten the job by default when the former mayor, his wife, died in office. Hana felt he had won the next election strictly on the sympathy vote. His speeches tended to be long.

He extolled the day, Hana herself, her entire

family, the year 1812, and the citizenry of Conover County. After that, a state representative spoke on the political symbolism of the azalea. Dr. Harold Reifsnyder told of his long and devoted relationship with the Shaner family, without mentioning his debt to them for his education. His speech focused on their debt to him as he conveyed the idea that the entire clan would have died before the age of ten but for his medical ministrations.

Finally the speeches were over and Hana again looked expectantly at Sergeant Kochen, so near and yet so far. The band struck up on a note of such discordant intensity Hana's teeth hurt. Marching in double time, the musicians parted like the waters of the Red Sea and a phalanx of Amish youths paraded through the opening. Behind them came the entire Conover Historical Society, each member carrying a county flag, which had been designed by a past president of the society. Against a green background was a stark yellow sun, the rays of which reached to the four corners, where the riches of the Conover soil were symbolized. The ears of corn were readily recognizable but it look a long time before Hana realized the white thing was a radish. (The county was occasionally referred to as the winter radish capital of the world.) A Colonial house remotely resembling Blue Spring Hill was emblazoned on another corner. The design was completed by a round brown ball representing earth and a round white one representing milk.

Parading with the society were Ghost and Crumb, each wearing a dog suit with the same logo on the back. The dogs were pulling Mr. Fred, who was attached to them by leashes, which probably explained the fact that he alone had no flag. Before Hana had recovered, she saw Bert Adams among the flagholders. She almost expected to see Josie too. After all, nothing would surprise her now. But no, apparently Josie hadn't joined the group. Ghost and Crumb began to howl. Then the band wound down and the dogs returned the favor.

Uncle Harold thrust the huge scissors into her hand. Obediently Hana turned toward the yellow ribbon. She'd get the damn thing cut, then immediately go to Kochen.

Snip.

The ribbon fell to the ground. Mr. Fred and the dogs hopped out of line to throw open the doors.

The band struck up their sprightliest number as they strutted forward, engulfing any of the crowd who had ventured into their territory. Officials, politicians, Historical Society, and flags were swept into the 1812 Annex, pushing Hana with them. Behind this VIP group surged the common citizens of Conover County.

"I've got to get to Sergeant Kochen!" Hana shouted.

Mayor Kleinhaus shouted back to her, "That's very nice! Good show!"

The number of people permitted into the museum was obviously monitored—trust Mr. Fred to think of everything—because the heavy doors suddenly clanged shut. Whether Kochen was inside this dungeon with Hana, she had no idea.

Incredibly, and apparently on cue, the band ceased. Unlike Hana, people around her seemed to know what a treat was in store for them. She wished she had read the publicity Mr. Fred had prepared.

"What's happening now?" she asked Mayor Kleinhaus, who was uncomfortably squeezed against her by the large drum in the uncertain hands of the enthusiastic percussionist.

He shushed her. Everybody stood squashed together, not talking, looking expectant.

The lights went out.

For a moment, Hana felt suffocated. Then Mr.
Fred's light show began. Weird metallic music echoed among the arches of the Annex. Lights flickered over showcases, highlighting skulls and
bones. The mauve glow flared in the coffin at the
end of the room. Fascinated, Hana stared at it. The
lid lifted. Mr Fred had obviously added a few
touches after her preview. The body inside the coffin was slowly being raised to a sitting position.

Only it wasn't a mannequin in a moldy uniform
dug up from the dirt of her lawn. It was Josie Adams dressed in Pocky Reilly's modified Amish
dress.

And Josie was very, very dead.

Nobody spoke. Everybody stood mesmerized,
staring.

Something stirred on Josie's lap, stretched, and
blinked at Mr. Fred's wild lights.

It was the hex woman's pale-eyed cat.

# Chapter Thirty-eight

LOOKING OVER THE top of his glasses, Sergeant Kochen glumly surveyed the scene. Hana, standing
beside him on the front steps of her mansion,
forced herself to look at the new intrusion. Extra
police had been brought in and were seated at card
tables. At each table a line of restless people waited

to give what information they had or report that they knew nothing of the crime. Hana wondered where all the card tables had come from. The police must have brought their own, because certainly Mr. Fred never could have . . .

But then, who knew what lurked in the bowels of Blue Spring Hill?

"This is worse than the other murders," Kochen said irritably. "I don't know why, but it is. The White Unicorn was impossible, so we didn't even attempt mass interviews. I wish you would arrange to hold these murders in an uncluttered atmosphere."

"At least you may have an eyewitness."

He turned quickly to her. "An eyewitness?"

"It's possible the cat saw the entire thing."

A series of odd emotions crossed his face. "I am going to forget you said that."

"We put her in the laundry room for safekeeping after I chased my cats upstairs. My cats like it in there. All facilities. Litter. You know. Anytime you want to see her I'll take you."

"Why would I want to see the damn cat?" he cried.

"Animals can tell you many things."

He growled. Hana was saved from his full fury by the arrival of Sal Nunemacher, herding her family in front of her.

"Miss Hana, I don't want these children to have to go through this!" She placed a protective arm about Honey's shoulders. The girl, rather than looking intimidated, grinned up at Hana. "This child that God sent to us for help has seen enough trouble in her time. I don't want her to have a setback just when she's doing so good. Sergeant, I want you to let us go home. Miss Hana can tell you where we live. My mother's terribly upset."

Mrs. Nunemacher, a stout woman with Mennonite cap and simple dress, had been peering about with excitement and interest but now obediently assumed a harassed expression.

"Go on home," Kochen said wearily. "We'll get to you later."

He scribbled a note, which he handed to Sal. Honey seemed about to linger, but Sal took her hand and trundled her away with the others.

"You didn't need to give her special privileges on my account," Hana informed him.

"Hey, you think we don't have enough to do here today? As she said, we can always get them another time."

"Since there's so much to do, why aren't you helping?"

There was just the trace of a smile at his lips. "I am. I'm interviewing you."

"Oh," she said, startled.

"Just, please, let's not talk about cats."

Hana shrugged. "Your loss. Josie was strangled, wasn't she?"

"Yes. That was obvious."

"With what?"

"The belt to that damned dress. What do you know about Josie Adams, Hana?"

She told him, holding nothing back. All she wanted now was for these awful murders to be solved so that Blue Spring Hill could be at peace again.

"It's ghastly," she said dully, "to have a murder here. I've always thought of this place as . . . well, like an island in a modern sea."

He followed her down the steps and over to a bed of azaleas.

"You might use those words to describe the Amish people too," he said. "They've tried to be an island in a modern sea. But the world is going to intrude in some way. And even if it doesn't, that island will get smaller and smaller until it develops its own seeds of destruction."

"I thought you loved the Amish people."

"I do. But that doesn't mean I look at them through rose-colored glasses."

Pocky Reilly came running across the lawn.

"Oh, Hana," she wailed. "I've been looking all over for you! I wasn't in there when it happened, but they told me Josie Adams was wearing my dress. The one I made. Is that true?"

"It's true," Kochen answered for Hana. "When did you last see the dress?"

Pocky seized Hana's hand. "I wish I'd listened to you! You didn't want that stupid design. You didn't like it. I know you didn't. You were just letting me go ahead because I thought it was so great. Oh, I wish I hadn't done it!"

"When did you last see the dress?" Kochen asked again in his official voice.

Pocky dropped Hana's hand and looked fearfully at him.

"Come on," he snapped. "The dead woman was wearing your dress."

"Not my dress."

"Same thing. It was in your possession."

"No. Not really. No, it wasn't," Pocky stammered. "That is, it disappeared."

Kochen warned, "Ms. Reilly, consider this an official interview. I want the truth, and if I don't get it, you'll be interrogated downtown at police headquarters."

Pocky stared at him, her mouth dropping open.

Hana inquired soothingly, "How did that dress get off the mannequin and disappear, Pocky? Just tell us in your own words."

Never too tall, Pocky seemed to be shrinking. "There was a disturbance. Bill was out talking to some Amish people. I think he wanted to take tour groups around their farm. And this fight broke out, right at the corner of my booth. Young fellows . . . some of them supposed to guard the property. I was afraid they'd upset the thing . . . I mean, my booth. They were shoving each other. Pushing against it."

"Did you recognize any of them? Like Jake Schwambach or—"

"No. I didn't."

"You never do," Hana said.

"What d'you want from me? They dress alike, look pretty much alike. Anyway, I went out to talk to them. I was trying to calm them down and . . . well, it worked. They left pretty fast. But when I went back inside, the dress was gone. I couldn't believe it at first. A naked mannequin standing there. I thought . . . I don't know what I thought."

"Did you see anybody inside the booth?" Kochen asked.

Pocky shook her head. "No, and you'd think I would have."

"You were very neatly distracted," Hana reminded her.

"Sure, I know that. But how did anybody get in there? I stayed right at the entrance. I wanted to be able to duck back inside if the fight got worse. And we had the rest of it staked down very well. Bill did a good job. It would have taken a very small person to slip beneath that canvas."

"A dwarf," Hana said.

Kochen nodded. "And he's Josie Adams's son. Could have been a lot of resentment built up there."

"If that boy stole the dress, it wasn't his idea,"

Hana said. "Somebody used him. Just like somebody's been using all these kids. They're not bad
but they're being influenced . . ."

"Hexed," Pocky breathed.

Angrily Kochen turned on her. "If they're being
influenced, it's by somebody with an ulterior motive but otherwise perfectly ordinary."

"A regular Bad Guy?" Pocky asked solemnly.

Kochen whipped out a notebook. "Ms. Reilly, I
want you to tell me exactly who looked at that
dress, who showed any undue interest in it, and
any pertinent comments that might have been
made. Especially hostile ones. Did Josie Adams
herself see the dress?"

"I'm not sure. She was very busy."

"Any idea how they got it off the mannequin?"

"That was easy. I used a lot of Velcro . . ."

Hana caught sight of Mr. Fred gesturing to her.
Murmuring an apology that neither of them
seemed to hear, she left Kochen and Pocky to their
interview and hurried to Mr. Fred, building up
fury as she went. It would be so soul-satisfying to
say, "See? I told you something awful would happen if we held this ridiculous Open House. I told
you so!" How good that would feel.

He had gone back into the house and was waiting for her in the front hall. Mr. Fred, overbearing
and assuming far too much power over Blue
Spring Hill, could, if the occasion demanded, hang
his big head so that he looked like a scarecrow. It
appeared he felt the present circumstances called
for this kind of body language.

Hana refused to be cheated. "See? I told you
something awful would happen if we . . . Will
you look at me?" He raised large soulful eyes full
of contrition. She quickly got in the last line, the
one that was most important. "I told you so."

Somehow it didn't come out with the ferocity she'd intended.

"You were right," he admitted. "We should have kept our museum private. During our lifetimes. I guess I did get carried away."

"You should *be* carried away! You should be put where you can't do any more damage!"

"Shh!" he warned. "He'll hear you."

But Hana had saved the best for last and she had to say it. Pulling herself to her full height, she intoned, "If my father knew about this, he would turn over in his grave."

Now she was playing his game. She watched him wince as the shaft hit home. She drew a breath to drive the next verbal dart more deeply, then stopped.

"He? Who? Who'll hear me?"

Mr. Fred, once off the hook, reverted immediately to his position of power. "Bert Adams. As soon as the police were finished with him, I took the liberty of bringing him into the house and offering him brandy."

"You take too many liberties, Mr. Fred."

"Would you have preferred to have him sit outside on a bench after the loss he's suffered? Your father always welcomed the bereaved into his home. I thought you would wish to carry on the Shaner tradition and speak a few words of condolence to the gentleman."

Score points in the game for Mr. Fred.

Hana decided the circumstances warranted a truce. "Take me to him," she ordered.

He had not, she noted with relief, put the man in her private snuggery. Instead he was in the Lafayette Room, swallowed up in a massive wing chair. He looked startled when Mr. Fred spoke gently to him.

"Ms. Shaner is here, Mr. Adams."

Mr. Fred eased himself out of the room, probably glad to get away from the man's sorrow. Hana recalled something Kochen had told her: that the police first of all look to the spouse when a murder is committed. It seemed obvious it was not the direction to look in this case.

"I'm so terribly sorry, Mr. Adams," she said.

He looked up. "You took her away. What the hell happened? Why didn't you stay with her?"

Hana pulled up a small, austere Shaker chair and sat beside him. "I talked to her. Tried to soothe her and calm her down." Tactfully, Hana refrained from telling him that she'd pegged Josie as the killer. "Then she ran away. She must have been someplace in the house but I couldn't find her."

"Somebody found her."

"Mr. Adams . . . Bert, she told me about her first marriage and the deformed babies. And about Eli."

He closed his eyes and leaned back as if exhausted. "That woman suffered in her life, believe me. But it never made her bitter. She was always trying to help. Never stopped trying to help. Did she tell you she was shunned?"

"No."

He opened angry eyes. "Before she left that sick fool they made her marry. Do you know what it means to be shunned?"

"I have some idea . . ."

"It's hell. Your own family isn't supposed to let you sit at the table and eat with them. They won't talk to you. You're completely isolated and if you're Amish there's not a hell of a lot you have outside the family. It drives some of them to suicide. I don't think even then she'd have left Eli, but she cracked. Couldn't stand it. Her sisters stuck by her, thank God. They risked shunning themselves rather than turn their backs on her. They helped her get away. After she was working she always went back, getting help for kids who were retarded or sick. Matthew and Aaron were violent and had to be kept locked away most of the time. She was always going over there to help out. She tried to get kids like that to real medical doctors instead of these witch doctors."

"But most Amish people welcome doctors."

"Most. Not all. And that family she came from was more backward than most. I wanted her to give it up, stay away. But she wouldn't. And they got her. In the end, they got her."

"Who got her? Surely you're not saying one of her sisters killed her?"

"It was that hex woman! Betty Schlicher. Who else? She hated Josie's guts. Josie was taking away her power to hurt. You saw that cat. That was the hex woman's cat. I wish I'd killed it."

"It isn't the cat that did the harm," Hana said. "It's the people, not the animals, that cause the hurt."

"Maybe . . . I don't know . . ."

"Did you notice the dress she was wearing when we found her?"

He nodded jerkily. "The cops talked about it. It was your dress."

"Not mine."

"Well, there was talk you were going to manufacture that kind of dress. Sell it to everybody. It didn't seem like a good idea to some people."

"Who in particular?"

"I don't remember. I can't even think right now."

"It was just a model. Actual manufacture of that dress may never have happened under any circumstances. But I believe it was her son Eli who took it out of the booth where it was on display," she told him. "I don't see who else it could have been."

"Could be," he agreed. "Eli's simpleminded. Not violent and crazy like those other two, just simple. That was hardest of all for Josie. If he'd been bright, she could have borne it better. It was why she left him on the farm. He was better off there."

"Somebody must have told him to take the dress. Someone he trusted."

"I tell you, it was the hex woman," he said irritably. "Betty. They take these kids to her and she gives them charms to wear—as if that helps. Gives them sweets too . . . candy. They love her. Go find her and you'll find him. You can ask him about it but don't expect much of an answer."

"What did you do after I took Betty away?"

"I went back in the booth, what the hell else do you think I did?" he cried. "That's what the cops asked too. Then I joined the procession just like I'd been told. So I could be in there when they lit her up and did that damn show with her body! Shit! You were the one with her. You were the one should have protected her."

Hana let him talk. Helplessly she realized she should have handled it better. Somehow she should have gotten to Kochen sooner and raised an alarm. She was guilty as charged.

Suddenly she realized he had stopped upbraiding her.

"Would you like me to call anyone for you?" she asked.

He was shaking as he lifted the brandy glass. "No. Nobody to call. I'm sorry . . . I'm way out of line."

"It's all right."

"No. Because it wasn't your fault. Knowing Josie, she'd have gone and done what she wanted or thought she needed to do and nobody could stop her. The police told me I could go. So as soon as I finish this . . . I'll . . . go . . . home."

Hana told him to take all the time he needed, then left the room. Once outside, she paused. It wasn't easy to face a man when you've let his wife run away and be killed.

Mr. Fred was nowhere to be seen. Thinking of Betty Schlicher, Hana went to the side door, hoping to slip out unnoticed. She had not seen the hex woman since the tragedy. For all she knew Betty and Barry and their two golden teeth might be in any one of those queues across her lawn. Then, too, they might be a dozen miles away. There had been a great deal of confusion immediately after finding the body, and Hana had faith in Betty's ability to disappear. Perhaps not into thin air, but certainly into the backwash of Conover County.

No one called her or even appeared to notice as she skirted flaming azalea patches and ducked into the woods.

# Chapter Thirty-nine

HANA MOVED ALONG the woodland trail, alert to sounds. As far as she could tell, she was alone and unobserved. When she reached the clearing the small shack sat quietly in lengthening shadows.

She stood still and looked about carefully. She was probably wasting her time. Betty would not be here any longer and almost as certainly she would not have left behind a clue. Hana felt foolish even considering the possibility.

She headed cautiously toward the shack. She was within ten feet of the doorway when the song started. It was a strange singsong, acapella, coming from the dark interior of the cabin. Hana stopped, listening to the words rising in trebles.

> *Come walk down this ancient road*
> *That leads to Endor town—*
> *The Witch of the Bible still lives there*
> *So come with me, walk down.*
>
> *Come when all the world is dark*
> *She'll tell of olden days—*
> *She'll make the morning come again*
> *She'll teach the olden ways.*

Stealthily Hana moved forward again. She tiptoed up the steps, paused to take out her gun, then quickly stepped inside the building.

Coming from the light into darkness, it took time before she could see anything. The singing surrounded her, almost stereophonically.

"Who's here?" she demanded, holding the gun, blinking, willing her eyes to focus.

The song stopped.

"Hana?" asked a small voice.

Hana squinted into a corner and recognized the singer. It was not Betty Schlicher who sat there on the floor in lotus position. It was Teddy Jolf. Teddy the New Witch, who was now occupying the Old Witch's shack and singing occult lullabies to herself.

"What are you doing here?" Hana asked, shoving the weapon back into her bag.

Teddy began to hum.

Hana walked closer. Teddy was swaying, smiling

as she sang, a strange vacant look in her eyes. Remembering her own reaction to Betty's teas, she reached down and tugged at Teddy's arm.

"Get up," she said urgently. "Do you know what's been happening?"

Teddy giggled as she got awkwardly to her feet. "I'm cured."

"You're drunk."

"Am not. Not a drop. Only good medicinal herbs. Mixed myself. Got the recipe from Aunt Sissy's wonderful, great, terrific notebook. Found the herbs here. I smelled them so I knew what they were." She stumbled to a shelf from which she took a thermos. "Have a swig. Good for sinus. Good for cramps. Good for—"

Hana took the thermos and sniffed the contents. Even the strong, aromatic odor made her feel light-headed.

"Teddy, have you seen Betty?"

"Uh-uh. Everybody's off at the thing. The whatever. The flower opening." She giggled again. "Oops. Going backwards in time. Everybody up there is a flower child. Sixties, remember? People always talking about them good old days. Aren't you going to drink any?"

"No."

"Then I will have some more my own self."

Hana pushed Teddy gently away, then went to the door and poured the liquid on the boards of the porch.

"That wasn't nice," Teddy pouted.

Eli wasn't here. Nobody was here except for herself and Teddy. The sense of urgency was strong. But she couldn't leave Teddy in her condition. If she drank more of anything, it could be dangerous.

"Come," Hana commanded. "There's someone I want you to see."

"Who?"

"Mr. Fred."

"I've seen Mr. Fred."

"Oh, but you haven't seen him the way you'll see him today. In charge here. Exercising his leadership abilities."

"I don't want to go."

"Of course you do, Teddy. Come."

Teddy Jolf was so relaxed it wasn't hard to propel her out of the shack, but getting her through the woods was a different matter. Teddy wanted to stop and smell the flowers. She saw nothing underfoot like roots and rocks which tripped her. And she continued to sing about the Witch of Endor. The song unnerved Hana. It gave religious sanctity to a belief in hexerei. For a people who lived by the Bible, here was the Word of God that such things existed.

"There are more things in heaven and earth . . ." Shakespeare. He had his witches too.

To Hana it seemed like ages before they reached the lawn. People were still milling about, talking. The lines of those waiting were still long. Hana was sure she saw Ghost and Crumb in one line and wondered if Kochen had changed his mind about interviewing animals.

Annoyingly she couldn't locate Mr. Fred. Teddy was an embarrassment. She refused to stop singing. People stared at her. Hana finally dragged her to the information booth, which was functioning now under police guidance, and had Mr. Fred paged.

While waiting for him to appear, Hana put her hands on Teddy's shoulders and peered into her fogged eyes.

"Stop. Singing. That. Song!" she ordered.

Teddy paused midsentence, her mouth hanging

open. Hana released her. Teddy swayed. Hana hoped the Good Witch would not pass out. But Teddy recovered, hanging on to the booth for support. At that moment Hana spotted Mr. Fred's ungainly stride as he ambled away from the portapots. Seizing Teddy's arm, Hana pulled her toward Mr. Fred. She literally thrust Teddy into his arms.

"Here. Take care of her."

"What am I supposed to do with her?" he asked, holding the young woman distastefully as if he had hoped for an archaeological skeleton and had been rewarded with a live body instead.

"Take her inside. Give her coffee. Sober her up. Or let her sleep it off. I don't know—you figure it out. Find Uncle Harold. Ask him."

She hurried away with no particular destination in mind other than to get away, to let Mr. Fred deal with the problem of Teddy Jolf. She felt close to something. She wondered if she should return to the shack. Or ask a police officer where to find Kochen. She had to think. There was something she could do . . .

She found herself at the rhododendron thicket that hid the offensively Victorian conservatory. When she was a child, this had been her place to be alone. A place where dreams and ideas came to her. She checked to see that no one was watching, then slipped into the thicket. Tangled, grotesque limbs tore at the flowing, flowery skirt. Nothing grew beneath the bushes in the soft loamy earth; it was a surreal world. She was within sight of the conservatory windows before she stopped.

*Through a glass darkly.*

Someone walked inside the conservatory. A shadowy figure, moving away from her. Stepping softly, Hana slithered around a particularly gnarled old plant and along the glass wall to the private entrance her ancestor had built into the windows.

Hana opened the small, hidden glass door, stepped through, and closed it behind her.

There was no sound but the dripping from a spray and the soft plashing of the waterfall. An odor of exotic flowers hung in the hot, moist air. Hana noticed that a scratch on her arm was bleeding. She wiped the blood on the ruined skirt, got out the Beretta, then padded along the bark-strewn trail in the direction she had seen the figure take.

Brandishing a pitchfork, the figure leaped out at her from behind a bed of giant ferns.

Hana screamed. The gun did not go off.

## *Chapter Forty*

BETTY SCHLICHER, THE hex woman, dropped the pitchfork.

"Shh!" she said frantically. "Hey, I'm sorry. I didn't know it was you."

Betty looked as scared as Hana felt. Hana, her Beretta still clutched in her hand, safety still on, took a gulp of air, trying to recover. She'd have to get used to this new weapon. Take lessons. She hadn't even gotten off a warning shot. Betty, very unwitchy now, sat on a boulder.

"What are you doing in here?" Hana managed to squeak.

"Hiding. My God, hiding. They got Josie Adams.

And Barry—that slob!—took the car and left me stranded. Here, with killers."

Just in case, Hana picked up the pitchfork. "Where did you get this?"

"Behind the shack we built for this damned Open House. Propped against it. Let me tell you, I didn't feel good when I saw it. I didn't want it to fall into the wrong hands."

But it already had, Hana thought, contemplating Betty. The woman was frightened. Either that or she was a terrific actress. But then, she *was* a terrific actress.

"You said 'they' got Josie. *Who* got Josie?"

"I don't know. God, if I knew, don't you think I'd tell the cops?"

"Would you?"

"Sure! This is terrible for business."

"When I went to the police because I thought Eli had drowned, you weren't so anxious to have them do anything," Hana said. "You put on quite a show."

"The sisters paid me to do that," Betty said nervously. "That kid can swim like a fish. Only thing he's good at. Nobody wanted you getting the cops looking for a drowned boy. These people like to be left alone. Eli wasn't your business or the cops'."

"I still don't understand why you're so afraid," Hana said, dropping the gun into her bag.

Betty leaned forward. "Listen, lady, look at that pitchfork. Who was it for? It was right behind my shack down there, so I got a good idea who they had in mind. Josie Adams was always hanging around those kids that were killed. She was always messing with any sick or retarded youngster. And who else was always doing for those kids? Me, that's who."

"But she tried to get medical help for them and

give support to the families. All you did was make trouble."

Betty bristled. "What do you know about it? Who's to say charms don't help?"

"Good charms might."

"So what's good and what's bad? I help people."

"No matter what they want done as long as they pay enough?"

Betty's pale eyes were shrewd. "Let's talk about murder instead. I don't trust some of these kids. Of course, I see mostly the worst cases. Plenty of normal ones out there too, but I don't see them all that often. Emotionally and mentally retarded, that's what I see. Some of them have to be locked up, like Aaron and Matthew."

"But they got out."

"Yeah. Okay, let's go back to that day at the quarry. I saw a boy sneaking around. Not one of the regular kids. At least, it didn't seem so, because the others were skinny-dipping. But there was somebody else in the woods that day you got pushed over the edge."

"An Amish boy?"

"Who knows? Chameleons, that's what they are. They change clothes, in and out. Who knows who's Plain and who's not? The kid was dressed Plain, that's all I know."

Hana contemplated her for a moment. "Eli knows, doesn't he?"

"Maybe. Eli knows a lot more than he lets on. I don't think he's as dim as they say."

"He's been working for the killer. He had to be the one who stole the outfit Josie was found in."

"Maybe he *is* the killer."

Hana shook her head. "How did your cat get in that coffin?"

Betty's face became as pale as her eyes. "Don't

think I haven't wondered about that. They must have picked up Hecate at the shack when they put the pitchfork there. Maybe so I'd come looking for my poor kitty. I tell you, I'm not safe here."

"Maybe it was a crude attempt to throw suspicion on you."

"Not so damn crude. I've got enemies," Betty said in a grieved tone. "And I can't imagine why."

"The cat—Hecate?—was so relaxed," Hana said. "I can't imagine any of my cats napping on a dead woman's lap."

"Hecate sometimes sniffs too much incense."

"That's terrible!"

"Cats enjoy it. Didn't you ever hear of those swinging kitties in the sixties that sniffed grass?"

Hana dabbed at the blood on her arm. So, she had a pitchfork, Betty Schlicher, and a lurking murderer. Josie must have known who the killer was, perhaps threatened him, and he had to act fast. If that same person was using Eli's help, how could the boy go on living? Probably Eli had not even known what use the dress was intended for. And what use *had* it been intended for? Had Josie been forced to put it on before she died?

It was all so crazy.

"I must go," Hana said. "Just tell me one more thing: how did you get into this conservatory?"

Betty flashed her gold tooth. "I'm good at slipping past people. Goes with the territory. Magic. You need a little magic."

"And a little herbal tea that sends even police officers on guard higher than the sky?"

"That too. Now where's my cat?"

"The cat is safe."

"You can't keep Hecate!"

"I can for now. The police haven't interviewed her yet. Hecate is a material witness, after all."

That seemed to make sense to Betty.

Hana did not want this hex woman roaming about Blue Spring Hill. Nor did she want the pitchfork. The most convenient disposal of both seemed to be the police. Hana escorted Betty and the pitchfork outside, where they bumped into Officer Alcorn; he located Sergeant Kochen for them. Kochen seemed reluctant to accept responsibility for Betty and the pitchfork. However, he finally agreed that a police car would return Betty Schlicher to Bruchberg, where she would be interviewed. The pitchfork, having committed no crime, was delivered into the custody of a junior officer for temporary shelter.

After Betty had gone with a policewoman, Kochen asked Hana, "What was that all about?"

She gave him a brief account of her talk with Betty, adding her own fears for Eli.

Kochen seemed tired. "It's probably one of those odd circumstances that clouds the issues in any crime. This boy is a problem child. Maybe he simply took a fancy to the dress, then was afraid of getting in trouble and dropped it."

"And the killer just happened to be there, found it, and gave it to Josie to wear?"

"Stranger things have happened."

"You don't believe that."

"I'm keeping an open mind," he explained patiently. "I'm investigating and collecting information. Maybe Eli is involved, but what I'm trying to get through to you is that we don't know. Not yet."

"I'd like to talk to him."

"Naturally. So would I, but I've never set eyes on the kid. He's a slippery one."

"Like in the old rhyme, 'Now you see him, now you don't'," Hana murmured.

"Something like that," Kochen agreed.

People were drifting away, encouraged by the police, assisted by Ghost and Crumb, to leave after their interviews. More lawn was visible. The azaleas were taking on the glow of late afternoon. It amazed Hana that the flowers were still blooming, unaffected by murder and crowds.

*Where would the boy go?* She was startled to hear Kochen utter the question she had just asked herself.

He went on, "I think he'd go home. I know that's where I'd have gone when I was a kid."

"I believe he'd go to the murderer."

Kochen tensed. "You sound as if you know who it is."

"Of course I don't know who it is! I'm just trying to figure out what these people would do. I don't think Eli's all that happy at home, so I believe he'd try to get to his friends. Betty Schlicher maybe. But she's gone. Or the murderer. If he couldn't find the murderer I think he'd hide, in the woods. That's where I saw him before. He seems at home there."

Kochen looked morose. "Okay, so he could be anywhere, but I still think he'd go home. Head right out over those fields."

Hana felt a web of ideas spreading through her brain. "Maybe we don't need him. Most people don't know Betty has left. We could announce over the PA system that Eli is in the shack with her and his family can meet him there."

Kochen stared at her. "Are you out of your mind? You're not even sure who brought him here or who might come for him. I don't like your games, Hana. You can't solve a murder with games. If I was a killer and heard something like that I'd never fall for it. Good Lord, woman! It's ridiculous. I'm going to send a police car out to the grandparents' farm and check if Eli's there. We'll be able to talk to them and the boy at the same time."

"And then wait for the next murder."

"Which could be Eli's if by some miracle you're right. You'd not only lure the murderer with an announcement like that, you might lure Eli."

"Not if it was worded carefully. Not if we didn't use his name, and used words he wouldn't understand but the killer would."

"No," he said angrily. "Absolutely not. No stupid traps. It's too risky. We'll use proper police procedures. Now I'm going to talk to my people, and get the police car on its way, and start going over the interviews that have been selected as relevant. And I want you to keep out of it."

Hana watched him stride away. His back still looked vulnerable.

"Have you interviewed the cat yet?" she called after him.

He paused for a moment, then squared his shoulders and kept going. Hana sighed. Kochen insisted on taking the long way around when it was obvious that the link to the murderer was Eli. And the cat. Hana's spirits perked up. Kochen wouldn't cooperate in using a spurious message to lure the murderer, but certainly he wouldn't object to her interviewing the cat. Obviously he wasn't going to do it.

She met no one on her way to the laundry room, but that didn't really surprise her. People and animals often became lost inside of Blue Spring Hill—and outside, for that matter. She hoped Eli would keep himself hidden.

Hecate was seated on top of a dryer. Large and black, with opal-like eyes, she was licking her whiskers carefully as if using a napkin. On the floor beside the dryer was an empty cat food dish.

"Hello, Hecate," Hana said. "Are you a nice girl?"

The cat glanced at her indifferently. Hana placed an experimental hand near the animal's nose. Hecate sniffed at her. Score one for Betty Schlicher. The cat was obviously not abused or frightened. Nothing on the neat, well-cared-for fur. No bell or amulet around the neck. Maybe Kochen was right. Whatever secrets Hecate knew, Hecate would keep.

Hana reached up to the top shelf where detergents and catnip were kept. The box of catnip was open and the odor reached Hecate, who leaped into action. With one swipe she struck the box out of Hana's hand, sending fragrant leaves spilling to the floor. Hecate leaped down after it, snuffling and sneezing. She batted the box again, then threw herself into the luxurious scatterings, where she rolled, belly up.

Hana stared down at her. Legs splayed, Hecate wriggled about on her back, having a wonderful time. And suddenly Hana saw clearly. Things that had made no sense were falling into place. An idea she had almost found when she'd been under the influence of Betty's tea surfaced. What Kochen had called her game was a necessity. She could see herself playing her role. She could see the murderer creeping in. It would work. It had to work, because maybe it was the only way to stop the killing. Because, if she was right, this killer would only lie low for a while before striking again.

"Thanks, Hecate," Hana said. "Have fun."

As Hana left the laundry room, Hecate was doing just that, chasing her tail in a swirl of high-grade catnip leaves and blossoms.

Hana ran upstairs to her room. In the large dressing area she again sought the last rack of clothing. Paging through them like the leaves of a book, she found things she had forgotten, like the tweed suit she'd bought in England in one of her Agatha Christie moods. Hana paged faster.

And there it was. Another skirt. Black. Fringed at the bottom in simulated tatters. Halloween—when?—ages ago. A party with Bill Longenecker. She grabbed it and ran to her blouses. Black turtleneck. And a shawl. Odd, ropelike material she'd received as a gift from somebody in the office a couple of years ago. The last thing she found was a black bag sturdy enough to hold her Beretta.

Hana dressed, added an assortment of beads and bangled bracelets, then tied a dark kerchief about her head to hide her white hair. Looking at herself in the mirror, Hana decided she could pass for an old-fashioned hex woman and, in a pinch, might be mistaken for Betty Schlicher.

Now she needed Mr. Fred.

After a brief dash through the downstairs, she was lucky. Mr. Fred, brooding over the remains of his Open House, was in the kitchen glaring into a cup of tea. Hana hoped it was not a brew Betty had left behind.

He gave a startled exclamation when he saw her.

"Where's Teddy Jolf?" she asked.

"Sleeping it off in a guest room. Are you in mourning for our Open House?"

Hana told him what she intended to do and what she needed from him. He shook his head as if the worst had happened.

He muttered, "You're just like your Aunt Sissy."

Hana carefully wrote down a message to be given over the PA system.

"Suppose they won't do it for me?" he asked sourly.

"Knowing your devious mind, Mr. Fred, I'm sure

you can think of some way to convince them how important it is."

He grunted and pushed away the offending cup of tea. They left the house by the side entrance. Mr. Fred headed for the information booth while Hana crossed the parking lot to the shrubs beyond. She walked swiftly to the woods and the path to the shack.

# *Chapter Forty-one*

BY THE TIME she reached the clearing, Hana was feeling quite witchy. Under other circumstances, she would have enjoyed the experience—a nice change for an executive and carpet spokesperson. No wonder Aunt Sissy had found hex a compelling hobby.

The dampness of the spring woods had created a low ground mist, which hovered over the meadow. In the slanting light of the sun everything seemed touched with gold, with magic. Deep within Hana came a sense of kinship with all those lonely women who had lived in shacks like these, dispensing herbs and medicines until hounded out of existence.

Racial memories. Echoes of danger. Along the edge of the woods Hana picked up handfuls of twigs, which she scattered in front of the cabin. Inside she breathed the spicy herbal odor, narcotic and powerful.

She struggled back from a primeval past. She

had come here because of a very real, present danger. She hoped Mr. Fred had broadcast her message. But of course he had. Mr. Fred was reliable.

Hana sat on a three-legged stool, her black skirt fanning about her. She wished she knew the song about the Witch of Endor that Teddy had been singing. But she needed to be alert and listen for an approach. She opened her bag, took out the gun, and placed it on her lap. It felt heavy and unnatural.

What if Eli had already been found by the killer? The murderer could be fooled only if the boy was in hiding or had run away.

Outside, birds were beginning their night songs. Inside it was already shadowy. What if the killer waited until night? She had to see. Hana rose and went to the door. Nothing. She had noted a kerosene lamp on the shelf. She lit the lamp and placed it on the other side of the room, opposite the stool. She had no intention of being silhouetted.

Tree frogs in the woods began a serenade. Spring peepers, that's what Aunt Sissy had called them. Dutch people shook their purses for good luck the first time they heard them.

Time passed. Through the open door she saw the mist swirling. She wondered if she should leave the shack and hide outside among the trees. She wished Kochen was here and not off chasing Eli's grandparents. She wished she had brought her dogs along. Dogs heard things people could not.

She was thinking of the dogs and straining for a sound of approaching footsteps when she became aware that the birds and the tree frogs had become silent. The birds' silence might be explained by the fact that the sun had gone down. But tree frogs sang at night.

Hana held her breath.

For a long time the silence continued.

Then she heard the crackling of her twigs as someone approached. Hana slipped the safety off her Beretta, rose, and stood near the wall.

"Anybody here?" he called.

Hana froze.

In another moment he was lumbering up the steps and into the cabin. She raised her gun, pointing it directly at him.

Dr. Harold Reifsnyder stared at her in surprise. "My Lord," he croaked.

"What the hell are you doing here, Uncle Harold?" she cried.

"Hana? Good heavens. Mr. Fred . . . he announced over the loudspeaker that a boy was ill down here in the hex woman's shack and that his family should come for him. I thought . . . You're always using me for these ridiculous medical emergencies. I thought this boy needed a real doctor. I thought . . . Will you please put down that gun?"

Outside a twig cracked sharply.

"Shh!" she hissed.

"Don't you try to shush me," he snapped. "Look at you. You're a disgrace to your family name. It's too bad you didn't marry and change it."

Behind the doctor, in the doorway, appeared the figure of a boy in Amish dress. It wasn't Eli. This boy was strong and perfect. She saw the raised pitchfork. The flash of motion as it descended. She jumped, shoving Harold Reifsnyder away. The gun flew out of her hand. She thought Uncle Harold said something like, "Have you gone mad?" before he screamed. The pitchfork caught him through the shoulder and upper arm. The boy jerked it out of the doctor's flesh and came toward Hana.

Her gun had spun across the floor. The boy was coming close. She saw everything clearly. The gun. Blood. The doctor's huddled form. The boy's face.

Most of all, the boy's face.

She didn't know him. It wasn't Jake Schwambach or Johnny Longsdorf or any of the other faces she vaguely recognized. His eyes were veiled with a gleam of evil triumph. He smiled as he raised the bloody pitchfork. In another second, he would rush at her and drive it through her heart.

It was four-pronged. She felt an urge to laugh hysterically. Here she was about to be killed and she was noticing that the murder weapon was a four-pronged pitchfork. An idea flashed into her mind: pick up the stool and hit him. But there was no time.

No time.

Hana seized a bowl of powdered herbs and threw it into the boy's face as he lurched at her. The bowl struck him, scattering the herbs. He cried aloud and fell. Hana ran across the room, stumbling as she scrambled after her gun, then whirling and pointing it at him.

His hat had fallen off, and long hair tumbled from beneath it. Mary Longsdorf sat there rubbing her eyes. Hana kicked the pitchfork out of the way.

Outside twigs popped and crackled. Police whistles sounded.

Kochen dashed into the shack. Behind him Hana saw more police and Mr. Fred.

"What are you doing here?" she asked inanely.

"You didn't think I'd let you do this without backup, did you? I knew you'd follow through with your crazy idea. I wanted to be here to pick up the pieces. I just hoped they wouldn't be your pieces."

He leaned out of the doorway. "Alcorn! We're going to need an ambulance! Call up for a stretcher." He turned back to Hana. "Which one do I put the cuffs on?"

Tears streaming down her face, Mary Longsdorf gave a loud wail, leaped forward, and sank her teeth into Sergeant Kochen's arm.

## *Chapter Forty-two*

IT WAS THE kind of day when Blue Spring Hill was at its best and to be savored, Hana thought. A day of sunshine and a blue sky, with just enough small puffy clouds to make it photographically interesting. The house loomed majestically above them against its backdrop of rolling hillside covered by a woodland edged with pink dogwood. The azalea flowers had fallen, and on the ground beneath the bushes were pools of colored petals.

Uncle Harold, his arm still in a sling, looked slightly mollified as Mr. Fred hovered solicitously over him, offering treats from a well-stocked cart. Will Kochen relaxed nearby in a marvelous two-tone turtleneck. They were sitting on the lawn, in the old wooden chairs Aunt Sissy had insisted were so much more comfortable than plastic or metal. The animals had been banished to the house in deference to Uncle Harold's injury and salty disposition. Hana had been tempted to wear her witch's outfit but also in deference to Uncle Harold had chosen instead a white shirtwaist dress with narrow red stripes and a red belt decorated with an ornate silver buckle. She consoled herself with the animals' absence at this meeting by reminding herself that they really did need their naps after a morning of frolic in the open air.

Hecate had not joined the family, although Hana had been tempted. It had been Hecate's rolling in an embarrassingly revealing position that had shown Hana that Hecate was a male, not a female as she had thought and the name implied. Then it had been a short leap to the memory of the change of clothing in the bathhouse at Mount Grunwald and the idea that if Amish youth could change from Plain to fancy and back again, why couldn't Mary Longsdorf dress as a boy? Mary had even left the boy's clothing in the women's side of the change house. Hana had derived a great deal of pleasure from telling Kochen that her interview with the cat had indeed been worthwhile.

As for Hecate, after Betty Schlicher's announcement that she was retiring as local hexeri to devote herself to opening a restaurant specializing in dishes such as powwow dumplings and hexburgers, the cat had been returned to her. Teddy Jolf wanted to take him since he had experience as a witch's cat, and she also had offered to rent the shack in the clearing. Both offers had been declined. Teddy was at present, Hana understood, negotiating with the owners of the White Unicorn to open a Witch Booth. Bill Longenecker was actively trying to persuade them to go ahead with the idea. Hana hoped that Teddy's interest in helping the Plain People, an interest sparked not only by her grandmother but by her own experiences as a school nurse, would not disintegrate into commercialism.

It was Harold Reifsnyder who, lacking the finer

sensitivities of civilized persons, brought up the subject of the murders.

"What's happened to that girl?" he asked. "Did you have to get shots for that bite?"

Kochen found his bandaged arm embarrassing and had been trying to ignore the injury. "She's not responding well to treatment, but she's young, so perhaps with time . . ."

"It's in the recessive genes," the doctor growled.

"It was also in the influence of her Aunt Josie," Hana said. "Mary listened to her aunt's tales of the genetic illnesses and deformities inherited by her people. God knows what she saw in her own family. Maybe she even felt the weakness in herself."

"One woman trying to stamp it out," Reifsnyder suggested. "Trying to cleanse the family by getting rid of the misfits."

Kochen shook his head. "I think it was more than that. Undoubtedly the two cousins, Matthew and Aaron, were mentally deficient. Their behavior was aberrant. Matthew nearly killed one of the other children last year by shoving her down a flight of stairs when she wouldn't share candy with him. He had to be watched whenever he wasn't locked in his room. Given to tantrums and smashing objects—that kind of thing. Aaron showed a lot of the same behavioral patterns. Mary saw what the boys were doing to her aunt and her mother. She had the opportunity to steal the antique pitchforks when she visited her Aunt Josie at the Historical Society.

"Josie was pleased with Mary's interest. Perhaps she saw something of herself as a girl in her niece. Mary read Josie's books about the medical problems caused by genetic inbreeding, but instead of trying to help as Josie did, she brooded and became pessimistic. Her mother told me she became more withdrawn after a particularly violent spell when Aaron injured his mother by striking her across the back with a chair. The youngest child in the family has something called—I can't even say it—Ataria-something."

The doctor cleared his throat importantly. "Ataxia telangiectasia. Usually we call it AT."

"It's got something to do with the immune system, hasn't it?" Kochen asked. "Like AIDS."

"Not like AIDS," Reifsnyder sputtered. "It's inherited as an autosomal recessive in a few groups such as an Amish isolate. Simply put for you laymen, it's something like Hodgkin's disease."

Kochen cleared his throat. "Yes. Well, Mary was given the care of that child a lot of the time. It seems she just couldn't take it. She cracked. She took the pitchforks from the Historical Society because she didn't want to use the ones belonging to the family. She's good at using pitchforks in the barn. Took pride in being the best in the family. Her mother said she used to meet her Aunt Josie at the Historical Society after hours and a few times left quietly without seeing her aunt. On one of those times she took the pitchforks. She left no fingerprints because she wore ordinary knit gloves her mother made for her. The morning of the first murder she went out to the Schwambachs' on her bicycle because she knew Matthew helped with chores in the morning when they were all working together and could keep an eye on him. Mr. Schwambach finally admitted that on that particular morning one of his bulls got loose in the fields—Mary's work. It effectively created a diversion so she could lure Matthew into the barn and kill him. She had candy. He had a sweet tooth."

"But Jake told me such a convincing story of the

whole family being together when they heard the boy scream," Hana said.

"Cover-ups, pure and simple, to give the family an alibi. The boy probably screamed all right, but the family was scattered about searching for the bull. So far as we can tell, Matthew Longsdorf did not scream when he was killed at the White Unicorn," Kochen said, glancing at the doctor. "When you think about it, you can sympathize with the way the Schwambach family reacted. They suspected one of their own had done it. They were confused, frightened, and being the religious people they are, prayed a lot. I think they were waiting for an answer from God."

"But Matthew was her brother and had hurt her mother. Why didn't she kill him first?" Hana asked.

The doctor allowed Mr. Fred to refill his sherry glass, then said pompously, "I think the murder of the boy Matthew was a rehearsal for killing her brother."

"Oh, for heaven's sake—" Hana began.

"He's probably right," Kochen broke in. "From what she has said about it, it was harder to kill her own brother."

"Then what about the sick child at home?" Hana asked.

"Same reason," Kochen said. "And she knew she'd have been suspected. But I believe she'd have killed that child eventually. She was getting bolder. Mary has admitted she threatened her brother. We think he became frightened and ran away from home. He'd been taken to the White Unicorn a number of times. In fact, it was the only outside place he did go. Mary followed him. We finally located a tourist couple who gave him a lift and even took pictures as he walked away from their van. Mary found him. We believe they fought. He may have been hiding in the barn. On the other hand, she may have lured him in there."

"More candy," Hana said.

"Right. Naturally she didn't have the other antique pitchfork with her, so she used one they had there in the animal barn."

"She must have been there when we found the body."

"Possibly. But would you have noticed an Amish boy melting into the crowd when you first went in? There were hundreds of kids around."

"You're probably right," Hana admitted. "By the way, I've seen Mary's mother. She visits Mary in the hospital and she's really supporting her. I believe she knew that Mary was dressing in boy's clothes."

"Why didn't the mother tell anybody?" Reifsnyder asked.

"Thought the girl was just wild," Kochen said. "Thought she could handle it herself with God's help. A lot of the kids knew of Mary's masquerade. But they still won't talk to us."

"They're a community that takes care of their own," Hana said. "They distrust outsiders. That's why Mrs. Schwambach wouldn't admit she suspected the second dead boy was her nephew. She hoped it would go away or . . . well, that God would take care of it."

"An unusual, odd group of people," Kochen said with something like awe.

"Has Mary admitted pushing me into the quarry?" Hana asked.

"No, but we're certain she did," Kochen told her. "Because of Josie. From what Bert Adams has said, her Aunt Josie was very upset with you."

"Why?"

Kochen frowned. "Despite the fact that Josie had

lost her church, her faith in its teaching remained.
She loved her people. Being around Mr. Fred at the
Historical Society brought her in contact with you.
She heard you were going to manufacture a dress
that she thought ridiculed Amish outfits."

"Did you tell her that?" Hana demanded of the
hovering Mr. Fred.

He bristled. "Certainly not! Of course, I may
have mentioned the dress a time or two in passing.
It was no secret, after all."

"And don't forget the Open House," Kochen said.
"Josie was afraid something would happen there.
Bert told me she didn't like the idea of having
Amish kids as guards. She may even have felt you
were exploiting them. She may have believed you
were using the Open House to continue your investigations into the deaths of the boys. Intruding into
a personal tragedy. There may also have been resentment on her part that you didn't do more to
help the Schwambachs that first morning when Sal
brought you over to their farm. You were the one
who insisted on calling the police."

"They had to be called," Hana said.

"Sure," Kochen agreed. "But we're talking about
a grieving woman who didn't look at things in a
rational manner. Not that she'd have done anything violent herself, but I think she worried out
loud in front of Mary. A lot. That day at the quarry
Mary saw an opportunity and gave you a shove.
She was skulking about because she couldn't go
skinny-dipping with the guys. It's possible she
didn't even intend to kill you."

"I believe Mary instigated the attack in the parking lot at the White Unicorn too," Hana said.

Kochen nodded. "Absolutely. She got the boys together to scare you. They liked her audacity. They
had not expected you to fight back or stand up to

them. By the way, Jake Schwambach wasn't involved. Neither was Johnny Longsdorf. Mary had her own little group and they weren't all Plain. Looks like she was more afraid of your investigation than ours," he added dryly.

"Somebody was in my office building one night when I worked late. Was that Mary too?"

"No," Kochen said. "Bert Adams told us about that little incident. Remember Josie had heard the news of her nephew's death from you when she was here at Mr. Fred's meeting to plan for the Open House. She suspected your motives and planned a little detective work on her own. She wanted to look in your files. From Mr. Fred she knew you hired private detectives for various things. It's possible she even suspected you of the murder. She got into your plant with some janitorial people. Better check your security, Hana. When she reached your outer office, something happened. I don't know if an office machine had been left on or what. But she heard something that she interpreted as a warning from God. So she got out of there. But she never stopped worrying about what you were doing. She had all the kids in the family stirred up about it."

"Who hit Pocky Reilly and dumped her mannequin into the quarry?" Hana asked.

"Josie was obsessed about that dress," Kochen said. "She hated the idea of copying their clothing. Mary and her gang stole the dress, took it out to the quarry, and had a good time destroying it for Aunt Josie."

"Didn't the woman suspect her niece of the murders, or didn't she care?" Reifsnyder asked.

"I think she did care," Kochen said slowly. "But remember she was very fond of the girl and wasn't the kind to believe ill of those she loved. She may not even have known that Pocky was hurt when they took the mannequin. Mary wouldn't have told her."

Hana nodded. "And at the Open House, Mary had Eli steal the second Amish outfit. But I still can't figure out where Mary got the cat to put into the coffin with her aunt."

"The cat's easy," Reifsnyder said. "Surely it must have been to divert suspicion. People saw that witch woman's cat, they'd suspect her."

"Well, the cat was certainly docile enough," Hana asserted. "He may have followed his mistress up here and been conveniently wandering around, or may even have climbed into the coffin by himself. They're curious creatures and Hecate more curious than most."

"You and your animals," Reifsnyder said testily. "Did you get to talk to Eli?"

Hana shook her head. "I wish we could do something for that boy. We found him hiding in the woods near the spring after everything was over, and I took him home to his grandparents. His Aunt Schwambach had brought him but couldn't find him after the police interview and had finally gone on home. I asked him why he had taken the dress. He wouldn't answer. I'm sure it was because he'd have done just about anything Mary or Josie wanted.

"Now let me see how close I can come to what must have happened. Mary saw me bring Josie into the house. She followed." Hana glanced accusingly at Mr. Fred. "During Open House the security around here was very sloppy and these kids were all over the place. After I talked to Josie Adams, she ran away. I think that was the first time she actually faced the fact that Mary had killed those boys. Maybe the fact that Matthew died at the White Unicorn gave her hope. But when I told her about the theft from the Historical Society, she knew it had to be Mary."

"Sounds about right," Kochen agreed.

"When Josie ran out of the room, Mary followed her. They got together somewhere. Mary had the dress."

"Really a dumb idea," Reifsnyder interrupted. "Amish dresses for the masses."

"We're not going ahead with that project," Hana assured him. "Dutch Blue clothing but no Amish dress."

"I think," Kochen said, "Josie Adams put on the dress."

Mr. Fred paused in the act of pouring more iced tea into the sergeant's glass. "Voluntarily? While she was alive?"

"No way," Hana objected. "She hated that dress. I'm sure Josie accused Mary of the murders and threatened to call the police then and there. Mary strangled her with the belt of the dress. Then I think she put the dress on her aunt's body."

"That's crazy," the doctor said.

"Well, yes," Hana agreed. "But maybe for her it was a way of destroying the dress. At this point her aunt became something like the broken manne-quin. She didn't just throw that mannequin into the deep water from the top of the cliff. She broke it and put it on a ledge. She *played* with it. And she played with her aunt's body."

"God," Kochen breathed. "If only the poor woman had come to us with her suspicions."

"Or told me and we could have confronted Mary together," Hana said. When Kochen scowled, she added, "With police backup, naturally. I think Josie had to confront the girl herself. That's the way she was. I wonder if Mary confessed. If she did, it must have been a bitter cup for Josie."

"But how did the body get into my display?" Mr. Fred demanded.

Kochen nodded his thanks for the iced tea. "Mary was a strong girl who did a lot of work on the farm. She just tossed out the dummy and placed her aunt in that coffin. In some twisted way it might have made sense to her."

Hana nodded. "Mary brought the second pitchfork here to the Open House for some reason. I wonder if she planned to kill Josie all along."

"No, I think she planned to kill Eli," Kochen said. "The poor kid is what they call an Ellis–van Creveld syndrome dwarf. It fits the pattern of her murders."

"Why did she leave the pitchfork at that hex person's shack?" Reifsnyder asked.

"She had to leave it somewhere," Hana reasoned. "She couldn't walk around with it. I think she got it here by hiding it in that old truck some of the kids came in. I'm more interested in how she got the pitchfork again after I turned it over to the police."

Kochen stirred uncomfortably. "The officer has been reprimanded."

Reifsnyder puffed indignantly. "I should think so!"

"Did Mary come on to him?" Hana asked.

Kochen nodded. "He's just a young officer. She's a very pretty girl."

"So she asked for the pitchfork and he just gave it to her?"

"It wasn't quite that simple," Kochen said. "She distracted him. Gave him a story and got him to desert his post for a couple of minutes, then slipped out with it. He didn't even notice it was gone."

"I hope she isn't that good with the staff at the institution where she's being sent," Hana said.

The doctor sipped his drink. "She should have been tried. She and Betty Schlicher. That woman has done a lot of harm and she's getting away with it."

"She's retired now," Hana said. "Both Betty and her cat."

"But somebody else is right there to take her place," Kochen sighed. "I understand Teddy Jolf has gone into the business."

"So maybe a little benign hex is a good thing," Hana mused. "Why do you suppose she acted so strangely when I asked her if the Schwambachs were at the White Unicorn on Good Friday?"

"I asked her about that," Kochen said, "and she told me she was so busy that day she didn't know if they were there or not. She didn't want to make trouble for them, so she just said they hadn't been around."

"I can buy that," Hana told him. "But what about our own Sal? She still swears she couldn't identify the Longsdorf boy, and even though she's as honest as anybody I ever met, I can hardly believe it."

"I can," Kochen said. "She never saw the Schwambach boy so how could she even know about the other one? The Longsdorfs live all the way over at the Scotch Mountains. She didn't know them. Actually, she didn't really know the Schwambachs either. Mennonites may be Plain but they're not Amish, and the groups don't mix that much."

"I suppose so," Hana agreed. "And speaking of the Schwambachs, you'd have thought they would have carried Aaron below to make it look as if he fell through that hole. After all, they hated having outsiders and police around."

"Don't forget they're very law-abiding people," the doctor said.

"Right," Kochen said. "And they're innocent about police procedure. Mr. Schwambach may well have thought they could report it, we'd take their word for everything, and that would be the end of it. Especially," he paused to glance at Hana, "if their good neighbor Sal had brought Ms. Shaner over to protect them."

Hana decided it was time to change the subject and turned to Uncle Harold. "I was surprised—and pleased—that you'd come to help a child when you heard the announcement over the PA system."

"After all, I am a doctor."

"Yes, you are, Uncle Harold."

"And I certainly didn't know what I was getting into. Although I should have guessed since it involved you, Hannah Elizabeth Clara."

She refused to take the bait. "I've been thinking of having Shaner Industries set up a program to help Amish who have genetic problems. A small rehab center right here in the county, near their farms."

"That's great!" Kochen exclaimed.

She continued to look at Reifsnyder. "I thought you might be just the person to run the place."

Now it was his turn to stare. "But . . . My word, you've never made a secret what you think of me as a physician or what you think of my practice. Which I will admit is heavily on the side of the wealthier, more obese inhabitants of Conover County."

"But I have always called on you in an emergency."

"Only because you can blackmail me into coming," he said sourly.

"So sometimes we don't agree, but you know that I do respect your curiosity—medical curiosity, that is—which is very necessary in genetics."

He was looking smug and self-satisfied. Hana
wondered if she was making a mistake.

"I'll think about it," he said agreeably.

"Maybe we can encourage them to reach out into
other Amish communities and hopefully tap into
other gene pools."

"That'll take time and education," Kochen commented.

"So we'll take the time to educate," Hana told
him.

Mr. Fred beamed down on them. "Perhaps we
could devote a special showcase in the museum to
this problem! Charts and graphs to show how inter-
related these people are. Start with a common ancestor . . ."

Hana stared him to silence. He murmured an excuse and huffily moved away toward the side entrance of the house.

"I'd get rid of that fellow," the doctor said.

"Can't do that. He's part of Blue Spring Hill,"
Hana sighed. "Look at this place. You'd never know
we had an Open House here so recently."

Reifsnyder fussed with his sling. "I trust you
have removed that offensive shack."

Hana smiled. "I rather like it. I think Aunt Sissy
would have liked it too. So it stays. At least for
now."

"A dead cabin," he snorted. "Dead Rooms all
over the upstairs and now a dead cabin."

Kochen looked dismayed. "What do you mean?"

"Really, Uncle Harold!" Hana turned to Kochen.
"It's just some boring family history. You wouldn't
be interested."

"Try me," Kochen invited. "We can talk about it
over an early dinner."

"We can talk over dinner," Hana said. "But I'm
not sure the conversation will be about that."

Politely Kochen turned to the doctor. "Would you care to join us?"

Reifsnyder beamed. "Love to."

Hana sighed and rose. "Why don't you two finish your drinks while I change?"

As she walked away the doctor had begun his favorite monologue about diets, which was, after all, his medical specialty. That should teach Kochen to be more careful about his invitations.

The air was sweet with locust blossoms. Hana paused to take a deep breath. She looked up at her elegantly sprawling house. She loved every brick in its walls. Every room, even the Dead Rooms. She wondered who had first called them that. It wasn't an appropriate term. There were no Dead Rooms here, just rooms in which the dead still, in a sense, lived on.

Hana wished them well, then returned her thoughts to the living. Uncle Harold usually went home early. After he left, she and Kochen could . . . What? The possibilities were endless.

This could be a very interesting summer, she decided as she went inside.

# A Message To Our Readers...

As a person who reads books, you have access to countless possibilities for information and delight.

The world at your fingertips.

Millions of kids don't.

They don't because they can't read. Or won't. They've never found out how much fun reading can be. Many young people never open a book outside of school, much less finish one.

Think of what they're missing—all the books you loved as a child, all those you've enjoyed and learned from as an adult.

That's why there's RIF. For twenty years, Reading is Fundamental (RIF) has been helping community organizations help kids discover the fun of reading.

RIF's nationwide program of local projects makes it possible for young people to choose books that become theirs to keep. And, RIF activities motivate kids, so that they *want* to read.

To find out how RIF can help in your community or even in your own home, write to:

**RIF**
Dept. BK-2
Box 23444
Washington, D.C.
20026

**Founded in 1966, RIF is a national nonprofit organization with local projects run by volunteers in every state of the union.**

# IF YOU HAVE A CASE FOR MYSTERY — INVESTIGATE THIS FROM PAGEANT BOOKS!

## A HANA SHANER MYSTERY

# ...Now You Don't
## Roma Greth

Set in the deceptively quiet Amish country, this galvanizing thriller features a corpse that won't stay dead. Remarkably shrewd Hana Shaner pieces together a complex puzzle that paints a picture far more sinister than a routine missing-persons investigation.

ISBN: 0-517-00625-1   Price: $3.50

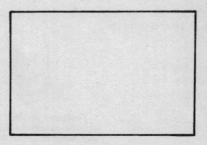

# AVAILABLE AT BOOKSTORES NOW!